The

Press

Secretary

Copyright © 2019 by Gokuren Publishing/ Stanley Ish

First paperback edition August 2019

Cover Illustration by Julie Horino

ISBN 978-0-578-53377-3 (paperback)

The Press Secretary

By Stanley Ish

GOKUREN PUBLISHING

2019

To my Mushroom. Boop.

About last night

It was a slow start back on Tuesday just after Labor Day, 2016.

I had just returned from a rejuvenating lunch when the office phone rang and before I got a chance to take a seat to rest. The southern belle on the other line woke the good old heartbreak tune that never seems to fade with time.

"How can I help you, Sherrie?"

"I was wondering if you knew about what time we were meeting for the gala tonight?"

How this was oblivious to her, I hadn't a clue. However, I was more than happy to oblige.

"Six-thirty, I believe. Do you have a way of getting there?"

"Yes, as a matter of fact I do. My cousin Charles, he will bring me."

"Lucky man." I could feel her blush on the other side of the phone. "How was your Labor Day, by the way?"

"It was nice you know. Daddy barbequed like always.......... Why don't you come by anymore? He's been asking about cha."

"........It's this job, I don't get much free time."

"Well then, you just gotta take it." She said it with such ease as if it were the simplest thing in the world to complete. This did nothing for my current mood, which had been teeter-tottering back and forth between being irritated and fucking pissed off.

"I'll take it into consideration," I said, letting steam outta the boiler below.

"Dad misses you," she finally said, allowing the true sentiment to pour through.

"You're dad misses me. That's funny."

"Why's that funny?"

"Cause you're dad hates me." I retorted.

"He doesn't hate you. He sees you like his son."

"But, Sherrie, I'm not his son."

"You think we don't know that? Johnny's dead. So what if you can't handle it, cause YOU ain't got no family, and don't know what it means to lose people you love. Your parents didn't abandon you; they just got a tough break. It was shitty, yea, but you know they were good. Only good people get taken out by a plane crash. Is it so hard for you to give him his happiness and act like his son? He's been a father to you, hasn't he?"

Well, she had me there. Sherrie's father had found me when I was ten, robbing a man whose head had been blown off at some point earlier in the day. Why this old man wandered into the alley, I'll never know. He says it was God's purpose or something for me to be found by him. I found out later, however, that after he took me home and fixed me up with a bath, clean clothes and the greatest meal ever, that his boy had been killed by a drive-by shooting a few months before. He introduced me to the whole family and then told everyone that I was going to live with them from then on. Beats the past 10 years of living wretched and lost in every sense of the word.

This was sure a shock to me. The whole time the old man was driving me to Evanston where his castle of a home was, I was afraid he'd be one of them freaks my friend Zenek told me about while we were in the foster home.

I guess I should explain myself a bit here. The real reason the old man even found me robbing a dead man, was because, wellllll, I had broken out of the Smitheran Sweets Adoption Agency. That place was the reason I had been living so wretched when the old man says God or whatever sent him to save me.

I can't say it was God, but that man did save me. And Sherrie had a point.

"I'm sorry, Sherrie," I finally said, feeling lower than a jackass.
"I know it's hard for you," she said. I could hear her trying to reach out with her voice through the phone and cup my head between her breasts to comfort me. This is how her voice made me

imagine it anyway. "But you gotta remember, we are your family. To Daddy, his son. To Mom, her son. To Laurel, her brother. And to me you're…"

"Your brother?" I said sharply interrupting her.

I could hear her stifle a sob.

"No."

"Then what?" Why is it men turn into such assholes when they're confused and vulnerable?

"…You know I've never loved you like a brother…. to me you are my lover."

Finally, it was all out in the open. But I felt no better. Clarity was not mine. In fact, all I wanted to do was cry with my face down pressed between Sherries bosom. But, I couldn't stop being mean to her. I had already committed to the complicated, yet misunderstood bastard of a child persona that was so familiar to me. Even though on that Tuesday after Labor Day, 2016, I was closely approaching thirty-two.

"I don't need any lovers. I'll try to see if I can take some time like you suggested."

After I let some moments of silence pass, I said my goodbyes and cut the line. It felt like I had just gotten off a fucking shrink's couch.

I checked the messages and made follow-up calls to all those that left numbers. Not everybody leaves a number, to the great dismay of my boss – The Press Secretary. After feeling a bit of accomplishment at finishing this task, I checked my book for the next one. There was always another task, waiting to be completed. And as I ticked off each task, and as the clock ticked off each second till quitting time, I slowly began to forget about the painful stew of regret rumbling deep in my stomach, ready to boil over at any moment.

Once five o'clock had chimed, I closed up and was guzzling down a Goose Island before 15 minutes passed. I was with my friend Dave, who had flown in from Turkey just the other day. Dave was originally from Chicago like me, but not quite in the same place. He married a Turkish woman and because of extraneous circumstances, had to tuck tail and return his wife to her home country. He seemed not to mind. Dave's a rater; how should I say, a very resourceful person.

"How's the Press Secretary treating ya?"

"She's treating me fine. It's just all the work that's being thrown on us. It's an ungodly amount of shit."

"Hey, that's why you're making the big bucks." Dave stated.

"I ain't making no big bucks. I'm an assistant for goodness sake." I snapped.

"And even as an assistant, you're still making the big bucks. That's something to be proud of man. Your boss is a woman, you're her assistant and yet you're making more money than most of the women in this room."

"One, I don't follow the logic or rationale of your pretty sexist comment. And two, dude, we don't know how much money any of these women make. They could all have more money than the both of us put together."

Dave gave me a quizzical look.

"It's possible," I said, shrugging my shoulders and finishing off my glass of Goose Island. With that, another chance at discussing the inherent sexism among men floated away.

This "oh so sexy" super sexy bartender, in cut-off jeans shorts and a very tight white t-shirt came over as she caught my eye searching for how she could be of service.

"Can I help you, darling?" When she spoke I picked up that she had to be from the south.

"Yes....dear. Can I have another glass of Goose Island and two shots of Italian whiskey, three if you'd do us the pleasure in joining?"

"Coming right up, and yes, I'd love to do a shot with you two gentlemen."

After the ritual was over and our stomachs were a little warmer. Dave coaxed the sexy bartender into general conversation with us. Privacy and intimacy were provided in the corner farthest from the single point of entrance, we had good positioning to enter into a blooming yet stimulating dialogue. The topic of the day? Gardening and sex toys. I'm not lying. Listen, it was Dave, of course, who set it up to happen.

"When I'm gardening I like to think about owning a huge lot of land that stretches as far as the eye can see; a garden so big it would take me all day, every day, to tend it."

"That sounds great, actually," the super sexy bartender said as she leaned in, resting her hand on her chin, gazing into Dave's eyes as he spoke.

This has been going on forever--Dave's seduction plays, as he was accustomed to calling them.

The topic of gardening came up very naturally.

"What'd you boys do for Labor Day?" She asked.
"I had to work."
"On Labor Day? Isn't that illegal?" She protested
"Not when you work for the Press Secretary," Dave said tapping me on the back in mock admiration.
"You work for the Press Secretary?" She stated with disbelief.
"I do," I said as modestly as I could.
"That's amazing. What's the Press Secretary like?" she asked focusing those wide-open hazel eyes at me. They were the kind of eyes that make you hate white women, for refusing to see the cloud of judgement that obstructs their view.
"She's pretty normal," I said, trying my best to summon up the life condition to deal with this line of questioning, without ruining Dave's Seduction Play. "She's got an incredible will. I've never seen her take a break, except when we take lunch. And even then, when we part ways, she's always holding a folder or two. She never stops."

"That doesn't sound too healthy," the bartender said with that deer in the headlights "Honest to gosh," little kid concern across her face. You knew this one was honest. Had to be, she was kind, a little imprudent. But that was just fine.

"She stays pretty fit, I mean she runs five miles a day and plays on a softball team, she even does Dragon Boat racing."

"Who, or What in the hell is Dragon Boat racing?" Dave asked, amazed while downing his beer.

"You want another?" She asked nippily.

"Yes, please." Dave answered.

We, of course, watched her walk away. There was no shame in admiring an ass that was obviously the product of thousands and thousands of squats.

"So what do you think?"

"You know what I think."

"Why can't you just take a break from your philosophy and moral, politically correct, mainstream media, blah blah blah, bullshit? For one day mannnnnn, please man, pleaseeeeeee." It actually sounded like an honest plea. I gave it some thought.

"I can't promise not to say anything else about it?"

"That doesn't work, you've got to finish telling her about the Dragon Boat racing stuff. Which I for one am actually interested in hearing about."

Right on cue, she returned with Dave's beer and three more shots of the same Italian whiskey.

"These are on the house, boys." She said with a cute smile and the sexist wink that told us she enjoyed our company and wanted more.

"Much obliged. I'm Cecil by the way. This is my friend Dave."

"Cecil, Dave, a pleasure to meet you both. My names Cassandra Dorothy."

"You have two first names?"

"You noticed, huh? Well, there is a funny story that goes along with my two names. And no, I'm not gonna tell you today. Far too long and far too sober for such a tale."

"Well, we can certainly help with that sober part," Dave said raising his shot glass. Cassandra and I lifted ours in kind, the ritual took place again. Others would follow and shot after shot we got Cassandra to tell us the story of her two names. Deeper and more comfortable the vibe had become after the many beverages and laughter.

It turns out though, that the story of her two names was as boring as she said it would be. She also got roaring drunk. The owner took her off our hands, even though I offered to drive her home as we lived in the same area. I'm sure he didn't believe that I lived in Evanston, but he also didn't know I made 200 K a year. Even if he did, I'm sure his Spidey sense tingled at the thought of a black man taking his drunk white employee home. And he was going to be protective, no matter who. But there was a look in his eye that I didn't like. It bothered me on the drive all the way to Dave's house and all the way to my home. Dave was oblivious to the confusion that I felt, being that he was white; no fault of his own. Nor, like I said, were my feelings based on the owner of that bar, per se. As I slowly drove home, praying to something that I wasn't going to be pulled over for a DWB (driving while black) was heavy on my mind. It's a common thing in Evanston, Illinois. But I grew up in this college town and at this point, all the police knew my car and my face, so I made my way home safely as safely as I could.

I woke with a splitting headache and a daze that put me off balance as I slowly rose from the covers. Damn, I missed the gala that Sherrie and I spent a few moments talking about on the phone. The thought pierced through the agony I was feeling in my head, the sensation so overwhelming snapping me all the way awake. Cassandra Dorothy was sleeping naked beside me with her beautiful yet unique features hidden from sight beneath the warm covers.

Now this is strange, I thought. As hazy as the night had been, I clearly remembered driving Dave home and then coming home alone. But the more I tugged at my memory, I found that I could only recall driving the car up the driveway. I couldn't remember opening

7

the front door, climbing the steps to the bedroom, undressing and falling asleep. I sure as hell couldn't remember having sex with the hazel-eyed gorgeousness beside me. The handful of condom wrappers scattered on the nightstand by me was a dead giveaway. The gold cellophane wrappers glowed as the rising sun bounced off them.

Cassandra stirred in her sleep. Let out a breath and then turned toward me. The grey sheets spread across the bed pulled away revealing her large breasts. Gravity sent them drooping to the side, enhancing them stupendously. I reached to grab hold of one. I figured I'd already handled them quite enough to qualify me as a return visitor. Just as I did, the iPhone buried underneath the handful of condom wrappers began to vibrate annoyingly. The pile of wrappers gyrated and fell apart as the phone crept its way toward the edge of the nightstand alongside me. I watched as it continued till the iPhone was hanging off the nightstand. Then the vibrating stopped with a cold silence lingering in the air.

"It was a text from the Press Secretary," I told Cassandra after I had woken her with a series of kisses and pecks at her neck. "I must go, post haste."
"Oh, that's too bad. I was looking forward to the breakfast you promised me."

I promised you breakfast? I asked myself as I hustled her out of bed and into the shower. She was already naked, so half the work was done. I re-entered a few moments later with a towel. She had slipped into the shower by this point and had the curtain wide open. Water was splashing onto the floor. I know this not because I looked at the floor because of the mess I would have to clean up when I finally returned for lunch later that day. No, I was far too distracted by Cassandra's body. Not only had she championed squats, but it seemed she was a pro at sit-ups, curls, dips, pull-ups and whatever else is needed to create one of the most athletic bodies I have seen.

She baited me into the shower by leaning against the wall and spreading herself open for me. Cassandra hurried to put me inside of her while the excitement grew more intense from the slipperiness of the shower. As the water poured down her breasts it started dripping between her thighs (ring ring ding).

It was the dingdong at the front door that cut our intercourse short.

I had Cassandra hang out in the bedroom, which she was happy to do. There was no telling who it was at the door. As I walked down the stairs, I tried desperately to piece together the missing links between coming up the driveway and waking up with a stranger next to me. She was drunk, and the owner of the bar had taken her home. Dave maybe? I'd have to call him to get more clues about what happened.

It turns out it was a priority mail package from the Press Secretary. This can't be good, I thought as I signed for the parcel and bid the deliveryman adieu. I went into the kitchen and read the stove clock. 8:00 Am. I wasn't expected into the office for another two hours.

I started a pot of coffee and opened the priority letter. This is what it said.

Cecil – Good Morning.

It's Antoinette Stalk.

I figured, as you have company, this would be a good time for me to fly up to London and take care of that thing I'm always complaining about putting off. Please take the day off and rest. I thought you didn't like white women? Well I don't see anything wrong with it. The only people who believe color exists are racist.

Do your best not to talk too much about politics and don't think too deeply about all that's happening. Just enjoy the company of a sexy woman who wants to drain you of all your sexual energy. It's not like I give you much time to enjoy the finer things in life anyway, though I have been responsible for you living kinda nice. I say "kinda" next to the way I live, of course. Compared to everyone else, you're on top of the world. Consider this a much overdue day to enjoy the spoils. It's not like you haven't earned it Cecil.

If you do happen to find some time in between your little sessions, would you mind looking over these papers for me? No urgency. Just curious as to what you think. As you know already, you can call me on my cell.

I should be back the day after tomorrow. I'll give you a call tonight and let you know if you need to come in the office tomorrow.

Have fun!

I put the letter back in the priority envelope and dropped it in the trash. I threw the papers that the Press Secretary wanted me to read over onto the kitchen table. It was a clipped stack of forty-some odd pages on a police oversight ordinance one of our clients had been drafting for what felt like months. I poured a cup of coffee and sat down at the table to begin reading. Never mind what she said about when I get the chance. She knew I was going to start right away. If she didn't want me to, she wouldn't have sent it. With this logic I started reading and forgot all about Cassandra chilling in the bedroom upstairs naked and wet, all the while filling the empty spaces of my homes nature with moans and screams of pleasure.

After some time, I can't say how long exactly-- I think I was on page five-- Cassandra came downstairs and walked into the kitchen. She had a towel wrapped around her bosom and another one around her hair.

She walked over to the coffee pot and poured herself a cup from the cupboard above. She sat down at the kitchen table facing me with those big adorable hazel eyes.

"Thought you had an urgent meeting?" She questioned.

"I did. But then the Press Secretary had an even more urgent meeting, so she sent this over and told me to go through it and write up a report."

"That's thick."

"It is. That's why I'm trying to get a start on it before the day gets going."

"Does this mean you're staying here all day?" Cassandra said pouting.

"Well, until I finish this, definitely. I need to run a few errands. But those can be done at any time. Can I ask you a question?"

"Sure. I like questions."

"We met at the bar last night, right?"

"Yep, sure did."

"And you were bartending, right?"

"Yes, Sir, I was." She was enjoying this. Her wide eyes behind the steam rising off the coffee in the cup pierced through me.

"And then, you, me and my friend Dave got drunk."

"We most certainly did. My boss was pissed, too."

"Was he?"

"What's the matter? You don't remember. I still had a couple hours left when you boys rolled in after work and started throwing shots of Italian whiskey my way. I have a weak spot for Italian liquor."

"And why's that?"

"My mom's from Italy."

"So you're Italian?"

"Si."

"I see. What's your dad?"

"Creole."

"Really, well, this just got interesting."

"Yea, it was pretty confusing for people growing up. My dad's a large charcoal black man from Memphis and my mother's a small little fiery Italian woman, white as hell, with huge tits."

"So that's where they come from," I said pointing to her towel-covered bust."

"Yep, all the women in my family have the burden of these melons," she said cupping them in both hands, lifting them ever so slightly.

I refilled our cups with fresh coffee and continued my line of questioning.

"How did you square things over with your boss?"

"Well, I have your friend Dave to thank for that. I think he could tell that I liked you, so he pretty much ran interference with my boss the entire night. After he told us his story about doing gardening work on some woman's lawn all the way out in Rosemont. How he stumbled upon her in a lawn chair by the pool enjoying a sex toy and offering Dave to join her, he got into some kind of in-depth conversation with my boss about something along those lines."

"And then what happened?"

"You and I talked. You told me a lot about your job, and the Press Secretary."

Anxiety grabbed me from somewhere deep in the background of my mind. I could feel my heart pounding through my ears, as I waited for the rollercoaster to reach its final point, before the fall.

"What did I tell you about the Press Secretary?"

"Honestly, you didn't tell me a whole lot more than I already knew. She's known to be secretive and everything you described about her seems to confirm that to be true. It was nice hearing about her work ethic though. You're so lucky to be learning directly under her tutelage."

"Do you remember anything about when we left the bar?"

"It was just before 11:30pm. I remember because you kept saying that you had to be in bed by 10:30pm and when I finally told you it was 11:30pm you paid the tab and swooped me out of there."

"So I took you home? What about Dave?"

"We met Dave at the Taco Burrito King a few blocks over."

"So, I paid the check, grabbed you and we went to Taco Burrito King?"

"Yup."

"And then Dave joined us later. How much later?"

"Not much later. You just ordered a bunch of tacos and Dave arrived right when the order was ready."

"And he didn't say anything about your boss?"

"Nothing important, I don't think. Dave did say that he convinced my boss to let me go early and give me today off, too. How'd he do that, by the way? He never would say."

"Money, the way you do everything in these parts."

"You mean he paid him to give me a day off?"

"We'd have to confirm that with Dave, but yea, probably."

"Why'd he do that for me?"

"I think it was more for the both of us."

"That's very nice of him."

"So, did anything else happen before we got back here?"

"Nope. We ate, had a few more laughs. The two of you are hilarious together. And then you drove Dave home and then us here. You really don't remember any of it?"

"I remember most of it. I just remember something a little different at the end."

"Sooooo, what do you remember?"

"I remember offering to drive you home and your boss saying something about not trusting no nigger to drive one of his employees."

"Well, yea. My boss did say that. But he was just joking."

"Funny way to joke. He's lucky I didn't knock him out."

"Well, you tried to. Your friend Dave was just faster and did it for you."

"Wait a minute. How long before we left did this happen?"

"Oh, it was still early on. I'd say 9 or 9:30pm. When we left though, Dave and my boss were on good terms. Like I said, you have a great friend."

"I just don't understand why I can't remember you being in the car with me and then coming inside together."

"Well, once we left Taco Burrito King, I helped myself to the back seat and fell asleep. Once we got to the driveway here, we popped two pills and smoked a joint before exiting the car. I don't remember leaving though, either."

I stood up from the kitchen table and walked to the front door. I hadn't glanced at the driveway when I received the priority mail from the Press Secretary. It was there alright, safe and sound. The driver's side door was wide open though. Only in Evanston would such a thing be able to go unpunished.

With the mystery of what had happened, the last part of the night was solved, I treated Cassandra to the breakfast I supposedly had promised her and made love to her on the kitchen table afterwards. I finished reading the ordinance from the Press Secretary's client and shaved, during which time an idea whispered into my brain to steal Cassandra away for a lunch date at 11:30am. We went to my favorite Italian place on State, Biondi, and indulged ourselves. With two bottles of wine in our bellies, we wobbled our way out of the restaurant and dove into a taxi to dart back to Evanston. With time left for one last roll in the hay, my half-day with Cassandra was lovely indeed.

I ordered her a Lyft car sometime after 1:00pm and she gave me a long kiss goodbye and a card with her number on it.

"I do hope you'll call me. Tell Dave I said thanks again for getting me the day off. I'm so happy you didn't have to go in today. I hope I was able to relax you a bit. It sounds like you have an awfully stressful job. You must be rather lonely." She mocked with a sad face.

I shrugged.

"I don't need a lover. I'm fine," I said.

We kissed again before she climbed into the car, but I felt nothing. It was already too late. The stone wall blocking my heart was already firmly back in place.

I watched the Lyft car drive away and walked back into the house, picking up the *New York Times* from the front lawn on the way back in. I went through the motions of cleaning up and washing the dishes before my thoughts could have their say on last night's and this morning's events. I had come surprisingly close to letting Cassandra all the way in but had to stop. The thought of it upset me. I had just met the woman and I almost opened my heart to her. It was only one reason, I told myself, thinking back to what Cassandra said, I was lonely.

After finishing the dishes, wiping down the kitchen table and sweeping the floor. I returned to the stack of pages I had set aside on the chair when I put Cassandra's sweaty, naked body on top of the wooden table, for one last roll. I was glad to be done with it. Dense reading, but interesting. The client was finally close to completing the ordinance that would change the paradigm on police accountability policies and procedures. Given all the young black men that were being gunned down and beaten in the streets, all the police officers being hunted and killed and the record high five hundred-and-counting murders that had taken place in Chicago at that point. A reform ordinance was definitely needed.

Somewhere around 3:30 pm, the landline phone rang. I still kept a landline because I didn't like using cell phones. I encouraged everyone that wasn't the Press Secretary to call the home phone. I didn't even answer the cell when I was in the house. It just made things easier for me. Plus, the connection will never drop on a landline and the call is always clear. At least, it is coming from my end.

When I picked up the phone, I found out it was my friend Dave.

"I'm glad you called man. Been meaning to call you all day."

"How'd the rest of your night go?"

"Good, I guess. I don't remember shit after dropping you off. Woke up with a naked woman in my bed. So I guess it wasn't entirely bad."

"Glad to hear it, my friend. I'm surprised you're not in the office. Early day today?"

"Didn't go in today. The Press Secretary had an urgent meeting. I had some stuff to read through, though, so that's been keeping me busy. Hey, Listen, did you really knock out the owner of that bar we went to last night?"

"Damn right I did. He called you a nigger. I felt it was my right as a proud upstanding citizen of America to correct him."

"And how did you manage to get Cassandra the day off?"

"Money."

"I figured as much. But he was all friendly with you even after you laid him out?"

"I explained to him who you were, and who I was, and why I had to hit him. He was a sensible man. He genuinely understood."

"You threatened him?"

"Well, I gave him options. One of those options involved a fair amount of pain and public embarrassment. Not to mention losing his cherished bar."

"Can we even go back there?"

"Why would you want to go back to a bar owned by a racist Nazi?"

"You make a good point. And you're sure nothing bad is going to happen to Cassandra? She can't lose her job over this."

"Well, well, well, look at chuuuuuuu, getting all protective of the lady and stufffffffff. Yes, I'm 100% certain that Cassandra is not going to lose her job. Listen, my wife is on the other line from Turkey. I gotta take this. Sorry bro."

"No problem. Tell the missus I said hello."

"Will do. I'll give you a call later, yeah?"
"Sure, I doubt I'm going anywhere today."
"I know, that's what I'm trying to change. Ciao."
"Ciao."

I realized I hadn't unwrapped the *Times* that I brought in after seeing Cassandra off. Pulling the newspaper out of the blue plastic, I spread it open on the kitchen table. Busying myself with reading, I let my eyes scan across each page and lost myself within the black and white ocean of words, looking for something colorful. I started to remember, once upon a time, that I had wanted to be a writer.

Sweets

It was a few years after Sherrie's dad found me in the alley. Having been saved from my wretched circumstances and seeing as how life was looking up, I started to dream again. The idea that I truly could accomplish something was no longer just a joke. I truly began to believe that I could do anything I put my mind to.

The one thing that was given to me from Smitheran Sweets Adoption Agency was a love for words. There was a janitor who worked nights named Smiley Wocket. He was in his sixties and had no teeth, to be honest, he was the nicest old man one could meet. He caught me skipping curfew one night. That was the first time I heard him speak.

"You're not supposed to be up at this hour." His voice was stern. And with no teeth, any child would be frightened by him ... even if he was offering candies.
"I couldn't sleep," I said softly, trying my best not to pee on myself.
"That's not a good reason to be out of bed. What'd you suppose you're going to find at this hour at your age, sneaking around this place?"
"I ain't sneaking?"
"You is too sneaking boy."

I started to shake with fear.

I guess I passed out because I woke up laying in a cot. I tried to speak, but it felt like I had aluminum foil in my mouth. I glanced around the room and was sure I was in a closet.

"You're in the janitor's closet," I heard a voice say. "You hit your head pretty bad. I let the headmistress know that you'd been sleepwalking. She seemed to buy it. Lucky for you. Told her I'd look after ya and then get you back into your quarters. So just lay there and be quiet. Ok?"

I nodded my head, yes. It hurt to all hell when I did it. The janitor started laughing at me. This seemed to make the pain worse, but I dared not make a sound. I didn't know how this was going to play out. I wasn't sure if the janitor was one of the freaks Zenek told me about when I first came to Smitheran Sweets Adoption Agency. It turns out he was not.

"I've got to go back to my job. These floors don't mop themselves. Like I said, stay here and stay quiet. Can you read boy?"

I shook my head, no.

"boyyyyyy, ohhhhh, boyyyyy that's a shame I tell ya. Boy, you know at your age you should know how to read by now. Well, I would say you can flip through one of them books from that stack over there. But seeing as you can't read, you can look through some of these with pictures in um. These are my little girl's. Sometimes she has to stay in here like you're doing when her mom works late at the brothel. Don't mess them up now. Do your best and try to read, sound it out. The longer you stay at this place, the less your chances will be to do so.

And with that, the friendly janitor Smiley Wocket left to finish his job mopping the floors of Smitheran Sweets Adoption Agency.

By the time Sherrie's dad found me in the alley, I was reading books from the stack Smiley kept for himself, with no pictures in them. Smiley had an array of tastes...everything from Anne Rice to Charles Dickens and even this crazy one by James Joyce called *Finnegan's Wake*. That was the first time I had ever seen sense made out of nonsense.

"Joyce wanted to make people think and confuse the scholars into not thinking so they could be like normal people that was thinking, "Smiley said to me before we said goodbye to one another, it was also the day I fled that wretched place.

Smiley knew as well as I did that once an orphan reached ten, they would never be adopted. You'd get one whole year as a last chance effort, just in case some lonely family wants to adopt an almost-done boy. On the eleventh birthday they toss your belongings; give you new clothes, new shoes, and a new toothbrush. And then you go to the basement where they give you a shovel and you start to dig. And you dig until you die. I never learned why you dig, what you're doing it for, or where the digging leads. I just know that's what happens from your eleventh birthday on.

I was getting the hell outta there, and Janitor Smiley knew it.

"I want you to keep this one with you, on your travels. I think it'll help you, wherever you should find yourself."

Smiley handed me his battered copy of James Joyce's *Finnegan's Wake*.

"Thank you," was all I could think to say.

Honestly, at that moment I was only thinking of escape.

"I'm sorry about your friend, Zenek," Smiley said after we hugged.
"Yeah, me too. We planned this escape together. He thought his birthday was six months later than it really was. I don't know if they lied to him or he just didn't know. He never spoke much about his life here before I arrived."
"That kid had demons I could never deal with. I was here when he got in."
"How old was he?"
"Two maybe? He was the only baby in the nursery his entire first year. He was totally alone. The mistress never entered the nursery. He told me once when he was older that he never knew

what she looked like till he was four. Up until that point he had only heard her voice through the loudspeaker. It was the nurses who took care of him. I'm surprised you never asked anything about him. I knew how close you was with him."

"I just felt it was wrong. If he had wanted me to know about him, he would've told me right?"

"Unfortunately, it's never that easy, Cecil. You've got to ask questions; as many questions as you can. Never stop asking them until you are satisfied."

With that, me and Smiley said goodbye. We both knew I'd never survive on my own in the city. I hadn't left those walls since I'd arrived.

Following the first months adjusting to freedom and comfort and an excess of everything I could ever want, including many things I didn't even know I wanted, I began to get to know my new family. Sherrie's father was the one who noticed I was always staring at the library in the living room.

By the time he found me in the alley, I had lost Smiley's copy of *Finnegan's Wake*.

"Do you like to read, Cecil? Tell you what, you can pick any book you want from the shelf and read it for as long as you want. But, if you want a new book, you have to put back the one you took first. Does that sound fair?"

It did.

"Well, go ahead. Pick a book."

I must've stood in front of that bookshelf for twenty minutes, mesmerized. I had never seen so many books in my life. It was an entire plethora of books. There were three walls alongside each other stuffed with knowledge and wisdom. Then another wall of books that were put strategically in the living room.

"Take your time," Sherrie's dad said, laughing intrigued by my interest.

My eyes flashed on a book with the word Tarzan. I had remembered Zenek talking about him one time. He was a man that was a gorilla. It sounded exciting, so I pulled that one off the shelf.

"*Tarzan, King of the Apes*, by Edgar Rice Burroughs. Interesting choice. Do you know anything about it?"
"No," I said feeling guilt in my stomach.
"Great," that's the best way to read.

Tarzan turned out to be completely different than what I had imagined it would be.

The Tarzan that I had imagined was a white man covered in dirt and utterly incapable of assimilating into British society. He was absolutely an animal and I figured the story would be about a man who was basically an animal and lived with other animals and it would be an animal story. Nope.
...

By the time I had gotten to the Editorial section of the *New York Times*, it was after 4:00pm. There were still errands to run and I wasn't going to let the events of the day stop me from completing the tasks I had to get done. I left the newspaper spread out on the kitchen table and after downing a shot of bourbon, jumped in the car and was on my way.

Drinking and driving had never been my thing. I was a sipper and driver. Sipping was easier to control. A few sips would jump start the internal engine and rev up the motivation within me to deal with people. I loathed being around people, almost as much as I hated being alone; but then I loved being alone and people energized me. It was the awful contradiction of my life that I was forced to reenact each day, over and over again. This push and pull of wanting to be around people and wanting to be around no one, or wanting to be inside versus outside. I didn't know what I wanted to calm the anxiety of residing in my own skin and listening to my brain think.

When I checked off–pick up laundry, groceries, light bulbs, new packs of underwear and socks (you can never have enough of these) and returned some tapes at Blockbuster Video, the time was 5:15pm. I wasn't thrilled about the idea of making dinner so I drove around Chicago for a while looking for something good. Sometime around when I was buying the light bulbs, it had started to rain. I fucked around and made a mistake getting on Lake Shore Drive instead of the Dan Ryan. It was the apex of rush hour which changed my mood from the, oh so productive day I was having. Being stuck in traffic was already depressing and with the rain pouring just made it the pinnacle of my life.

I flipped through station after station until finally I was forced to settle on the default, 91.5, where classical music is played endlessly. It was broadcasting a Schubert week. As I listened, the music pulled the negative me from my body. I watched it soar up above the endless line of cars, stretching both north and south. Everyone was trying to get somewhere, when most of them didn't even know who they were. I watched my negative self-swoop Peter Pan-style just above the rows of cars. It was exhilarating yet consoling at the same time.

A loud horn sounded from behind me. The noise broke apart my lovely vision. I watched my negative self, swooping and diving, dissipate into a pool of nothingness. The driver behind me punched the horn again. A car-length space had been revealed in front of me and the driver behind me was desperate that I fill it immediately. I waved my hand in thanks for snapping me out of my daydream and inched the car forward.

I was in no hurry. I hadn't even wanted to get on Lake Shore Drive. In a brain fart moment, I jumped on the drive in the hope that I could bypass a few lights. I definitely was not trying to come as far as I had into the city. When I finally was able to get into the far right lane, I drove off at the first exit I passed which happened to be 35th Street.

I hadn't been over here in quite some time. My high school was Hales Franciscan at 4930 S. Cottage Grove. That's where I received my last official degree. All the rest are stolen or counterfeit. Sherrie's dad thought it important that I go to an all-black high school when I came of age at 14.

"The boy's lived in that orphanage all his life and now he's been surrounded by white people for the last four years. He's gonna have to learn what and who he is and that's just something we can't teach him Diane."

Diane was Sherrie's mom. She treated me like her own and was always kind to me. I believe she missed me more than Sherrie's dad did honestly.

"I just don't want him to feel like we're kicking him out or that were ashamed of him."

"I don't think Cecil feels that way at all. He's a bright boy. He knows that he's black and we're white."

"Then, why do we have to do anything more?"

"Diane, you know as well as I do that life is going to be a lot harder for Cecil then it will ever be for us."

"I don't want to believe that. Cecil's not like the others that you hear about, shooting up laundromats and using dope."

"You know there's a lot more to it than that. And, whether you believe it or not, Cecil is a black boy and he will soon become a black man. I can't teach him how to be either. He's got to learn it on his own. At least this way he can be exposed to his people and be in the environment where hopefully he will learn what he needs to in order to survive."

"And if he doesn't? What are you going to say when he gets shot coming home from school one day?"

"That's not going to happen. Where is your faith, Diane? Why do you have no hope that good will prevail over evil?"

"As long as they keep letting these savages run wild, there won't be any good."

"Well, how will it ever end?"

"I don't believe it will ever end, but the only way I can see it happening is once they all kill themselves."

"Most of these people doing the killings, and being killed, are young black boys. Just a little older than Cecil is now."

"And you want to send him into a school with those same kids?"

"Diane, I think we should stop speaking about this tonight. Your racist father is starting to come through."

"How dare you!"

"It's true, Diane. Just listen to yourself. You sound like a driveling idiot; a scared, stupid white woman living the happy life of a housewife in Evanston. You don't know anything outside of this little bubble that I've created for you."

I heard a slap from my hiding place at the top of the stairs. Sherrie and Laurel were already asleep in the room they shared. I had my own room that used to be Johnny's, the dead son. I had been eavesdropping on Sherrie's mom and dad since I was taken in. They always had a husband and wife conversation at the end of the night. They didn't always end in fights though.

"You bastard," Diane said to her husband after I heard her slap him. I was pretty sure he was the one who was slapped, but I couldn't confirm it until the following morning when the left side of his face was red. "You act like you're the wise white man who knows what's needed for the black community. You're no different than any of us. So you took in a black orphan, Wow, good for you. That doesn't mean you know anything about what's right and what's wrong. You have no right to stand there and judge me."

"I never said I knew what's right and what's wrong. And I'm not judging you either; not at all. It's exactly for that reason why I don't have any answers to the matter of why I think Cecil should go to Hales Franciscan."

"I think it's a stupid idea and we're going to fuck his life up if we do it. He may not even be able to get into college. Did you ever think about that?"

"You really don't believe schools in the black community can produce excellent students, huh?"

"It's not that I don't believe. Of course I believe. But I'm also realistic."

"Spoken like a true white woman. Listen, let's talk about this tomorrow. Nothing's been done yet, we haven't even spoken to Cecil to see how he feels about it, I don't want to keep arguing with you."

I took this as my cue and walked down the stairs into the living room. The silence between them standing in front of the bookcase was thick. It felt like walking into a hot oven.

"Cecil, why are you still up? Is everything ok?" Diane asked me. She walked over to where I stood and knelt down to be on an eye level with me. "Are you not feeling well?"

Diane went through her regular "make sure my child is ok" routine. After my temperature was checked, my tongue was examined and my eyes proved not too cloudy or reddish.

"We're you listening to us, Cecil?"

I couldn't lie to Sherrie's dad. I nodded my head.

"Oh God. How much did you hear, Cecil?" Diane asked, putting a hand over her face.

"He heard everything, I'm sure. He's always listening to us talk."

"Why haven't we taught you it's not nice to listen in on other people's conversations?"

"I don't think he meant any harm, Diane."

"It's not right."

"You know not to listen in on anyone else, right?"

"Of course." I confessed.

"See, Diane. It's just with us. I don't see anything wrong with that. I used to listen to my parents when they would talk at night. I learned a lot about how to talk to adults and how to talk to my wife."

"Well maybe you should've listened a little more."

"Really, Diane. This is why I wanted to end our conversation. Never go to bed angry at each other. Wasn't that our rule?"

"Look, we can discuss rules later. Right now, I'm taking this boy back to his bed."

Diane picked me up and carried me back up to my room. I assume they made up eventually.

After ending my little reminiscence tour, I got back to my home in Evanston around 6:00pm. The phone began to ring the moment I locked the front door from the inside.

"Hello."

"Cecil, its Dave."

"What up man?"

"Just checking in. Said I'd give you a call back later in the day. How are things?"

"Things are ok. Got some work done. How's the wife?"

"She's fine man, a little under the weather though."

"Cold?"

"I guess so. It's the traveling you know. Turkey's different. Different climate, different food, different people."

"Yea, it's a different country."

"Indeed. What are you up to?"

"Right now I'm polishing off a forty-year-old Scotch and about to pop open some box wine."

"The rich and the poor unite."

"Precisely. Care to join me?"

"I don't think I've got enough energy to drive out to where you are. I literally just stepped in the house."

"I can come get you."

"Sounds like you've been doing a lot more than sipping. You know how I feel about drinking and driving."

"Sipping's about all I've been doing today. I'll head out now, put the box wine on ice for us when you get here."

"Where are you staying again?"

"Rome?"

"Uh huh…."

"I'm at the Hilton, downtown. I guess I should be able to get to you in about forty. Traffic depending."

"Sounds good. I'll hop in the shower.

"Cool, let's shoot for 7:00pm."

"For sure."

"Ciao."

"Ciao."

I felt a lot better after taking a shower. It had been a pretty long and eventful day. As I sat in the living room, I went back over the day from the beginning. It had been a habit of mine to replay the entire day's events and see how much I could remember. It was an exercise I had been doing for quite some time now. Everything from Cassandra to driving by Hales Franciscan, it all rolled on the reel of memory recorded in my mind's eye. I drank Italian whiskey I had found in the cupboard above the coffee maker when I was cleaning up this morning and I realized that I had forgotten all about the Press Secretary saying she'd be calling tonight.

Pulling me away from what was beginning to look like a negative thought, the vibrating in my pocket went off, letting me know I had a text message. I figured it'd be from Dave, turns out it was Sherrie.

'What happened to you last night? I was so worried. My cousin Charles thinks you're a dick for ditching us, by the way,' the text message read.

I remembered again that I had forgotten all about the gala last night. I went through my head trying to think of a proper excuse to give Sherrie besides the "I got drunk with Dave and took a bartender named Cassandra home." Unable to think of any, I wrote just that. Her reply wasn't nice.

The landline started to ring and I drained the whiskey I had been sipping. I walked over to the phone and considered answering it; then I thought better of it and poured another two fingers of Italian whiskey. The answering machine picked up the call and after the cordial request for a name and number, it recorded longer than I cared to remember. Click.

"Cecil, its Sherrie," the voice being recorded into the machine said.

This should be good, I thought.

"How could you be so rude to me? What's been going on with you? You've canceled every date I've tried to schedule with you. This time you didn't even give me the courtesy of letting me know what happened or even think up a clever excuse like you usually do. It's like you don't even care anymore. Did you ever?" Sherrie paused as if there was someone there to answer. Or she knew I was listening and paused for my benefit. "We stood outside the gala for an hour waiting for you. I ended up getting into a fight with my cousin Charles and taking a cab home. I called my cousin an asshole, and do you know why? Because he said you were a dick. I was so angry at him. But then, in the taxi ride back, I started to think about it, and it's you that I should be angry with, not my cousin for pointing out something that I've been too blind to see all this time. You really are a dick. Or should I say you've become one. Cause you didn't used to be. What happened to that sweet boy I grew up with; that boy who became a man and went away to China, learned the language, came back and started working for the Press Secretary?"

This was a greatly abbreviated version of my biography, but Sherrie had gotten the gist down pretty concisely.

"Anyway, that's all I wanted to say. I'm glad you found some time and relaxed. I wish you had called me instead of taking home some bartender. I would have come over instantly. It's amazing to me; you have the option of having a woman who believes you are the direction her compass points to, a woman who would spread her legs for you at any moment, and you don't want me. Do you know what that makes me feel like, Cecil? It makes me feel like a………"
Click.

The robot voice let me, and I assume Sherrie knows that her message had passed the allowed time. Thank God.

I looked at the two fingers of whiskey in the glass I was holding. The honey golden liquid swayed in the glass to my pulse's movements. I let out a breath that I hoped would rid my body of the regret, which was trying hard to overwhelm me. It didn't help much, but the whiskey did just fine as I discovered after swallowing the two fingers in a single gulp.

The landline began to ring again when I put the glass down in the sink. For a second I thought that maybe the phone would stop ringing if I picked the glass up. I tried but it didn't work. I figured it was Sherrie calling back because she wasn't able to finish leaving her message, which was just starting to get good.

My voice from the recording blared throughout the silent house. Leave your name, number and thanks, followed by a friendly bye-bye. Click.

"Cecil, its Dave. I'm outside. Let's go." Click.

That's odd

Just in the nick of time, I thought, grabbing a jacket and heading out the front door toward the driveway.

Traffic was light on the drive back into the city. By 7:00 pm most people have gotten to or away from wherever and whatever it is they had been so frantically trying to flee earlier in the day. Dave was driving a rental from Enterprise. As fortune would have it, they gave him a Ford Mustang GT.

"I don't know what year it is. But this beauty is slick as hell."

It was.

"All black: black leather, chrome wheels, Bose stereo. I can't believe they just handed it to me. I was expecting a Camry or something. I don't even understand how this can qualify as a rental." "Some people have expensive taste and they must indulge it, no matter where they are."
"Well, here's to them," Dave said, removing a flask from his left jacket pocket.

He handed it to me after taking a nice swig. I wasn't ready for the Tito's vodka that poured down my throat, burning all the way down. My stomach relaxed and started to warm. Suddenly, life was beginning to drift away into Feel Good Land. I leaned back in the leather seat of the black Ford Mustang GT and listened to the engine as Dave gunned it down the expressway.

"When are you heading back to Turkey?"
"Next week."
"Did you take care of everything?"
"I did, but with the wife getting sick, I figured it best to just take it easy for a few days and chill; make a visit up to my mom's grave."

Dave's mom had died of tuberculosis. He wasn't able to make it to the States before she died. This sparked a binge that lasted the better part of two months and almost destroyed both of us.
"Is this Pandy's first time to the United States?"

"No, she came once before with her family when she was in grade school. She says she didn't like it so much, actually."

"She say why?"

"Oh yes. She was very vocal about the woes of that visit. From everything she's told me, I've gathered she had her passport stolen in the airport lavatory, or, she left it in there. I've heard both."

"That must've sucked."

"Yea, it's an inconvenience, but it wasn't like the end of the world. She explains it like she was violated in some horrible way."

"Well I'm sure she was worried."

"Panicked is more like it. The entire trip she was a neurotic mess. Drove her parents crazy. So all her beef with America is her own bullshit."

"I see. Is that why she's sick?"

"Probably. Anyway, it's given me a chance to take a break, which I needed."

"What are you doing again over there?"

"Consulting."

"You speak Turkish?"

"No, the company has a translator. They've made it so all I have to do is what I was doing at my other company here."

"Which was consulting?"

"Bingo. It's okay; a little boring. But it pays, and I make tons of contacts. It's all about the contacts. Networking is a lot like the stock market."

"How so?"

"Well, you gotta play to get paid. That's all there is."

"Aren't most things like that? You gotta get to the table and press your agenda if you want to create change."

"Yes, that's true. But, when it comes to the stock market and networking, you really gotta play."

"How can you say you've got to do one thing more than the other?"

"I didn't really think we were going to get into a whole debate over this. All I'm saying is you make great contacts through consulting."

"It wasn't being made into a debate. What contacts have you been able to make?"

"So far I've been mainly helping a couple executive directors expand their companies. One of them has to rebrand, we just found out."

"Yeah? What happened?"

"It's this nonviolent program that the company sponsors; it's like the main thing they do. The rest of the company is geared towards research on violence and looking at it from the angle of public health."

"Violence as public health?"

"Yeah, basically. They've been around for two decades and the program's been active for about five years. But in those five years when the program was alive and active, violence went down in all the districts where the program was based. The research base is designed to stretch across nations, so it's globally connected. Started out at UIC, ironically enough."

"That's crazy. What's the name of the company?"

"Confidentiality agreement."

"What's that?"

"I signed a confidentiality agreement. It means I can't talk about shit as far as details are concerned. You can Google them. They just don't want their competitors knowing that I'm working for them. What they don't know is that my other client, the other executive director, is their top rival."

"How'd you make that happen?"

"I didn't make shit happen. They both called me. In the same week."

"Lucky."

"Yeah, I guess. Anyway I'm basically playing myself in a game of chess and they've both thrown a lot of money my way to win. So I gotta put in an equal effort on both sides."

"How long have you been keeping this up?"

"The project's been going on for nine weeks and I'm exhausted."

"Well, sounds like you deserve a break then."

"Yeah."

"What've you been doing with yourself while away all this time?"

"I picked up a copy of the complete James Baldwin essays in a bookstore at the airport."

"Really! What airport?"

"In Turkey, before we left."

"That's crazy."

"Not as crazy as you think. There's tons of good books scattered throughout airport bookstores all around the world. You just gotta take the time to browse through."

"Point taken. How'd you like it so far? You ever read James Baldwin?"

"Just that one you let me borrow."

"Speaking of which, can I get that back?"

"Sure, just remind me when we get back to the hotel."

"You brought it with you?"

"Of course. I was planning on giving it back."

"How'd you like it?"

"Oh, it was great. Very smart, and bold for its time. Simple you know. It's like Hemingway's prose infected everyone after World War II."

"I think there were a lot of other people besides Hemingway that influenced 20th century American literature."

"Yea, I do too. Stylistically, contextually, yaddda yaddda yaddda, but never influenced like Hemingway. Just the craft of putting words on a page simply was hypnotic."

"This existed in other's writings."

"Like who?"

"Langston Hughes."

"That's poetry."

"Langston Hughes wrote novels, short stories and essays too. These were versatile renaissance people back then. All of them, white, black, brown, Latino and Asian, they did everything."

"Point taken. Anyway, *Giovanni's Room* was very good. I enjoyed it. Thank you much. But having now read Baldwin's essays, I like them a whole lot better."

"I could agree with you on that actually. How many have you read?"

"Three. *The Fire Next Time, Notes of a Native Son* and *Nobody Knows My Name.*

"What about his essays did you like so much. I haven't read any; I think maybe one at Hales."

"Well, they're so sharp. Many are angry. But it's not a wild anger. It's a very suppressed and tamed anger. A conscious anger, fiery, yes, but not enough to cause immediate alarm. Like someone who never speaks above a whisper, but is feared by everyone."

"Sounds frightening."

"It is. Especially for me."

"Why for you?"

"Because I'm white."

Dave offered no follow up as if waiting for my response. I said nothing and realized I still had his flask full of Tito's Vodka sitting in my lap. I let the last statement wash over me and allowed contemplation its chance to have its moment. Afterwards took a strong shot of Tito's Vodka.

"Go on," I said handing the flask back to Dave. He quickly tucked it back into his left jacket pocket, then flipped on his right turn signal, exited the expressway at Roosevelt Road and stopped at the first red light.

I watched as Dave handed the keys of the Ford Mustang GT to the valet without looking at him. I took the time to thank the guy and slipped him a twenty. He seemed most grateful. I would find out how grateful when I left the Hilton hotel the next morning.

Pandy, I guess heard us walking down the hall and opened the door when we were in front of it and greeted us inside. Dave's wife was wearing a grey bathrobe the Hilton hotel had provided. Her graceful strides around the hotel suite provided faint glimpses of her bare thighs leading all the way up to her peach. It didn't surprise me to see that she was wearing nothing underneath.

"It's been such a long time," Pandy said, drink in hand, after we had gotten settled on the large sofa tucked into the far corner, overlooking the balcony view of downtown Chicago. The windows of the suite were an entire wall of glass. We were so high up, it mattered not what you did. There was no way anyone could see you up here. "What've you been up to?"

"Just working for the Press Secretary. Same as always."

"You've had that job for a while now, yes?"

"Yea. A few years."

"Well, you must enjoy it. David here tells me the most fantastic stories about you, they can't all be true, now can they?"

"I'm not sure which stories Dave's been telling you."

"Oh, any will do."

"Oh, I see. You want me to tell you a story."

"Yes. You're quite right. I have been looking forward to seeing you again. The last time we met you told us the most delightful story of you and David's first meeting."

"Yes, that is quite a famous story. But perhaps that one's become too bland. Popularity does have a way of reducing the value of a thing."

"Or person," Dave chimed in, refilling his glass and offering to do the same for whoever else wanted more vodka.

I did. And so did Pandy.

"So, come on now. If not that story, then any will do. Just tell me something daring, dashing and dartfully sexy."

"Dartfully sexy? I don't think I quite know what you mean."

"Oh you know. Sexy shit that darts in artfully."

"Haha. Thank you for clarifying."

"Now you're laughing at me. I'm a sick invalid. You shouldn't be giving me such a hard time."

"You're right, my darling. My sincerest apologies."

"You're forgiven. Now, on with the story."

"Seems I haven't a choice. Well, if that's the case, allow me to bring your attention to the year. It is 2013 and I am on my way to make my fifth journey to Japan. Little did I know the trip would last three years, but it wouldn't have been an adventure if I had known what was going to happen at the start?"

"David, will you pop some popcorn."

"Hee hee. Sure thing, my darling.

"You were saying?"

"Yes. Upon my arrival at Narita Airport, I took the Skyline to Nippori and then transferred over to the JR Yamanote line."

"Ooh, that's the green one, right?"

"You remember."

"Sure do."

"Well I rode that to Shinjuku and exited there. I had time to waste, so I decided to reacclimatize myself to Tokyo. I wandered into alleys and into every broken-down liquor store I could find. By dinner time, I was drunker than I can remember. I wobbled this way and that for a long time, trying my best to get my internal compass back online. There didn't seem to be any harm in stopping and having a drink. After I was sure I was lost, I figured eventually I'd be able to make my way to the Hilton in Shinjuku and I'd check in. No problem."

"Why did you go to Japan in the first place," Pandy asked. She had been listening intently.

"To be honest, it was to shuffle the deck of my reality. Things were getting pretty grim for me here in Chicago at that point in time."

"How so?"

"Well, shit with my 'family, everything was deteriorating because I was pulling away from them and they were taking offense to it."

"You don't think they were just worried?"

"No, I know they were worried, but it's the way that they went about expressing that worry. There was a lot of guilt and blame thrown my way, and I didn't ask for any of it."

"Well, none of us choose our families."

"No, what I mean is....Ah, that's right, you don't know that I'm adopted."

"No, I had no idea about that."

"Yeah, I was adopted by the family that you know of as my 'family' when I was ten."

"You were so old. What were you doing before then?"

"Living very miserably in an orphanage."

"That's terrible."

"Yea, it was pretty horrible."

"Popcorn's ready."

"Right on time. Cecil was just getting to the story. Weren't you, Cecil?"

"Ah, great. If no one needs anything else, we're all set then."

"Thanks, Dave. After my night of drunkenness ended and the sun began to creep its way over the horizon, I woke to my first morning in Tokyo since returning. I was in a love hotel surrounded by an assortment of Japanese men and women. All naked. Except for one guy in a suit tucked away in a far corner. His dick was hanging out of his trousers through the zipper. It was a strange sight, he was leaning his neck one way and his limp dick was leaning the other. The juxtapositions of the leaning was what I remember most alarming when I woke to that scene. There were more women than men, thank God. And I was buried underneath an array of asses and tits. As I climbed my way from the bodies that were sprawled atop me, two women moaned when I moved their exposed love muscles out of the way. One woman woke, and grabbed hold of me by the balls. It was startling to say the least. It froze me in my climb out of the pile of naked Japanese woman I was surrounded by."

"This story sounds like bullshit to me," Dave broke in.

"Why do you have to be so rude to your friends?" Pandy said, trying to defend me.

"Cause it sounds fabricated."

I laughed, grabbed the popcorn from Pandy and watched them squabble, happy I didn't have to continue telling a made-up story. Being put on the spot sucks.

Their bickering continued for some time and it's not necessary to record it here. I fell asleep at some point. When I woke on the couch, the sun was just beginning to rise. I walked over to the giant window wall and looked down at the city below me.

All those people down there running around, losing their minds for no reason at all, I thought to myself. There was a half-smoked joint in the ashtray on the table near the end of the sofa nearest me. I noticed it and indulged in a little wake and bake, smoking while overlooking the vastness of downtown Chicago was liberating. An idea sparked in my mind. It would be this idea that brought about the change so many in our field of thinking had been waiting for to come about.

I hastily searched the suite for anything to write on. I found a pen and notepad in the drawer of the large dresser at the entrance of the suite. Franticly writing, over and done with it, I pocketed the jewel of my future and snubbed the joint that had gone out a while ago.

I wrote one more note to Dave and Pandy, thanking them for their hospitality, and left the suite.

Outside the hotel, the valet I had tipped a twenty to the previous night was just coming in to work.

"Yo, long time no see, my friend. How are you?"
"I'm good. What was your name, man?"
"Hector, amigo."
"Hector. Cecil."
"Good to meet you, brother."
"You too, my dude. You just coming in?"
"Yeah."
"Didn't you work late last night?"
"Si."
"How much could you have possibly slept?"
"About as much as you, I assume."
"Good answer. You work here every day?"
"Every day except Sunday."

"Busy, busy."

"I gotta family to feed, bro."

"I understand."

"You got kids?"

"No."

"So what the fuck do you understand?"

"Another good point taken."

"Yeah, you takin' all these points, but I'm not sure if you're actually getting what people be telling you."

I said nothing at that point, any answer I gave would further prove his point.

"At least maybe now you're listening."

"Thanks for the lesson, Hector."

"Anytime, Cecil. Come back through later. I gotta break between shifts at 5:00pm."

"I'll see if I can get over here then."

"Yeah, ok."

"Have a good morning, Hector."

"You, too, Cecil. Peace."

I walked down Michigan Avenue looking at my feet, oblivious to all that was going on around me. I kept replaying the great idea that I had written down in Dave's suite at the Hilton. If I played it out correctly, a shift in the political climate of Chicago would take place. All the plans were tucked away in my left jacket pocket along with Dave's flask of whiskey. I told him that I'd taken it for the road in the letter I left him and Pandy.

I was on my way to death in the form of being hit by a bus if it weren't for this beautiful French Cuban nurse who intervened and saved me.

"Why don't you watch where you're going sir? You drunk? You high?"

"All of the above, Madam."

"Look, if you want to die, then shoot yourself, but don't put other people in danger just cause you can't take living here no more."

"Yes, Ma'am. I do apologize."

"Apologies don't mean shit. You're a bum."

"I have a job."

"I don't give a good goddamn if you do or you don't. You're still a bum. What're you doing?"

"Actually, at this very moment, I was just working out a plan that will shift the political climate of Chicago for black people."

"Now I know you're crazy. Did you hit your head or something? I'm sure that's what it is."

"No, Ma'am. I left my friends' hotel suite and I've been walking and thinking about my plan ever since."

"Well, you almost walked your way in front of a bus."

"I know, and I'm super grateful to you for saving my life."

"Well, you better be. Almost killed myself trying to do it."

"Why did you?"

"Because I'm a nurse."

"That's the only reason?"

"I need more reason for wanting to save your life? Perhaps I should've just let you get hit by that bus."

"Perhaps you should have."

"You really are crazy, I ain't got no time to be talking to no crazy people on this or any other morning."

"I'm sorry, please don't leave so agitated. I really am grateful that you saved my life. I would like to repay you in any way that I can. My life is not worth much money, but enough to be able to offer you compensation for saving it."

"I couldn't possibly take your money. Now, I've already spent far too much time idling away the morning with you. I'm sure I'm late, so I have to be going."

"Very well, at least let me take you out to lunch. You did save my life. It's the least I can do."

The French Cuban nurse paused, analyzing.

"Perhaps if you meet me at the Couplet Parch at noon, I could consider letting you pay me back."

"Couplet Parch at noon, got it. Thank you for saving my life, Ms......."

"Susanna 'son."

"I owe you an eternities of thanks, Ms. Susanna 'son. My name is, Cecil. I will meet you at noon at the Couplet Parch, and very much looking forward to it.

And with that I was off, feeling much more chipper, indeed.

The Press Secretary hadn't called me the night before like she said she would. This didn't concern me. Probably she just got caught up in whatever, that could possibly include sleep. Which was just fine, good in fact, because I knew the Press Secretary didn't get much sleep at all.

As I thought about the Press Secretary not calling me last night and some other things, I glanced up at the sky and was stunned at what I saw above me.

"It's purple, umm, why's the sky purple?"

I wasn't the only one that took notice of the strange scene that was happening around me.

"Excuse me," I said to a random passerby I had stopped. He was transfixed by his smartphone and hadn't looked up at the events taking place overhead, I assumed.

"Yes, can I help you?"

"Did the sky turn purple just now?"

"What? Are you crazy? Let go of me."

"Now, sir. All I'm asking you to do is to look up. That's not really out of the ordinary. If you see blue then I will agree that I must be crazy."

"Holy shit. The sky's purple."

"I told you!"

"What the fuck's going on? What's happening?"

And so the chaos ensued. Not everyone noticed, but not too long after, it was impossible not to notice all the people on the street and in their cars and on the busses looking up at the purple sky.

The purple sky had affected the perspective of every person I passed as I made my way to the Press Secretary's office. It had passed the point where I would be able to run home, shower and change clothes. I kicked myself a bit for not going through the motions of utilizing the wonderful hotel suite that my friend Dave had gotten for his wife Pandy and himself. It was a wonderful thing that we had been able to spend time like we did. However, the fact of the matter of the sky turning purple erased all other coherent thought from my and I'm sure many other brains.

As I strolled down Michigan Avenue under the vibrant purple sky, there seemed to be something ominous that would tell me exactly what was happening. This, however, was not the case for those of us who are unlucky. I happen to be one such person, luck, or fortune as many would call it. I am not attuned to linking fortune and luck into the same category of positivity directed from the universe, this theological perspective creates a misunderstanding as you shall see when all of my words have been written.

Not knowing what to do, I stopped into a Walgreen's somewhere along Michigan Avenue. As a rare treat, a piano ballad of 'summertime' was playing through the overhead speakers.

It can't be this easy, I thought. I wandered through the aisles in search of what I knew not. The thing was, all I was doing was passing time for this secret meeting I had been waiting for to happen.

Ah, I see. I understand why you have such a look on your face. You're wondering what the fuck I'm talking about. Listen carefully, because this is some back to the future, Bill and Ted kinda shit.

Everyone took notice of the purple sky, but there was something different about the way they looked at the clouds above them. People's intentions reveal quite a bit about them that isn't noticed in the day-to-day activities.

Walking and staring at the recently purple sky along with all the other bystanders, although not everyone took immediate notice of what was happening. To be expected, they were staring at their smartphones and not watching where they were going. These people looked up only when they started to get Facebook notices about the purple sky. So it was everywhere and everyone could see it. This confirmation did wonders for me as I was beginning to slip toward believing I was losing my mind. Insanity isn't something you want to embrace or admit to.

I felt the iPhone in my pocket vibrate. It was the Press Secretary.

"Good morning, Cecil."
"Good morning, how's everything? You back from London?"
"No. Heavens, no. I'm going to be stuck here until next week, you haven't gotten to the office yet, have you?"
"No, not yet."
"Great. Don't worry about coming in. I just want you to read over the ordinance on revamping the police review system. Did you get a chance to look at it yet?"
"Yes, I read through it when you sent it yesterday."
"I figured you would. How was your day, by the way?"
"Good. Almost relaxing."
"Why, almost?"
"Well, it had to end."
"It must, too much work in the world to do with so little time."
"How did you know I had company?"
"Come on now Cecil, you know who I work for?"
"Yeah, that's true, it's just a bit disconcerting though."

"Just try not to think about it, Rest assured, I've made sure your surveillance has been tapped with a priority sticker."

"What's so good about that?"

"You'll find out if there's ever a situation when people must be rounded up for their own protection."

"Like the sky turning purple."

"Yes, we've known this was going to happen for some time. It'll pass in a few days."

"Why's this even happening? It's purple in London, too?"

"Cecil, it's purple across the entire northern part of the planet. It has something to do with rocks and dust in outer space creating a lens that when the sun shines through, the effect of it turns the sky purple."

"Sounds fabricated."

"Has a lot to do with global warming, too. Of course."

"Global warming seems to be what's going to do us all in, in the end."

"It very well might be."

"I have to go into a meeting."

"Ok, don't work too hard."

"Thank you, Cecil. Enjoy your day off, figure out everything you can with that ordinance, will ya?"

"Sure thing, boss."

"Thank you kindly."

The call had ended.

The sky being purple had quickly become just another rarity in a world chock full of them. Almost everyone walking on Michigan Avenue that early morning had their smart phones out and were clicking away at the purple sky. I considered hailing a cab to Evanston, but the thought of paying the fare frightened me. I, of course, could afford it, but why should I when the Purple Line el train would take me close enough to walk. I suddenly had time on my hands. Getting back to my place and showering was the most important thing at that moment.

I caught the el at Clark and found a seat tucked in the very back of the car I got in. Settling down for the hour long ride, watching the people below on the street, almost all constantly glancing up. I thought it was funny that I was riding on the Purple Line while the purple sky was stretched out above us.

As the train approached the north side of Chicago, the Cubs stadium, Wrigley field and Loyola University passed. I got off at Davis and walked the rest of the way to my place.

The walk was a bit far and by the time I arrived at the house, the only thing I wanted was a tall, cold beer. The clock above the stove read 11:14am. I would have been at work for over an hour already, if the Press Secretary hadn't called me. What a morning it has been!

After doing absolutely nothing--and I mean nothing--over the next three hours. I tossed my 12th beer into the rubbish and stole another glance at the clock above the stove. 2:30pm. Shit, I totally forgot the date I had at noon with the French Cuban nurse Susannah-son at the Couplet Parch paying her back for saving my life. Starting to feel the twinge of sadness creep its way in. I saw Cassandra's number stuck to the refrigerator by a magnet and decided to give her a ring. I can't quite say why I did this, perhaps I was horny, lonely or both. Whatever the reason, it would turn out to be the greatest mistake I would make. Certainly not the only one, though, and definitely not the last.

I picked up the landline phone and dialed the number Cassandra had written down on a piece of paper she had torn out of her day timer just before she hopped in the Lyft car the day before. Listening to the rings, I lost myself in thought.

"Hello." Her picking up startled me.
"Hi. Can I speak with Cassandra, please?"
"This is she."
"Hey, this is Cecil. You hung out with me yesterday."

"We did a lot more than hang out. Or don't you remember."

"Feels like it was all ages ago."

"Well, perhaps you need me to refresh your memory."

"Refreshers are always helpful. Sounds nice and fun. Do you have to work tonight?"

"I do."

"What time do you start?"

"I clock in at 10:00pm"

"So that leaves you about seven hours to reenact yesterday."

"Sounds like plenty of time."

"How soon before you can come over?"

"I can head out now, if you want."

"I want."

"Ok, let me order a Lyft and then I'll let you know when I'm on my way."

"Sounds like a plan. See you in a bit. Looking forward to seeing you again."

"I've been hoping you'd call me. I don't usually give myself completely to men I just met."

"What was so special about me?"

"I don't know, at first it was your spirit, you have a very pure and natural spirit. Then you were funny and hospitable, hard and soft in bed."

"You mean I couldn't keep it up?"

"No, you were just fine at keeping it up. Kept me going, too."

"I must say, Cassandra, this conversation is starting to get me a little excited."

"Me too," as she let out a longing breath. "Let me order the car so I can get to you."

The line went dead and I hung up the phone.

The prospect of seeing Cassandra again brightened my day. Even though I wasn't necessarily sad or anything and with the sky turning purple all over the northern part of the globe, there were lots of interesting things to distract my thoughts. But whenever I thought of Cassandra, a feeling of having to see her overcame me.

I wasn't too keen on this feeling arising. It reminded me too much of love. So I grabbed a pint of whiskey and polished off two fingers to push the thoughts of love and happiness away. As the whiskey relaxed my tummy, I spotted the *New York Times* that I had brought in when I got home after taking the Purple Line el train under the purple-blanketed sky. I removed the blue plastic wrapper and unfolded the entire paper on the wooden kitchen table.

I was halfway through with the international section when the phone rang.

"Hi, it's me."

"I'm sorry, I don't know any ME's. I know a Cee."

"Well, this is not he."

"How do you know it's a he? Cee can be a woman's name."

"Is your Cee a woman?"

"No."

"So, like I said, this is not he."

"Then who are you?"

"I already told you. I'm me."

"Well, as least you know who you are."

"Definitely took a while. I can assure you of that."

"Takes us all a little while to figure out who we are. Then you gotta figure out who you want to be. That's the real hard part."

"This is getting a little too philosophical for me. I'm just a lonely bartender. I don't read many books. I don't even have a whole lot of opinions on anything."

"That's not good, Cassandra."

"So you did know it was me?"

"Of course I did. Are you on your way?"

"Yep, just hopped into the Lyft now. Can you give me the address?"

"Aren't you supposed to put that in before you order?"

"Well, I didn't have it."

"So, what'd you put in?"

"This random Barnes and Noble I go to from time to time on Davis."

"Ah yes, I know the place. I'm in there a lot. Listen, why not just meet me there. We can grab lunch and a cold one. Then come back to my place and embark on this refresher."

"Okay, that works. I'll see you there. I can't wait. It's going to be hard to contain myself. I might just jump on you, wrap my legs around you and push your face into my chest."

"Now that would be a lovely greeting, you've officially gotten me excited. I better get off the line or else I'm gonna be poking out down the street."

"There is an awful lot to poke out."

"Yeah, this was a good idea."

"I agree."

"I think we're about to have a great time before you go to work."

"Yes, I think so, too. And what about you? The Press Secretary is just handing you all of this free time."

"No, actually. She's just traveling, so I get to work from home."

"That's lucky."

"Not quite. The Press Secretary's modus operandi is when working from home the load is larger than normal. She figures you're at home so you are comfortable and therefore should be able to be more productive. You get to make your own hours, can work in your pajamas and can even be drunk or high as long as the work doesn't suffer."

"Still sounds better than going into the office."

"I like the office."

"But if you were going in you wouldn't be about to be returning back inside me."

"I guess working from home has its perks."

"Speaking of perks, how's your poking. I'm getting closer to the Barnes and Nobles on Davis."

"Sure thing. I'll see you in a bit."

"Bye."

"Bye."

I made it to Barnes and Noble before Cassandra arrived. I grabbed some coffee from the Starbuck's and went upstairs to the literature section. All the old friends were there: Dante, Fitzgerald, Keats, and Shaw. I lost myself walking through the aisles and forgot completely that I was supposed to be looking out for Cassandra's arrival. I'm not sure how she did it, but – it seemed like I had been in there an hour when in fact it was only five minutes – Cassandra snuck up behind me and reached around and grabbed hold of my penis through the slacks I had on.

Her grip was firm and the shock of it sent me into a fit of insecurity. If I were white, I'm sure I would've blushed; probably was.

"Hey," Cassandra said smiling wide showing me her crooked but pretty white teeth.

"Hey," I said pulling at my crotch through my pants. "Readjusting everything."

"Did I hurt it?"

"No, just gave it a little shock. I thought you were going to jump on me and mash my face into your breast."

"I couldn't resist when I saw how intently you were browsing."

"How long were you watching me?"

"Not very long. I was really just looking for you and happened to come straight upstairs first. When I spied you and could see how oblivious you were to the environment around you, I started to think that I could do that. I'm sure you wouldn't let anyone else get away with it."

"And you thought to grab my dick in public?"

"Exactly. What's the matter, you didn't like it?"

"Now, I didn't say that, I just would've been able to enjoy it more if I had known it was coming."

"Where's the fun in that?" Cassandra said, showing that erotic smile of hers."

We took the opportunity to walk a bit once we left Barnes and Noble. Once our stomachs began to rumble, a suggestion of pasta was brought up by Cassandra. I saw no reason not to respond positively to this. Her Italian heritage was much stronger than I would ever have guessed.

"What have you been up to today?" Cassandra asked me after we settled into a table for two tucked away in the corner facing the front door.

"Today was rather dreamy and vague."

"In what way?"

"Well, I woke up with a hangover all the way downtown, far from home. I lagged too long at my friend Dave's place."

"Oh, your friend from the other night."

"Yes, that's him."

"I thought he was in town from Turkey."

"He is."

"Oh, he has a place here in Chicago, too?"

"No, he was at the Hilton."

"Oh, I see, it all makes sense now. Please, continue about your day."

"I left too late to run home and change, so I was in the process of making my way over to the Press Secretary's office when she called me herself and said not to come in for the rest of the week. She's tied up with something in London, so I've basically been given an assignment."

"What's the assignment?"

"Do you remember that stack of pages I received the morning you were over at my place?"

"Yes."

"Well that's my assignment."

"But I thought you already read through it."

"I did, but now I've got to do more than just read."

"What else is there?"

"It's really too technical to talk about right now, there'd be no follow-up conversation that could save us from the boredom we would fall under if I began to talk about what I'm supposed to be doing." I found this last statement of mine to be very amusing and ceased talking.

Feigning being parched, I drowned the glass of red wine before me. I hadn't touched a drop of the sauce since sitting down. Cassandra on the other hand was getting her third glass filled by the waiter when I asked for my second. The silence continued and Cassandra was giving me an opportunity to go on. Maybe she figured I was thinking about something terribly hard that I wanted to say and if she interrupted me I'd lose the thread. Just as she looked as if she were about to say something, the waiter arrived with two large plates of pasta.

"Here you are, Ma'am and here you go Sir. Can I get you all anything else?"
"No, this is wonderful. Thank you."
"Very good then. Please do let me know if you all need anything. Enjoy your meal."
"I'm sure we will," I said more to myself than anyone. I'm sure Cassandra heard me but she didn't seem to be bent on hearing this story about my day. She did observe some form of cordiality and let me eat my meal in peace and silence.

"More wine?" I asked Cassandra, pointing over to her empty glass. While devouring our pastas I had caught up to her and was now on my fifth glass. I remember thinking, "It's a good thing I live so close to here."

"Yes, please," she responded.

I signaled the waiter and he came over with a new bottle in hand and a dessert menu. It was amazing how on top of his shit this man was. He truly was a professional waiter. Maybe they imported him straight from Italy.

We clinked glasses and enjoyed sipping. I refused to break the silence, Cassandra seemed just as stubborn. So the rest of our date floated by without a word spoken. She smiled the entire time and then before we knew it we had worked out a very effective form of communication using just our eyes and hand signals. It was talking with our eyes that excited me the most. There was something mystical about it all, I swear I actually could hear her voice in my mind as I read her lips. It was with my silent lips and a few hand signals thrown in here and there, that I told Cassandra about the rest of my day.

Strangely, the fact that the sky was purple didn't come up a single time. By the time we exited the Italian restaurant, the sky was black with night. As we walked along the neighborhoods in Evanston, admiring the beautiful houses, we found ourselves at the edge of the lake. The sound of the waves cascading in and out brought a steady consistency to the jumble of conversation we had been gesturing. Cassandra was still not talking because I wasn't. It was strange, though, I didn't feel in the least bit upset or frustrated. Or that she was making fun of me. More than anything, it felt good, as if she was respecting me so much that she wasn't going to talk because she figured I didn't want to. But she didn't want to know for sure, so she just let it go.

The absence of any real alarm for the purple sky worried me. I couldn't understand why the sky being purple was being taken so nonchalantly. It was real, not something happening in my mind. I had watched earlier today as countless people glanced at the sky and saw dozens of smart phones snapping up photos to post on Facebook. There was even a snippet about it on the news playing from the television at the entrance of the Italian restaurant, but it was mainly just reporting. The sky was purple because of space rocks and dust and air pollution. Somehow I had a feeling that it had more to do with air pollution than anything else.

Well, the Press Secretary said it'd clear up soon, I believed her if she said it. The Press Secretary had the direct link to about a dozen operating intelligence agencies located throughout the world. That's why it wasn't such a shock to me when she knew that I had met a bartender named Cassandra and she had spent the night with me the Tuesday after Labor Day 2016.

Cassandra did not spend the night again. I walked her home, which wasn't very far from the Barnes and Noble. She lived in the Evanston neighborhood, so we promised to link up again sometime soon. And after a prolonged kiss we parted ways, her entering her home and bolting the door and me returning to the life of a pedestrian where I had spent most of my time this day.

I decided to walk home, which would turn out not to be the wisest choice, but I'll wait until we get to that point. Walking home was the most exhilarating of all the choices available to me as I drifted in a semi-intoxicated sense of delight after parting ways with the bartender Cassandra.

Hobbling down the boulevard was not the smartest thing for a black man to do in Evanston, Illinois, in September 2016. But at the state I was in, there was no telling me that. So I walked home from Cassandra's.

The good old thoughts which I had been trying my hardest to avoid for the entire day--well really every day--pounced on me with a ferocity I had not felt since college. In the beginning, it was just a slight annoyance, but as I put each foot in front of the other, the thoughts began to press down on me. After a while it began to feel as if two giant hands were pressing on my cranium.

I tried my best to redirect my thoughts, grasping for anything positive I could find or anything neutral for that matter. I stumbled upon a lost memory in some plane floating in my mind left to be discovered or never recovered.

Boom

Memories have a way of taking over reality. They meddle in and wreak havoc upon the accurate recall of the events as they actually happened. It is for this reason that I say memories are unreliable things. How do we know that the memories we have are in fact from us? Often times I have experienced, as I'm sure you have as well, things that you are sure didn't happen but you know you experienced them. Many people I've spoken with have tried to classify these things as lost thoughts or suppressed feelings. However, I don't believe in that mumbo jumbo. I think that we are just recalling memories of things that we have imagined, made up or even dreamed.

At this moment the alarm on my wrist watch began to ring, not sure if I have mentioned that I wear a watch very religiously. It's always a Hamilton, leather band, if I can help it. I have a bit of a budding amateur watch collection as well as shoes, ties and hats, if you were wondering what to get me for my birthday.

"What are you doing around here, Boy?" the cop asked me as he shined the flashlight in my face.
They had snuck up on me. I figure it was the alarm on my Hamilton wristwatch that caught the police officers' attention. I can't imagine what I looked like at that moment. Based upon the mug shot, I didn't look all that bad, if I do say so myself. But looks can be deceiving, I suppose, and maybe they knew something I didn't know.

It turned out what they knew was that I fit the description of a perp who had robbed a liquor store. As cliché as this all sounded, it actually happened to me. I tried my hardest to explain who I was and who I worked for. Also, that I owned a house not too far from where we stood. All of this fell on deaf ears and the only thing that mattered was that I quickly and slowly (something I thought absolutely impossible) produce proper identification. I did as I was commanded and even then the abuse did not abate.

I looked into the eyes of the two police officers who were accosting me. In each of their blue eyes was a fear I couldn't place nor had ever seen before. It was a far-reaching fear that predated their lifetimes or mine, for they were older than me. It was a collective fear felt by all white men and this fear terrified me; not for them, but for myself. Because within their fear the only thing I could see was my destruction, there was no positive outcome for me in the eyes of these two police officers of the law; only a distinct fear of the unknown that caused their blood to boil and their lips to curl.

After that they ran my identification and patted me down for weapons or paraphernalia, something I allowed them to do. Unsatisfied with all that they found, they started physically jostling me. This quickly escalated into a full-on shoving match. I wasn't one to let myself be pushed around and after a certain point, when I thought I was about to lose my balance, I unconsciously swung on one of the officers near me. He was old and fat and no match for the instinctual fist I launched at him.

The connection of my left fist against the cop's right check was priceless. The silence as I broke his jaw was deafening. Without a doubt the thought that pierced my mind was the same that shot through the other officer's head. "Holy shit," he screamed and reached for his piece.

I knew it was all over then and told myself to put both my hands above my head. I did nothing of the sort. Before the cop I didn't punch could remove his pistol from the holster, I had my hands on his gun. The piece was in my hands and it went off, but it didn't hit him.

Luckily, I was able to get a hold of the Press Secretary still in London. She wrestled up some police that she had a few things on to scoop me, clean the scene and erase the memories of the two officers I assaulted. How they wiped their brains, I have no idea. I didn't ask too hard, as it were.

When I was finally back home and in bed, free, it was a quarter after three in the morning.

As I drifted away into that place of dreams, I thought semi-hard about why the hell I had even though it a good idea to walk home so late and drunk as well. I don't think I would've done that anywhere in the United States sober. But there I had been.

When the sun finally tiptoed its way onto my closed eyelids, I inhaled the sweet smell of freedom. It tasted great ... so great I decided I wanted a cigarette. I had ceased the lethal habit some years before and only occasionally indulged in the practice of pulling drags off tobacco. As I lazily made my way around upstairs searching for papers and tobacco, it dawned on me that I'd be much more useful and alert if I got some coffee.

After sitting down and enjoying a cup, I got hungry and boiled a few eggs. While I waited for the eggs to cook, I went to the front door. I opened it, walked halfway down the driveway where the *New York Times* was waiting for me wrapped in blue plastic. I splayed the paper onto the kitchen table and poured another cup of coffee. The front page was scattered with the usual sensational reports of the presidential race, coined the most important in history. It seems each presidential election is the most important in history.

As I sipped coffee and flipped through the *New York Times* pages, skimming over articles, I was so happy I didn't have to go in to work and that I wasn't in jail for shooting a cop. When the eggs were ready, I poured the hot water from the pot into the kitchen sink. I had never been good at peeling eggs, so it took a lot longer than it should have.

By the time I finished peeling and eating the eggs, reading the entire *New York Times* and polishing off the whole pot of coffee that's automatically made by the machine every morning, the clock above the stove read 11:22 am.

I folded the newspaper and threw it on a chair closest to the entrance by the stairs. Even though I could come down into the kitchen directly from upstairs, for whatever reason, I always came down the steps in the front of the house and walked from there into the kitchen through the entrance. I sat in the chair and thought about this for a while. As you can clearly see, I was deathly bored.

I sat in the chair staring at the sink and began to think……

Consider all of the time put together to make this house. I wonder what it would cost to destroy it or if I started to take it apart piece by piece with just my hands, how long would it take? Maybe I would need more than a hammer; perhaps a sledge would do the trick. Sledge always makes me think of sludge; messy old things stuck up in the tail pipe or any pipe for that matter. How can I even find out to call a plumber? I wonder if a plumber has a diagnostics test just like you would get done on your body to see if you're sick, but I guess that's called a physical and the body is so complicated that they miss a lot of things a lot of the times. When's the last time I even went to the doctor? When I started working for the Press Secretary, I guess I never would've imagined I'd be working for the Press Secretary this long. I really don't miss it in the beginning. Honestly, it's starting to get to the point where I don't want to do the work anymore. Maybe that's why I'm happy about not working. I do miss being able to sit like this and do absolutely nothing and just think and be able to eat breakfast which I am never able to do. These past few days have been great. Let's see, if I stopped working what would I do and how long it would be before I ran out of money. Well, how long the money would hold up would determine what exactly I'd do when I quit because I've got to do something; can't sit around all day on my ass and wonder if the mailman with my check came today. Mailman is such a tough job. That's another thing I really don't want to ever do again. Working for the Press Secretary is definitely not as bad as that job was. What a horrible way to make a living! I guess, in part, that's what makes it a noble profession and it is a trade, if you will; not as useful as painting, hammering or plumbing, but the only thing mattering in the evenings is how listening to the little things glowing between the brightest of corners tucked away in the shade of all that. I would like to see my mind wandering through the hula hoops of life, attacking and crashing together the remarkably kind softening rays of all that is observable in this day and age. How is it that even now the regret of losing her pulls at me always, even getting in the way of this time when I just let my mind wander and no, we can't go in that direction because it will make me unhappy and today is a good day so far? So it'd be very nice not to ruin it in any sort of way; just waddle through it as best as I can without making any waves or doing something stupid. It's always the stupid things that tug at the only real reasons that exist in these parts for the outcome is never worth the crime and now my thoughts have wandered into that other place. It's that place I seldom wish to go and it's because of the sadness and her pervasive sweet scent and her beautiful behind, so firm and so bubbly all mixed together into the tightest little compact lover I had ever had; no one like her before. She seemed to be sent especially for me, there could not be a very strange and very hard slap to the face as the last remembrance I have of her and how I had broken her heart and how she was going to give me everything. She really loved me and I loved her and I broke her heart because I was broken and hurting and I keep hurting and breaking those dumb enough to let me in. I let them in and wonder what it takes to lose, the breakdown of all of this is being put into focus and I wish there was no more sadness. All of the pain is overwhelming and it does in fact seem to be overpowering me. This is how we always gather all of the words and put them together. What is it that I am trying to say when I think in this way? There aren't any reasons why we were not good together. It was me that was bad in the head, me and my mind, and it was because of you, my wonderful friend, who insisted on thinking everything that's presented as negative and pointing it all at me and making me feel like I'm nothing and feeling like nothing makes you do stupid things like not to respect your queen who was willing to lay it all down and left another man for you, but she wanted to leave him in the first place. I doubt I am that powerful of a seducer to really truly do that, and come to think of it, I can't possibly forget about the way she treated me, the way I let her treat me, the way I let them all treat me. It was audacious the way they were always so suspicious and then the get-backs and put-downs and lashes in anger and frustration. I prided myself on being fair, calm and collected. It seems like no one else was concerned about such things and now I can't stop thinking, "Ain't that a bitch, the damn things took over again and those wonderful negative thoughts, I can feel them creeping along, trying their best to break through and pour it all down the long narrow display of cleavage representing my heart exposed for vultures to pick at as they pleased.

A loud rattle sounded from the door, knocking me thankfully from my stream of thinking.

I rose from the kitchen table and went to see who it was at the door.

It was another Priority letter from the Press Secretary.

I thanked the deliveryman and opened the envelope. A thin manila file was contained within it. I pulled it out and tossed the empty envelope, which I would to my dismay discover later wasn't completely empty.

Returning to the kitchen, I tossed the file on the table. Pulling down from the cupboard above the coffee machine my stash of Italian whiskey, I poured myself a glass three fingers-full. I was out of the thought stream, but they were still there in the back of my head, feeding the reel of the movie through the projection screen reserved especially to play these horrible movies in the theatre of my brain.

The whiskey burned the back of my throat, causing me to choke a second later. The slow descent of the liquor into my gut warmed and relaxed the tense muscles in my stomach. I realized I was close to an anxiety attack. I poured another two fingers and put the stash back up in the cupboard. I nursed this second glass of whiskey as I wandered around the house, willing my mind to be blank and think of nothing. Thinking of nothing is a very difficult thing. Nothing doesn't mean absence of thought, but rather not attaching oneself to the thinking being done.

After twenty minutes of nursing the second glass of whiskey and walking around the house like a crazy person, trying not to think, I remembered the file I had received from the Press Secretary. I like this working from home thing, but it all was starting to make me wonder what exactly was happening with the Press Secretary. I tried to wrap my head around London and recall whatever was going on there. The Brexit vote that had taken place a few months ago was the only thing I could think of as far as London politics was concerned. My knowledge of foreign affairs was certainly lacking, something I made a mental note to improve upon over the next few days I had off.

Putting a halt to all the guessing, I opened the file that had been sent to me by the Press Secretary. It was a single sheet of some very fancy, heavily decorated gold paper. It always amazed me how she was able to write the most concise messages enfolded with tons of information. This letter was no different. Well, there was one difference. She wrote it in ink. It was the first time I had ever seen the Press Secretary's elegant penmanship.

The letter read simply.

"Cecil, Pack your bags. I need you here in London tomorrow night. Plan to stay at least a week."
     -Antoinette

By nine o'clock that evening I was on a United Airlines flight heading to London. I always loved flying. The best is when you happen to get trapped in the window seat by a beautiful stranger named Janelle Muberty.

"Are you coming or going?" she asked me after the Captain turned off the fasten seat belt sign.
"Going."
"First time to London?"
"Yes, actually."
"Vacation?"
"No, business."
"Oh, too bad. I was thinking of taking you to bed with me when we land."
"I'm sure I'll have a little time before I have to go in to the office."
"Oh, so much to look forward to, what do you do?"

I don't know why, but that question always makes me feel uneasy, like I'm being investigated all of a sudden.

A few hours into our flight, after Janelle Muberty and I small-talked our way into silence and grabbed some much needed shut-eye, I was up and about. Walking up and down the aisles of the plane, stretching my legs along the way, I scanned all the passengers that I could see. Most were sleeping, s few looked up and smiled, mostly women. A few men nodded sternly, what is it with men and insecurity making us act mean? When I made it to the back lavatories I found them both occupied, so I waited.

Idling my time rummaging through the different drawers and shelves of the flight attendants' quarters, I spied a small cooler with no top sitting on the counter next to the coffee machine. The cooler was filled with a great assortment of mini bottles of vodka and whiskey. Like a kid in a candy store, I tucked about a dozen into my suit jacket and pants pockets. As I got the last of the small bottles into my hand, the flight attendant who had helped me with my seat belt entered the flight attendant quarters.

I stood there looking like a kid caught with his hand in a cookie jar laughing it off as if I was just looking. She smiled politely and pointed to the coffee machine.

"Would you like a cup?" the flight attendant asked me after grabbing the pot and a tray of cups.

"Yes, please," I responded, not seeing much of a reason to turn down free coffee.

"Let me take care of all the other passengers and then I'll come back to you. I should be finished by the time you finish in the bathroom."

"Thank you, that's very kind of you."

"I'm here to serve you." This last bit she said with a lift of her eyebrow and a glance down at my feet. She turned to return to her duties, then abruptly turned back and took a step in, leaning closer. "Just so you know the liquor is free and you can take as much as you want. So you don't have to tuck any more bottles in your crotch."

"I haven't stuffed any in my crotch, just my suit jacket and pants pockets."

"Oh, how embarrassing."

"Don't be embarrassed, it's rather flattering."

"Very funny," the mocha-skinned woman with an afro flight attendant said, visibly blushing, she turned again and went about fulfilling her duties.

As I watched her walk away, hips swaying as she kept her balance with the slight turbulence of the plane. Both the lavatory doors unlocked at the same time. I was beginning to get excited at the wonderful spirit I had just spoken with.

A large white man and a very small old Asian woman exited the lavatories simultaneously. The man let the woman pass first down the aisle to return to her seat, acknowledged me with a nod and followed a sensible distance behind the old Asian woman to his seat. I entered the lavatory the woman had just used and urinated.

Draining all the pee I had in me, when I exited the lavatory, the wonderfully spirited mocha-skinned flight attendant with an afro stood waiting for me with a cup of coffee in her hands. She handed it to me and smiled.

"Is there anything else I can do for you," she asked.

I very briefly thought about pulling her into the lavatory and making out like high schoolers tucked away in some stairwell, ditching class to press our bodies against one another and discover the new sensations arising from the exploration of each other's sexuality. This was just a fun thought to have, though. Nothing to act upon, I took the coffee and smiled.

"Have a drink with me."
"We're not allowed to drink while on duty."
"You mean to tell me you've never had a drink while flying."
"Well, I can't say that."
"I thought so, no reason not to have a quick drink with me," I said removing one of the mini liquor bottles from my outside left jacket pocket. "Would you hold this," I said handing her back the cup of coffee.

Breaking the seal on the bottle I took a step closer to the flight attendant and poured the whiskey in. I heard her take a surprised breath when I moved toward her. I re-pocketed the empty whiskey bottle and offered her the first sip.

"Ouch, it's hot."
"Blow on it."
"You blow on it."
"Sure."

I got even closer to the mocha-skinned flight attendant with an afro. Putting my hands over her own, I blew lightly on the cup of coffee we were now holding together. This went on longer than it needed to, but I saw no reason to interrupt the moment.

"There you go," I said taking a step back. "Should be good now."

I watched the flight attendant take a sip, closing her eyes as the now luke-warm liquid made its way down, warming her belly.

"You can go ahead and finish it," I said, taking another bottle out of the same jacket pocket.

I spotted a trashcan behind the wonderfully spirited flight attendant, who I was beginning to take a liking to. I fished out the empty mini-bottle of whiskey and tossed it. The bottle I pulled out this time turned out to be vodka, which would determine my mood for the remainder of the flight to London. I swallowed it down in a few gulps, tossed this second bottle behind the first in the trash bin. Then troubled the flight attendant to pour me some more coffee.

It was a good thing, too, for just at that moment one of her co-workers made his way into the flight attendant quarters.

"Hello," the man said to me. He was medium height and build, with excited rosy skin. He looked as if he had been running on a hot day. His smile was authentic and calming.

"There's a customer in First Class who would like a cup, as well."

"Thank you, I'll get right on it. Take care, Sir," she said politely to me before fleeing down the airplane toward whoever it was that wanted a cup of coffee--if they even existed in the first place.

I took a sip of my coffee and eyed the male flight attendant, smiling softly at the hilarity of the scene before me. I was beginning to get the feeling that this Jack liked the mocha-skinned flight attendant with an afro and a naturally formed juicy booty. Her body was accentuated perfectly in the tight uniform United had required her to wear. And I was blessing them for it as I sipped my coffee and replayed the feeling of having my hands over hers as I blew on the cup of coffee she was holding.

"I'm going to have to ask you to return to your seat, Sir," the male flight attendant said. I guess he got tired of my sipping.

"I thought we were allowed to stretch our legs."

"Yes, of course you are, Sir. However just at this moment the captain has turned on the fasten seatbelts sign. Perhaps you didn't notice because you were using the toilet."

"I suppose. Well, thank you, I've got my coffee, so I'll skedaddle."

"Very good, Sir. Do watch your step, it's expected to get a bit bumpy from now until we land."

"Thanks for the heads up."

The male flight attendant nodded and smiled his comforting smile. I nodded to him and returned to my seat.

"I thought you'd fallen in," Janelle said as I climbed over her to get to the window seat.

"They were both occupied but I was able to pick up these while I waited."

I pulled out two mini bottles that turned out to be one vodka and one whiskey.

"You got goodies."

"You want vodka or whisky?"

"Oh, vodka it would have to be."

"An excellent choice Madam, Here you are," I said handing her the mini bottle of Grey Goose.

I pocketed the mini bottle of Jack Daniels whiskey and pulled out bottles until I found another vodka. I had four mini bottles of whiskey, all different brands, sitting in my lap. Johnnie Walker, Jack Daniels, Makers Mark and Bushmills.

"Nice selection," Janelle said as she watched me stuff the four whiskey bottles back into my suit jacket and pants pockets.

"Shall we," I said after cracking the seal on the bottle of Absolute vodka I grabbed out of my pants pocket.
"Yes, we shall indeed."

We clicked our mini bottle necks together and swallowed our liquor. Savoring every drop, I felt the tension in my stomach melt away.

"That's nice, just what I needed. I'm not very good at flying," Janelle said to me.
"Really? You could've fooled me. Thought you were the height of cool and collected."
"No, that seems to be you. I can't tell what you're thinking, even when you were sleeping, your face was like concrete. Hard and unchanging."
"You were watching me sleep?" I asked with a smile.
"I wasn't watching, I just glanced from time to time. You coughed once, just made sure you were still breathing."
"Oh, you were worried about me. Are you always like this?"
"Like what?"
"Showing concern for strangers you've only just met on airplanes?"
"I try to care about all those I meet."
"Even those that stick you up and rob you?"
"I've never been stuck up or robbed."
"Well, now that's lucky."
"I would say it's fortunate."
"Same difference."
"No, actually they are two entirely different things."
"Really?"
"Yes, one is controlled by the environment and the other by the heart of the individual experiencing it."
"Now, that's fascinating, let's have another drink and you tell me all about it."

We ended up having way more than just one drink. We talked for the rest of the flight. The mocha-skinned flight attendant with an afro stayed on the other side of the plane and I didn't get a chance to talk with her at all for the last half of the flight. It wasn't until exiting the plane that she stood there smiling that wonderfully spirited smile, thanking me for flying with United Airlines. I drunkenly mumbled something and slipped her my card. She seemed to take it enthusiastically, which I appreciated a great deal.

Janelle was a few steps ahead of me as I was in the window seat and she had the aisle, so she didn't see me slip the card to the flight attendant.

As I walked down the tarmac with the other passengers, I wondered if the flight attendant was from the States or London. I hadn't detected any sort of accent, but ways of speech can be stripped and changed.

Getting off a plane after being jettisoned through the clouds at an alarmingly fast speed always leaves me discombobulated. Being drunk didn't help matters, but its better being drunk than sober going through this experience. I stopped off at the loo and rinsed my face in the sink. Looking at my reflection in the mirror, my eyes looked tired. That was ok. I just got off an international flight. And was drunk. I was allowed to be tired. I looked at my Hamilton wristwatch and shook my head because I was still on Chicago time.

Janelle was waiting for me at the entrance to customs. The line was zig-zagged with people filling the entire room. The worker at the beginning of the line let Janelle and I and everyone else in shouting distance know that the wait would be at least forty-five minutes.

Janelle nudged me in the ribs with her elbow and said, "Let's pretend to be a loving couple that can't keep their hands off each other, but are respectful with our PDA"

"1960's PDA."

"I like that you figure things out so quickly," Janelle said, leaning her body back into my chest and letting her entire weight fall on me.

When we stepped out into the London air, it mattered not that the sky was still purple around the world. There was no light to see the sky.

One of the bolder countries had set off electromagnetic bombs systematically throughout North America, Europe and Australia. The pulse went off right at the moment Janelle and I stepped in front of the automatic doors to exit the baggage claim area onto the street. The doors didn't respond.

I remember it all so clearly because I slammed my face into the glass doors that didn't slide open because the bomb had just gone off. There was no force, no explosion; absolutely nothing to indicate that the power of all the First World countries had been switched off. The bombs sent a pulse through everything electrical, burning out everything.

I forced the sliding glass doors open and Janelle and I exited the London airport. Darkness covered everything, silence usually filled with the hum of motors and the rumble of electricity pervading any Super Power city engulfed everything.

Behind us, the darkness was no less. Certainly worse being that the lights in the airport had just been on. Cars, taxis and vans were all stalled. The drivers and passengers inside the vehicles were all trying to piece together, just as we were, what was going on at that moment.

The planes started to fall not too long afterward.

The first plane hit the highway in a puff of fire illuminating the scene. There was no time to think when that first plane crashed into the earth. The second boom knocked me awake. Before we knew it, planes were falling all around us. The ground was shaking. The noise was unbearable and wave after wave of force generated from the exploding planes pushed all around us. I remember there being so much dust.

I grabbed Janelle by the hand and ran forward, trying to get as far away from the airport as possible. She was keeping good pace with me, so I let go of her hand and picked up speed. With our feet pitter-patting against the pavement, I was scanning my mind for options on what to do next.

"We'll need a bicycle," Janelle Muberty said to me through a hard gasp as we were pumping our arms and legs, running as fast as we could.

Janelle's suggestion set my mind toward a proper destination.

"You're right. We're gonna have to steal one, I'm sure we can find one not being used closer into the city."

"Where are we going to go, the Embassy?"

"That seems like the best bet at this point, you wouldn't happen to know where it is would you?"

"Yeah, I know exactly where it is. I work there."

"You work at the Embassy?"

"Yes, I thought you did too. You said you work for the Press Secretary. She's in and out of the American Embassy constantly."

"What exactly do you do for a living?" I asked Janelle as I spied a bike and pointed at it.

"I'm in law enforcement," she responded, taking the hint and running toward the bike.

"At the Embassy?"

"Yep. At the Embassy."

"So what were you doing in Chicago?"

"I'm from Chicago. I was visiting my parents for Labor Day."

When we got to the bike, it was chained to a telephone pole. I broke the lock with a rock and then Janelle mounted on the seat. I climbed up onto the handlebars and away we went down the street. Janelle drove since she knew the way. Otherwise, I wouldn't have had to deal with balancing my weight on the uncomfortable handlebars.

"How long is it going to take to get there?" I asked Janelle, trying my best not to tip us over. I was skinny, but muscular, and a slight shift in the wrong direction would definitely cause us to topple over, given the circumstances of barely being able to see, I'd say Janelle already had enough trouble other than worrying about my ass knocking us over.

"I'm not sure, given the circumstances, usually it takes about forty minutes by car and that's with traffic. I've never tried to bike there. I don't even know if you can."

"Well, we're going to find out either way."

"Lucky us," Janelle said.

We made our way through the dark maze of stopped cars and confused pedestrians. Everyone was wandering this way and that, trying their best to make sense and figure out exactly what was taking place. The air was stale and the hum of electricity was nowhere to be heard or felt. Even the panicked murmurings of the pedestrians around us could barely pierce the silence that had enveloped reality.

I knew it wouldn't be long before the looting started. It's never long before people figure out an advantage to be exploited. It was comforting to know that hoodlums in London were just the same as back in the States, predictable, dumb and slow.

As Janelle peddled us closer to the Embassy, I kept a sharp lookout for approaching danger. Perched atop the handlebars as I was, my left butt check started to fall asleep. I wriggled a little more than was necessary to keep the balance of the bicycle and did exactly what I had feared, toppling us over onto the concrete. Almost as quickly as we were on our feet, the bike we had stolen was stolen from us by someone we couldn't even see as they rode away.

I kicked my left leg trying to jiggle my buttock to get the sensation back.

"We lost our ride because you had to adjust?"
"No, my butt fell asleep riding on the handlebars."
"You couldn't just deal with it?"
"Have you ever had one cheek fall asleep? It's bloody uncomfortable as hell."
"If we get murdered because of your ass falling asleep, I'm going to be angry."
"You'll be more than angry, you'll be dead."
"Let's start walking."
"I'm following you."
"Thanks."

So we walked. It ended up taking us two hours by my Hamilton wristwatch with a light built in to illuminate the clock hands. During that entire time Janelle didn't say a word. Not necessarily minding the silence, I said nothing as well. At first I thought a lot about whether or not I had ruined my chances of getting cozy with Janelle, but then the reality of no electricity smacked me square in the face. The two of us knew nothing of the circumstances of the massive power outage. We had no way of knowing that America had considered the attack an Act of War and the country responsible was in the crosshairs of us and our allies.

I figured, I'm sure Janelle did too, that this was some kind of terrorist attack. It certainly had caused enough havoc. With hours before the sun would be thinking about rising, there was no telling what London or the rest of the First World countries would look like by morning.

I kept a respectable distance behind Janelle as we walked. I knew I really had pissed her off by causing us to fall off the bike, but a numb butt cheek just ain't nice. I didn't mind walking behind her so much. Both her butt cheeks were just fine, firm, plump and round. Janelle had a booty that was worth taking the time to admire. Luckily, she was wearing highlighter orange yoga pants that were tighter than a nun's love for God.

Once we finally arrived at the American Embassy, we walked up to the gate and showed the soldiers our IDs. As to be expected, the place was swarming with faces filled with fear and confusion. The stoic, unexpressive faces of the young warriors poised to protect us with their lives was calming amongst the cowards hollering, "Save me, please. I'm important, I must get back to America."

For some reason, many people were under the stupid belief that America still had its lights on with no understanding that the electricity was out, thus preventing any and all communication, especially since we had put all of our freedom into electricity.

"Now what do we do?" Janelle asked, speaking for the first time.

I knew she was talking to herself but I figured I'd answer her anyway.

"Let's go find someone with some rank and get some answers."
"That's about the only idea I had. Come on, this way."

I happily followed her as she took off in a sprint down the atrium toward the stairs. I watched as people stupidly looked at their cell phones, they weren't going to work. Nothing with a switch, button, microchip or electrical wire was working. It was as if a giant magnet was put beside the central computer connecting the First World together. The Second and Third World countries didn't suffer because they weren't targeted. But even if they had been, there wouldn't have been much of a difference. It is for this reason of unbalanced and unfair politics and justice that the boldest country in the globe decided to level the playing field and make all countries equal. Relatively speaking, it was the easiest way to shut down the world order and cause enough mayhem to insure a declaration of martial law which would narrowed the playing field significantly.

As I watched Janelle work her way through the crowd of people oblivious to the others around them, their own concerns the only thing of importance, I spotted the Press Secretary.

I should say, she spotted me. And I shouldn't have been surprised to find her in the midst of a meeting with what looked like generals. It was a quick glance from her that let me know she had seen me. She tilted her head up slightly and I grabbed hold of Janelle's hand and lightly pulled her along in the direction of the Press Secretary.

Janelle protested meekly using her mouth. She allowed me to lead her. The way she submitted herself let me know there was still a chance we might become cuddle buddies. We approached the circle of generals listening intently to the Press Secretary.

"Ah, Cecil, good, you're here," she said to me as we arrived at the back of one of the generals. He was at least six feet tall and his shoulders were as wide as an oak tree. He turned slowly and looked down at me. I nodded and stepped forwarded, moving as if I was able to walk through him. The general stepped aside and let me and Janelle into the circle. I walked up to the Press Secretary and greeted her.

"Cecil, you're just in time. I was just catching the generals up on what we know so far. You and your friend need to know this."

I pulled out a notepad I use for such occasions with the Press Secretary. These occasions arise quite often when we are together outside the office.

"Ok, my apologies, Gentlemen. As I was saying..."

"Wait just a minute," one of the generals interrupted.

"Yes," the Press Secretary calmly answered.

"Just who are these two and what makes them think they have the security clearance to be in this meeting?"

"Very good question General, I am glad you asked, this is Cecil. He is my assistant and this is Ms. Janelle Muberty, General. If you had been paying attention, has been working here at the Embassy as a security guard at the entrance for a while now. Isn't that right, Janelle?"

"Yes, Ma'am, It is. I appreciate you for noticing."

"You're very welcome. I see I'm not the only one to have taken a notice to you. Eh, Cecil?"

"Can we get on with this?" another general blurted out.

"If there are no further questions, I would like to continue, there's a lot of information Gentlemen, so I won't have any more interruptions. Is that understood?"

They all nodded like obedient bobble heads.

Now that our credentials had been clarified, the Press Secretary went on with her briefing. We learned exactly just what the hell was happening.

The nefariousness of the situation was astounding, following the briefing with the generals, Antoinette Stalk, the Press Secretary, scuttled Janelle and I down the stairs to an emergency exit into a bunker under the American Embassy.

"Things are about to get pretty hot upstairs," the Press Secretary said. "It'll be best if we stay down here until we're given the all clear. None of us is trained for what's about to take place."

"It's the purple sky." I said.

"What? That doesn't make any sense," Janelle, uncharacteristically, interrupted.

The epiphany moment happened.

"Why is it that you say it doesn't make sense?"

"Because it was explained on the news everywhere that it occurred because of a storm of space dust that gathered around the planet."

"And that explanation makes sense to you?"

"I'm not a scientist. They said it was going to be over soon, so there was no cause to worry. Why would the scientists reporting on what was happening fabricate a story? Why wouldn't they just tell us the truth?"

"It's called misdirection," the Press Secretary chimed in.

"I'm familiar with the term. Not quite fluent in it, however. Perhaps you'd be kind enough to further enlighten me."

"Cecil can do that for you. Can't you, Cecil? I have some business to attend to."

The Press Secretary pulled a cell phone from her suit pants pocket.

"You can't use cell phones, remember?"

"No, you can't use cell phones, I'm afraid, this phone's connected to the only working source of electricity in London, completely disconnected from any outside source. There's no way in."

"How is that even possible?"

"It's been made so, Cecil, do you mind catching the young woman up on the misdirection of the purple sky?" the Press Secretary said, pressing a button on the phone. Putting it to her ear, she turned her back to us and walked slowly out of the scene.

"Sure thing," I said to the back of the Press Secretary, covered in shadows tucked in the corner of the bunker on the only working cell phone in London. "It's like this," I began to explain to Janelle.

"Before you start, who the hell is that woman?" Janelle said pointing to the Press Secretary.

"That's the Press Secretary," I casually responded. She didn't seem to appreciate this.

"The Press Secretary of what?"

"Oh, what? Why, the United States of America, of course."

"Oh?" Janelle responded, stumped as to what to say next.

"Any other questions?"

"No, please continue."

"Thank you. The purple sky that occurred a few days ago was the result of the bold country's attack on the First World countries around the globe. The one thing that all super powers depend on is electricity. This simple function can destroy a single republic, especially any that have designed their infrastructure to be solely dependent on the function of electricity. There didn't seem to be much of a problem with deciding to rid our systems of paper. The environmental people seemed to think it was a good idea, but to not back anything up with paper and store it in the archives just in case the day arrived when there was no electricity was utterly stupid. So the day arrived, the purple sky was the way of letting the outside agents know that a massive shift in the power structure was about to take place."

"Who are the outside agents?"

"That, Janelle, is the mystery."

"No one knows who the outside agents are?"

"No, they are outside our reality?"

"What the fuck does that mean? They're aliens or something?"

"That's actually neither denied nor confirmed."

"You must be kidding me."

"It would explain why the signal was in the Earth's atmosphere."

"What's going to happen to our atmosphere now that you bring it up since this shit was put up in the sky to signal the 'outside agents'?"

"I'm not really sure about the ramifications of making the sky turn purple. I imagine that whatever was used to make such a thing happen around the entire planet was a strong chemical that will have awful effects. But what do the super powers care? They've lost everything and they know it. They're reaching out in hopes that they will be bailed out by the 'outside agents.'"

"How could the 'outside agents' possibly bail out the previously First World countries?"

"Simple, by removing them from this reality."

"Ok. Now you've lost me."

"Brace yourselves!" the Press Secretary yelled out.

The ground shook with ferocity. In the blink of an eye, I was on the hard, cold concrete of the bunker underneath the London American Embassy. The earthquake did not abate for several moments. I couldn't get a clear picture of anything. My vision was blurred. The earth was shifting. When it finally stopped, the silence overtaking the bunker was astonishingly loud. After a while, I realized my ears were ringing.

I slowly lifted myself up and assessed the damage to myself, then I scanned the bunker for Janelle and the Press Secretary. I heard a cough to the left of me. I spied Janelle lifting herself up like she was doing a push-up from the concrete of the bunker.

"Are you alright?" I screamed over to her.

"Not really," she said, still coughing.

I got to my wobbly feet, balancing myself, my gaze shifted forward and then dropped down to my feet. In another blink of the eye, I realized I was on the ground again. Fuck! I must've hit my head, I thought.

I tried to move, but my limbs were not obeying me. My shoulders moved up and down in a hopelessly sad Harlem shake. Face down on the cold concrete, I was without feeling.

"Cecil!" I heard the Press Secretary yell out.

"Over here," I said, happy I had been spared movement above my shoulders.

"Janelle?" I heard the Press Secretary ask.

The sound of shifting stone grated against my ears. I rested my head on my chin, trying my hardest to look left and right and trying to find the Press Secretary or Janelle.

I saw nothing.

"Listen to my voice," I heard Janelle say. I didn't know who she was speaking to. I decided it was me.

"Cecil, I'm coming to you, I'm touching your leg. Can you feel me?"

I couldn't.

"It's ok, just keep getting ready to feel me."

I would later find out that Janelle rubbed her hands from my ankles to my neck. Her hands rubbed against the tattoo on my neck and that's was when I felt her hands. The sensation crept only through my head, but my thoughts immediately went to tying her body to mine.

"How do you feel?" Janelle asked me.

Looking into my face, she smiled and cried and at the same time she seemed to know something that I didn't.

"I feel alright, just can't move. I stood up one time, but I fell back down."

"Can you feel this?"

"No, I don't feel anything."

"OK. It's ok. Your feeling will come back in a bit, I'm sure."

It didn't.

For the next three days, trapped in that bunker underneath the American Embassy in London, I was chained to the bed, afraid I was paralyzed from the neck down for the rest of my days.

As you can imagine, I had a lot of thinking time on my hands. This is what I thought about that first night as Janelle and the Press Secretary enjoyed their pleasant slumbers. I was forced to stare at the ceiling and ponder the disaster that I felt had unfairly struck me. Never mind that the world was crumbling above the bunker I was in.

I thought: "The ceiling is so dirty. Would it bother them to try and wash it every now and then? I guess it would be too much worry and then you'd have to pay someone and that would just make things even more inconvenient. No one likes to pay money, but money must be paid even to make it, although, spending it is fun. Well, it can be, I guess, if you spend it on fun things. Even those fun things have a way of becoming something less fun than could be lost in the breeze of discovery and that is the only real chance I will have at happening upon my own fortune in winning the lottery. At this point, look at me. I've lost everything. I'm sitting here, not even sitting, but laying here, and wondering, not even wondering. I want to sleep. I want to stop thinking. I can't even give myself the benefit of entertainment because I'm so bummed at my current situation. Anyway, long story short, who am I talking to? What is the point of any of this? I'm going to die or, if I have something to look forward to in terms of living, it's as a paraplegic "cause that's what it seems I am and I don't like that. Seems like the cruelest joke any god could impart on a person. Good thing I'm Buddhist, but even from a Buddhist perspective, why the fuck do I gotta deal with all this? I guess its 'cause of karma, we would say, but why did I create this kind'a karma and then that's a whole other conversation I need to have with myself and that's not something that other people, or anyone, or you reading this for that matter could answer, and yes, I'm speaking to you in my thoughts because this is what I was thinking about when I thought about what I'm telling you I'm saying happened and I knew we would be speaking, so listen close to the words I'm saying and you'll maybe walk away feeling livelier and fresher than you set out to be."

My thoughts froze as footsteps approached.

The Law of Cause and Effect

The clump, thump of the boots above echoed down. Their sinister tromp crept its way slowly down, filling the bunker where we were trapped underneath the London American embassy.

I stared at the ceiling. Chanting to myself the prayer Sherrie and her family practiced daily, "Nam-myoho-renge-kyo" I remembered the first time I asked about the practice.

It was the first day I moved in with them; that day I told you about earlier when Sherrie's dad told the family that he found me in the alley robbing the dead man and I would be staying with them. It was just as much a shock to me as it was to the rest of the family.

"What do you mean, he's going to live with us?" the youngest daughter, Laurel, asked.

"I mean he is going to take the place of your brother Johnny and live with us."

"Daddy, how can you be so cold," Sherrie exclaimed in disdain at having a scavenger like me replace her honorable brother, Johnny.

"Sherrie, this boy is good," her father defended me. "He has had a tough beginning, but together we can inject enough love into him to bring him out of his misery. I found this boy in the alley robbing a man that had no semblance of a head. He didn't flinch; he didn't seem to feel any pity. He was just hungry and hoping he could eat. He's got no one. It's not fair that this happened to him and plus he's been handed to us by God."

"Daddy," Sherrie butt in. "It wasn't God that brought this boy to you, but your karma, according to Nichiren Buddhism, the two of you are fused by it."

"That seems to reinforce my point."

"I'm afraid it does, Sherrie," her mother said as she approached me.

"What's your name?" Sherrie's mom asked me. Stooping down to my height, her eyes squinted in pain as she leveled her own with mine. "Don't be afraid now."

"My name's Cecil," I responded.
"Cecil, that's a lovely name. How old are you, Cecil?"

"I'm ten," I answered.

"The best age. I remember when I was ten. Things were a lot different way back then."

"Back in the olden days," a little girl said from somewhere tucked away in the corner of the living room where the television was blaring.

"It wasn't that long ago, Laurel. You, too, will be old before you know it. So you should be nice to your mother."

"Yes, Ma'am, I'm sorry."

"It's ok. I know you were just trying to be funny. Come over here and meet Cecil, he's going to be your new brother."

"He's going to replace, Johnny?"

"No, Sweetheart," Sherrie's dad said. "Johnny can never be replaced. God has sent us this child because he took pity on us for having to take Johnny away."

"When've we talked about this?" Sherrie's mom said to the man who found me in the alley robbing a dead man.

"I'm really not trying to get into this right now. Look, I believe in God. You can believe in whatever you want, and our children can believe whatever they want also, but I'm not going to change the way I speak because you don't think God exists."

"I've never said God doesn't exist. I said I don't believe we are dependent upon some being outside ourselves."

"And I can't tell you how many times I've said that is not the way God is. God is not outside you. He is within you."

"Yes, but you believe it is because of him that everything happens."

"God allows us to be as we are and do the things we do. If we serve his purpose then we will be protected in life and rewarded in death."

"Why can't we be rewarded in life as well?"

"Are we really going to have this conversation in front of this boy on the first day I've brought him into our home as our son?"

"We might as well let him see honestly what kind of family he's walking into from the get go."

"Will you two stop fighting, please," Sherrie interjected. She was coming down the steps as the voices of her parents began to rise. I stood there with Laurel still watching television, ignoring the whole episode. I didn't know what to think, Sherrie took charge of the scene.

I watched her long, slinky frame as she walked down the stairs. Her undeveloped breasts pointed two little points through the blue tank top she wore. White sweats pulled tightly over her waist accentuated her shapely athletic legs.

"Mom, Dad. I'm sure, Cecil is probably really hungry. Why don't you all go into the kitchen and make him something. You can continue to discuss there."

The parents obeyed their daughter. After they went into the kitchen, Sherrie walked down the rest of the stairs toward me.

"My name is, Sherrie, Cecil, welcome to the family. Would you like to sit down on the couch and watch TV with Laurel?"

"Can I use the bathroom? I've been holding it for over an hour."

I watched as Sherrie gave me a truly genuine smile. It warmed me and brought about a sensation of comfort that still appears every time I see Sherrie. Even though it's been over ten years since I've seen her, I imagine that if I did see her again the same feeling would come over me.

There was a certain amount of pleasure in living with Sherrie's family. They lived on a routine and were always punctual. The father was a computer programmer at Sky-Tech International. You remember the little devices that came about after the iPhone 7's were released? They turned your phone into an automatic remote for anything that needed a remote. Sky-Tech International was the company that introduced the prototype. Apple would eventually steal the prototype and swear they never worked with Sky-Tech International, but they did give them a significant amount of money in exchange for their silence about the truth of it all.

Sherrie's father was part of the team that made the prototype. For his part, he received a substantial amount of money. Sherrie's mother was a public health consultant for Mt. Sinai Hospital in Chicago. She had been a nurse in the US Army once upon a time. She even served in the Gulf War and the Iraq War. Her pinky was shot off as she saved the life of a soldier. She was a bundle of cheer and I only saw her angry when she spoke to her husband.

Laurel, Sherrie's younger sister, was in the seventh grade when I was 'adopted' into the family. There wasn't a whole lot to her in the beginning. She went to school, was a good student and had a healthy number of friends ... guys and girls. It wasn't until high school that Laurel began to experiment with drugs. She would eventually get pregnant during her senior year and drop out with a semester left before graduation. This was after I left the house for China. I was updated once a week by post card. It was only Sherrie and her mother who took the time to write me. It was for this reason that I knew Sherrie's father didn't care for me. As much as I owed him for saving my life, he was an angry man. I didn't like angry men.

The first night I stayed in the house, I was given their dead son, Johnny's, room. It had been kept exactly as it was before Johnny had died, I assumed. Sherrie was the one that told me this. She walked me upstairs and opened all the closest doors and showed me inside all of the drawers.

"All of this was my brother's, he was killed a few months ago. Now that you are going to be living with us, it's all yours now."

"Does that make me your new brother?"

"Let's not jump to any conclusions, I don't know how long you're going to end up staying here."

"I really appreciate that you all are letting me stay here."

"Thank my dad, he's the one who found you and brought you here. It's because of his faith in God that he believes you've been sent here to replace Johnny."

"Do you believe that?"

"I don't believe in God. I'm Buddhist."

"I've never met a Buddhist before. What's that like?"

"It's very liberating. I am free of the guilt and suffering so many seem to feel is part of being human."

"I know a lot about guilt and suffering. It's no fun."

"Yeah, I can tell. Perhaps you'll tell me about your travels sometime later when you're settled and feel ok."

"I don't mind talking right now."

"Don't strain yourself too much. I'm sure you've had a long day."

"It's been a long ten years."

"Well, would you like anything to eat before you sleep?"

"Well, I'm not very sleepy; more excited than anything else."

"Yea, I can imagine, but, it doesn't matter if you're sleepy or not, you've got to be in bed by 9:00 and it's already after that. You're actually making me late."

"I'm sorry."

"It's ok. My dad said I was allowed a bit of leeway in order to help you get settled."

"Well, if you're allowed some leeway, will you keep me company for a little bit?"

"I guess I could do that." Sherrie sat down on the edge of the bed, I sat at the top near the pillow. We sat and stared at each other, she was older than me, more mature, and, there was something in her eyes that demanded a certain level of respect that I had never experienced in a young woman. "So tell me about yourself, Cecil."

"Well, up until a few months ago, I was a sad tenant of the Smitheran Sweets Adoption Agency. "Where forgotten children are found" was their motto. It should have been, "Where forgotten children go to disappear.""

"Do you remember anything before that?"

"Not much. I was sent there when I was really young. My parents, I was told, died in a plane crash. I found a news clipping of the accident one day and kept it. I assumed based on the dates and the low frequency of plane crashes being reported that it was probably them. The head mistress found the news clipping and made me burn it. 'There is no room for sympathy here at Smitheran Sweets Adoption Agency,' she said to me."

"That's horrible, how is such a place even allowed to exist?"

"I don't know, but it sure does exist. When I turned ten it was time for me to escape."

"Why when you turned ten?"

"Because on your eleventh birthday they sent you underground to work in the mines."

"The mines, underneath the adoption agency, my goodness. Why do they do that?"

"No one knows. Well, I'm sure the head mistress knows, but all the other workers didn't seem to know anything about what's under the building. It was talked about with such fear and dread and learned quickly not to question it. Nor anything else for that matter."

Sherrie noticed the book I had grabbed from the bookshelf in the living room.

"Have you read that before?"

"No. Never, I did hear of the name, though. Tarzan, king of the apes. The janitor used to tell me stories. He's how I learned to read."

"They didn't teach you to read at the school?"

"It wasn't a school, it was an adoption agency. When kids were given up for adoption they were shipped to Smiterian Sweets. It is a horrible place, in the main lobby and on the first floor, they kept all the well-behaved kids. All ages. They put them on display. There is a great reception area that is welcoming and attractive, and from the appearance of the lobby, Smitheran Sweets seems like the greatest place for unwanted children to be cared for and nurtured, at least until a family comes in and takes them away to a better life. Once the doors are bolted and the lights are turned out, it becomes a detention center."

"Why!?"

"I have no idea? Well, after all that occurred, I finally escaped after my friend Zenek was sent to the mines. Zenek and I had been working out a plan to escape for three years. Really, it was Zenek who put together the plan, he was Russian and really smart. They said he was a genius, even though he didn't read or anything. He just knew everything he needed to know. Out of everyone, I heard that Zenek was the one who was there from the youngest age. Basically, from the womb, he was sent to the adoption agency. I never heard anything about his parents and I never heard anything about where he was from. I don't even know if Zenek knew where he was from or who his parents were. "

"This is all very horrible. I'm so sorry," Sherrie started crying.

Her sobs filled her dead brother, Johnny's, old room which had just become my room. As I listened to her, I was filled with an overpowering emotion I had never felt before. This feeling stayed with me for the entire time I stayed with Sherrie and her family.

"Are you ok?" I asked, not sure what to do.

"Yes, I'm fine, I'm sorry, it's just all so sad. You've been through so much in just ten years. I can't imagine it."

"How old are you?"

"What? Me? I'm fourteen. I just started my freshmen year of high school two months ago."

"How is high school?"

"So far, it's ok," Sherrie said, grabbing a tissue from the desk that was now my very own desk.

That indescribable feeling that creeps in each night, every night, began on that first day. The Godfather Part Two was playing on the television in the living room when I woke up the next morning. It was right at the beginning of the movie ... the funeral scene. I came down the stairs at the point where Vito Corleone's mother is crying over her eldest son whose been shot down by the men who killed his father, her husband. The boy had screamed for vengeance, so he was killed. The mother would later go to the Don responsible for all the killings and plead to save her youngest and last child, Vito. The Don refuses and the mother puts a knife to his throat. Vito runs, but not before watching his mother get gunned down by one of the Don's men.

I had never seen the Godfather Part One and I definitely hadn't seen the second movie either. It was good timing that I woke up when I did.

"Ah, you're finally awake," Sherrie's father said as he heard me coming down the stairs. "Come join us on the sofa. The movie just started. This is a good one."

I tucked into the corner of the sofa. There was plenty of room for me to spread out. Sherrie's mom and dad were cuddling in the other corner. Sherrie and her sister, Laurel, were laying on their stomachs on the floor, facing the television. Sherrie's legs hung in the air, swinging back and forth, hypnotizing me for a brief moment. It didn't matter that I could stretch out on most of the sofa and that I was encouraged to do so by Sherrie's mom. She was always kind to me.

When I returned my attention to the movie, young Vito Corleone was quarantined on Ellis Island after fleeing Italy by boat after the Don killed his entire family. This then cut to the present; all of that was a flashback. There was a party going on at a beach house. That scene I would later learn was a mirror image of the beginning of the first film that started with a wedding going on ... the same, but different. Foreshadowing the ascent to prominence of Michael Corleone and the simultaneous destruction of his family.

I could barely follow the plot. The vocabulary was beyond me and the acting was so superb that the entire production went over my head. The movie was so engrossing that I didn't stir for the entire film, all three-plus hours of it. After it was over, I suddenly realized that I had been holding my pee for a long time.

I carefully got up from the sofa and made my way to the toilet on the first floor. There were three toilets in the house. This certainly was an upgrade from the disastrously horrible one toilet shared by all of the orphans at Smitheran Sweets Adoption Agency. After emptying my ten-year-old bladder, I rejoined the family in the living room.

"Did you enjoy the movie?" Sherrie's father asked me.
"Yes, Sir." I said, realizing the dilemma of wondering what on earth to call this man who saved my life the previous day. Luckily, he answered the question for me.
"You don't have to call me, Sir. You can just call me, John."

John—as ordinary a name as any. But John, the father of the family, was no ordinary Joe by any means. Evens his job as a computer programmer was a misnomer that confused many. During his college years, John had served as a gatherer of information for a government agency. The reason I became privy to this information is that one night when Sherrie, Laurel and their mother were on a girls' night out, John got roaring drunk. I had seen John drunk and had even been allowed myself to get drunk with him, but that night he revealed his secret to me, I was fourteen.

John had set a glass filled with four fingers of whiskey and three cubes of ice on the coffee table in front of me as we watched reality TV.

He sat down in the chair opposite me with a long sigh that was typical when he sat in that particular chair. Sherrie told me once that it was the first chair John had bought when set out on his own, independent from his family.

"Daddy worships that chair. When he sits in it, he says all of the memories that chair contains come flooding back to him and he reviews his entire life from the beginning until whenever it is he's sitting there."

I tried on many occasions to sit in that chair and feel the same thing, but to no avail. I guess the mojo only worked with him.

By the time John placed that glass in front of me, he was already half a bottle ahead of me. After falling into his chair with a sigh and, I imagine, scanning through the Rolodex of his memories, John slumped his chin into his chest and fell asleep. At least, I thought he had fallen asleep. It turns out that he had fallen into deep thought concerning the mystical nature of how I had appeared in his life.

"The only reason I even walked down the alley," John began, startling me to the point where I almost dropped the glass of whiskey I had been taking nips of while I thought he was taking a nap. "The only reason I walked down that alley was because I had a thought. It was more like a vision. I saw you laying with your face up in a pool of your own blood. The snow was falling down on your small face and you were so close to death you weren't even shivering."

This morbid beginning captured my attention.

"I'm not sure if that was you sending me a signal or if that was God showing me what was to become of you. It wasn't snowing the day I found you; it wasn't even winter. It was just the beginning of fall. School was back in session and overall it was a very good day, not too hot and not too cold. I was on my lunch break from the office and had gotten into a rhythm of walking. The walking was supposed to improve my health and keep me from thinking about drinking.

"Drinking has always been a problem for me. I could never just stop cold turkey, but I did have to take breaks every few years or so. On the day that I found you, I guess that was what, four years ago, I was sober as a bone for three months. Before that, I had been drinking the worst of my entire life. That was after Johnny had been murdered.

"When you lose a child in that way--and I hope neither you nor any of my daughters ever have to experience this-- a piece of your heart is torn away and most of your soul dies. You wander through life with half a heart and very little soul to call your own. It's interesting that at that time I was the most productive at work. Maybe it was the sympathy everyone was giving me and ignoring the fact that I was drunk as a skunk every time I walked into the office. But I did my work and I delivered.

"But you can't keep that type of lifestyle up for very long until your slips starts hanging. Luckily, I have a wife who didn't mind letting me know without hesitation when I was fucking up. And she did. She straightened me out and I quit drinking, cold turkey. Or she was going to quit me. When your wife is about to walk out on you-- again something I hope neither you nor my daughters ever have to experience--when this kind of decision is put in front of you, you must respond to it seriously for this is God giving you a chance to alter the course of the path you have been paving before it hardens and you're no longer able to change things.

"Drink your drink, Boy. Don't let the ice sit there and melt and water it down," John said to me, standing up and grabbing the whiskey from the minibar tucked in the corner of the living room, besides the fireplace.

He poured himself some more and waited for me to finish drinking my own. The liquor burned its way down my esophagus and splashed into my belly, warming and relaxing me. He poured me another four fingers and put the bottle back on the minibar. He sank into his chair with the same long sigh of remembrance and continued telling me about the time he found me robbing a dead man four years before when I was ten years old, months after escaping from Smitheran Sweets Adoption Agency, that awful, horrible place.

"You were no bigger than a small tree. Skinnier than that. I couldn't believe you were even alive. The look in your eyes told me everything. Like I said, God had put the image of you lying in a pool of blood into my mind as I came to the alley. When I turned into it, I knew I was going to find you, but I figured you would be the way I saw you in my mind. I was happy that you weren't.

"After Johnny was killed, I began to see visions more and more frequently. I also started to be visited by Johnny in my dreams. It was part of the reason I was drinking so heavily. You don't want your dead child to be visiting you, even if those visits are good. When you wake up covered in sweat, not sure if what you dreamed was real or not, and being unsure if you wanted it to be real or not and unable to share it with your wife for fear of driving her crazy because you know she is already going through her own pain.

"When all of these things begin to feel happy, life isn't where it should be. So I was deeply happy that you weren't lying in a pool of blood. Do you remember when I found you?"
"Very vaguely. I remember you walking into the alley and I remember being afraid because I was robbing the dead guy."

"Yeah, you had his wedding ring and a few dollars of cash clenched tightly in your fist."

"I didn't know who you were and I knew what I was doing was wrong."

"What you were doing, you were doing to survive. There was nothing wrong in what you did. I was happy that you were trapped in the alley by the dead end. I knew if there was an opening you would have run. And if you had done that, there's no way I would've caught you. Maybe twenty-five years ago, but not four years ago. And definitely not now.

"The look in your eyes told me that you had seen more than you ever should have seen. It also told me there was a remarkable amount of fight in you that most adults didn't possess. As I watched you realize you weren't going to escape and assess whether or not I was a threat to you, for the briefest of seconds you were transformed into my son, Johnny. It was as if his form was draped over your own and I was looking at my son. Johnny smiled and then he faded away. You were yourself again and more afraid than an injured puppy that's lost its way. That was the last time I saw Johnny and that was when I knew God had sent you to replace my son."

"You remind me a lot of my son, Johnny, just in the way you hold yourself, Cecil. Johnny was quiet like you and funny. He knew how to relieve the tension in almost every situation. Johnny had an ability that he said he got from the ghosts he would see."

"The ghosts?"

"Yes. Johnny could see and feel ghosts or spirits or whatever you wanna call them. I can't remember how old he was when it all started. He was young, maybe three or four years old."

"How did you know he could see ghosts?"

"Well, the first night he was in his room, your room now, he started hollering for his life. I didn't know what had happened, but when my wife and I opened the door and went into the room, it was as cold as a freezer. Johnny was tucked into a ball in the corner of the room near the closet. I grabbed the blanket off his bed. I heard the door slam and then looked at my wife. I figured she had closed the door. But when I looked at her frightened face, I knew that she hadn't touched the door.

"The door jerked open wide and then slammed shut again. The sound of the opening and shutting of the door was deafening. Johnny started to scream. My wife was frozen in fear. Somewhere in the midst of all this, I thought in the very far back of my mind, if Laurel and Sherrie were ok. Just as quickly as this thought entered my brain, there was a yank on my hair. Johnny was pulling on my hair. He had a handful of it and his clenched fists were beginning to turn white. With a strength that was not of his three- or four-year-old body, Johnny pulled my head down to his face. He began to whisper in my ear over the sound of the slamming door."

"What did Johnny say?"

"It was the hardest thing to make out. But he said it over and over again so many times that it has been etched solidly in my memory. He said, 'It is already too late.' It was at this point that my wife collapsed to her knees and began sobbing uncontrollably. The door slammed shut again and then just as suddenly as the chaos had begun, there was silence. Being engulfed in that silence was terrifying. The thickness of the quiet could be felt everywhere. Every breath I took sent out puffs of cold vapor. Johnny's erratic breathing and my wife's sobbing did the same.

"Then the door jerked open. As the echo reverberated throughout the house, a dark figure slowly poked its head around the door. I remember its eyes the most. They were bright yellow. There was no feeling in the eyes, no life whatsoever. But the black creature with the yellow eyes was absolutely there just as certain as you are here now. We stared at each other and it was then that Johnny started to have a seizure. I felt him trembling in my arms and tried my hardest to look away from the creature but couldn't. The yellow eyes had trapped me. It wasn't long before I began to hear the creature in my mind.

'There's no reason to fight,' it said. 'Give me your son and I will leave you in peace. If you refuse, I will take him and then haunt you until every member of your family has gone insane.'

'I will not give you my son,' I yelled back at the creature.'

'I'm not asking for your son. I'm taking him. There is nothing you can do to stop me.'

"And it was right," John kept speaking to me. He had poured us both another four fingers of whiskey and resumed his place in the chair. With a sigh he launched back to where he had left off in his story. "There was nothing I could do to stop the black creature from taking Johnny. But Johnny, little did I know, knew exactly how to get rid of the monster. As his seizure began to subside, Johnny sat up and looked directly at the monster. The yellow eyes for the first time broke their gaze at me and narrowed sinisterly on Johnny.

'I told you I would find you,' the black creature said. 'You thought you could get away so easily, but there is no escaping me. I've been collecting little boys like you for centuries. Now it's time. Come with me, Johnny.'

'No,' I said to the creature, grabbing Johnny and holding him to my chest. I motioned to my wife who had barely breathed from the moment the creature made its appearance. She was in a daze, but I was able to convince her to scramble over to Johnny and me. Together we knelt on the ground, huddled together, watching with fear as the black creature with yellow eyes stepped into the room. The creature's legs were bent backwards at the knee like a bird's. Its toes were talons and the razor sharp nails scratched the wooden floor as it dragged its feet across the floor. Its yellow eyes darted back and forth between Johnny and me. Lips snarling in disgust, the creature came within inches of us. I never took my eyes off it and I felt Johnny doing the same."

'You can't take him, I shouted again, forcing myself to stand in front of my family to protect them.

'And who's going to stop me? You? You don't even know who I am, or what I am, for that matter. You're way out of your level of expertise here. You should stick with computers.'

"Then Johnny stood up. He stood up so abruptly that it startled both me and the creature. We both jerked our heads back. Johnny's breathing had calmed to a slow rhythm and he seemed to be completely comfortable with the creature. There was no fear in my son."

Fried Chicken

Back in the bunker underneath the American Embassy in London.

The heavy footsteps that had me scared enough to start chanting Nam-myoho-renge-kyo and recall my childhood continued to approach. They belonged to Janelle Muberty.

"How are you feeling?" she asked me.

"I feel ok. What happened? Why can't I move my body?"

"A piece of the ceiling broke and landed on top of you. There was a big earthquake. The Press Secretary says she thinks it was probably a bomb. She figures they blew up the embassy. Since the power's gone it seems everything is up for grabs. We have no idea what's happening aboveground, but it's safe to assume that whoever is responsible for shutting the power off in the First World has further plans that I'm sure are being put into action as we speak."

"Am I paralyzed?"

"I don't think so, you just need to rest for the time being. None of us can leave anyway, so there's no reason not to rest. The hard part now is going to be sustaining some type of sanity while we wait here."

"I finished checking the supplies," I heard the Press Secretary say, coming from somewhere far away. "How's he doing?"

"He's awake."

"Good. I thought you'd sneak in a nap before the real work begins, huh?"

"You knew this was going to happen?"

"We received a tip that something was going to occur. We had no idea in what form the attack was going to be. We knew the purple sky was a sign from whatever order of bold countries and organizations was responsible for this."

"Why did you send for me?"

"Because I need you, Cecil, and you're the only person that I know I can trust. You also are good at what you do."

"I think it's time you explained to us exactly what you know is going on. It's not like we're going to have to be worrying about security clearances anymore."

"You do have a point. Why don't we eat something first, maybe have a little wine, and then I'll tell both of you everything I know, and what I think is going to happen next as well as what our next step should be, because we certainly can't stay down here forever. Though given the amount of supplies I found, we could safely remain locked in here for the next four months. I think that would be a mistake, though, and besides, there's too much work to be done."

"How long do you think the power will be out?"

"Indefinitely, I'm afraid."

"You mean to tell me you don't think we have a way to get the power back on?"

"It's not so much that there isn't a way. I think the bomb fried everything that generates power. Everything is scorched, I'm afraid."

"How can that be?"

"Oh, it's something that's been available for decades. It's one of the many alternative weapons we designed with the United Nations during the last terrorist attack."

"That proved to be a disaster," Janelle said.

"Right you are. In fact, it was such a disaster that the majority of the information about it has been sealed as classified, not to be opened until fifty years from now. It's what we do in America whenever we do something we're not proud of; lock it up for half a century. Hopefully, all those who took part in it will be dead or on the way to their graves. All others were children when it happened and they won't even know to ask about it."

"So if this weapon, this electricity bomb, if it was so classified, how was someone able to get hold of it and use it to shut down the superpowers of the world," Janelle asked the Press Secretary.

"Let's eat first."

"No!" Janelle yelled, jumping to her feet. "The world as we know it is falling apart. We're trapped down here in this bunker. Cecil is injured, and come to find out that you knew all this time and didn't warn anybody. My family, my friends, are all probably dead. I didn't even get a chance to warn them."

"Janelle, everyone's friends and families are dead. Everyone's injured or with someone that is injured. From the few reports that trickled through before the embassy was blown up, aboveground the end of the world is taking place."

"What about your phone, does it still work?"

"No, the phone stopped working after the earthquake. That's why I assume the embassy was blown up above us. The embassy had the link to the emergency distress satellite in the Quinton space station."

"So, we can't communicate in any way?"

"Not at this moment, no. They know we're down here, though. They'll triangulate our last known broadcast and then track us. They'll probably have to dig us out."

"How long do you think it'll be before they rescue us?"

"There's no way of knowing for certain. It'll definitely be some time; it really depends on who is conducting this operation. So, you might as well sit down and calm down. We're gonna be roommates for some time. Help me make some food and then I promise I will tell you every single detail I know and every possibility I've thought of so far. Cecil has a lot of information, too. He probably knows more than I do. He's been my main researcher for the last three years."

"Four," I said trying to sit up and doing nothing but straining my neck.

"Come on, Dear. Everything's going to be ok. As long as you're with me, you'll be safe," the Press Secretary said to Janelle.

Johnny's dad had fallen into a drunken sleep in the middle of his long speech on how I was just like his dead son who talked to ghosts. I sat staring at him with the untouched glass of whiskey still in my hand. The ice had melted away minutes ago. I placed the glass on the table beside me. Replaying the crazy story John had told me, I wondered if Johnny could talk now that he was a ghost. Then the fear in my imagination created an image of that black creature with the yellow eyes that came to take Johnny away and Johnny somehow stood up to it. That wasn't explained. I cursed at him for being so drunk and not finishing his story.

It was always like that when he had something important to say. I guess once John found me, he figured God was telling him he could move on and return to his life with me as his son. So, the grief of losing Johnny was gone and drinking once again became a pattern in his daily existence. Always jovial and gay, John never lashed out in any way when he was drunk. The only real cause of concern when John was drinking was the inevitable stupor he would fall into when he drank beyond his limit, which wasn't so great. Nothing would abate his shift into oblivion but sleep.

He would get a certain look in his eyes that let you know he was floating somewhere in the cosmos in his mind. It's in this way that I learned discipline from John.

John was a routine freak. He had a routine for everything. Everything had a way of being done and it had to be done the right way.

"You kids are too young to create your own routines," he would say whenever we questioned why we had to do things his way. "Once you move out of this house, then you can have your own routines. You'll see soon enough that having to make your own routines ain't all it's cracked up to be. The responsibilities are going to get piled on you and you're gonna have to put those into your routine, too."

He wasn't lying about that one. When I ran away from home my senior year of high school, I had no idea what was in store for me. Never mind that I fled all the way to Wuxi, China.

Sherrie's family tried very hard to satisfy me and all of my little wants. There wasn't anything I needed. Everything was taken care of.

When I was sent to Hales Franciscan at 4930 S. Cottage Grove, it was at the tail end of the gang wars that had been ravaging the city for the last five years. People were dying in atrocious numbers, far more than the tragic numbers happening at the time of the shutting down of the First Powers' electricity around the planet. At that time, I was merely a teenager and couldn't comprehend all that was taking place. I was fortunate to be embraced in the protection of Sherrie's family.

John assigned two independent bodyguards who shadowed me everywhere I went. They were seldom visible when I was with friends. The three of us would converse quite a lot when I was alone, which was most of the time. During high school I wasn't talkative or outgoing. I followed the routine that John had laid out for me and I cooperated with the agents on loan from wherever John had gotten them.

Every day after my last period, I would head toward Harold's Chicken Shack a few blocks down. I would buy a bag of fifteen wings and then head into Washington Park. There was a picnic area that was our usual spot. I would sit down and start eating chicken. One and then the other of my bodyguards would come up and sit down on either side of me.

"How was school?" Bodyguard Number One asked me as he grabbed a piece of chicken from the bag. I passed a cup of hot sauce to him. "No, thank you, I can't do the hot sauce. I have an ulcer."

"That's too bad," I said lathering up a wing with hot sauce.

"Yes, It is, I sure miss it."

"Just a taste won't hurt you," Agent Number Two said, grabbing a wing from the bag.

"No, Man. I have to be careful. There was a point not too long ago when I had a heart attack; you remember that, don't you?"

"Yeah, I do. I thought you were going to die."

"What happened?" I asked.

"We were on a routine training exercise, moving along the battered remains of a street that had been designed to look like some war-torn block. It was quite good work, almost like it was done by a Hollywood production company. We were running through drills and then I collapsed. I hit the deck harder than I have in my entire life. I felt as if all the air from my lungs had been sucked out of me. My arm went numb and between the elephant that I thought had sat on my chest, I was gasping for air. I was certain I'd be dead in no time."

"I thought you were going to die, too," Bodyguard Number Two said, grabbing more chicken."

"You didn't even notice me when I first collapsed."

"That's true. We were in the middle of an exercise and I thought you just stumbled. You do stumble often."

"You didn't even look back."

"You didn't make any noise."

"I was having a heart attack and I couldn't breathe."

"So you can't jump on me, then."

"At least you finally did notice and came to help me."

"Yeah, that was the point when I thought you were going to die."

"But you didn't," I said finishing off the last piece of chicken in the bag.

"No I didn't. Been going strong ever since. That's why I stay away from the hot sauce. Not even supposed to be eating fried chicken much. But seeing as its part of the job, I don't think it hurts much."

"How is eating fried chicken with the client part of the job?"

"Making sure the chicken's not poisoned."

"You're ridiculous. You know that, man."

"What? It's the truth. I had a client who was killed by poisoning. We had an ironclad bubble of security around this man, too. One morning, while he was eating his cereal, his heart stopped and he plunged face first into the bowl. What little breath he had sucked up the milk."

"He died in his bowl of cereal?" Bodyguard Number Two asked with a look of utter disgust on his face.

"Yeah, what a way to go, right?"

"We should probably change the subject. I'm sure we're freaking the kid out."

"No, I'm doing ok. You all know what school I go to, a lot's happened this first year and a half."

"You're a sophomore now, Cecil?"

"Yeah."

"How is that?" Bodyguard Number One asked as he balled up the white paper bag that now contained only fried chicken crumbs.

"It's ok. Basically the same, I'm just more used to the place."

"Got any friends?"

"Not really."

"You don't talk to anyone?"

"I talk to a few people. They talk to me. I don't really talk much."

"The people that you say talk to you, are they nice? Do they have interesting things to talk about?"

"Yeah, for the most part. They are definitely nice. The conversations aren't necessarily all that interesting, though."

"Sounds like you've got yourself some friends."

"Yeah, but we don't hang out outside of school. On TV, your friends are people you hang out with once school's over."

"Yeah, but Cecil, you don't hang out with anyone after school."

"I hang out with you guys."

"No, technically, we hang out with you. And we're hired to be around you. Do the other kids say anything about the fact that you have two bodyguards?"

"No, I just tell them that my dad's a diplomat and travels all the time."

"John does travel all the time."

"Leaves you all alone with a house full of women. I don't admire you, Cecil."

"It's not all that bad. I just do what I'm told."

"It's good you've learned that so young. It took us a long time to learn that."

"Hell, I'm still learning. I think my wife has pretty much given up on me."

"She still loves you very much."

"I know she loves me. Been together twenty-five years. When you're together that long, you just go on living together, no matter what."

"That doesn't sound like very much fun," I said rising from the bench and heading toward the El toward home.

"Well, marriage is a lot of things. At times, it is fun, but it's not gonna be fun every day. I think people forget that marriage is just a contract between two parties, a merger of two private companies investing in the production of heirs to carry on with what would be a profitable way of combining assets."

"Sounds like running a business."

"It's worse than running a business, Kid," Bodyguard Number Two said as the three of us walked toward the Green Line. "Its way more pressure for one thing. If you make a mistake in business, you just lose money and standing. However, in a marriage, if you make a mistake, you deeply hurt another individual. I don't care how cold you are, you're gonna feel bad about hurting your wife."

Once we finally arrived at the Green Line stop on Garfield, the two bodyguards were out of breath from the long walk.

"You sure love walking, don't you, Cecil."

"It's good for the health."

"It's also exhausting. You know, we could occasionally drive you home. It takes you such a long time to get home this way."

"I like reading on the train."

"What are you reading now?"

"To Kill a Mockingbird."

"That's so heavy and depressing."

"It's history."

"That is true. What are your thoughts on white/black relations in your age group?"

"I don't know. It's ok. Could be better. I'm in a very different circumstance, you know. I don't really feel any connection to anyone."

"What do you mean?"

"I'm an orphan. I ain't got no peoples."

"Sure you do. You have John, his wife and the two daughters, Laurel and Sherrie. They all love you so much."

"But they are not my family. We are not from the same place."

"Why do you say that?" Bodyguard Number One asked as the sliding doors parted and we stepped onto the train. Bodyguard Number Two went to get the car and drive it up to meet us at the house in Evanston.

"I say that because they're white and I'm black. I don't even know who my parents were, what kind of people they were. I don't know anything. All I know is me."

"And what about the family that's taken you in, the family that's taken care of you, the family that's provided security, leisure, health care and a trust fund? What about them, Cecil?"

"I'm grateful to them and I owe them a great deal, but I am not chained to them."

"No one said you were, Cecil. But you're just a sophomore in high school. You gotta be patient, Son. Once you graduate, you'll be on your own. You won't have to answer to anyone."

"Why do I have to wait that long?"

"How old are you? 15? It's only two-and-a-half years, maybe three if there's a hiccup along the way. Just be patient."

"No, I don't think I'm going to wait that long."

And I didn't. I cut it down six months earlier than Bodyguard Number One's projection.

As you can tell, my high school experience was not ordinary. The school I went to exacerbated matters greatly. Hailed as one of the last, if not the last, all-black all-male Catholic high schools in the United States, Hales Franciscan was designed to instill discipline and positive values into impoverished young men. It was also intended to contribute to low-income families so that their children would be able to raise their community's income level. A world where schools support individual growth and encourage community development sounds great, but it was both idealistic and naïve..

Alas, the reality is that money is always the issue when it comes to schools, especially those in the quote unquote ghetto.

Ah, yes. The ghetto. That was the reason John saw fit for me to learn about my people by sending me into the ghetto. The irony of it all was that Sherrie's father saw himself as somewhat of a progressive leader. The neighborhood saw it as that, too. I'm sure having adopted a runaway black boy helped his popularity there.

Hales Franciscan, John believed, was the most suitable place for me. It was in the heart of what in his eyes was certainly the ghetto. Historically, Cottage Grove nurtured some of Chicago's most successful people and businesses, black-owned and black-operated. If Cottage Grove was a ghetto when I went to Hales back in 1999, then its history is that of a paradise. As far as I was concerned, I was sitting on my heritage. It took Ms. Brown to instill this in me, though.

It was during my freshman year that I met her. By my sophomore year, she had quit teaching to open a jewelry shop with her good friend, Ms. Bradley. Ms. Brown was the one who more than anyone else encouraged my writing, just as I was discovering this was what I wanted to do.

I had a cheap, green, spiral notebook that I purchased from Walgreen's around the beginning of my freshman year. There was a three-week period in the summer before school started when we were to get adjusted to being in high school and make friends with others in our freshman class. After the first year, we were then grouped together by GPA. I remember those first three weeks as being a lot of fun, but I didn't feel like I belonged to any one group or fit in with any one person.

The beginning of school was always exciting for me when I was younger. The adventure of something new drew out my curiosity, the wonder of unknown journeys and new discoveries all colliding together with possible danger and irrevocable doom. This is what living was made of. For me, the closest I could get to it was the start of school. By my junior year that had all been worn off and I was planning my escape to Wuxi, China.

During that three-week orientation, Ms. Brown was assigned to my group's home room team. I think the groups were selected based on the entrance exam which I probably took in the 8th grade to get into Hales Franciscan High school. It was the last placement exam I ever took and that I was excited about taking. High school really took the fun out of school for me.

Somewhere within the second week, while we were on a break. I was engrossed as I had been on every break and every moment away from the classroom, writing and drawing in a notebook. I had seen the hip hop movie 'Beat Street' for the first time two years before and at that point in my freshmen year, I was fully emerged in the hip hop culture. Breakdancing fell into place for me quite naturally so that's what I did. But I loved the wonderful art of graffiti most of all.

One of my friends at my elementary school was a graffiti artist. They were all white at that school … white and Asian. Back in the 90's, there hadn't been as much of an influx of East Indians and Middle Easterners as now. There were a lot of Japanese Americans and Chinese Americans. That was the Evanston I experienced and remember.

We had been in the same class since I first entered the school at ten years old after John discovered me robbing a dead man in an alley. We didn't become friends until my twelfth birthday, which was a special one for me as I was supposed to have been tossed into the mines at that point and who knows where I'd be if that had happened; probably dead. We had been cordial and civilized to each other; as polite as 5th graders could be.

It was Timothy's art that caught my eye and made me want to become friends with him. His art was truly extraordinary. He was always drawing from the moment I first met him. I watched him during those two years, everyone watched him. He would sit tucked into the corner and just draw, never showing anyone what he was doodling. It was a rather free private school in that the teachers didn't enforce a lot of boundaries on us. We were allowed the space to try and figure things out. The kids were free to experience life without worry or want and without the weight and tension of poverty and all the baggage that it brings.

I was unusual because I was black. Timothy was unusual because he was an artist. During lunch sometime after that special 12th birthday, Timothy was sitting next to me. He wasn't quite speaking, but made noises every now and then. For no reason, he pulled out his drawing pad and started doodling. He wasn't making much of an effort to cover up his work and I was trying my best not to seem like I was looking over his shoulder to catch a glimpse of what he was drawing.

Timothy very abruptly leaned back and allowed me a proper view of the work he had done.

"What do you think?" he asked me.

What did I think? How could I answer that? I didn't know how to describe what I saw. I had never seen anything like it before. The colors were majestic and swallowed me into a sweet swirl of silliness. I started giggling uncontrollably. It wasn't long before the hiccups started. I wasn't laughing at the drawing and he knew it. I was laughing uncontrollably because the drawing made me feel that way. I felt the pleasure of someone telling a perfectly timed joke that encompasses everything about a particular moment in time. I couldn't stop giggling. Timothy was no help, as he started giggling uncontrollably, too. Our giggling and hiccupping started a wave of laughter through the entire cafeteria until the whole room was laughing uncontrollably; all different types of laughter. Loud, soft, squeaky, coarse. Even the adults who were eating with the kids and serving lunches were laughing despite their best efforts to contain themselves. It's too hard not to enjoy a cafeteria full of kids laughing and enjoying themselves to no end. It wasn't very hard for the principal, however.

When he found out that it had been Timothy and I who had caused the ruckus, he called our parents and demanded to see us. It was a frightening experience, waiting in the office with the large man who was the principal sitting at his desk, eyeing us with anger and suspicion. When our parents finally arrived, we were soaked in nervous sweat.

Yes, we had been laughing. Yes, we were the first ones laughing. No, we didn't know everyone was going to start laughing. We were laughing at what Timothy drew. We told them everything truthfully. We hadn't known we were being bad, honest. Timothy and my adopted parents--both John and his wife came-- were trying their best not to laugh at how pathetic we looked. The principal was not going to let us off the hook, however.

"I demand that they be suspended for two days."
"Suspended!" Timothy's mother exclaimed. "Sir, are you out of your mind? Look at them. They're sorry. They didn't even know it was going to happen and honestly, children laughing? What exactly is wrong with that? This is a school. Wouldn't you want kids to be laughing?"
"This is a school. We want kids to be learning."
"It was during lunch," John chimed in. "What do they need to be learning during lunch?"
"They need to learn how to behave like civilized young people so that they can integrate into a civilized society. I'm sure it was your son who made Timothy laugh. You know how they are so naturally funny."
"What the hell do you mean by "they"? Did you just make a racist comment toward my Cecil?"
"Yep. That's just what he did," said Timothy's father stepping in.
"What do you care?" the principal pleaded with both gentlemen. "He's not even your real son."

"Sir, I'll have to warn you," Sherrie's mom jumped in. "If you say one more bad thing about Cecil, I will jump across this desk and slap you with both of my hands."

"Ma'am please. I didn't mean any harm or disrespect. Right now, the most important thing is the next step. What do we do from here?"

"I don't think the children need to be punished. You can look at them and see they've been traumatized enough already, just sitting in here with you," Timothy's mom said.

"As a matter of fact, I'm traumatized from sitting in here with you, too," John's wife piggybacked.

"If there is nothing more, Sir," John said rising to his feet, prompting the other three parents to spring to their own.

"No, we still must punish them."

"We've already agreed they've been punished enough. You two have learned your lesson, haven't you?" Timothy's dad asked us with military sternness.

"Yes," we feebly responded.

"That's not good enough," Tim's dad barked. John's wife was startled. "Have you two learned your lesson?"

"Yes, Sir," Timothy responded, which sounded stronger than anything I had heard from him before. After a few moments of staring at Tim in disbelief, I realized that everyone in the room was staring at me, awaiting my response.

Fear grabbed hold of me. I knew I had to bellow out a baritone "Yes, Sir" in order to make sure the principal felt it, but John and his wife disarmed me. They made me feel weak and insecure. I hated myself for feeling that way. They did everything for me and I never thought they didn't love me and wouldn't defend me, but I still refused to acknowledge them as my parents and they never insisted that I do.

"Yes, Sir," I mustered up with whatever strength I had. It was weaker than Timothy's, who I learned later was used to his father's military character. But I got an A for effort.

Both our parents took us out for pizza after we got the hell out of the principal's office.

"That guy was an asshole," Tim's dad said to anyone listening. The two dads had put back a pitcher of beer while the rest of us sipped cokes.

"Chad, watch your language," Tim's mom said.

"No, it's ok, Elise. Chad's right. He was an asshole."

"Now, John, Elise's point isn't whether or not it's true. It's to set a better example for the boys."

"They know not to talk like us," Chad said taking a mighty swig from his drink.

"They know that, but that doesn't mean they don't want to. They look up to you two."

"Goddamn right they should, me and John are real American men.

It was in my junior year at Hales Franciscan high school that I learned my biological grandmother was still alive. The city had a policy that adopted children could request information concerning their biological parents once they turned 17. I was unaware of this and honestly cared less about whether or not I had real family somewhere. It turned out that I did. It was John who took me downtown to City Hall on my 17th birthday.

"Now, when we go in you're going to show them your state ID, birth certificate and your Social Security card."

All of these, John made sure I had within the first month of him finding me in the alley robbing a dead man.

"Just answer all the questions and be polite. You'll do fine."

"You're not coming in with me?" I asked suddenly, realizing that I was to do this alone.

"Nope," John said sitting down on a bench outside the staircase leading up to the large building. "You're a man now. It's time to go your own way, alone."

"What are you going to do?"

"Me? I'm going to sit right here. Read my newspaper." He had a copy of the *Washington Post* tucked under his right armpit. "And smoke a cigarette."

"I thought you gave them up?"

"I did, and that's all you'd better say to anyone else, too, that I quit smoking squares."

"But you didn't," I answered, confused.

"Yes, I know," John said lighting up a square. "But, as far as anyone else is concerned, I have."

"Isn't that a lie?"

"Yes, it's absolutely a lie. But it's a lie I'm trusting you with. So it's imperative that you never speak a word of it to anyone. Do you understand?"

"Ok," I didn't understand why he was hiding the fact that he was still smoking, but I saw no reason to keep going back and forth with John when I had business to attend to.

Inside City Hall, the process was simple and straightforward. The hard part was the waiting. I must've stood in line for over an hour. I thought I was going to pass out on my feet by the time I got to the counter where the meanest, ugliest-looking woman I can remember sat. The woman stared down at me with stuck-up prickliness behind gold-rimmed glasses with the thickest lenses I had ever seen, making her face look like a google-eyed fish.

"Can I help you?" she said in an "I'm ready for my lunch break" tone of voice.

"Yes, I have these papers and I'm here to pick up some information you're holding for me on my biological parents.

The woman scrutinized the papers with her face scrunched up like Kermit the Frog from the Muppets. She kept looking back and forth between me and the papers. Furrowing her thick, dark brown eyebrows, she stood up and said she'd just be a moment, then she disappeared. I was left alone before the massive counter. It seemed to become even more massive. I felt as if every eye behind me was staring, wondering how I could be so dumb. There was nothing for me to do but stand there and the wait heightened my anxiety until I could feel my heart pulsing in my ears.

The google-eyed woman returned with a nicer looking man. He wore a suit that shined like none I had ever seen. It was as if the very florescent light above was reflecting off whatever material the suit was made of.

"How are you, Cecil? Why don't you come with me into my office? We have a lot to discuss."

I nodded my head and took one last glace at the woman behind the counter. She smiled and all the fear and anxiety I had been feeling was gently washed away.

I followed the man with the reflective suit into a room I presumed was his office. He left the door open and had me sit in the chair opposite his own across the desk.

"So, it seems it's time for you to find out where you come from?"
"I guess so."
"Well come now. You don't sound anywhere near excited. This is a big deal, young man."
"Well, I already know my parents are dead. So I don't know what more information I will learn from you today."
"Well, aren't you interested in details concerning your parents? Where they were from, what they did for a living. You know how they died, I take it?"
"Plane crash."
"Yes, I see here, it was certainly fortunate that you yourself weren't on that plane."
"That's yet to be determined, I'm afraid."
"You don't think living is better than dying?"
"I've never died before, so I really don't know."

"Quite right, but life so far hasn't been all peaches and cream, then?"

"No, Sir. It has not."

"It says here that you were adopted by your current family after they found you in an alley robbing a dead man."

"All of that's in there?"

"Everything's in here, Cecil. We know everything there is to know about you and your workings and dealings."

"Well, I don't do much."

"It was just an expression. So this file is now officially yours," the man said, closing the folder, giving it a tap to neaten the pages. He slid the folder over to me. "There you go," he said.

I picked up the folder and slowly opened it. A wave of excitement flowed over me. The first two pages were on both my mother and father with individual profile photos of them. I had never seen pictures of my parents. I hadn't a single memory of them. My father was named Wellington Pittsburg and my mother was Yvonne Pittsburg. They were both born in Memphis, Tennessee. They attended the same high school and started dating during their senior year. My father went on to Howard University while my mother went to the University of Illinois in Urbana Champagne. It seems my mother was the most educated among the two of them. She had a doctorate in clinical psychology. My father had a bachelor's in communication.

My father's build was strong. His eyes were steady set and he did not smile in the picture. He was bald, which gave him a military intensity that from the picture terrified me.

The picture of my mother was just as intimidating. Her eyes pierced through the photo into me and made me feel as if she truly was staring at me. My mom had the widest and most beautiful smile I had ever seen, however. I could see why my father had never let her go after high school.

As I flipped through the files on where they had lived, the work they did and the traveling they had done, an unexpected feeling of warmth came over me. These are my parents, I remember thinking. Without warning, I started to cry.

I had forgotten all about the man whose office I was in, but as soon as the tears began to fall, his presence returned to the center. I looked up at him and tried hard to stop my tears, but the more I tried to stop them, the more they streamed down my face. I put my head into my hands and began to sob uncontrollably.

I heard the man stand and walk around the desk. He put one hand on my shoulder and squeezed it tightly.

"Let it all out, Cecil. This is a lot to take in."

After my fit had subsided, the man handed me a box of tissues.

"Are you feeling any better?" he asked me after some moments of silence passed as I tried to return to breathing normal.

"Yes, a little," I responded, blowing the snot that had flowed out of my nose along with the tears from my eyes.
"Are you here by yourself?"
"No, my guardian is outside."
"Why didn't he come in with you?"
"Because he said that I'm a man now and it was best for me to open this door on my own."
"That seems a bit harsh, but I guess you two have an ok relationship. Do you feel he knows you rather well?"
"I'm not sure if anyone knows me rather well, but John has been there for me since he found me. He's treated me like his own son who was shot and killed."
"Yes, Johnny, correct?" the man asked flipping through another file he pulled out of a file cabinet behind his desk. He returned back to his seat after he grabbed the folder. "It was very

generous for John to adopt you, especially being as old as you were, and all the trauma that you had gone through at Smitheran Sweets Adoption Agency. By the way, you'll be happy to know that they shut down that agency earlier this year. The police had been trying to build a case on them for over a decade. It was their claim that they shipped children over ten years of age to their main building in Paris, France. There was a trail that had been sending law enforcement in circles until finally the truth was uncovered. When you were there, did you know anything about the mines?"

"I had only heard of them, we all knew about them. It's the reason I escaped when I turned ten. They send you down into the mines below the school on your eleventh birthday. They had already sent my friend, Zenek, away. We were going to escape together."

"Well, when the police finally shut down the adoption agency, they went into the basement. There were no mines. But there were buried underneath the concrete the remains of over 400 children. It seems they would drug those who were over the adoption age limit and then throw their bodies into the furnace. Then they would dig out their bones and bury them in the concrete. They had been doing this for a very long time with an elaborate system, the reasoning, sadly, was financial. It was cheaper for them to kill the unwanted children who didn't have any family that would be looking for them."

"What happened to the Head Mistress?"

"Oh, you mean, Eliza Huffington? She hanged herself while awaiting trial earlier last month. She was the one who would kill and burn the children, but not before sexually assaulting those that she grew a liking to. You were a very lucky boy to have escaped the way you did."

I felt a shiver run though me as I recalled my long decade trapped at the Smitheran Sweets Adoption Agency.

"Unfortunately, I have another appointment coming up that I need to head to," the man said, glancing at his wristwatch. "But before I go, there is one other thing I must tell you." He pulled out another folder from the drawer behind him and placed it gently in front of me. "If you're interested, your grandmother is still alive, your father's mother. She is living out her last days in a nursing home on the north side. She suffers from dementia, but the nurses have told me she is aware of your existence. They think it would be beneficial for both of you if you could take the time to go and speak with her. She's pretty much been living in the home for the past decade. Right after the news of your parents' death, she had a mental breakdown."

And that's how I spent my summer days after finishing my junior year of high school, solving small mysteries around the nursing home for my 96-year-old grandmother. She was a contradiction of senility and sharpness. She went to college when she was 16 in the 1920's. No small feat for a black woman.

Candice was my great aunt's name, was among the greatest of the mysteries revealed to me by my grandmother; a treasure trove of galactic proportions. She had information unfolding layers of generational skeletons, tucked away neatly in a closet of iniquity. The burns of memory scalded me 17 years later. It was funny that she died in an insane asylum, burned to death in a fire that she started. It reminds me of Francis Scott Fitzgerald's wife, Zelda. Zelda died mysteriously in a fire in the mental institution where she was being held. She had a breakdown when she was desperately trying to become a ballerina at a time when she was too old to do anything. Such things happen when you piss your life away drinking.

My grandmother, Lucy, told me about it all while we played a game of Scrabble on the day she decided to die on me.

"Candice was a monster of a child. We were five years apart. I remember distinctly her wailing and hollering, always considering about nobody but herself. It was amazing that nobody slapped her around. They slapped me around just fine. I do remember that, vividly, but smacking Candice was a no-no, you hear? It wasn't that, 'We don't hit kids.' Hell, they beat the shit outta me, but Candice was something special for everybody. I admit that she was special for me, too. But the way they treated me wasn't fair and I didn't see no reason why I should take no shit from my own little sister."

My grandmother, Lucy, scrutinized her Scrabble pieces and, after much speculation, decided to pass. I connected four words and gained bonus points. Lucy was quite pissed, but not upset enough to discontinue her story of my kinship.

"When our mother," Lucy continued, "went travelling, she would always take the youngest of her children: Candice and my little sister, Bee. They would bounce around the world while our mother, your great-grandmother, would perform in grand productions. She was a stage actress at a time when that meant something."

I didn't follow what she meant, but I went along with it. The story of my great aunt, Candice, was playing out to be a very interesting scandal.

"Her downfall came when she slipped into bed with my husband." And this is when the story began to get interesting.

"She had been trying as hard as she could to get close to my Sydney. He was your grandfather. She was walking around the house conveniently forgetting to put on her clothes. And this is a woman who since she was a little girl refused to wear shorts, period. Whenever she could find the opportunity, she took advantage of your grandfather's hospitality. He was an overly gracious person, and he fell easily for the charms of an attractive woman. Under other circumstances, my husband was a saint and utterly unbreakable when it came to his fidelity. However, when it came to my sister, he was at a loss as to how to proceed.

"Candice was thinking, she was always thinking. That was the problem: the thinking. It was such a constant thing that it wasn't until she was in high school that she learned that her way of thinking wasn't like others. The twists and turns of her mind would pull at the strings of her heart, would send her spirit spiraling downward into oblivion, all along the road toward insanity. Banks counted the money spent on her therapy and the like.

My grandmother, Lucy, was born into a wealthy family. Her mother, my great-grandmother, I guess, was a singer and actress during the Great Depression. Her movies spanned a global reach at a time when black women were barely allowed to make a name for themselves. Listening to the tales of my grandmother brought me into a train of thought and that was right on time as I prepared to leave Chicago and travel to Wuxi, China in the next few weeks.

The trip was one no one thought I could do. Sherrie's parents agreed to it because they figured I would never be able to raise the funds. Even if I did, they figured the school wouldn't consider sponsoring such a ludicrous proposition. But when I showed them the letters from both the study abroad agency and the school and Sherrie's parents which I had myself gotten done, they had no choice but to let me go and spread my wings.

The wings that I spread were the limitations I had been placing upon my self-confidence. It was appalling to the degree that I didn't believe in myself. Others could glide through the universe without a care in the world, but I would care about the world and the universe. It wasn't a good thing to be so young and worrying about everything. When I moved to Wuxi, China, I figured it was time to shed the burden of all that.

It took a long time, and I'm not even sure I accomplished anything during my time there beside plant the seeds for the future, which one way or the other, was on its way. Worrying was something that crept into me from my earliest memory. They were about nothing I can remember that was of importance. For me, the significance of the feeling was that I held onto it for so long.

It was something I have never experienced before; something mind-boggling and even though I was young, I was sure it was there and no need to question it. Of course, over time there is always a person who will question it. The alternative to that question shall prove itself in the grand scheme of things.

Mission of Purpose

Listening to the jazz recording playing through the audio speakers overhead, I was pulled from my remembering and brought back to the bunker underneath the American Embassy in London.

We had been in the bunker for over two weeks. It was a terrible place to be. Each of us experienced a significant increase in nightmares and waking memories, tormenting us with greater intensity each day. By the two-week point, we were pretty much insane. We had the ability to keep track of time through my chronograph watch that continued to tick as long as I kept moving, but the absence of space made time seem inconsequential.

To have time with no space or space with no time is a ponderous thought that I took into consideration at about the two-week point. I exhausted myself with the inability to stop the reel of memories being fed through the projector inside my mind. Every day, every second of the twenty-four hours, I was thinking. In the past I was always able to relieve myself of thought by sleeping. Inside the bunker, when I slept, I was thinking even harder and not only my mind, but my body, was succumbing to the stress of it all.

Both the Press Secretary and Janelle Muberty were equally showing signs of wear on their faces. Bodies slumped over and backs bending over, lower and lower, and each tick of the Hamilton wristwatch I wore ticked away.

"How are we on food?" Janelle asked.

She and the Press Secretary, in spite of going crazy as I was, had devised a system to ration the food supply. An inventory was taken of every item within the bunker during those first days after we entered following the cutting of power to First World nations around the globe. It was a good thing they did this, too. As much as we lost track of our minds, there's no doubt that without the order and control of the Press Secretary as architect and Janelle as operator put together, we would have died a long time ago.

As our luck would have it, that obviously would not be the case. After what we approximated ended up being about six weeks, a loud click sounded and then echoed a deafening gong of release throughout the bunker. The large steel door that had kept us enclosed in what was beginning to look like our tomb slowly opened to reveal a small contingent of twenty soldiers. Their manner was not friendly at all.

"Identify yourselves!" the leader of the crew barked his command.

The Press Secretary stepped forward and did just that. After an exchange of credentials took place and we were searched for weapons, the soldiers escorted us out of the bunker and up the stairs to what could only be described as another dimension.

It was bright outside. When we opened the trap door in the ground of the American Embassy in London we were greeted with the rich nourishing rays of the sun. There was no longer an American Embassy in London. In its place was a steel wall. A series of bunkers were set up along the inside of the wall where we were standing.

We were led into one of these bunkers, which to tell you, I was very reluctant to do, having just spent the last two weeks in one under what used to be the American Embassy in London.

When we walked in we were saluted by a superior officer and told to sit.

"We're going to get right to the point here seeing as we don't have any time to waste. As I'm sure you've already ascertained, two weeks ago, we were hit with a device that severed the primary power source from every First World nation on this planet. What you don't know is that a week following the attack, a ground force of one hundred thousand invaded those countries that were without power. As you can imagine, a vicious battle ensued; one which we are still fighting. The normalcy you knew before you went into the bunker is no more and you had better face the harsh reality now, instead of later, when it may cost your life and those you hold near and dear. Any questions, so far?"

"Are we winning this war? And who the hell is it with?" Janelle asked.

"No, we are not winning this war. Whom is a bit more complicated to answer, I'm afraid. We know the enemy is made up of a coalition of nations that for most of history have been exploited, shunned and left to rot away."

"Well that's almost every nation."

"Exactly. So we have been forced to unite with all the other nations that are without power and forge our own coalition."

"General, are you saying the world is split between two coalitions?" the Press Secretary asked.

"Yes, that is what I am saying. The powerless First World and those with power."

"How were they able to mobilize an entire coalition of nations without anyone catching wind of it?"

"That would be one of the thousands of questions we can't answer because there is no electricity."

"Don't we have generators or something that could pump juice into our infrastructure?" Janelle asked.

"You're not understanding the devastation this electronic bomb has caused. We've basically been knocked back to the steam engine days. When the bomb went off, it fried every single thing that uses electricity. That includes items that used batteries. Imagine if you will, all across the First World nations, individuals with battery powered hearing aids, the pulse or wave or whatever the fuck it was that they set off, short-circuited and exploded the hearing aids in their ears and their heads exploded. The reports were unbelievable and late, given that now the only way to send and receive messages was snail mail. You couldn't even send a note through Morse code because it hadn't been used in so long that it wasn't preserved just in case of such an emergency. So we travel now by steam and wind and live at night by candle light."

"We're back in the Dark Ages," I said.

"Precisely. So now that we are all up to date, Sir, you will have to go with this gentleman," the general said to me pointing to a soldier who put his hand on my shoulder. "And ladies, we'll have to escort you to the women's bunker where you will be processed and placed."

"Placed? Placed into what?" Janelle asked.

"Why your positions, of course."

"And where am I going?"

"You're going to where all men go, the military."

I gasped and could no longer breathe. I couldn't inhale or exhale. That last breath I took was locked in my lungs as tight as a prison. Or maybe it was a protest from my lungs themselves, saying, and "We're not going to be killed. We'd rather take our last breath and then cut ourselves, die on our feet.

But I didn't want to die, I wanted to breathe. As I struggled to will my body to breathe like normal again, my life force slowly and painfully drained away. I felt my knees wobble, then buckle. I fell down on them hard. The pain shot up through my legs to my whole body. I wanted to holler out, but that just made not being able to breathe that much worse. My vision became more and more hazy and I eventually gave up and fell on the floor of another bunker.

I woke in a cot surrounded by rows of empty cots to the left and right of me. The room was large and dark except for a single hanging light above me. There were other hanging lights, but the bulbs in those were all out. I sat up and realized there was an IV stuck in my arm. I took some breaths, happy that I could do so, and pulled the IV out of my arm. It was an awful feeling that I've never experienced, although I had two surgeries before I fled to Wuxi, China.

The first surgery was a hernia on the left side above the base of my penis. It was there since I was at the Smitheran Sweets Adoption Agency. It was Sherrie who saw it and told her mom when I first was brought in by John, her dad. She used to peek in on me when I would take baths. Her mother, being a mother, was concerned and demanded that I show her. I demanded that Sherrie leave my room, Sherrie's mom told her to leave and then told me to show her.

I pulled my pants and underwear down and showed her the hernia. It was a golf ball-sized bump sticking out. She pushed it in and watched as it quickly re-inflated again. She frowned and asked, "How long have you had this?"

"Few years," I said shrugging my shoulders and about to pull my pants up.

"Not yet," she said still inspecting. "We're going to have to call the doctor."

"The doctor? Why?" My experiences with the doctor at Smitheran Sweets were horrific.

"Because that means something's happened inside you that needed to be fixed."

"How do you fix it?"

"Surgery, probably."

"Surgery?"

"Yes, surgery. The doctor is going to have to tell us for certain what should be done, but from what I know about hernias, they almost always have to be surgically repaired."

"What's a hernia?"

"You know, I'm not well versed on it. From what I remember, it's when the stomach lining punctures and your bowels spill out. That's what's inside of that bump, your bowels."

"Is the surgery painful?"

"The actual surgery, no. You'll be drugged up for that. Afterward you will feel pain as the pain killers wear off."

"When is the surgery going to happen?"

"I don't know. I have to call the doctor, Cecil. Don't worry, Sweetie, it's going to be ok." Sherrie's mom had a special way of relaxing me. She always was extra kind and treated me as if I were her own son.

When I woke after the surgery, I looked around and there was a nurse tinkering with the heart monitor machine I was hooked up to. She hadn't noticed that my eyes opened and was engrossed in whatever it was she was doing. She pulled something and the calming beep-beep stopped and the screen flat-lined with a blaring alarm. I thought I had just died and screamed, startling the nurse. She spun around and looked at me, then at the machine, and smiled.

"It's ok, Honey, you're alive. I just took out the cord connected to your pulse. I'm happy you're awake. How do you feel?"

I leaned back in the bed and struggled to grab hold of my breathing. Unable to do so, I passed out.

After the hernia surgery I was stuck in bed for three days. Sherrie's mother took off and nursed me back to health. She didn't let me just sit idle, though. She insisted that I read a book a day, which was no problem. I had intended to do that anyway. My reading increased after I was taken in by the family. I had access to whatever I wanted. She also insisted that I write a review of each book, typed and double-spaced. This significantly changed things for me. She also didn't let me pick the book; she picked the book. For those three days I was in bed recovering from the surgery, I read *The Great Gatsby, Crime and Punishment* and *Of Mice and Men*.

"Ah, you're finally awake," the general said, standing over me. "You had quite the freak-out there when I told you it was time to serve your country."
"So that wasn't a dream?"
"No, no dream."
"Then how is there electricity in here?"
"This place is protected. The power's run off a generator buried deep underground. It's designed to last one hundred years."

"But what about the electrical cables and components? I thought the bomb was supposed to wipe all that out."

"You're on a military base, Son. This is the most secure place in London. There ain't no other facility in the First World that's safe."

"So, there's no way out of this, huh?"

"Nope. You either fight or we take away your citizenship and toss you in the coalition and let them do whatever they please with you. From the reports I've read, not many, but definitely a few, have been accepted into their coalition and joined the fight to destroy their First World enemies. But there ain't much more than a few."

"How many have chosen not to fight?"

"Oh, thousands. That would be all the rest. Out of those that were among the few lucky individuals given the opportunity to join their ranks, about half said, 'Fuck you!' to them to the other half that crossed over. The rest of the poor bastards were locked in barns and burned alive. The coalition has been doing sick things like that, and we don't even know about it because they've knocked out our means of connecting to the rest of the world. We can't even contact our allies who are in the dark as well. The world's laughing at us and the coalition has every nation by now, if they didn't already. They've done without direct confrontation what no other power could: stop the flow of electricity to the First World nations."

"So what happens now?"

"Now, we return to the basics."

"What are the basics?"

"Guerilla warfare. There will be no mercy. We will be invisible. And we will kill swiftly and viciously."

"I don't want to kill anyone."

"I've already told you what will happen if you don't fight. The Press Secretary tells me you aren't without some skill. She speaks very highly of you, actually; thinks you're going to make me glad that I met you. We'll see about that. I'm not in the habit of being happy to meet new people. Now, what's your answer going to be?"

"Excuse me?"

"Are you going to fight or aren't you?"

I didn't see much of a choice.

"I'm going to fight," I said.

"Good. Well, it's time to get your lazy ass out of bed, then."

"What?"

"Move! Move! Move!" the general began yelling over and over again until I was standing straight up like a stalk. My eyes rolled in my head as I desperately tried to click all of my functions back together. I stood before him at attention, unable to process what was going on. The general eyed me hard.

"You're not going to make it through this program, Son," the general said. "I can smell the fear wafting out your pores. You're a sweet sugar fairy whose gonna miss his mommy too many nights. Sensitive to the tear as you hear strong me yelling in your ear. This is going to be a waste of my fucking time."

As the general yelled at me, his spittle splashing against my face, I slipped further and further into the back of my mind. It began to occur to me that he was going to be my personal drill instructor and I was going to have to go through this 'training period' all alone, which thankfully turned out not to be the case.

"Private, why are you not responding to me when I am asking you simple fucking questions? Are you retarded? What the hell is wrong with you?"

There was nothing wrong with me. I just wasn't there in mind or spirit. I let myself leave my body and astral-plane away to another dimension, one that was pure and where I didn't have to worry about anything. The dimension was similar to our own, but it was peaceful, joyful. I usually could stay in that dimension for a while before remembering that it was all in my mind and this peaceful place didn't really exist. Of course, it exists, but the thing about it is that I'm from here, so with the choice of picking reality or not reality, I'm always going to pick reality.

When the charm of being in another dimension in my mind wore off, I checked back in to see if the general was still going at it.

"...little maggots like you feel entitled to some sort of royal treatment. Do you think we care about you? You think you can just say nothing and stare through me? I can do this all day. I am a general, Son. I've killed men with my bare hands. There isn't any way you are going to leave this room without showing me the respect you are required to show a superior officer. You will learn the chain of command and adhere to it always, or else I'll strip you of your citizenship and send you to the coalition. This war is no longer about all your little liberal working class, black poverty struggles. This is now about those who wish to live free with the powerful knowledge that there is no other place that should be the sole super power than here and the United States."

So that's what's happening, I thought. England and the US have merged into one. Things are becoming confusing. Confusion did little to help the infernal clicking's and ticking's of my brain. I tried hard to not lock onto the words the general was spewing. I didn't want his life force to grab hold of me because then I knew I would break. If I gave him nothing, there'd be nothing for him to gain. So I slipped back into my brain.

I figured since I had this time to think, I should try to figure out what was taking place.
This is what I thought:

"Pardon the curiosity of all those ponderings that have decided to catch me in the middle of a thought that was overlapped onto a memory in between a dream and lost in the forgotten exchanges seldom given a chance to develop into the caring and sharing type of experience we all search for. Searching is what I was supposed to be doing; what I set out to accomplish and I'm searching for meaning, but even with the searching, there isn't much that can be accomplished. It seems almost an untruth that if you work hard you will be rewarded. All the hard work seems only to grunt in the space and pull you back and then you're stuck in bed for weeks and probably will lose your job which sucks 'cause you've got kids to feed. I'm glad I don't have any kids to feed. Children would be a bad thing for this period and it's the beginning of a change. The First World and the Third World have switched, but, no, that in itself isn't even true because now there just is no First World. Everyone is just third, but the old one that formed a coalition is not going to back down an inch and now they want me to fight in this war that honestly isn't going to happen. I don't know how I'm going to be the one who gets out of this because it's important to stand by your principles, but first you've got to learn what your principles are and if they are sound and when you discover them, there is a certain moment when you must push beyond all of it and try your hand at things you've never done or repeated, nor should they be and that is the entire point, really. Allow them to introduce themselves; learn their names and try hard to continue where your parents and grandparents left off. Coming from the type of family that I....."

The general socked me in the face, breaking my stream of thought.

My head reeled back and my hands snapped up to my nose, but not fast enough to catch the rivulet of warm blood that gushed forth from my freshly broken nose. I stumbled a few steps backward and then fell on my knees. I let my hands move away from my bloody nose to the floor in order to catch myself from smashing my face into the tile. In a matter of seconds, a pool of blood had developed. It spread quickly and I felt a surge of anger building up in me. My nose was still bleeding profusely and my vision was impaired from the tears that wouldn't stop falling. It didn't even hurt at that point, but my eyes continued to water, so there was nothing I could do about it.

I stood, and for the first time since saying I would join the First World Coalition's army, I looked the general directly in the eye. The anger boiled over from deep in my belly, burning my insides and the pain made me even madder. It seemed the general sensed my intention, but all he did was raise his eyebrow. I took a moment to ponder what I should do.

129

If what he said about killing people with his bare hands was true, then I'd be a fool if I tried to swing on him the way he did me. The blood from my nose still flowed and the front of my clothes was covered in it. I thought, but what if he's just bluffing? Well, he already did hit me. Yeah, but I wasn't paying attention. I should knock this joker out right now and call it a day. I'm sure I'll feel happy if I can get him square in the nose the way he did me. But if I go for it and miss or he senses it and is too quick or blocks it, would officially be the end of me.

But this motherfucker punched me in the goddamn nose, I thought. I'm not sure how long all of this took, but by the time I realized what I had done, or attempted to do, I should say, I woke up in the cot again. It was like Deja Vu. I was exactly in the same place I found myself when I woke after passing out after having been told that I was going to have to enlist in the army. There was a wondrous moment when I thought for just the briefest of moments that I was back in Evanston sleeping in my bed that used to be Johnny's. I decided to let my mind indulge itself and allowed myself to fall into my memories.

When I woke the day after my grandmother, Lucy, died, I was pulled from a pleasant dream. Surrounded by honey-skinned-with-a-touch-of-cinnamon women, I was floating on a cloud above the Atlantic Ocean. The waves could faintly be heard from the height we were at. There were six in total of the honey-cinnamon-skinned women on the cloud with me. For some reason I was a king and they were serving me. It was like a scene from Aladdin or something. I began to take notice of the cloud we were floating on and watched as it slowly began to dissipate into nothing. It wasn't long before each of the honey-cinnamon-skinned women began to tumble off the cloud, one by one. The very last one looked me in the eye seconds before her time came. It was a look of acceptance. Then down she went, splashing into the ocean.

Following the six weeks of basic training I was forced to endure, I was fully indoctrinated into the First World Coalition military. There wasn't a whole lot to say after graduating, so I stopped speaking. During the six weeks, I gained the casual acquaintance of a few rather fascinating individuals. Each of them was from different points scattered across the globe. Somehow each one of us found ourselves serving an ideal, strictly because of where we were born. Out of all the enlistees that were run, yelled at and beaten, there were four that I truly made a solid connection with. One of them was an orphan, like me.

Christian was born in San Paulo, Brazil. His family immigrated to London when he was two years old.

"I've never been back since," he told me one night after we finished PT and had downtime. "I've always wanted to. Just to feel the sun. Swim in the ocean. Lay in the sand with a beautiful woman. You know what I mean, right, Cecil?"

"I've never been to Brazil either."

"No. Not just Brazil. But home. It's where I was born. To not be able to return to where you were born is hard, man."

"I know a little something about that."

"Do you, now. Tell us a little something about it."

"There's not really much to tell. Both my parents died in a plane crash when I was two years old. I have no idea where I was born. I never met my parents. My grandmother, who was the only one left in my bloodline that's known to me, I didn't get to meet until I was seventeen and then she died a few months afterward. And as far as my family is concerned, that's all there is to it. There was a family I stayed with that took me in after I escaped from the orphanage. They were kind and nice and very rich and gave me the opportunity to experience things I otherwise would never have had the chance to."

"Sounds like you've been a very fortunate man."

"Yes, I would have to agree with you on that. There isn't a village, rural or urban, that can compare to the harsh tutelage of Smitheran Sweets."

"Was that the name of the orphanage?"

"Yeah. Rather strange, don't you think?"

"Not really. The one I was tortured in was called Uncle Gatsby's Home for Lost Children. I think it's something that they do. Kind of a cheap labor, sweat shop type of operation. That's why they're in the business in the first place. They want to hire ten- and eleven-year-olds to work in their different factories, producing whatever the hell it is that needs making. So far I've been able to determine that a large number of these orphanages' funding sources were from both of our countries."

"You mean the United States and here?"

"Yes, that is exactly what I am telling you, Cecil."

"Oh my god. How could they be allowed to get away with something like this?"

"Easy. They do whatever they want. That's exactly the reason we're in this fucking situation in the first goddamn place. Look at us. We're covered in mud and shivering while trying to eat week-old bread."

"It's boot camp, Man. They gotta get us ready to go in and do what we gotta do. We're fighting an entirely different war this time around."

"You don't even know what you are talking about. They've got you brainwashed just right. You really believe the shit they've been pouring into your ear. That's amazing, Cecil. Well, if they can get another chance at being in control of the world, perhaps then what you seem convinced of is a good plan will turn out to have been just that. As for now, from what I see, we are heading into a suicide mission situation in which the probability of us returning is absolutely doubtful. And do you know why we are covered in mud preparing to fight a battle we cannot win? Because the powers that be did not want to help those less fortunate countries around the globe. And instead of leaving them the fuck alone if they weren't going to help them, they chose to exploit them and create problems where there were none and drain these countries of everything while they made billions. You know what's a real funny thing? All of the information that I've heard about the coalition is that it's made up entirely of black and brown soldiers. You understand what I'm saying? Black people have united and are taking over this planet. Taking it back, I should say."

"If that truly is the case, surely the coalition is going to kill both me and you."

"No, that's not true. I've heard so many stories. I've heard that if the coalition sees a brown or black person, they immediately disarm themselves."

"I don't believe that."

"Well, why not?"

"Because they are the enemy."

"Whose enemy?"

"The First World Coalition."

"That neither you nor me wanted to be a part of; which never even existed until a few months ago."

I had to admit that everything Christian was saying sounded very much like the truth. And given the polarized stance of the United States at the time of the electromagnetic bomb going off, there wasn't much of an argument as to who the real forces fighting to maintain their power were. And, it's like Christian said: All of the coalition looked like him and I.

"If you feel all this strongly," I finally said. "Then why are you here with me covered in mud eating week-old bread and complaining? Do something about it."

"Why don't you do something about it?

"Because I don't feel the same way as you, so I'm not going to do things that will make me break again."

"What do you mean, break?"

"That's not really important right now."

"How could it not be important? Breaking just once is a trip. You broke and rebuilt. What's that like?"

"You know, I'm sorry. I really don't feel like talking about it?"

"I wasn't asking about what broke you. I was curious about the rebuilding and then maintaining. When did you break?"

"It was when I divorced my wife."

"You were married?"

"Yes, I was; happily married and looking forward to the years to come. It would've been ten years this year."

"How long did you all last?"

"Nine months."

"Any kids?"

"No. Though she has one that I know of for sure, now. A daughter."

"Do you stay in touch?"

"Nope. I don't know. I never felt that calling would be something she would want."

"What do you mean?"

"I mean hearing from me. I always feel like any and all feeling that my ex-wife ever had for me has been scorched from her very soul by me, so there's no blame or victimizing. It's just something that I live with. Along with a deep regret that plunges into my kidneys and digs a dark gash that I'm sure will eventually puncture and give me more problems than I need."

"But it's been so long. How long since you last spoke to her?"

"Oh, it was a long time ago. I'd probably say four or five years ago. It was just after I had returned from China. Interestingly enough, I was on my way to Japan."

"Why were you in China and Japan?"

"I was in China the first time for my senior year of high school and second time for study abroad at Uni. I was studying Chinese and exploring like any good young lad that's given the opportunity should do. Japan came about for a slightly different reason. I was raised by a family that were Nichiren Buddhists and the philosophy of Buddhism, specifically as taught by Daisaku Ikeda, president of the Soka Gakkai International."

"What's the Soka Gakkai?"

"The Soka Gakkai is a lay Buddhist organization that's in 192 countries and territories."

"Wow, that's a lot."

"You bet your bottom dollar it is?"

"What?"

"Don't worry about it."

The general came into the mess hall and announced that dinner was over. It was time for the evening run. I never understood why they always made us run after we ate. I guess that was part of the training. It just seemed unnecessarily cruel and counterproductive. But we ran. We ran ... and we ran. For a total of sixteen weeks, we hopped, skipped, jumped, crawled, swam, climbed and whatever else you can think of, we did it. We learned our trade crafts and we were formed into a self-sufficient, fully responsive tactical unit.

Barry was the second of the good friends I made during my time in the First World Coalition military. Barry was a construction worker from Gary, Indiana. He had three kids once upon a time. The oldest was killed in a drive-by shooting. He was a gang member and had shot a rival gang leader's girlfriend in the head a week earlier. So they retaliated on Barry's oldest. Barry's second oldest was a boy who was gifted in drawing. He could draw almost before he could walk. His abilities made him pick up the aerosol can and he made a bit of a name for himself in the streets. But a rival crew that was tagging and doing burners didn't appreciate Barry's second eldest expressing his art. So, they shot him as he walked home one night. The last of Barry's children was his little girl. She was the apple of his eye. Barry's little girl could do no wrong. By the time I met Barry in boot camp, his baby girl had been grown. They hadn't spoken in over ten years.

"She asked me to respect her space. What more can I do besides that? There weren't any arguments that I can remember. There wasn't any difficulty or harsh words or anything of the like. All that happened was that she said she couldn't take it anymore and that she wasn't about to continue the chain and watch me die, too."

"What made her say that?"

"I had started drinking a lot again."

"So what she said was justified?"

"Oh, absolutely justified. I was a wreck. It's amazing that I didn't kill myself, to be perfectly honest. It was only that the gun I had was buried so deep under the bucket of clothes that I didn't have the motivation to deal with retrieving it."

"Seems like you were protected."

"Yeah, by laziness. Anyway, I packed up all my stuff and moved out."

"You moved out of your own house?"

"Of course. I gave it to my daughter. I felt like that was the least I could do after being such a horrible father and her having to deal with as much as she did those first eighteen years plus all the others were shit that continued to be fucked up."

"I would say that makes you a good man."

"Well, reserve judgment on that until at least after we graduate from this hell hole. How much longer we got before we're outta here?"

"I think its one more week. Unless they have a surprise for us."

"Which they might. They seem to be having a lot of surprises for us. It's been quite annoying actually."

"No reason to get annoyed."

"That's easy for you to say. You're a Buddhist. You're always calm."

"That's not true. I get pretty ticked off from time to time. In fact, I would say that I have a pretty bad temper."

This turned out to be the greatest joke in the world to my friend. Barry started howling to such a degree that he started to embarrass me. Caring enough to be sensitive to me and my insecurity, Barry stopped laughing and apologized to me.

My other two compadres were Tammy and Jason. Tammy was from Minnesota and Jason was from Arkansas. They were both on a college semester abroad in London when the electromagnetic bomb went off, silencing the First World around the globe. I have no idea how long they had known each other before they were drafted along with Barry, Christian and myself, but from the moment I met them, you could tell they were fresh on each other. I couldn't blame Jason, either.

Tammy was beautiful. Carmel-skinned with dimples you could steal. She was obsessively athletic and had the body to prove it. But it was her eyes that stood out the most. She had majestic eyes that captured you into a cocoon of happy haze. Dipping into Tammy's orbs was like smoking hash on a cool autumn day.

By comparison, Jason was tall. Taller than any man should be. And he didn't even play basketball. I have always taken offense to being short. It's always those individuals blessed with height that are so un-athletic it's embarrassing to watch them play. Jason was one such individual. Lanky and skinny, he looked as if his bones were ready to crumble. He was always injuring himself, which made him being in our unit the greatest of challenges. But Jason was a great guy who just appeared in the wrong age. He would've been better suited for the 1930's, not the crazy time we found ourselves in 2016, finishing up training and preparing to enter the war against the coalition.

Between basic training and graduation, I suffered from nightmares. The terrifying dreams were filled with poisonous rage lying dormant somewhere deep within me. The stress of the days combined with the unresolved abandonment issues of my life threw me into a spiral of depression that I only experienced when I closed my eyes and went to sleep. They kept us too busy and there wasn't a single second left to wander in ponderings, which was a good thing. But a release had to come and there was nothing that could prevent me from being on the edge of insanity.

Filled with a multitude of changes, there was never a night that I did not wake up screaming for dear life. If this is how it's going to be in training, how will I possibly be able to perform in war? Even that thought: War. What was war? What was this war going on between the coalition and the First World and how did the coalition get such an upper hand and take out the First World, thus transforming us back to the Stone Age. These questions and dozens more flashed through my mind during those last days before graduating.

In order to finish our training, we were sent through a crucible of tests that lasted for one week entirely. There were all types of scenarios thrown at us in hopes that we would slip up. I would later learn that we were all receiving specialized training and because of my work with the Press Secretary I was tagged to be a covert operative; a fancy word for being a spy.

Yep, I was a spy during the polarized war that started after the coalition dropped the electromagnetic bomb on the nations of the First World. There wasn't a single moment of rest once we graduated.

I was immediately sent back to the States. Because the electricity was still fried, it would take a total of four months to get things back in working order again. I was forced to travel by steamboat.

"I didn't even know they still made these things," I said to a woman I had struck up a conversation with out on the deck. I was never a good boat person. I didn't have my sea legs, as they say. The trip from London to the States took a total of two weeks. It was quite a lot like a cruise I took with Sherrie's family before I made my exodus to Wuxi, China at 17. The only difference this time around was that I was a solider for the First World Coalition on my way to my first assignment.

"Well, I certainly am glad they do still make them. Otherwise I would've been trapped in London. I still can't believe all that's happened. I mean, we don't even know what condition the United States is in." The woman had an exceptionally good point. "Have you heard any details?"

"Nothing more than word of mouth gossip I've heard from people on the street and so far on this boat." I, of course, knew way more than I could let on to her. She was the first person I'd even spoken to after graduating and receiving my assignment

"I wonder if people have gone crazy and are looting. I bet they are. It's always like Americans to take advantage of a disaster to be selfish and try to get some free stuff. I bet those poor communities where they were doing all the shooting look worse than Iraq. Especially Chicago."

"Why especially Chicago?"

"You know why? Cause of all the gang shootings and the black kids killing each other."

"Why on earth would they do that?"

"I don't know. I'm not poor. Nor am I black. But all I know is before this electro bomb thing went off, the only headlines beside the elections were about black men killing black men."

"What about all the police killing black men?"

"That was all trumped up political stuff. There's no way the police were getting away with killing unarmed people. They all had to be doing something. Did you see the pictures of most of those guys that were shot? They were some scary thugs. If I had a gun and they approached me, I probably would shoot them, too. What I mean is, they didn't look like you."

"And what exactly do I look like?"

"You know."

"No, I'm afraid I don't. Can't see myself. Perhaps you'll be my mirror and tell me what I look like. And how the way I look doesn't warrant being shot for no reason compared to the thugs that seem to deserve to die, according to you."

"Did I offend you? I'm sorry."

"No, you didn't offend me. I'm thirty-one years old; way past the point of being shocked by the stupid things white people say to black people that they think are their nigga. And you say all these black men being killed by the police. What about the 14-year-old boy that was killed playing with a toy gun? What about all the other children that find themselves in the wrong place at the wrong time being the wrong color. That's truly what children think when they watch the world; when they are in a good school and they look around and none of the kids look like them. It's unfathomable that you at this point don't realize how horrible the treatment of black people has been."

"I know blacks have had a tough break."

"A tough break? You call slavery a tough break?"

"Why is it when blacks talk about race they always bring up slavery?"

"Because it is the most important factor when it comes to America's schizophrenic relationship with itself and black people. Inside the communities that are being terrorized by these 'thugs,' as you put them, and then being gunned down like cattle by police who don't lose their jobs or get punished for killing someone for no reason. And the lack of remorse coming from the police and the department and from you, quite frankly, is mind-boggling. Here we are on a damn boat trying to get back to America because of the coalition-- a group that until the bomb was unleashed on the First World nations no one had ever even heard of. But you're sitting here wondering if black people are rioting and stealing shit. Don't you think black people are just as terrified as you are?"

You all are naturally attuned to the dark, I thought.

At this point, I stopped talking to her ignorant ass and stopped speaking altogether. I looked out onto the ocean as we drifted our way back to the States. The birds flew beside the boat for a time and we exchanged a kind of communication. It was Laurel, Sherrie's younger sister, who taught me how to talk to birds.

"You have to let them know that they can trust you," she said as a giant crow flew down from the telephone wires in the back yard of Sherrie's family's home. "If they know they can trust you, they will come to you. Most birds are fascinated by humans."

"What is it about us that fascinates them?"
"From what they tell me, it's the fact that we can't fly. They want to know how we can be in charge of the entire planet and not be able to fly."

"But we have airplanes. What do they think about that?"
"All of the birds that I have spoken with don't like planes very much. Almost every bird has a relative that was killed by a plane, either by smacking against the plane and breaking their necks or plunging headfirst into the engine."

"They hate airplanes, but they like humans?"
"No, birds don't necessarily like humans. It's just that there are so many of us and they know that we have ways of killing them easily. Birds don't know how to kill us, so they stay in the cut and play their part. But I'm sure they are trying their best to devise a plan to take control, if they knew how to kill us the way we do them. I'm certain if we give them enough time, they will figure out a way to do it."

"That's a pretty scary thought. But you'll be ok because they trust you, right?"

"That is my hope, but so far, there has not been an attempt by the birds of the world to take over the planet and kill all the humans. But yes, when that happens, I just might be in an advantageous place. And so shall you, because I'm going to teach you how to talk to birds. So, after you've established their trust, then—and this is probably the hardest part and the part that requires the most patience—you have to be able to make the bird believe that you are a rock."

"A rock?"

"Yes, a rock. Or a branch or a door. The main thing, is to become something that isn't alive. Once the bird trusts you, it'll let down its initial guard. Once the bird no longer senses you, period, it will recall the feeling of trust that you sent out and be drawn to that area. It took me about six months to master this part."

"I think it'll take me a lot longer than that."

It didn't. By the third week I had birds knocking their beaks on the window of my room that used to be Sherrie's dead brother, Johnny's, room. It wasn't long before the neighbors and then the whole of Evanston knew about me. The Bird Boy is what they used to call me. John didn't like the fact that they were calling me a boy. He said it was racist to call a black man a boy, but then his wife would correct him and say that I am a boy and that it's not an issue until I leave the house. And then it's up to me to correct whoever is saying it to me.

It was cool to be known as the Bird Boy, though. I gained something of a reputation. I was cool in the eyes of all my friends, which weren't very many at the private school I was attending.

When we finally arrived in the States, the Press Secretary was there to greet me at the dock. Janelle came with her. The Press Secretary looked her usual elegant-mixed-with-powerful self. Janelle looked considerably different. Her dress was sharper. I'm sure spending time with the Press Secretary had a lot to do with that, but the way she held herself was not the same.

When I first met her on that plane ride from Chicago to London, she had seemed sure of herself and confident. Now, that confidence was gone. She seemed submissive and modest. It felt as if she was holding back a storm of emotion that would burst out of her violently if she ever lost control of it. It was when I looked into her eyes that I understood. Boot camp for her was far worse than it was for me. I would later learn the truth of this.

"So good to see you again, Cecil," the Press Secretary said, embracing me in a warm hug.

I hugged Janelle. It was very awkward, but I could feel the sexual tension that had led to the two of us shacking up after the First World's power had been severed by a terrorist network called the coalition.

"How was your trip over?"
"Incredibly long and incredibly boring."
"Yes, traveling by boat across the ocean isn't very pleasant."
"Especially if you're sick most of the time."
"Oh, you poor thing. Well, you are home now. No need to fret any longer."
"Does that mean the power's back on?"
"Don't bet on it," Janelle said.
"So, then I'll continue to fret."
"Now, don't be like that," the Press Secretary said. "There's still plenty of fun to be had in the good old United States."
"Fun?" Janelle said.
"What's wrong with fun? Poor people know how to be happy because every day is a gift and any gain is a great gain for the community. There is no individual when you are poor with a family, when you live in a community. Here, when you get poor you are shunned by the community and forced into solitude because you couldn't make and hold onto your money."
"Ok, Jesus. Forgive me for missing the way things used to be."

"I haven't really had a chance to even think about the way things used to be," I lied. I had thought about the past every night for as long as I could remember.

"Yeah, I heard they were keeping you busy," the Press Secretary said.

"How'd you hear that?" I asked as if it should have shocked me that Antoinette would know exactly what was happening to me. For all I knew, she orchestrated it for some reason that will be revealed later in the course of this game called life that we play. It turned out that I didn't have to wait very long to confirm what I already knew.

"First, I'm sorry for all that you had to go through in training," the Press Secretary said to me after we took our seats in an empty Indian restaurant not far from the dock in New York City. I had so many questions as to how the country had been able to keep moving with no electricity. As far as I could see, there wasn't a single electric anything working. From the dock we took a horse-drawn carriage. They were everywhere. We were truly back in the Dark Ages.

The Press Secretary continued after the waiter poured out three glasses of wine and left the bottle chilling in a bowl of ice in the middle of the table.

"I was receiving daily updates on your progress and Janelle and I were analyzing everything being done to you and your progress. The atrocities you were forced to experience were necessary, however, in order to wean out the weakness locked deep within you. You had to be broken and then rebuilt. The passion that you contained within your heart needed to be released before you would ever be able to tap your true potential. So, that is why you received the training you did. There were only three dozen in total around the world who were selected for the special training program you went through. You are part of the first graduating class. So now they will be watching you carefully."

"Why will they be watching?"

"They've invested quite a lot of money in you, Cecil. They need to know that it was worth it."

"So I have to perform for them?"

"Don't think of it as dancing. Just focus on the fact that it's the right thing to do."

"I'm not even sure if I totally agree with this whole war between the First World nations and the coalition nations. I haven't had to opportunity to really sit down and dissect just what the hell is going on."

"Well, you're going to have the next few days to do just that. We go operational tomorrow, January 1st, 2017. Are you in?"

"Am I in what?"

"You weren't briefed?"

"Of course not."

My answer caused the Press Secretary to furrow her brow.

"You know, I can't depend on nobody to do shit right. That's all I asked them to do. And after how much I paid them. The nerve of them not doing their fucking job. Well, I don't have time to brief you, so Janelle is going to have to do it. Is that alright, Janelle?"

"Yeah, that's perfectly fine."

"Great. So, since you are going to go over everything, there's no reason for me to do so. Now, let's lift our glasses as another year passes us by."

"That's pretty good," I said finishing off the glass and pouring myself some more. "So, what's on the menu?"

"We ordered a vegetable curry with cheese naan for you."

"Sounds great. I've been eating bread and cheese for the past few weeks on that damn boat."

"They didn't have any other food?" Janelle asked.

"No, they had other food. I just didn't have my sea legs, so I couldn't keep anything down. It was really an awful trip, one that I would rather not take again."

"Well, I'm sorry to say, you're going to have to be taking that trip and many others quite often," the Press Secretary said. "You've been promoted to my Number Two. Well, you've always been my Number Two."

"There's only ever been two of us."

"Yes, that is why you've always been my Number Two. But now, I'll have your title reflect that."

"I don't understand why you're talking like business is just going to continue as usual."

"No, it won't be as usual. But it is going to continue. There's too much money and too much power bouncing around, especially now that the world's class just split between the First World and the Third World. And those of us in the First World are going to be feeling the effects of living without electricity for many, many years to come."

"Even when they get the juice back and running again?" Janelle asked.

"Yes, even then."

"Wait, they are going to get the electricity back and running again?" I asked both of them.

"Yes, Cecil. But, like I said, Janelle will cover all of that when she briefs you tonight. Here, have another glass of champagne," the Press Secretary said, topping off mine and her own.

I glanced at Janelle's glass as the Press Secretary paused to take a sip from her own. Janelle hadn't touched her flute once. She looked so subdued, as if she was being controlled. I flirted with the idea that there was some type of mind control device implanted in Janelle's head. Seeming with everything that's occurred, from the sky turning purple to the electro bomb going off and the melding of two opposite factions that have split the world into poor and rich with the rich living like the poor, anything was possible.

There were so many questions and I didn't want to wait until later to start having them answered. But I was forced to. So I had to endure. The restaurant never saw another customer. I would learn later that since the electro blast, businesses have folded left and right. Those whose records existed only digitally lost everything. Thousands and thousands of people lost their entire fortunes.

"Everyone's had to return to the ways in which work was done back in the Dark Ages. The problem was that every First World citizen had fully assimilated to technology in such a way that they knew nothing of life before electricity. What's worse is that the technology from the days before electricity has been forgotten and those pieces of equipment stopped being made more than a hundred years ago in some cases."

"So how've we managed to get on?" I asked. Our food had arrived and the vegetable curry was as good as advertised in the window of the restaurant.

"The government issued an order to raid the museums and historic exhibits that contained working models of things like a printing press. They also shifted about a billion dollars to the post office and hired ten thousand citizens across the nation to work in the mailroom. The post office has become the most important of all our communications. Now everyone has finally learned to write and send letters."

"What about the schools? Hospitals? All the services that we knew, loved and took for granted?"

"Well, the schools are in the process of adjusting their curriculum. But what you have to remember is its winter. From the time it started getting cold, the countries had a hell of a time trying to keep their citizens warm. So many have frozen to death. So far, I think the count is about 40% of the population has died."

"Jesus," I exclaimed.

"Yes, and the remaining 60% are sick in some way."

"So, basically, we're fucked," Janelle said, downing her glass of champagne and pouring the last of the bottle into her own glass.

A waiter's spider sense must've gone off somewhere, for one appeared and popped the cork on a fresh bottle and replaced the empty one in the bowl of melting ice. Then, he skated away, out of sight and eventually out of mind … until we wanted something more.

"This is why it's of the utmost importance that we get the power back on and destroy the coalition and return the global economy to order and control."

"So how do we do that? I assume you already have an intricate plan in place."

"Actually, no. We have a very limited supply of quality information. Our governments of the First World powers have been having a bastard of a time trying to juggle a dying population, rebuilding our defenses and designing some sort of counterattack to take down the coalition."

"I just don't see how there could be no working electricity in the United States or any other First World nation."

"Well, let's not get carried away. Of course the United States has contingencies in place for such attacks. It's just that that they consist of only a very small percentage of the United States. I'm talking 3 to 4%. The rest of us are not essential enough to know about nor benefit from these resources, which are very limited and must be kept secret."

"So, what exactly is it that we're going to start tomorrow?"

"You will learn all of that when Janelle briefs you tonight. How was your curry?"

"Splendid. Good. It's incredibly expensive to eat out now. To eat anywhere for that matter."

Silence engulfed the table and none of us bothered to do anything about it. My mind floated to the seemingly infinite ramifications of the current reality. The world had shifted to a tremendous degree and nothing would ever be the same.

The next day the three of us-- Janelle, the Press Secretary and me – strolled out of the Hilton Hotel where the Press Secretary kept a permanent residence. It was a nice arrangement. Even though the entire time there was no light, with candles everywhere there was no way we could gather enough equilibrium to even consider it a pleasant rest. In the morning, upon waking, there was a great welcoming by the sun as it rose and granted us light for a time. We took advantage of the gift and did our best to collect as much as we could in terms of information regarding what was happening in the current area. The Press Secretary had skirted her way somewhere before either I or Janelle even woke. It would be something that would be lost in the looking glass reflections when we never know it, but what is considered all of the light shining down on us all. In the morning, when there is no electricity in New York, there was no way that we could ever be considered tourists. This was my first time in New York. I wondered if I hadn't wasted all of those other times before I came and now I never will know because it has all been decimated, but that is when the second bomb–the real bomb–goes off. For now, it is only about the electricity going off.

In the meantime, a pause to consider what exactly is going on. If you look at it all–and I have been trying my best to pay attention to it–there is something that hasn't been adding up. If you really listen to the plays, you will see for yourself, and that is why I'm trying my best to tell this story to you in a way that would make sense, but for now, I feel that my words are going to fall on deaf ears. Still, nevertheless, I forge ahead.

When I received my first assignment, I was wondering what it would feel like taking a life, for that was what I was tasked to do. I had never heard of the woman I was to murder. Apparently, she was a key member of the coalition. It was my sad luck that she would be my first kill. I never made that kill and the beginning of my life as a fugitive became the real world experience dealt to me by the universe.

All things considered, I would say that being chased like I was made me become someone who was unbreakable in every way. There's something lost in the nature of lost causes. Paying attention to details is forgotten and, for that reason, I take advantage of the openings. Weaknesses are everywhere if you just seek them out. And when the sirens wail, it would be that what you always forgot was lurking in the background you reminded yourself to remember, but always forgot. That is why you remind yourself to remember, but wouldn't it be so much better to write it down and remember it. Nevertheless, it's an end and there you go.

Strange Fetish

Into the morning and evening I fell as we searched out clues in libraries and dug through files and files of documents lost to the antiquity of forgotten remembrances. All things considered, I would never have acquired the skills to read like I do now nor the ability to write these words if I had not forged on with those two women, following the Press Secretary's direction, looking for something that I was never sure what it was.

Knowing mattered not. That reminds me of college and this French philosophy professor I had. Speaking of knowing and not knowing, he would go on and on, sampling different theories and offering up a helping of discovery in a cloud. It was as if he had given us a bow and arrow and instructed us to shoot at the cloud and try our best to hit the bullseye between the clouds, hidden beneath it all.

Janelle wasn't doing well. After about five weeks, I began to take notice of Janelle's frequent trips to the bathroom; at least a dozen times in a single working day. In the beginning, I didn't think anything of it. My stomach was messed up adjusting to a diet based solely on no electricity which was no easy feat in this modern world, let me tell you. But we managed and yet oftentimes there were stomach aches. Later I heard horror stories of people who poisoned themselves by eating spoiled and all types of different foods that weren't fit to be eaten by people.

"How did you survive?" Laurel asked me.

I had been with her for the past two days. After Sherrie, her mother and her father, John, died in a car crash.

This all occurred after the electricity was restored.

But where we are now, I am about to embark on my first mission as a spy for the First World Coalition.

They had trained me to be the best there ever was. I was a cold blooded, emotionless assassin and very proud of it. There was no simple way, but perfection is what I delivered and when the job was done, the satisfaction far outweighs the pleasure of gaining more money than a person would earn in a single lifetime of honest living.

"Remember, there can be no trace that you were there," the Press Secretary said to me as she tossed my knapsack onto the beach. The boat that we rowed bobbed in the water. I grabbed hold of it and walked it out, back into the open water. When I was waist deep, I pushed the small rowboat off with all of my strength and watched Janelle and the Press Secretary float away.

"Remember," the Press Secretary said. "If you need us, just break your pinky finger. You'll activate the tracking device."

I couldn't understand why they put my emergency tracking device in my pinky finger. To be more specific. I wondered why the only way to activate it was by breaking my pinky finger. I thought of the silly question that I should've asked before, any time between the month and a half that we were travelling from New York to Chicago to get our briefing and then to ship me off to this island where I was dumped off for my first assignment.

"Which pinky finger is it?" I kept saying to myself, as I walked onto the beach and headed inland. There wasn't a soul in sight, so I didn't pay any mind to anything around me. That was my mistake, for eyes were scorching my back without my knowledge. It would be true that if you tried to sense someone watching you, you'd have a better chance looking in the mirror and discovering your long lost relative. Basically, what I'm saying is that it's very hard. But what isn't hard, is giving, and giving is free, so, if you give, you will receive, and that is a basic fact of life.

This was Thomas. Thomas was always good to tell you useless information that he pulled off Facebook. Thomas lived on Facebook. There was no other way for Thomas to survive, but on Facebook. In actuality. Thomas was a 40-year-old virgin who lost his way a long fucking time ago and gave up trying to find his way back home. But these things considered, it would be those of us who are climbing stairs on a daily basis that would consider what a new day looks like.

"Cecil, how many days have you been with us?"

"Eleven, Sir."

"And why is it that you're better at this than any other man I've had on my crew in the last two years?

"I couldn't say that, Sir."

"Are you calling me a liar?"

"No, Sir."

"Then what exactly are you saying?"

"All I'm saying, Sir, is that all the guys you're saying I'm better than taught me how to do the job you're saying I'm better at them than. It's hard for me to say that, Sir. That's all I'm saying. Surely you can understand that."

"I suppose I could. Where you coming from, Cecil?"

"Originally, Chicago, Sir."

"Your folks around that way?"

"My folks are dead, Sir."

"That a boy. Mine are too. Liberating isn't it?"

"They been dead since I was a baby. I never knew them."

"Well, you ain't missing much, I'm sure. Not to say that your parents weren't fine and everything. It's just from my experience that most people older than us don't know how to take care of children … except for the grandmothers, but ours are dying and they are the last ones, really. All the others are having babies when they're still babies. They never got to try and snuggle up next to me.

You'd better back on up before I put you down. I'm sitting here fighting for your ass and you think that's just because we're buddies, but let me tell you, there is no line. It's just about how you know someone and you have the credentials, then, that is all that matters and you go and take whatever job you want."

The woman who was supposed to be the contact to the Press Secretary said they would meet me if I wandered inland on the island and take me to the main house where the county sheriff was stationed. The sheriff was the one who oversaw all things as far as the island was concerned, so it was of the utmost importance that I meet with this man.

The sheriff welcomed me with open arms.

"We have been waiting for you, Cecil?"
I was shocked that this man I had never met knew who I was.
"I'm honored, Sir."
"Sir?
Hush away these formalities. There isn't anything that should separate us from being equal. My friend, please, you've travelled very far. Rest. You must rest your loins."
"Rest my loins? No thanks. I should say that I am at a disadvantage."
"How's that, Cecil?"
"Well, I have no idea who you are. And I have no idea how you know my name."
"The Press Secretary was right. You are green."
"Ah, thank you. I'm glad you and the Press Secretary are cracking jokes on me."
"No jokes. She has much respect for you. You would not be speaking to me at this moment if it were not for the trust the Press Secretary has for you. I think you should consider this. For I don't think you know that the path you are walking is essential for the pulling together of humanity."

I must admit that this was all pretty heavy. I looked at the sheriff and nodded my head as if I understood what was happening. He knew I didn't and so did I. But we forged ahead.

Butterflies swarmed majestically in my stomach as I lifted the last ounce of energy up and out of myself. The Press Secretary lay in a pool of her own blood. Bleeding from her stomach, the bullet buried deep into her spinal cord. There was no hope for her. I knew it. She knew it. And so did Janelle.

"Well, seems like this is it?"
"I don't understand. Why is this happening?"

"Things happen, Cecil. The world has changed drastically and the echo of destruction that is to come will give a reverberation that will be felt for decades. Unfortunately, I guess I can't be there to work things out with you. So, now it's up to you to rebuild the world. It'll be a lot of work, but I definitely think you're up for the challenge. This is what I have been training you to do."

"Yeah, I figured something like that."

"But you had no idea it would be like this."

"Who the hell could've predicted this shit show we're faced with now?"

"I could."

"Then why didn't you say anything?"

"Who would've believed it?"

"Well, you do have a point."

"And with that point. I shall leave you, Cecil. Don't look back. Don't mourn me. Change the world. And become known for eternity as the arrow directed toward peace."

And with that, the Press Secretary faded away. Her last breath exhaled in a final exclamation of a life well lived and anticipation for the next to come.

I tried my best to hold back the tears, but nothing could stop the hurt from pouring through. I realized at that moment that the Press Secretary was for me the mother I never had. No, she was more than just a mother. She was my teacher, she was my friend. The hurt exploded from me and I was overcome with such grief as to wonder if it ever would cease. It never did.

After the Press Secretary was killed. I fell into a spiral of depression. Realizing that the woman who was the closest thing to a mother that only after she passed was devastating. Janelle checked us into a motel we passed on the highway. I don't know where she had been intending to drive us. She just told me to get in the car and went straight. Once we were in the hotel, I went into the bathroom and stripped down naked. My clothes were soaked in the Press Secretary's blood. I piled soiled clothes up in a ball and tossed them out the window above the toilet into the alley behind the motel.

The shower scalded my body and returned me slightly to myself. I hadn't realized how far outside of my skin I had felt I was. There was no change in my thoughts, however. They raced. When I got out of the shower, Janelle was on her way to getting drunk. I caught up to her in no time and before we know it we were passed out in our underwear on the bed.

The dreams I had. Oh, what they were! Scary doesn't even do justice to describe the horrible things I was forced to see that first night and the many nights to follow. We scrambled along the next morning. It was late afternoon when I finally rolled out of bed. Janelle had just showered and walked out of the bathroom naked.

She saw that I was awake and started.

"I'm sorry. I thought you were still sleeping," she said making no effort to cover herself.

"I'm sorry, too," I said, averting my gaze and trying my best to be respectful.

"Cecil, its ok. I just came to get a towel." She grabbed a towel and covered her dripping wet naked body. The towel did nothing to take away from her voluptuous figure. I watched her walk back into the shower, trying my best not to, but failing to not stare at her ass. After she waddled her behind back inside, I realized that I was hard. Feeling self-conscious, I got up to search for my pants and cover up my shame. It stuck out comically as my penis strained to be released from the boxer briefs I was wearing.

As luck would have it, just as I found my pants laying underneath the bed, I grabbed them and yawned. I extended the yawn into a stretch and bent backward, stretching my back as well.

Just as I was arching my back with my pole sticking out at rock solid attention, Janelle came out of the bathroom, again without a towel and dripping wet.

"Sorry, I forgot my toothbrush," she said walking over to her bag, not directly paying much attention to me at first. "Got it," she said and made to go back into the bathroom. She glanced at me with a casual smile and then looked down at my erection.

She froze and I froze. I watched as droplets of water fell from her hair onto her breasts. Amazingly, I got harder. The tension was beginning to ache. Janelle kept her eyes on my dick poking out of my underwear for a long time. A smile began to stretch at the corners of her lips. She licked them and I felt a wave of pleasure wash over me. It was brief and intense. Vanishing as quickly as it appeared. Her gaze never wavered and her breath became short as she forgot to breathe.

"Seems you've got a bit of a problem there," she finally said.
"Just a little bit."
"There's nothing little about that."
"Thank you, I guess."
"Is that for me?"
"Depends. Do you want it?"

Janelle nodded her head in the affirmative and took a step toward me. Her hair continued to drip rivulets falling down her body in patterns I would later trace with my tongue. When she arrived within a hair's breadth of me, our lips barely touching, her breath exhaled onto my lips. My dick wedged its way between her legs just at the bell of her lady. And there we stood. Enjoying the energy bouncing between us. My dick pulsed as my heartbeat quickened. I could see Janelle could feel my heartbeat through my dick as it rubbed up against her exposed clit. Janelle closed her eyes and sucked up my lips and tongue. I wrapped both my arms around her naked body and pulled her close to me. My underwear started to get wet from her still wet body. I took a step back, breaking our kiss and removed my boxer briefs. My penis sprang free, bouncing in happiness. Amazingly, now that it was free, it had room to grow fully. I walked back to where I was and Janelle opened herself to let me back in. I grabbed hold of her ass and squeezed it tight.

She let out a moan deep into my ear just before licking it and biting my ear lobe. This sent a shiver of pleasure from my head to my toes. I shook as if I was cold. Janelle grabbed me by the hand and led me into the steaming shower she had left running.

Once in the shower, our lips and tongues danced frantically as if life depended on keeping the momentum of making out high. Janelle pushed my back against the wall the shower faucet was on. I stood under the stream cascading down and watched as the water hit against Janelle's breasts. Gravity hadn't done much to her cantaloupe sized-cups. She grabbed them both and squeezed them together for me.

"Do you like?" she asked me.
"I like"
"I'd like you to put that between them," she said lowering herself to her knees.
"I aim to please," I responded for lack of anything better to say.

She grabbed hold of my weight and held it in the palm of her hand. She raised and lowered it as she were weighing it for market. She seemed to be impressed and then began to stroke it very slowly. She alternated between squeezing the shaft hard and stroking it very softly. When she felt she had gotten to know my penis a little, she licked the very tip and then put it between her tits. As she smooshed them together, I felt I was in heaven. Janelle had hazel green eyes, honey bronzed skin and light brown hair. As my dick slid up and down between her breasts, she looked into my eyes with the greatest, 'I'm going to fuck the shit outta you face' I had ever seen.

And that is precisely what she did. In the shower, on the bathroom sink, on the bathroom floor, in a few of the chairs and on every part of the hotel bed. We even did it in the car before we headed out to our next destination.

The plan that we were following was the last one ever made by the Press Secretary. The plan was simple, masterfully put together, and if done properly, would be able to set foundations to make a sustainable peace. We just first had to get to DC. The Press Secretary gave us a letter of invitation to speak with the President of the United States. Then she gave us the best gift we could ever ask for: a prototype car that had no electrical or metal components and ran entirely on water.

Apparently the car was invented in the event of such things happening like the electro bomb going off. The engineers were tasked with the impossible goal of using no wires, no metal, to build a car that would run entirely on water.

Ours was the only car running, which proved to be a great hazard to our personal health and wellbeing. There were countless cars scattered throughout the roads, all abandoned exactly as they were when the electro bomb went off. Many of the highways were zigzag mazes of destruction. Between the time we had waited in the bunker and all the wandering we did with the Press Secretary, the country, along with all the other First World nations, had been in ruins for almost half a year.

Rotting, decaying bodies were scattered everywhere. Crows plucked at the eyeballs of corpses that perished in ways rendering them indistinguishable to any relative seeking them out as so many were searching for lost loved ones.

It was in Montana that our plastic nonelectric car that ran on water decided to die.

It was 2:13am, about when the noise of the engine struggling screamed against our ears causing an inner panic that bellowed forth a multitude of stressful worries I could've done better without.

"I think it's dead," Janelle said to me as she peered underneath the hood. We rode the buggy as long as it would last.

Once we finally stopped, Janelle popped the hood and I looked in the trunk to see if we had more water. I was sure it was out of gas.

Finding none and nothing we were able to do, Janelle and I set out from the broken down prototype car for a future that no longer would exist, if any future would ever again exist in the first place.

"Do you really think this plan is going to play out?"
"What do you mean?"
"I mean it all sounds so intricate. So grandiose, that I just can't believe it will work out."
"I wish you would have just a little bit more confidence."
"You have confidence and I have rationality. And rationality tells me that this isn't something that can be done by two amateurs like us. We are not professionals. We are just the hired help. Don't you get that?"

I could see that things were beginning to fall apart in Janelle. I was sad that she was hurting, but happy I was finally able to see exactly what was going on inside her. She was rotting and wanting to die, but refusing not to fight. Janelle was a great fighter. Our wanderings after the Press Secretary was killed in the prototype car that ran on water afforded me the opportunity to get to know Janelle intimately.

Janelle was born in Oklahoma into a family of Mormons. When she was ten, her father took her away to Cuba where she lived for the next twenty years. She never was able to find out why her father just up and left for Cuba with her in tow. Janelle had two sisters and a baby brother. She has never seen them since that day when her father made her say goodbye to her family. It was a strange thing to have happen to a ten-year-old kid. Janelle told me it was something she thought about constantly.

In Cuba, Janelle excelled in school, picking up Spanish as if she had known it in a previous life. She also took up and became a master at the Japanese martial art of karate. Janelle's father had been a Green Beret in the Army during the Vietnam War. Through his experience, he learned the value of self-discipline to be able to control the environment. He taught the same principles to Janelle, who took them on as naturally as she did Spanish.

By the time Janelle was sixteen, she had already won every national and international competition she was able to qualify for. Her fortune shifted when she was nineteen. Her father was stabbed twenty times in a robbery and left to bleed to death in a gutter outside a barn.

It would take Janelle eighteen months before she was able to learn of her father's unfortunate ending.

After Janelle lost her father, she spiraled down into a field of self-destruction. 'Fuck the world' became her motto.

Janelle traded her passions for alcohol and drugs. There wasn't a day she was not drinking. Snorting was in the evenings. Smoking was habitual and popping pills was done with friends. One of those friends, her best friend, she said, until that friend stabbed Janelle's boyfriend sixteen times when he wouldn't cheat. She was a pharmacist and had access to every drug known to man, or worth taking, I should say. She supplied the pills.

A treasure trove could be found in her purse whenever she returned home from work.

"What'd you bring from work, Michelle?" Janelle would ask her best friend and roommate at the time, like a little kid jumping up and down when Santa Claus comes down the chimney.
"I've got something that'll make you pop. It's got a hidden treat at the end of the ride."
"Oooooo! Now that sounds enticing. Gimmie, gimmie, gimmie!"
"Now, now. Is that how you ask? Where are your manners?"

"Yes, Ma'am. May I have some, please?"
"That's much better. Yes, you may."

When Janelle was telling me about Michelle as we drove in the car powered by water after the Press Secretary died, I felt I had known so much about Michelle. I felt like she was my best friend. The sense of betrayal, and the fact that Michelle tried to sleep with Janelle's boyfriend and then killed him when he wouldn't, began to come to the surface while we drove.

"Michelle had so much control over me. I would do anything for the drugs and she controlled my supply. It was a double control; the drugs got me and so did she. She wasn't abusive and she treated me good, but I was as her slave or dog more than anything. I guess not slave because I wasn't working for her. I never did any work and neither did she. Michelle had a maid from Peru named Claudia. Claudia was beautiful. Michelle and I were intimate occasionally, but that was usually drug-induced and a convenience. I didn't have any romantic feelings toward Michelle. Claudia was something else entirely, though. From the moment Michelle hired her and I first laid eyes on Claudia, I knew I was in love and she was the one for me. It didn't take long for me to confirm for myself that Claudia felt the same. I tried my best to keep our relationship a secret from Michelle. I didn't have any immediate reason to be worried, but I just thought it was poor taste to be dating the maid. But I didn't care about appearances. We were in love."
"Sounds like things were going good. Until, what happened?"
"What makes you think something happened?"
"Well, just your tone makes it seem like things are about to fall to shit."
"Oh yes, things absolutely fell to shit. Fast and hard. But Claudia, no. Her mother got ill back in Peru so she had to leave. We said goodbye and I never saw her again. As far as I knew, Michelle didn't know a damn thing about it. But she did know about my boyfriend, Steve. Steve was a good guy and about a year after Claudia left, I gave this boy I met in a bookstore while I was high on

cocaine, a shot. We started dating and after a few weeks I let myself fall for him.

"He was perfect in almost every way. The one flaw to this total package of a man was his breath. It was amazing how a man could have such funky breath. It didn't make a stitch of sense and it wasn't like he didn't brush his teeth. He had a germ phobia to the highest degree. A lot of his time was wasted worrying about washing his hands or how to open the bathroom door without touching it. But for some reason, his breath couldn't be fixed. It got so bad that I even encouraged him to see a doctor and make sure there wasn't anything medically wrong with him."

"You sent your boyfriend to the doctor because he had bad breath?

"I mean, when you say it like that, sure. But it was just because I was so concerned."

"And you also wanted to kiss him without gagging?"

"Well, yeah. But I would never have thought that he had a rare form of bad breath that is a collection of bacteria in the back of the throat that takes months, if not years, to rid the mouth of. But we had invested a lot of time in one another and besides that, he was a perfect specimen for marriage. So I went ahead and let the relationship grow and flourish. He knew his breath stank and felt that I was settling for him. I thought he was settling for me because I was a drug addict."

"The perfect couple," I exclaimed sarcastically.

"Actually, yeah, we were."

"Until?"

"Until Michelle decided to intervene. I had been spending less and less time with her. My boyfriend started helping me get off drugs. He had such a beautiful way of encouraging me to try to take a day off. One day led to two and then to three. After a week of being drug-free, my boyfriend looked at me and all he said was, 'Now that you've done a week, you can do anything.' And when I looked into his eyes, I not only believed him, I knew that he was right. The surge of power that overflowed from inside of me was the greatest feeling ever. It was a feeling I hadn't felt since I was a child. And then after that, I weaned myself off everything except weed."

"Your boyfriend didn't mind you smoking weed?"

"He smoked all day, every day."

"So he was against the pills and hard drugs, but not against weed?"

"I wouldn't say he was against any drugs actually. It's just that he didn't like the fact that I was addicted. I never hid it from him. On our first date, I told him I was struggling with addiction; that I loved to drink, pop pills, snort and the only thing positive I had going on in my life was that I was somehow keeping a house plant alive."

"A house plant?"

"Yeah, a house plant. Something Claudia left. That house plant helped keep me thinking about drinking water. I made sure the house plant had water and that I had water. Staying hydrated absolutely kept me alive. I was doing so many drugs every day that there is no way I would have been able to survive unless I was drinking water."

"So water became your religion?"

"Water is my religion."

"Well you must be struggling since we left the bunker. Water is hard as hell to get now."

"Why the fuck do you think I've been breaking down? I know you've noticed and been worrying about me. You say so yourself when you sleep."

"I talk in my sleep?"

"Yea, all the time."

"Why are you just now telling me this?"

"I figured you knew. You never mentioned it, so I just thought it was normal for you and you just didn't pay attention to it. You are pretty aloof."

"What else have I said?"

"Well, mostly in the bunker you talked about your family. It seemed like you were replaying conversations or talking to them just as you are now. I'm not an expert on dreams. You're always talking about Sherrie. Who's she?"

"My stepsister. But she's in love with me."

"Kinda strange."

"Very strange. What've I talked about since we left the bunker?"

"You talked a lot about the orphanage you were in and I think you imagine talking to your parents, although I know you never did 'cause you said they died when you were two. Oh, one night, and only once, you were weeping badly."

"I was weeping?"

"Yeah, and over and over you kept whispering, 'Tiffany, don't leave. Please. I'm sorry. I love you. I want you.' Over and over this went. Who's Tiffany?"

"My ex-wife."

"Man, you've got an awful lot going on up there in your head. How do you deal with it?"

"With great difficulty. From now on, if it's alright with you, please tell me what I say if you hear me talking in my sleep. I'm curious as to what my subconscious is really focusing on."

"Sure, that's no problem. I can do that."

"Very much obliged. So I mentioned that I've been worried about you when I talk in my sleep. Which is true. I have been worrying about you. I've grown rather accustomed to your essence."

"That's nice of you to say. I kinda like you, too."

"I figured as much."

"Yeah, sure. You know everything."

"Not everything. Just everything so far."

"Humph, nobody likes a smart ass."

"That's funny. You just said you did."

"You gonna keep this up or can I finish talking?"

"Please continue."

"Thank you," Janelle said sarcastically as the car zoomed along the abandoned highway as we tried to make our way to Washington, D.C.

The personal invitation that was a dying gift to me from the Press Secretary was burning a hole in my vest pocket. I tried to ponder what wonders lay ahead of the door this invitation would unlock. Wandering through my imagination, nothing would prepare me for the journey we were about to embark on. The stage was set.

The world was split between the powerful and the powerless. The powerless had found a way to take away the powerful main source of power: electricity itself. Water was the new currency and the two coalitions of First World and Third World were gathering numbers and galvanizing groups as the strategy for global domination was set to begin.

Once I finally got my shit together following my breakdown after the Press Secretary's murder, I was able to think more clearly and returned my focus to the basics taught to me at the beginning of my employment with her.

I had just returned from Tokyo after being denied a third renewal of my visa status. Uprooted again, I left a booming job where I was teaching hip hop dance to children and young adults. My operation had expanded to include studios in Tokyo, Gumma, and all the way up to Hokkaido. I was especially proud of the studio in Sapporo, Hokkaido. It was the largest by far and had the largest number of students. Hokkaido also had the three individuals who probably would have become major influences in the hip hop dance game had humanity decided not to throw a temper tantrum and knock the planet back into the Dark Ages.

When I landed back in the States, I was at baggage claim waiting on all that was my life that I could fit into a medium-sized duffle bag. I was a minimalist. Watching the conveyor belt go round and round, I started thinking of the places where you can eat sushi on a conveyor belt. Suddenly, I began to understand that a chapter of my life had closed once again. I had lost count of which chapter I was on at that point.

I remember it as clear as day. At just that point, reminiscing on the joy of eating sushi and drinking sake, the Press Secretary nudged me with her booty as she reached to lift out her large bag. I quickly snapped out of my reverie and grabbed her bag and pulled it out onto the floor.

"Thank you so much," she said looking at me through Ray-Bans."

"You're very welcome."

I lingered for a moment and smiled, enjoying her smiling at me, then moved a polite distance away and returned to waiting for my bag.

When I left on my self-imposed exile to Wuxi, China, I was seventeen and as disconnected from life as a teenager could be. The last known roots I had in my grandmother had died and she took with her every memory that I might've learned about my parents and family in general. I packed a small duffle bag with a week's worth of clothes and three big books that would keep me occupied for at least a few months: *Don Quixote, War and Peace* and *The Odyssey*. I didn't let Sherrie and her family come with me to the airport. I hopped on the Purple Line at Clark and Lake, transferred to the Blue Line and got to O'Hare on my own. When I walked through security and got to the gate, I sat and waited.

This was it, I thought, as I watched passengers arrive and board the planes around me, my departure from this failure of a life I was born into, I thought. I had over two hours before the flight to Canada where I would transfer and head directly to Shanghai, China. From there, I had no idea what would happen. I would land and then get my bag and hope there was someone there who would be able to help me get to the family I'm supposed to be living with. But for the present, I had time and for the first time I didn't feel the pressure I had always felt since my time at Smitheran Sweets Adoption Agency. With that, my mind raced on and I let it.

This is the stream I followed:

Today is the day I embark on an adventure that will surely change everything about me to no longer be the same, which is not the goal, but the random effect that occurs and now I am sitting with nothing to do but watching these people walk all around me. In the corner, there was a woman in a bright yellow dress who is naturally attractive and my eye can't help but focus on her features. All these days, I have been pondering about the woman of my dreams, but I have no loves to claim as my own now or before. It would be a treat for me to enjoy as I serve her the way a partner does, but it's not proper for me to be going around hitting on every woman who walks by and who would leave you, us, me, looking like a dog and who wants to be known as that, but then, I guess there are those that just don't give a fuck and it would probably be the way that is happening when there is no greatness in the polls of life. How is it that I was handed these cards that don't seem to be getting better, but I guess they are now that I've taken my life into my own hands and have set out on an adventure that I can't even comprehend.

I took a break from thinking and decided I might as well eat as much food as I could. I had no idea what kind of food I would be eating, but I figured it wouldn't be like the Chinese food we eat in the States. I was very right, but the place I chose was a poor location 'cause it turns out there were more than you could count in China: McDonald's. Everywhere.

After getting a Big Mac Meal and devouring it at the gate, I sipped on my Coke and went back to watching travelers. I wasn't looking at anyone in particular, just those that caught my eye. And it would be funny little things that I was fortunate enough to turn my head toward just in time. This happened so often that it was almost like I had a sixth sense about things. A woman's heel would break for no apparent reason, causing her to drop her cup of coffee that she was balancing on a book, the coffee splashing onto a seeing eye dog that just so happened to be right under where the coffee landed. The dog gets scalded and freaks the fuck out. The blind man is pulled and people freak out 'cause they just see a crazed dog. A chain reaction of freaking-out ensues until calm is restored by the police and in ten minutes, it's like it never happened. A janitor has come and cleaned up the woman's spilled coffee. The dog's been taken to a vet, I guess. I don't think the airport has a vet. And I'm the only one that's spaced out enough to stare at the same spot and watch the many changes that happen in just that one spot as I wait for the plane to take me away to China.

"Where are you headed?" the jovial plump man to my left, asked me as the plane started to taxi away from the gate. It had been a long wait and I wasn't necessarily in the mood to talk, but I figured this is a new start and I might as well reach out beyond my comfort zone. Little did I know how uncomfortable I was about to become.

"I'm heading to China?"

"China? What are you doing over there?"

"I transferred to school there."

"What year are you?"

"Going into my senior year."

"You look a little young to be in college."

"My senior year of high school."

"I see. Your father in the military?"

"Why couldn't it be my mother?"

"I'm sorry. Your mother's in the military?"

"No."

"Oh, so you're going to an international school?"

"Nope. Chinese school."

"So you speak Chinese?"

"Nope. Not a lick.

"So then, what exactly are you doing? How are you going to survive?"

"I'm going to live with a family and the school is going to teach me Chinese."

"And your parents just let you do this?"

"My parents are dead. And I'm seventeen."

"Point taken. So, why China?"

"I don't know. Spun a globe and that's what it landed on."

"Why did you even want to go anywhere?"

"Why would I not?"

"I mean, it's not something that's usual for a seventeen-year-old kid to just up and go live in a different country."

"What're you talking about? So many teenagers travel around the globe. Look at all the young people on this plane. Can you tell me, what's the main difference between us?"

"I guess I see your point."

"No, actually you didn't. You see, the difference between them and me is that they are all white. There isn't a single young black person on this plane. You didn't even realize that, did you?"

I could watch the jovial plump pink-skinned business man in a suit redden in the face and glance around to try to disprove what I didn't even have to look to confirm. I challenge you, Reader, on your next international flight. Count how many black Americans versus whites. It's also funny when actual things black folks experience aren't believed when they are reported. That just can't be true, marginalizes say. They fight to maintain their happy ignorance of the American citizens' inner racist tendencies.

"Now, I tell you. It's strange you're so embarrassed now. It really is ok. It's not quite your fault. But now that you know, you should try to pay attention more and do what you can to point it out to others. It's a misconception that it's us against you or them. There is no separation amongst humans except those we put in place. And those separations that are forced in place, as human beings it's our responsibility to unite and put them out of the way and continue with the unity."

"I don't think that is realistic and I don't feel like a racist."

"Well, you're white, so you are."

"That is such a blanket statement."

"I just proved how you didn't think it strange that there was only one black boy on this plane headed to Canada. And you were so shocked that I was going to China for school and not 'cause my 'father' was in the military. All because I was black."

"Son, I think you've been reading too much Malcolm X. I understand what you're saying, but you can't just throw out conjectures. Is this your first time out of the country?"

"No."

"Where else did you go before?"

"Japan tour, just before I went to high school."

"That's nice. So, when I look and talk to you, I see a young man who is incredibly independent, exceptionally well-educated and intuitively street smart. But you are inexperienced. I was politely trying to engage you in conversation and before this plane has even taken off you feel that you've got me all figured out and insulted me by calling me a racist. I agree, white people and all Americans do have an inherent fear and distrust of black Americans. We put you down in every way. We don't believe you can ever be on an equal level with us because of your impossible circumstances. And those of you who do make it out of the ghetto, which in itself is a horrible thing because white people are basically telling you that your neighborhoods aren't as good as ours, so if you want to be successful, we're the scale for what success is. You're not accepted and you've removed yourself from your own village. So once you wake up to the fact that you're not equal, even though you thought you gave up everything that was yours by birth–family, friends, neighborhood, beliefs, human rights and the very right to be free– you still are a nigger. This isn't a fair world for you to be born in. It's not fair and it should never be. But it is. You yourself have tendencies that have been programmed into you to hate black people just as much as any white or other color citizen. This isn't just about black and white. It's about saving humanity as a whole. So you should step back and study history a little more. Talk to more old people and learn who your enemies are and aren't."

With that the jovial plump pink-faced man smiled and shook my hand.

"This is the part of the flight I always hate," he said slouching into his seat.

He closed his eyes as the airliner raced down the runway and took off. The feeling of gravity disappearing as we soared up toward the clouds overtook me. The weightlessness combined with my own weight in the airplane caused my body to feel crazy. There was a point where I felt like the plane was losing its thrust in its ascent and

I was sure the engines stalled and we were going to die, but then we leveled off and all was well. The man to the left of me didn't stir until we landed in Canada.

It was as if in a blink of an eye that I was on the next flight to China. The flight was to last fourteen hours. As luck would have it, a woman who had sat to the right of me but was asleep from before I even got to the middle seat of the flight to Canada, was in the aisle seat of the flight to China. This time I was sitting in the window seat when she arrived. We both looked at each other and could see in one another's eyes that we had seen each other before. She tried and I tried and we both wondered who it would dawn on first. It turns out it hit us both at the same time. The woman was all smiles which made me smile even more.

We exchanged our cordialities and prepared for our personal rituals for takeoff. Once the captain turned off the fasten seat belt sign after the plane leveled off, she kicked off her black boots and I unhooked my seat belt. I'm ashamed to say that I had a great deal of trouble not looking at her rather large bust poking through the tight green turtle neck she was wearing.

The rains started a day before the hurricane hit. Cascades of melancholy pushed me through the tunnel vision of my heart as I met the woman who would steal my heart for the first time in life. Tokyo's rainy season was upon the island. Hurricanes and typhoons were a norm that passed through with such frequency that there was usually little cause for concern. I was entering the second year in my Japanese exodus and the natural storms and earthquakes were as much a part of my life as eating with chopsticks.

Heading back from teaching my last dance class, I rode the Chuo Line (the orange one) toward Shinjuku, allowing myself to drift away into my thoughts as Tokyo glided by. It was past 9:00pm and the intake of sake from the konbini had me melted into the seat. There were plenty of seats. Thursday is always one of those days when by 7:00 pm people are done for the week. The boost of knowing its Friday is what usually carries me over to the weekend. At that point, having taught three one-hour dance classes to over fifty kids, I was done.

My life had reshuffled the deck of my destiny and dealt me a hand that landed me in Tokyo at first as an English teacher, and then, as luck would have it, a dance teacher. I maintained both gigs the entire time I was in Tokyo, which was three years. I made something of a name for myself, too. Not famous; just well-liked and appreciated.

Japan was much different than China. But then, some things were the same. Most of the similarities were because of the region the two countries share. Similar areas have similar customs and there's more interaction and cross-breeding among neighboring countries. The differences could be attributed greatly to poverty. In Wuxi, China, where I fled when I was seventeen, I was trying to reset my life from the horrible existence I felt I had been handed by fate. There was poverty in Japan, of course. And there was some poverty in Tokyo. However, the Japanese did a far better job of covering it up so it wasn't seen. I'm not sure if the Chinese even cared. And if they did, there's no way they could hide reality.

As the train glided through Tokyo, my mind raced and wandered. I wondered what direction my life was heading. There was no telling at this point. The sudden shock of a bad memory forced its way into the field of vision in my mind's eye. It was just at this point when I was beginning to regret this life and accept that hope was hopeless and I was useless, she walked onto the train at Shinjuku. I was standing at the sliding door waiting to exit. She was standing to the left, waiting to board. When the doors opened our eyes met. And then we were stuck. When the music began signaling the doors would be closing soon, I took a step backwards and she got on. The doors closed and the train continued on its designated path.

We slowly took seats next to each other and our legs brushed. She was not Japanese. I didn't know what nationality she was, but I didn't care. All I knew was that I could not and did not want to stop looking at her. Feeling the warmth from her body as we sat staring at each other, waiting for the other to finally say something. Anything would do. But neither of us said a thing. I was already on my way toward being way out of my way to get home. That didn't matter. It would later. Later wasn't now. The silence didn't bother me. It didn't seem to bother her, either. It is hard to explain, but it seemed like the two of us were having one of the most in-depth conversations ever. I can't imagine what the two of us looked like, staring at each other, smiling wide.

Twenty minutes passed. We both occasionally stopped staring at one another's eyes and enjoyed spacing out in the company of an existence that made you happy. It was a wonderful feeling, to say the least. When her stop approached, she finally spoke.

"My stop is next."

I didn't know what to say. I'm not even sure if what she said registered in my brain. I didn't want her to leave and I guess I showed it in my face.

"You want to join me for dinner?" she asked rising from her seat and walking to the sliding doors where we met at Shinjuku.
"Yes, I would love to join you for dinner."
"Great. I need to stop at the grocery store to pick up some things."
"No problem," I said, standing next to her as the Chuo Line slowed to a stop.

The doors slid open. We exited the train. Our hands brushed and instinctively I grabbed her fingers, intertwining them with my own. It happened so naturally that I don't think either of us recognized that we had only just met and were now holding hands. Those things didn't matter. This was right. We both knew it, and decided to enjoy it for as long as it lasted.

"I feel as if I've been searching for you for such a long time," she said to me after she bought groceries, took me to her home and cooked a great dinner that we devoured in silence.

"I feel the same way," I said after swallowing a gulp of Sapporo beer from the bottle.

"Where did you come from?"

"Chicago. Where are you from?"

"Australia."

When she said this, I was even more confused. She had no accent that I could place. Her completion was such a tan that it could spread across the spectrum of almost every ethnicity. But thinking about such things was the last thing on my mind as I watched her sip Sapporo beer from the second bottle on the table where we were sitting.

"What are you doing in Tokyo?" I asked.

"I'm an accountant for Mitsubishi."

"That sounds nice."

"No, it's pretty boring."

"Well, I'm sure it pays nice."

"It pays a decent salary. But looking at numbers all day isn't my idea of fun."

"Yea, I can't imagine it'd be anyone's idea of fun."

"You'd be amazed. As a matter of fact, there is a guy in the cubicle next to mine who literally gets off on numbers. It's like porn to him."

"What do you mean literally gets off?"

"I mean, he jizzes in his pants as he crunches numbers."

"How do you know this?"

"Funny you should ask. When I started working there about two years ago, he was there before me. He was very polite and soft spoken. I thought he was going to be a nice neighbor to have. And he is. Except that, at least once a day he lets out an exclamation of pleasure that could only be an orgasm. I thought maybe this is how he stretched and it just felt that good. Or he was exhaling a deep, healing breath. But one day after what I thought could only have been an orgasm, I bumped into him as he came out of the restroom and he had a large wet spot on the front of his trousers. It was unmistakably cum. And if I hadn't been sure when the smell of the ocean hit my nostrils, I knew exactly what was happening."

"That's crazy," I said, polishing off the bottle of Sapporo. She rose from the table and walked to the fridge to get us another. I watched her walk away, admiring her behind. It was very nice. She definitely kept in shape.

When she returned with two new open bottles of Sapporo, she continued her story.

"At first, I figured the guy was watching porn on his phone or something. Not the greatest crime in the world, just pretty disgusting. But why not do it in the bathroom or somewhere else besides your desk. And why be so vocal about it. These are questions I admit I usually thought about on my train ride home from work."

"When did you realize it was because of the numbers that he was busting his nuts?"

"That was the funniest, actually. The two of us had been assigned to a project together and, like I said, beside him having an orgasm at his desk, the man was very friendly and I felt relatively safe with him, which was ironic because I knew what was happening and under normal circumstances that should've cut him off any list of trustworthy men. But it didn't and we did the project together.

"It was when we were finished, reviewing the material, he started to make these noises. After a certain point I stopped reading my section and just observed as he read each number and came closer and closer to climax. When he finally exploded, he screamed and reached out to touch my hand. I snapped my hand back and jumped up away from him. 'What is wrong with you?' I asked him. 'It's the numbers. I'm sorry. I can't contain myself,' he told me. 'You know I should report your sick ass.' 'You're right. You're right. You should.' His response threw me off and I paused. Perhaps he said it because he knew it would cause me to hesitate. Either way, he could tell that I was not amused. I asked him if he needed to go to the restroom and clean up. He, of course, did and graciously bowed to me as he skirted away toward the men's room. When he returned, he hadn't done much of a job getting the semen off his pants. But given that he was in the office, there wasn't much he realistically could do."

"That's hilarious. I guess there are people that get off on numbers then."

"Yes, there are."

The conversation died away and we drank our beers in silence. I replayed the story she had just told me about the man who got off on numbers. I imagined what he must've looked like and how she was able to stay calm during all of that. I probably would've flipped out on the guy, but that's just me. I glanced at my Hamilton wristwatch and saw that it was 11:00pm.

"I better start heading home if I am going to catch the last train home."

"Where's home?"

"Sugamo."

"Sugamo, where's that?"

"One before Komagome."

"Ok. I don't know where that is, either."

"It's about twelve minutes from Shinjuku, give or take."

"Oh, ok. Not too far away, then?"

"No, not far at all."

"You've made me very happy."

"But I didn't do anything?" I said.

"You got the groceries. And you make me feel nice."

"That's only because we just met. I'm sure in not too long at all, I'd be more annoying to you than a mosquito."

"I highly doubt that."

"I don't. I've seen it before."

"I feel like things are changing."

"That I will have to agree with. I also am very happy that I met you and have been happy this entire evening. Can I say I don't want to leave?"

"Of course, you can say that. Can I say you don't have to leave?"

"But you just met me," I said, wanting to jump at the invitation of sleeping with her.

"Should I not trust you?"

"No, I have no intention of taking advantage of you."

"Then you will stay the night with me?"

"Can I use your shower in the morning?"

"I only have enough hot water for one shower in the morning."

"Oh, ok. I guess I can do without a shower."

"Why not just shower with me?"

"I didn't want to impose."

"You're about to sleep with me. You should impose all you want."

Old Friends

As hurricane Matthew picked up its pace, autumn rolled through in the east. Rain was an ever-frequent friend. At the final bend of the corner in our journey to Washington, D.C., to deliver the letter from the Press Secretary that was burning a hole in my vest pocket, negotiations were taking place. We would later learn that an arrangement was made between the First World Coalition and the Powers. They changed their name at some point after the First World was forced to submit to the Power's demands. Power was handed over and we in the United States were no longer in charge of shit.

We were back to the basics whether we liked it or not. On our journey to D.C., we met people who were thrilled that the country had been pushed back to zero.

"It's a restart for us. No credit. No debt. Just living off your own spirit and the spirit of your family."

"What about friends?" I asked the family we spent a night with when we got caught in a storm out in the cornfields of Indiana. The house appeared out of nowhere. We hadn't seen a single living soul or building for two hours at the point the house came into existence.

"Friends?" the father of the two little girls and husband of the kind woman asked. "We're back to zero. There are no friends. Only family."

"But you've trusted us and let us in," Janelle said.

"I don't trust you. But yes, I did let you in. Because my Muslim faith obliges me to care for a fellow human being. You two are on a mission, I can see. My family is my mission. That is the difference between us."

"Thank you for letting us in," I said for lack of anything better to say.

"Are you hungry?"

"Yes. Unfortunately I can't remember the last time we ate."

"Two nights ago," Janelle said. "We stole a few cans of chicken pot pie from a grocery store. The entire place was cleared out. We searched it from top to bottom and all we found were four cans of chicken pot pie. We made those cans last ten whole days."

"I don't know how we did it," I added.

"Well you two must be hungry," the woman and mother of the two little girls and wife to the man who opened the door and let us in, said. "Kids, please set the table and light the candles. We have guests. Bring out the silverware and the nice plates."

Janelle and I watched as the children dutifully obeyed their mother. They went through their preparations with practiced comfort. Candles were lit and the atmosphere of the house changed dramatically. We began to see how large the place was on the inside. The sun had set some hours before we'd arrived which increased the drastic nature of our plea to seek shelter under the family's roof.

After we ate the great meal prepared for us by the two daughters, the mother and father entertained Janelle and me. The father told us how he used to be a carpenter and that because of that he sympathized with the Nations.

"I don't understand how being a carpenter explains why you are a sympathizer with the Nations," Janelle said, sipping on a glass of white wine that the mother kept a constant flow for her and all of us.

"You see, my young lady," the man explained, "I appreciate the value of working with one's hands. Having two hands is a great thing. Hands can be used to create or destroy. The things hands create can also create or destroy. Hands bring life into this world and hands take life away. There is no slight of worth that having two undamaged hands can offer to a community. Hands themselves, of course, aren't the end all, be all. There must be a work ethic in place. There must be a strong spirit inside the heart of the individual, or else the hands being wielded will be weak and useless. They'll be controlled by other hands that will more than likely use them to do more damage to humanity. Those of us who work with our hands deliver services the community cannot do without. At a basic level, those services make up the bulk of our resources. Now that there is no electricity, what we can build with our hands is what will prove the worth of a man, now that we are no longer judged based on the dollars in our bank accounts. Now it's about what you can actually do with your own hands. With that said, I sympathize with the Nations because all of them work with their hands. It's not like here, or the way here used to be before the electro bomb. Here is now, these are people who have been exploited, taken advantage of; entire nations. It just isn't right what's been happening. You yourself should understand that."

I knew the man directed this final sentence at me. I'm sure he figured if anyone would agree with what he was saying, I would. He wasn't wrong. I did. And thus began the scourge of doubts and confusion that would plague my mind for as long as I can remember. Even until now, there hasn't been a pause or break from the tension that I cannot ever be relieved of. Writing this is helping me finally relieve myself of all that. This is probably my last opportunity to tell my story, so I might as well take the opportunity while it's still available to me. My hope is that someone, some day, reads this story and learns how the new world was formed.

The doubt the man planted in me didn't break when Janelle and I finally laid down to sleep. The family had an extra room. They had candles set up everywhere and were the neatest and most organized people I had ever seen. They figured we were a couple and at that point I think Janelle and I felt like we were, too. Janelle stripped down to her underwear and climbed into bed. I did the same. After a certain point, as I stared at the ceiling, Janelle asked me if she could sleep on my chest. I said, 'Yes,' and felt her weight press on me. It was relaxing, but not enough to stop my mind from racing.

This is what I thought:

Another day, another night, another bed with a woman beside me. Janelle has become inseparable to me. I guess it's because of everything we have gone through and the arguments we have had. It's almost like we are a long-term couple, but it's only been—I don't even know how long it's been—and the only way I have been able to tell time is with my watch. Thank goodness, it never stops. It's a wonder that we came across this house or else we more than likely would've been killed by something, if not by the flooding, and it's these difficulties that build character. The rains have continued. It seems like it's raining everywhere, like every place we go, we find ourselves engulfed in the night and when the morning comes, water is everywhere and the rains are lighter, but continue to fall. All of this began out of nothing and I think that the most amazing point out of everything is that it all starts from nothing, even the way the First World went at it and I don't think there is an answer to the equation other than to look within yourself and follow the inherent law locked within every human being. It's these basic principles that we have forgotten and maybe that's why this happened because, on face value, citizens of this country haven't given a shit about them for a long time. If they give a shit now, it's because they've got no choice and are either sick or hungry or about to get sick, but there ain't no in-between.

Janelle stirred in her sleep and threw her leg over on top of me. Her lady smashed against my crotch and I tried my best to not think about all the things I had been imagining for so many weeks since we met on the plane to London. Alas, to no avail, my willpower collapsed. It wasn't long before I was poking Janelle Muberty with me. She must've been half awake and felt me growing 'cause I felt her adjust slightly and ever so subtly jerk her hips up. But then she lowered herself back onto my penis and began to grind herself on top of me. It wasn't long before we were full on dry humping. Janelle was fully awake and straddled me. I didn't know what to think and opted to think nothing. I let Janelle do what she wanted and I grabbed her ass and enjoyed the ride she was driving on top of me. I felt her clench and shake, then quake spasms of pleasure as I came.

She laid back on my chest and without a word continued to straddle me, got comfortable and fell back asleep.

This is what I thought next:

Well, that certainly was a strange series of events. It felt so great that I can't believe it even happened. I guess it was a physical thing. Neither of us had had sex for a long time and I'm sure she's just trying to relieve some tension. I'm flattered that she feels comfortable enough to do that with me, but it's like she's just using me and I'm not sure how I feel about that, but then again, she's attractive and smart and strong and we've been through the world transitioning into another world together, so that has some significance. I've shared something with her that will never, ever, be repeated and she's listened to me talk about who knows what beyond what she told me that I said while asleep. That shit's made me worry about going to sleep with her or anyone else around.

"Now, there are some things that I cannot repeat unless I'm awake to assess the audience to which I am speaking. A highly attuned ear overhearing a piece of this information could scoop it up and turn it over to someone who will use it against us. But even now, with the way things are, is my job even important anymore? I suppose my job isn't important, but the tutelage of the Press Secretary is the invaluable resource that makes me qualified to do whatever it is that she wrote in the invitation to the president that I am going to deliver. I wonder what it is and I wonder if I really can do it. Yeah, I was learning directly under the Press Secretary for the past four-and-a-half years and during that time I have learned how to see beyond the surface and even beyond the narrative hidden underneath. The Press Secretary taught me how to see the next move and now I am the only one who knows the truth that I don't even know, but have to uncover and for that reason, I'm the one who has to get to it and this letter to the President from the Press Secretary is the most important of the keys. I wonder what it says. She gave me strict instructions not to tamper with it. It's my only authorization to get into the room, so I better not fuck it up. I wish the man hadn't said that about siding with the enemy. That confuses me. Who is the enemy? What is happening? What am I supposed to do?

When we arrived at the White House, we were shown straight into the Oval Office. It was strange. I wondered why we were let right in after showing the letter from the Press Secretary to the guard at the gate. The urgency with which they showed us in revealed a host of things that I could never have anticipated. Janelle and I were suddenly summoned in. Past memories of dreaming of being in this position overcame me. It was the only thought I had. I couldn't touch base as to why I would have had such a dream. And it was something I hadn't thought about for quite some time. The Marine opened the door for us and the emptiness of the space beckoned us to enter. So we did. And there he stood.

His hair was gray, a salt and pepper display of what could only be described as a distinguished look. It was amazing how after seven-and-a-half years, he had aged so much. But those are the effects of the job that must be done and the sacrifice made to command the position of chief.

"Come in, please. You've had the longest journey of anyone."

"Unfortunately, Mr. President, I doubt that we are the only ones who have had the worst experiences."

"I have to agree with her, Sir. There is no way that what we went through was any worse than the horrible situations faced by so many who are struggling throughout this great country, Sir."

"Yes, I understand there are a great many Americans and other humans across the globe who are struggling in ways that are unimaginable. This is a great travesty and the main problem is that this so-called coalition has refused to discuss things with us."

"With all due respect, Sir, I believe the coalition has a lot of reasons to give resistance against the First World powers, or used-to-be powers. Where do we stand, as a matter of fact, Sir?"

"Not at a very good place, Son. Not very good at all. There are numerous attempts to overthrow the order of our republic taking place from multiple sources."

"Do you really think that the republic is still standing?" Janelle asked. "Let's be real, Mr. President. Look around you. There is no longer an American democracy. We are back in the Dark Ages. What republic are you thinking is still standing?"

"My dear young child, the republic has withstood greater crises than this. You don't know your history, young lady. There has been an attempt on the republic every year since its founding. There isn't a single threat that we have ever folded under since our inception. Do you realize how effective we are at dominating? There is no other nation that can do what we do. And that is why all other nations employ us to take out those who they can't kill."

The evil of it all sickened me. How could a human being remain so insidiously woven into the patterns of a quilt blanketing the freedom we enjoy?

"I see you sitting there judging me," the President said after pausing from his speech and walking over to the bar near the large oak desk that forty-three others had sat at before him. "You don't understand the sacrifice that public service makes on your soul, the type of clientele you must deal with, the types of people you would never associate with. They have to be my closet advisers, my closest aides."

"How could you keep such horrible people close to you?" Janelle asked.

"It's basic strategy, young lady," the President replied. "There is a simple code laid out by Sun Tzu in his treatise *The Art of War*: keep your friends close and your enemies closer."

"I've heard it before."

"Well, this is that concept happening in real time."

"Congratulations!"

"Well, you asked."

"And I'm glad you answered." Janelle didn't seem to be very impressed by the 44th President of the United States.

I had been an avid admirer of him since his inauguration, and after the preceding exchange, my opinion hadn't changed. I was confused by the hostility Janelle directed at the President. I couldn't place the condescension she felt that lapsed over time into something that could be described as half-sarcastic and half-facetious. Her tone was so gangsta,' I struggled not to laugh. It was amusing to me to watch her rattle off vicious questions that I knew from my previous experiences with the President that he couldn't or wouldn't answer. The tutelage of the Press Secretary screamed forth reminders in the area of my mind reserved for those things that arose in the course of the hard battles aiming to extinguish life.

Seeing as how she wasn't a fan of the President and how I had nothing better to do at the moment, I had delivered the letter from the Press Secretary to the President of the United States, I humored him and listened to his soapbox image of why it all wasn't his fault. It mattered not to me. I rose from the seat in the Oval Office and walked toward the minibar beside the President's desk.

When I sat back down, I was considering just getting drunk and falling asleep. When else would I have the opportunity to get sloppy drunk in the Oval Office in the company of the 44th president? But humanity was in the unsteady balance of life and death and there was no time to enjoy the feeling of a life without responsibilities. So throwing away the thought of throwing away restraint, I downed the two fingers of whiskey I poured myself and refilled both Janelle's and the President's glasses. The Prez had hooked us up with drinks when we first walked in. Then I returned the large decanter that was the Presidential whisky bottle to the minibar.

I chose to sit back and enjoy Janelle and the 44th President of the United States bantering back and forth. Everything I knew about Janelle at that point was enough to know that this was a great therapeutic release for her. For the President, I'm not sure what the hell it was.

"This is the greatest opportunity for us all," the President said. "We are faced with the actual opportunity to reach forward and grasp the little snatches of peace that we have been reaching for all this time. It should be a great way for all of us as Americans to embrace the life we want to live."

"Mr. President, with all due respect, so many people have died. How can you sit there and talk to me like you do, calmly and coolly?"

"Would you rather I be freaking out? Would you rather I be incoherent? Would you rather I be reacting like a small child throwing a temper tantrum? Is that what you want me to do? Well guess what? I'm not Donald Trump. "

"Oh, no, he didn't," I said. I was drunk. Yes, I admit it.

I wasn't trying to get drunk. Janelle and the President were just having such a great conversation, I didn't want to interrupt and kept getting thirsty. So, I kept going back to refill my glass. The first two times, I offered both the President and Janelle refills. The President took one and Janelle took two. She was in the zone and growing even sexier as she went in on the President. He was a seasoned vet and I can imagine that he hadn't engaged with many people since the electro bomb had gone off.

The exchange was great. Had I not lost track of time, I'm sure I would've interjected. But between the whiskey, the entire days and weeks that had transpired since the bunker, after the Press Secretary was killed by the Bikers, after wandering through the Midwest on our way to Washington, D.C. and finally delivering this message from the Press Secretary to the President, I was in absolutely no place to be of any help, so I said nothing and listened to them speak.

"I'm glad we are having this conversation. It's something that I am not able to have often enough; never, in fact, if I may be honest. These days have changed my life, the lives of all the American people."

"Sir, honestly it seems as if you are deflecting."

"Deflecting from what? I am not going through anything that I would need to deflect."

"What do you mean?"

"I mean, you are not questioning me to tear me down; you are questioning me as Janelle. You are coming to me as a concerned citizen."

"Yes."

"So why is it that you feel the need to attack me?"

"Because you are responsible for my parents being murdered."

"And how is that?"

"Because both of my parents were in the military; they were in the Iraq war and both died there. And you are not even sympathetic to that."

"I understand that this is a painful thing for you and it's not something that can just be glanced over quickly. But I must remind you that the entire globe is faced with something that is a lot bigger than your personal problem that seems to have taken over your entire being. I'm sorry for the loss of your parents. I'm sorry for every single service member who has lost his or her life, but right now, we need to figure out what the next step is to move our country and the world forward in the direction of peace. This letter ..." the President said as he held up the envelope that had burned a hole in my vest jacket pocket ever since the Press Secretary gave it to me before bleeding to death, "This letter from your mentor," the President said to me, "contains the location of the Coalition's base of operations. These are the very coordinates we've been searching for."

"What good are coordinates when we don't have any power?" Janelle asked, not letting the President go an inch without questioning him ... as she should have done.

"My dear young lady, there is still electricity in the world. It is just owned by private companies."

"But I thought the electro bomb short circuited everything that was electrical," Janelle said.

"It did. However, we have for a long time been running systems that are entirely plastic and in some instances organic."

"I don't understand what you mean."

"I know you don't. But that's ok. You don't have to understand. You will in time. Just sit back and relax. Have a drink. Your friend Cecil definitely has taken the bait."

And with that, for the first time I began to feel the narcotic that had been slipped into the whiskey. I felt the world grow dim around me. As I recalled my training in poisoning from the Press Secretary, I tried my best to control my breathing. This was something that I hadn't considered happening. And here I was being poisoned. The first time the Press Secretary brought it up, I took the entire thing as a joke. Luckily, I did remember the steps. She spelled them out for me in a way that I had no choice but to remember them.

"First, you need to induce vomiting. If you can get the poison out of your system, you are halfway to surviving. The best way to get yourself to vomit quickly is to drink a glass filled with salt water.

I don't' know if I remembered the Press Secretary's directions wrong or not, but it was too late. Either way, I collapsed from the poison and blacked out in the Oval Office at the feet of the President of the United States.

When I woke, I was in a cellar chained to a seat. The day's events had begun to get interesting, I thought to myself as I scanned the dank area I was in. Not a sound was heard except the drip of a leak from a pipe in the ceiling. It wasn't something one would normally notice, but having the rare opportunity to indulge in such pleasantries as counting drops from leaking pipes, I counted an even ten thousand before I heard footsteps.

"That was a close one," the voice in the black mask said. "We thought you were going to die on us. It took a bit of medical magic to reverse the effect of the poison you drank. You unknowingly saved the life of the President of the United States. Someone from the Coalition, presumably, placed poison on the rim of one of the President's whiskey glasses. You picked the lucky one."

The humor of the situation was lost on me.

"Suffice it to say, you're a hero. A dumb lucky hero, but a hero nevertheless. The President would like a word with you when you are able."

The President's advisor left the hospital room I was in. I guess it was somewhere in the White House. To my shock, the bed I was in was fully functional. All the beeps and ticks of a modern hospital being run on electricity were present. I heard my pulse blipping off each time my heart muscle beat.

I skittered across flickers of disjointed memory, flashes of what I assumed were whatever emergency procedure had saved my life, viewed from a high vantage point over the scene in some omnipotent vision, more than I cared to see, showed itself as always. I tried to signal for a nurse, but nobody came. I desperately needed someone to help stop my mind from doing what it was trying so hard to do. Taking over had always been my mind's one and only goal. Nothing would be spared. There can be no resting. My mind is always watching and waiting for the opportunity to pounce and take control.

I made a few feeble attempts at getting out of the hospital bed. It was so painful that I passed out after the third try. Upon reawakening and realizing once again that I was indeed in a hospital bed and it wasn't just all a bad dream, I started willing my mind to think up a next move that could lead me out of here and be able to walk again. There was nothing to be done. Whatever had been done to save my life and whatever damage the poison had done to me was done, so there wasn't a single thing I could do about it.

Accepting this fact, I surrendered to my mind. It was a washing over of emotions that took hold of my entire being. There wasn't a single trace of what I had been fearing for so long: the pain of my mind taking over. It was, in fact, rather exhilarating ... until the visions in my head moved to scenes I'd kill to never see again.

I don't remember his name, but I do remember the way he smelled. It was this cheap cologne they used to sell at JC Penney. I never smelled it again after the day he molested me when I was three at Smitheran Sweets Adoption Agency until I was shopping with my ex-wife while we were still married. She was trying different perfumes and suggested I look at colognes. I had no desire to do so and told her that. However, the saleswoman must've overheard us and offered herself up as a solution and whisked me off to the next display where the men's' colognes were arranged.

"There's not as broad a range for men as for women, but these two rows are the favorites among customers who shop with us."

"And what about these other rows below?"

"Those are an assortment of flavors, mostly experimental."

"So they're newer brands than these?"

"Precisely."

"Well, out of these bottom shelves, which do you recommend for me?"

"If I were picking for you, I'd select the orange bottle."

I reached down and picked up the orange bottle.

"Chateau Di'if?"

"It came out two years ago; very rare. It's the only product they've made. It's already become a staple among those who follow the likes of Kanye West."

"This is Kanye West's cologne?"

"No, I didn't say that. I said that people who follow him buy this cologne."

"Ok, thank you for clarifying. That is very different indeed."

"It's important to me to be clear. I've noticed so often when communicating with people that there is a disconnect originating from a certain point and from then on the message is lost."

"Isn't that the shame of this age?"

"It's more like the shame of our race."

"Black people?"

"No humans. But, yeah, actually, black people, too."

"How can you have both? I thought that once you ascribed to one thing you were obliged to stick to that particular forum until it was stupid to continue in that direction."

"Kind'a like voting for Donald Trump."

"Ten points for the mystery man."

There was no mystery man. We were just drunk. I had been a frequent patron.

The pomp and circumstance of the White House was still in effect in spite of there not being a single lightbulb on.

"Makes me think back to the days of George Washington and Abraham Lincoln. Everything was done by candlelight and electricity hadn't been harnessed yet. The failure in our history by becoming so dependent on electricity is apparent now, more than ever," the President said as he showed Janelle and me into the guest rooms.

There were so many Secret Service men and women dashing around the White House that I nervously began to think that something big was about to take place, but I couldn't put my finger on it and couldn't find any clue that would explain it to me.

The Press Secretary and the President had been close. I watched him process the news as I told him about watching the Press Secretary bleed to death after getting shot in the stomach. The President was visibly shaken while Janelle and I briefed him on all we had done and all that we had seen as far as the country was concerned.

"I appreciate this update. I haven't left the White House in a number of weeks. They won't allow me to leave. Thousands upon thousands of citizens are suffering in unimaginable ways and I am being contained within my own home like I'm a prisoner, but I have no place to complain. When I took the oath of this office, I gave up my life to the service of this country. If being locked inside my own house is what that means, then I will do it."

Once we were settled into the guest room, Janelle stripped naked and climbed under the sheets while I was still taking a shower. When I came out of the bathroom with a towel around me, Janelle looked to be asleep. I figured she was and took the towel off my warm body. There wasn't much light, but I could see my outline in the soft hue of the moon shining in from the window. I walked over to the window and looked out. A cold breeze came from somewhere and wisped across my bare skin, causing goose pimples to sprout up all over my body.

"You should get in here before you catch cold," Janelle said staring at me as I stood naked before the window.
"I don't have any clothes on."
"I can see that. It's ok at this point, Cecil. We've been through too much together for you to be shy at this point, don't you think?"

She did have a profoundly good point.

"I guess I can concur with that," I said, walking over to the bed where Janelle was tucked in. I pulled the sheets up and saw that she was just as naked as I was.

"You've been waiting for me, I see."

"I figured we could keep each other warm."

"That's a splendid idea," I said slipping underneath the sheets. Janelle moved her body toward me and once again laid her head down on my chest. I was harder than Chinese arithmetic in no time at all.

"I don't think you're going to be able to sleep with that poking up so sternly," Janelle said, wrapping her hand around my erection. She helped me bring it down each time it popped up, which I thought was fair, given that most of the time it popped up because of Janelle. When we finally passed out, we were allowed to sleep well past noon. That was good because at that point, we were both more exhausted than we had ever been. Given the sheer amount of Secret Service who were around as well, it was the first sleep since the bunker when the two of us could truly shut down and just sleep.

My dreams while cuddled up with Janelle were a mixture of fun and terror. My mind kept trying to replay the entirety of the events that had taken place from landing in London until now.

The Cecil who got on a plane from Chicago to London just hours before the electro bomb went off is not the same Cecil who was laying naked with Janelle wrapped around him. This new Cecil has seen death, lots of death; so much death that I was becoming immune to it—maybe not immune to death. I'm not sure if death is something you can become immune to, but I will definitely say that I had become desensitized and indifferent to the extinguishing of another soul.

It was the countless bodies we saw on the road. Some had been murdered. Others had rotted out. There was no telling how so many had died. There were tons of children; entire families left to die in their cars. Looters tossing aside their corpses as they tried to find whatever could be salvaged. Many of the bodies had begun to peel from the sun. The skin was literally being lifted cleanly off the bodies by the sun. That image is forever burned into my brain.

Some of the bodies we passed were actually still breathing. These usually were the victims of the flu that began to spread a couple of weeks after the electro bomb went off. Because there was no way to preserve food, bacteria spread quickly and people started getting sick. The hospitals had no means of doing anything that required electricity. They were forced to just respond to those who were being dragged in by whoever. The best that they could offer was pain medication, patching them up to the best of the doctor's ability. And then on to the next one. There wasn't a single stopping point for the invalids coming in.

The bodies and faces of all that I had seen continued to wash over my mind's eye as I tried desperately to sleep. Eyes open or eyes closed, it mattered not. I would've given anything for a television and a stupid movie that I could stare at and stop thinking about what was more and more looking to be an absolutely hopeless situation. I didn't want to feel hopeless. I didn't want to give up. But I couldn't see what could be done. Furthermore, based on the letter the Press Secretary had written to the President of the United States, I was supposed to be the one to take her place and work directly with the President in order to bring order out of this chaos.

It was all too big. And my mind wouldn't let me rest. The thinking had taken over. And this is what I thought:

Why can't I stop with the thinking? It's a constant thing that has to stop. I'm thinking about things that don't even matter and things that do matter, but thinking about them isn't going to do nothing for me but cause me not to sleep which is what's happening right now and I'm so tired and I should be happy I'm alive, sleeping next to a beautiful woman that I just had sex with who seems to really enjoy my company or is it that we've just experienced this life or death situation so many times and have been surviving? I'm not sure what's going to happen. Everything was geared towards getting this letter to the President. I don't know why I thought that once I got this letter from the Press Secretary to him that all would be good.

I guess because they used to be lovers. I wonder if the President knows that I know he and the Press Secretary used to fool around before he was elected. He's got to know I know and he's got to know everything there is to know about me, however Antoinette was pretty good at discretion and the fact that she hired me lets me know that at least he had to approve and this isn't where I would have ever imagined I'd be. I'm sure the current standing of the globe is a place no one thought we would come to, but I guess that just goes to show you that with the flip of a coin the entire world can be turned upside down. In this instance, it was just the press of a button.

There was a loud clatter outside the door. Janelle jerked awake on my chest and I popped out of bed. Forgetting that I was completely naked, I ran to the door and tried to open it. It was locked from the outside.

"Did they lock us in?" Janelle asked, panic beginning to rise in her voice.

"Seems like it. Makes sense though. Best way to make sure we are protected."

"But how the hell are we supposed to get out if something happens."

"I think something is happening."

Just as I said this, a large explosion sounded from somewhere not far from the door. The floor underneath us shook. I fell to my knees. Fragments from the ceiling above crashed down. I crawled over to where Janelle was. She had rolled out of bed to dodge the falling plaster from the ceiling.

"Are you ok?" I asked, pulling the sheet off the bed and wrapping her in it.

"Yeah, I think so. Something cut my forehead."

Blood was pouring down from Janelle's head.

"Shit, you're cut pretty bad," I said. I ripped strips off the sheet and tied them around her forehead to stop the bleeding. It was too dark to see if it made any difference. I crawled around on the carpet, frantically groping in the dark for our clothes. We had to get the fuck out of the room. That I knew for certain.

Another large explosion sounded and the entire wall where the locked door was blew away. A large hole appeared after the dust settled and the hallway with candles running down the wall was filled with Secret Service and marines frantically running every which way. I grabbed Janelle's wrist.

"We gotta get outta here. Put these clothes on," I said handing her what I had been able to find.

All in all, I was able to gather up both of our pants, shirts and shoes. I couldn't for the life of me find our underwear or socks.

Janelle and I climbed our way out of the large hole in the wall and exited the guest room in the White House into the chaos that was swarming the hallway. More explosions went off in the distance, shaking the foundations of the White House. I stopped one of the Secret Service agents who had greeted us when we arrived earlier that day.

"What's happening?"
"We're under attack."
"By who? The Coalition?"
"No, this is from inside."
"Inside the White House?"
"No, inside the United States," he said. I heard a loud pop from behind me and watched as a hole appeared in the Secret Service agent's head. A puff of blood splattered onto my face. I blinked twice and shook my head, trying to return to reality and not slip into shock. I glanced at Janelle, who was wide-eyed with fright. I turned around in the direction the shot had originated from and received a gun butt to the head for my troubles. As I hit the ground, I

heard Janelle scream and another shot fired. I felt her slump against my ankles. I heard the gun cock and reload and felt it pressed against the back of my head. I waited for the cacophony of sound that would bring this all to an end.

"Don't kill him," I heard a familiar voice say. The pressure of the gun against the back of my head was removed and I felt two sets of arms wrap themselves under my shoulders and left me up. The gun butt to my face caused me to have trouble opening my eyes.

"Everything's going to be ok, Cecil," I heard the familiar voice say.

"You killed her," I mumbled out.

"No, we just knocked her out. She'll be fine in a little bit. It's a good thing that I was able to find you. They were about to turn you all into one of their agents.

I was beginning to focus a bit more and quickly recognized who it was speaking.

"Dave? What the fuck is going on?"

"Revolution, mi amigo. Revolution."

David was in charge. This didn't surprise me. Dave was always in charge. He was one of those born leader types; an operator if there ever was one. As I watched the men floating around him, I could see the respect he commanded from each of them. This didn't surprise me either. As the two men holding me up stood on either side of me, the fogginess cleared and I could see the destruction and death that surrounded me. I stole a glance at Janelle who was still knocked out on the ground.

"I can't say I'm happy to see you here, Cecil," David said after he pulled out a Newport from the pack he took out of his pantsuit. He offered me one that I tried to take, but the two men holding me didn't budge. "You guys can let him go," Dave said. He handed me the pack once I got my hands free. I took a square and handed the pack of Newport's back to him. There was a flash of light from the Zippo Dave pulled out. He offered to light mine first and I took advantage of the gesture. There wasn't much that could be said about the lighter, except that I had bought it for him when he got married to Pandy.

That was a wedding I thought was never going to happen. Dave had never been the settle-down type. I watched him go through more women than some lesser-admired presidents notorious for their promiscuousness. I couldn't understand how he was not only able to stay on good terms with all of them, but he also let it be known that he was involved with someone else. It was this part that I never understood.

"I just am very honest," he tried to explain to me one night when we were out playing darts.
"But isn't that too honest?"
"There's no such thing as too honest. And it's best to get that out of the way from the start. Think about it. You tell everything: your flaws, your failures, and your opinions that you know she doesn't agree with."
"But then how do you get them to talk with you if they don't agree with what you're saying?"
"Argue with them. Women love to argue. Listen to their points and, if they have a good argument and present the facts in a well-polished presentation, then they have won and there ain't no shame in being beat by a woman."
"Unless your opponent is a woman."
"Well, in that case it has nothing to do with the opponent being a woman and more to do with just losing in the first place. If it stings more because the person who won is a woman, good; more power to the fact that it hurts men so much because they are insecure as hell."
"You've put a lot of thought into this, I see."
"You always have to put a lot of thought into women. They're putting in thought on everything else. You might as well contribute

and learn as much as you can about the gender that's more than likely going to take control of the globe by the next generation."

"Do you really think we're ready for that?"

"I'm not sure about America, but I know the rest of the world is more than ready for a steady stream of progressive woman leaders as the majority."

"Seems like a fairy tale."

"Well it's not. And it's for that reason that I am trying to sleep with as many women as I can before it's too late and you really have to work to get a date. That's going to change the competition."

"What do you mean?"

"Well, look at the state of women and men's affairs at this juncture?"

"What about it?"

"It doesn't exist. There is no respect. There is no incentive. Women carry around the two things men want from them and they give it away for free."

"Most women hold themselves to a pretty high standard, I would have to say."

"And that is true. They hold themselves to a high standard. Women follow strict decorum practices and, of course, dress with respect for themselves and courtesy to others who glance at them. But when it comes to men and sleeping with them, they'll let any confidence man swoop in and woo them with fancy words and a quick wit. And they'll open their legs for the man. Don't matter if he ain't got no car, if he ain't got no home of his own. A lot of times, it don't even matter if he got any teeth."

"So you feel because of that, you might as well take advantage of those women who are settling for bums before they all wake up to the fact that they hold all the power?"

"Precisely!"

"But, you're still taking advantage of them."

"No, I'm not. I'm honest, remember? I clarify from the beginning that I am intent on having fun and I'm seeing many women at once and I have no time for commitment, nor do I want to."

"What happens if they don't want to deal with that?"

"Then they don't deal with it."

"Does that happen often?"

"What?"

"That women turn down your proposal."

"No, actually, it doesn't happen often at all."

"That's not encouraging. You mean there are women who actually go for this?"

"You'd be amazed, Brotha."

"I'm already amazed. Has it ever happened to you?"

"What?"

"That you've been turned down?"

"Not since I've adopted this philosophy. I think a lot of it is that I ended up getting involved with young, insecure women as well. It doesn't hurt that they have been dropped on their asses by some man they were in love with, but it's interesting that they're not as many as I would think who would have a problem with it."

"None of this makes you uncomfortable?"

"Maybe if I stop to think about it for too long, but I have so many dates during the week, that I don't have to suffer much with self-reflection."

"How long are you going to keep this up?"

"Until I get bored I guess."

"I still don't see how this is a good way to treat women."

"I never said it was a good way, but I don't think it's all that bad either."

"How can it not be bad? You're using them."

"Well, I wouldn't go that far."

"What would you call it then?"

"We use each other."

"And that's better?"

"Hey, like I said, as long as you're honest and upfront with everything what does it matter who is using who?"

"I can't condone the way you're bending the rules because everything is so confused and backwards."

"What do you mean?"

"What I mean is, if you talk like that about one of my daughters, I'd probably punch you in the face."

"But what if all your daughter is interested in is a good time, no commitment and freedom?"

"As her father, I'd still have a problem with that as a choice. And I think it's wrong for you to encourage such unhealthy behavior."

"Man, it always amazes me how you strive to be good."
"Well, of course."

"Naw, Man. Most guys don't give a fuck about women. They'll say they do, but they don't. Now, granted, I'm sure there are specific women who they worship and the ground they walk on. But women as a whole, naw, Man. Most guys are dicks and think women are here on this planet to serve their needs."

"So, if you know that, why not help support women and educate those men?"

"That's too much work. And I am providing these women with another option. I put it all on the table from the first date."

"But you do the same thing to them that gets done to them by these asshole guys."

"No, it's different. They know it's the case, so they don't let their hearts get involved."

"Now, that's a lie. You told me yourself just the other day that one woman with a lazy eye fell hard for you. You said she almost tried to kill herself when you told her to stop calling."

"That was a bit different. She chose to fall in love with me."

"I didn't know that was something you could just choose to do."

"Women can."

"And you know this because you're secretly a woman?"
"Of course not."

"Then how the hell do you know what women do?"
"Observation and perception."

"Whatever happened to that woman with the lazy eye, anyway?"

"She was committed to some psycho ward."

"Are you serious?"

"Yeah, Man. She tried to kill herself. That's what happens when you do that."

"Have you talked to her at all?"

"Hell naw, Man. Are you crazy? That chick is nuts. I don't want a goddamn thing to do with her. If I never see that woman again in this life or the next I'll be a happy man."

"Are you boys doing alright?" the bartender said as she walked over and collected our empty Goose Island bottles.

"Yes," Dave replied enthusiastically, scaring the shit out of both me and the bartender.

"What would it be?"

"Two shots of Jameson for me and my mate here. Would you like one?"

"No, we're not allowed to drink while on shift."

"That's too bad."

"Can I get anything else for you guys or is it just going to be the shots?"

"Can we get two more Goose Islands, too?" I asked.

"Sure, coming right up"

We watched her walk away. It was a decent enough show.

About a quarter to two, the only thing still moving in the bar was the hired help. This would've been the smart time to hail a cab and get our asses home. However, there wasn't a single smart cell swarming in our brains at that point. Dave was drunk and I was drunk as a skunk.

"Ok, Gentlemen," the well-built owner of the bar said to us. "We're closing up and we're gonna have to ask you to leave."

"Is it that time already?"

"It's been that time for a long time. That time's come and gone, as a matter of fact."

"I see," I said. "Our apologies. Would you mind calling us a cab?"

"What the fuck do I look like, your secretary?"

"Sir, that wasn't necessary?" Dave said. He'd had his head down on the bar for the past twenty minutes complaining about a headache.

"Look, Buddy, you don't need to be telling me anything. You need to pay your bill and get the fuck outta here."

"Really, sir. Why must you treat your patrons like this?"

"You're not a patron. You guys are a damn nuisance. I hate customers like you two. Just get drunk off your ass and then linger around. It's always your type who get into fights and harasses my bartenders when they get off."

"It's not our fault that you've got such great taste in picking your employees. That's it, isn't it? You hand pick them. Do you get to taste, too?" Dave asked with a big smile across his face.

The owner of the bar wasted no time in knocking the shit out of him. Dave collapsed onto the bar floor as his legs gave out from under him. I tried my best to retaliate and lay a haymaker that was dodged by the owner. He countered with a right that connected perfectly, shattering my jaw. When I woke, I was in a jail cell and couldn't open my mouth. Dave was pacing back and forth in front of the cell bars. There was more fog in my brain than there had been before and, for a moment, I didn't even know who the hell I was.

"I see you're awake."
"How long was I out?"
"Too long. I have been so goddamn bored."

Dave snapped the Zippo shut after lighting his Newport cigarette. He dismissed the two large men who had been holding me up. We sat and smoked in silence. Well, as much silence as could be found in the midst of the raid on the White House.

The Three Stooges'

"Are you with the Coalition?" I asked Dave after snubbing out the spent Newport.

Thoughts and ideas spun in my mind. Dave had traveled to Turkey to get married. He had converted to Islam. Turkey, before the blackout, had been a conduit of terrorist activity with the group ISIL taking the lead in the media. This was the same time that the police in Chicago were shooting people like porn stars.

"No, I'm not with them," Dave said completely shattering my dreams of him being a super terrorist genius fighting for peace and justice, even though killing people for peace is a strange concept.
"Then what exactly is happening?"
"This is my own thing that I've put together."
"Your own thing?"
"Yeah, my own thing."

Another explosion sounded and gunfire was exchanged. It seemed to be getting closer to where we stood. Dave calmly pulled out two Newport's and handed one to me. He lit them both again with the Zippo I bought for him as a wedding present. I wasn't able to make that wedding. The Press Secretary was riding me and the clients were riding her. Work popped up and never ceased to flow from that point onward. The lighter wasn't anything special in the material sense, but Dave knew that it came from my grandmother who he knew was the only member of my family I had ever known.

To see him carrying it in the midst of what he called his 'revolution' touched me.

"Well this is the part that's going to hurt, I'm afraid," Dave said, puffing on the Newport between his lips.
"What do you mean?" I asked.
"Well, protocols must be adhered to."
"What protocols?"
"Well you've seen my face. Under normal circumstances, I'm supposed to kill you."
"Kill me?"
"Yeah, Man. I'm the leader of an independent progressive organization that kills people. We work in silence and invisibility. And

we have a strict protocol that must be followed. For you, however, the rules will be bent just a bit, much to the dismay of my members, but I rule with an iron fist and they all know I kill without blinking."

"Except for me?"

"Come on, Cecil. You're my best friend. How could I ever kill you?"

"What if I don't agree with the way you conduct your operations?"

"You've rarely agreed with the way I conduct my operations. And you've been outspoken about it."

"Well, I'm your friend. Wouldn't be much of a friend if I didn't tell you the truth."

"And that's why I'm bending this rule for you."

"What about Janelle?"

"That's why she was knocked out before I made my dramatic appearance. This way she's been spared. You would've been knocked out, too. But I just wanted the chance to talk with you. We haven't seen each other since that last night at the Hilton in Chicago. A lot's happened since then."

"Who are you telling?"

A soft rumble sounded and a flash of blinding light followed, filling the room and causing me to shut my eyes.

"Just on time," Dave said. I saw him glancing at his wristwatch when my vision returned.

"Time for what?"

"So, yeah. Sorry, my Man, but this is going to hurt."

"What, argh," I exclaimed as I felt a blunt object bash the back of my head. I heard the footsteps and felt being caught by whoever hit me lower my crumbling body beside Janelle's. Before I blacked out, I stared into her face and thought how gorgeous she looked, almost as if she were peacefully sleeping and had not been bashed on the back of the head like I had just been. Then darkness overtook me.

For a time, I swam in a pool of disjointed memories as my mind tried to make sense of the bizarre shifts that had taken place since the day after Memorial Day. It all seemed so long ago, when normalcy existed; then that was wiped away by the purple sky which in turn became normal. Then the blackout and the slow descent into the Dark Ages the planet had endured.

Cassandra's naked body graced the swirl of liquid that was whirling through my brain. I wondered how she fared in the days and weeks following the electro bomb that blacked out the First World powers. Or even the French-Cuban nurse I accidentally stood up. I couldn't remember her name, as hard as I tried, it continued to swim around and around in my head.

When I started to come out of the daze, I felt like I was in a vehicle of some kind driving straight. I gathered we were on the highway as there were only soft turns left and right and the fast pace of acceleration with the engine steadily roaring forward. My hands were cuffed together in front of me and a hood was over my head. I reached to remove it. Just as I was lifting it up I heard Janelle's voice.

"They'll hit you if you take it off."

I thought for a moment about how I didn't care. I wanted to see her face. When I removed the hood with my cuffed hands. Janelle's puffed up black and blue face smeared with blood met me. Her eyes were tearing and lips quivering. Rage boiled from deep inside me.

"They did this to you?"

She nodded her head, yes. I stood up from the seat and moved closer to Janelle. I reached out and put my cuffed hands in her lap. Janelle lowered her head and began to sob. Then, she leaned her head onto my shoulder.

"I'm so happy that you're awake," she said to me. "I don't think they'll hurt me now that you're awake."

"What do you mean?"

"When I woke, we were in the van. One of the guys up front--I think there's just two of them--he peeked back and saw that I was up. I tried my best to not make a sound or move, but he came back and started talking to me. I'm not sure how long I had been out or how long we've been in this van. He said that he'd un-cuff me if I sucked his dick. I kicked him in the balls and then he punched me a few times. I heard the other guy, who I assume was driving, say that the boss would be angry if he found out they had roughed us up. He told the driver to shut up and as long as you were knocked out they could do anything because they boss was only concerned about your opinion; says he gives two shits about women and then smacked me around a little more before he returned to his seat up front. I've been staring at my shoes counting ever since."

"Hey, up front?" I yelled, startling Janelle.

"What do you want?" a voice yelled back.

"Have to piss."

"Piss in the van."

"I'll piss on you. Come on, Man, stop the car."

"Listen buddy. Just 'cause the boss is your childhood friend doesn't mean we got to do what you say."

"Is that why you beat the shit outta my woman?"

As painful as I'm sure it was, I saw Janelle smile when I said this. That was a happy moment. Brief, but happy. Maybe if we survive this, I might get the chance to explore all that Janelle had to offer. But first, this asshole.

I heard the rustling as the man who beat the shit out of Janelle moved to join us in the back. Once he removed himself from the black curtain separating the back from the driver, I saw that he was a monster of a man. He had that military glean in his eyes. He was taller than the van and had to bend his head down. His chest was bigger than my arms' length. It wasn't that big, but he was built like a tree trunk, solid as hell and powerful to boot. There was no way this was going to end cleanly.

I glanced over at Janelle and saw her focusing her non-swollen eye at me. Her other was swollen shut. With her swollen pierced lips done by this monstrous man's fist. Janelle smiled at me. That was all the encouragement I needed.

"As a matter of fact, yes. I'd much rather beat the shit outta you, but the boss has ordained you an untouchable. Lucky you. Unlucky for your pretty little thing over here. As soon as we dump you off at the boss's quarters. I'm going to take little Miss Attitude over here and give her some good sex. Not to say that you haven't done a great job, but she ain't never had no man before. Just boy, from the looks of you."

"Didn't anyone ever teach you not to call a black man, Boy?"

"What would you prefer? Nigger?"

I heard something snap. It was like a twig. I'm not sure if I made the sound in my head or if there really was something that snapped. When I tried to recall what I remembered, the little that I remembered, Janelle said there was no snap.

"It was dead silence after he called you a nigger. And then I guess you heard a snap which released you. You got this sadistic grin on your face. It was such a wide smile and your eyes were sparkling. It was such an abrupt change that the man took a step back. Then without any warning, you lunged at him, slamming your head into his stomach and pulling his legs out from under him. You and the man tore down the black curtain and fell onto the dashboard. The driver swerved to the left and then regained control as you and the man that beat me wrestled on the dashboard of the van. Somehow the man, or the driver, got you off the man you tackled and you tripped over a black bag that was sitting between the driver and passenger seats. The large man stepped forward and then the driver screamed. He must've sped up and was looking back 'cause he didn't see the stalled truck and didn't know he had pulled the van so far over onto the shoulder. It was just the side of the van that struck the 18-wheeler. But the van was moving fast enough to propel all of us forward. The impact was shattering; unexpected for you and me 'cause of the big hairy monster standing in front of us ready to kill me, I'm sure. The driver hadn't been paying attention to the road. And the monster had his back to the windshield. He went through it and severed something in his throat. The driver went through and was decapitated. And you and I were smashed straight into the dash."

We were both knocked out for some unknown time in the van. I opened my eyes first and saw that the sun was setting. It had been high in the sky when the crash occurred. I picked Janelle up and carried her out the back of the van. It was a deserted highway. The stalled truck the van collided with, saving Janelle and my life, I'm sure, was decaying with rust. It probably had stalled right at the time of the electro bomb. The van ran on water and had over half a tank. All of its components were run on steam, but after the collision it was just as useless as the truck. I checked the bodies of the two men that flew out of the van. They were dead. Taking their clothes and belongings, I put Janelle in the back of the van and set up a makeshift bed for us. Then I stood guard and waited the night out. There was nothing that could be done until the sun crept back up into the sky, hopefully illuminating a path forward.

The wait for the sunrise seemed like a lifetime. The rains returned as a flash of light spread across the sky, followed by the rumble of thunder. Then the sky started to cry horrible tears of loss. I listened as the rain cascaded on the roof of the van. With Janelle cuddled in my arms, I tried to make music out of the chaos of the storm.

Janelle woke some time later, but as she did so, wrapped her arms around my waist and squeezed tight.

"Everything's going to be ok," I told her. "Just get some rest."
"I know. When I'm with you I feel safe."

"We've been through a lot together since the first meeting, haven't we?"

"Too much."

"I was thinking, it's been just enough."

"Well, I am glad we've been able to be together for it all."

"Me, too."

"You know I like you, right?"

I laughed.

"Yeah, I could tell."

"Usually I don't sleep with anyone for a long time after meeting them."

"Well, it wasn't exactly like we slept together right off the bat. There was a bit happening around the world, if you recall."

"Yes, but if the blackout never happened, I would have had sex with you that night. I was planning on it."

"Well, that makes me happy. I was hoping we would have been able to from when we first met on the plane."

"And now we've lived through the destruction of the First World, together."

"I like the sound of that. Together. You think I'm going to lose you once everything settles down and peace is restored?"

"Do you honestly think that peace is going to be restored?"

"Of course I do. Always the optimist, I must be. We can never lose hope, for then we are without a future."

"I can't imagine how we're going to come back from this. I don't even see how we're going to survive. Where are we, even?"

"On an expressway."

"Heading where?"

"No idea."

"What time is it? No idea?"

"How do you not know what time it is?"

"Janelle, open your eyes. Do you see how dark it is? The light on my watch is powered by the sun, no sun means no light on the watch."

"Can I close my eyes now?"

"Yeah, I'm sorry."

"It's ok. I really am scared, Cecil. I don't know where my family is. I don't know where my friends are. I don't even know where we are."

"Yeah, I understand how you feel."

"How could you understand? You don't even like your stepparents."

"That is true, but that doesn't mean I don't love them. They took me in when no one else would when I was ten years old, too old to be adorable. Rich folks only want adorable babies. I guess I don't understand what you mean though. I've been alone for as long as I can remember. My step-family tried their best to envelop me in nurturing love. But at ten years old having lived a wretched life, I just wasn't up for the challenge of confronting my inner demons."

"What about now?"

"Now, things are simpler, ironically enough."

"Living in the Dark Ages is simpler?

"Yes, it is. Less choices. Everything is up for grabs."

"If it hasn't already been blown up."

"Or been taken already."

"Come on, gotta maintain that positive forward thinking, none of this depressing, woe is me..."

A loud whoosh followed by a cacophony of sonic booming sounding above cut my words short, splitting both Janelle and my heads'. The ringing was deafening. All I could hear was ringing in both ears. I saw Janelle in my lap, holding both hands over her ears with her mouth wide open. Her eyes were shut tight and it looked like every vein in her neck was popping out. I couldn't hear her screaming. I didn't realize I had been screaming too until my hearing returned.

We looked at each with alarm on our faces. My heart was slowly trying its best to return to a normal pace. Janelle looked as if she was on the verge of hyperventilating.

"Hey, Janelle, look at me," I said. She stared down at the corner at nothing. She was slipping into shock. "Janelle, Baby, look at me, please," I said snapping my fingers and trying hard to make her blink and get the motor running in her brain again.

She finally looked up at me and smiled.

"Hi sexy," she said smiling drunkenly.
"Hey, Beautiful. Are you feeling ok?"
"My head hearts a lot and my ears won't stop ringing."
"Mine, too, Love. It'll pass soon. What the hell was that?"

I watched as Janelle's eyes opened wide with alarm.

"It's ok. You don't have to worry yourself about that. Can you wait here and I'm going to step outside and try to find out what the fuck that was that flew overhead?"

Before I got a chance, however, the back door of the van snapped open. It was difficult to see, but the sun had just begun rising and the first moments of dawn were beginning. The silhouette of three men in masks could be seen. They stood in a triangle, unmoving, watching Janelle and me. I could hear their breathing. These guys were serious.

"Leave it up to them two idiots to crash into a stalled truck on an otherwise empty stretch of road," one of them said.
"I told the boss we shouldn't have trusted some newbies with transporting such high-profile subjects," another said.
"I don't see what's so special about this guy. The woman though, I hope he lets one of us have the woman," the last of the triplet said.
"He's not letting us have anything. We're not in this for spoils, remember. This is about justice," the man who spoke first said. I gathered he was in charge of this motley crew.

"See, that's where we differ," the squeaky-voiced man said, who seemed to have eyes on Janelle. I wanted to rip his throat out. "You're here for justice. I'm here to have fun."

"Man, I don't see why the boss let you and your little thugs into The Flawed." The masked man who wasn't too keen on letting newbies transport Janelle and I, said.

"It's like the boss said himself," the squeaky-voiced man responded. "We're all flawed."

"Eh, that's such a horrible answer, Pete."

"Now why would you say his name, Ray?"

"Marvin, you just said Pete's name."

I could see right away that this was a very sharp bunch of goons! Janelle and I listened to the Three Stooges bicker and, as the sun came up, we were able to see just how large they were. The masks they wore were made of black cloth. They were all light-skinned by their hands, the only piece of skin not covered by black.

"Why do I always get saddled up with you two?" the man who seemed to be in charge, who Marvin let us know was named Ray, said.

"It's no picnic for us either, Buddy Boy."

I continued to hold Janelle and we listened as the three men continued to argue. It would've been a good show if not for the fact that I couldn't remember the last time we ate, we had just been in a serious car accident, we'd been knocked out before the crash and Janelle had been beaten as if she were a man. All of that was in less than forty-eight hours, too.

Once the Three Stooges finally were reminded by Ray, their fearless leader, that they had come to do a job, Janelle and I were cuffed and brown paper bags were placed over our heads after taping our mouths shut. I heard Janelle cringe as the top was put over hers. I appreciated Ray for doing it himself and keeping Marvin away from her. I'm pretty sure that he heard me say that if Marvin put a finger on her I'd rip his throat out.

We were escorted out of the van and then, with our hands cuffed behind our backs and brown paper bags over our heads, we were herded down the highway. We walked for a long time. At some point we veered off the road and were on dirt. I fell a few times. For the most part the Three Stooges kept their mouths shut. I figured they felt stupid about having their little squabble in front of Janelle and me. I tried to feel for Janelle with my shoulders, but couldn't find her. It was part of the reason I kept falling 'cause I wasn't walking in a straight line.

"Ok, we are here," Marvin, the squeaky-voiced henchman said. The paper bags were removed and the tape ripped from our lips. Janelle muffled a scream of pain and I glared at Marvin, daring him to try something.

The sun was directly above us. We were in what could only be described as a desert. Sand dunes were spread 360 degrees around us. I had no idea where the hell we were. The cuffs were unlocked from our wrists and we both rubbed where the steel had cut into our skin. I grabbed Janelle's hand and pulled her close to me.

"So what now, fellas?" I asked, getting tired of not knowing what the hell was happening.

"Now, we wait."

"What was that plane that flew overhead? I thought there wasn't any electrical working anything anymore."

"Yes, in the First World nations," Ray spoke for the first time since the van. "But theirs's electricity was left intact. So, it would seem that we flip-flopped, but it's not quite that straightforward."

"Where's Dave?" I asked, finally beginning to get annoyed.

"I don't know who Dave is," Ray answered.

"Your boss. You don't even know your own boss' name?"

"We have no reason to know his name."

"So you just follow blindly?"

"No, we all know the plan. We all know the schedule. We just don't know much about the boss."

"Isn't that kind of strange to you?"

"Why would it be strange?"

"Because you don't know who the fuck this great leader of yours is."

"Like I said, we don't have to know."

"Do you want to know?"

"No, not really," Ray said, a little too quick to be convincing.

"Now, wait just a minute, here," Marvin pitched in. "I, for one, would like to know who this guy is that's been ordering us around for almost six months now following the blackout."

"Marvin, you're starting to step out of place," Pete said, with a stern look on his face.

"Who's going to stop me from stepping out of place? Who's to say that it's not our place to ask questions? Isn't that what the boss has always encouraged us to do, question everything? But no one thinks to question the boss. That's strange, don't you think?"

"I reluctantly agree with you, Marvin. I still want to bash your fucking face in, though."

"Unfortunately, I don't think you're going to get that chance to be embarrassed in front of your little squeeze over here."

"Well, I could tell you a little about your boss, my friend Dave. And then if there's time left while we're waiting for whatever the hell it is we are waiting for, you and I can do a little dance ending with my foot up your ass."

"Marvin, stop talking to the prisoner," Ray said with authority.

"Now wait just a minute. You ain't got no power over me," Marvin barked at Ray, getting into his face.

"Marvin, calm down, Man," Pete said trying to keep the peace. He put his hand on Marvin's shoulder. Marvin aggressively shrugged him off and then got back in Ray's face.

Ray looked away from Marvin and pointed his eyes directly at me. He winked a signal of comfort and then head-butted Marvin in the nose, sending a spray of blood into the air.

Marvin wheeled back and Ray pulled a silver revolver from the holster in his vest. The three of us—the other henchman Pete, Janelle and I—watched as Ray steadied himself, took aim and blew a hole in Marvin's head. Marvin's corpse crumpled to the ground. Ray holstered the silver revolver and inhaled deeply through his nose.

"Well," he said exhaling. "Shouldn't be too much longer now."

As he said this, the silence of uncertainty wafted over me.

"What the hell is going on?" I finally whispered.

"It's about self-preservation, Cecil. Old Marvin here was a thug for hire. Same with good old Pete," Ray said nodding in Pete's direction. You know what the difference is between them?"

"Pete's not dead," Janelle said.

"Funny. No, the difference is what caused Marvin to be dead."

"And what's the difference between them?" I asked Ray.

"The difference between these two men, uneducated, unrefined and unwanted henchmen, is that, Pete here, doesn't make unnecessary conversation."

"So, Pete keeps his mouth shut."

"Now, I wouldn't say that. Would you, Pete?"

"No, I wouldn't say that."

"See. Pete speaks. He just doesn't speak unnecessarily. The only time Pete opens his mouth is if there is something useful to say. Ain't that right, Pete?"

"That's right," Pete responded, giving nothing more.

"So, there you go."

"Ok, so that's why you killed your friend, Marvin."

"Pause. Marvin was not my friend. He was a henchman."

"Henchmen aren't your friends? What about Pete here?"

"You see that, Pete? You should take notes from this little guy here. See how he's trying to flip what I said against me and get you to raise doubts about my leadership. But what he doesn't understand is that the two of us are clear on who our leader is. Aren't we, Pete?"

"You are most certainly correct, Ray."

"You see that, Cecil? That's called loyalty; that's called respect. It's something this country could only wish its citizens were able to follow. Now, to answer your question, I never said henchmen aren't my friends. I would say Pete and I are fairly close. Especially given the short time we have been associated with each other. Would you agree with that, Pete?"

"Yeah, Ray. I'd have to say that I agree. You're a pretty good guy. I'd consider you my friend."

"Now look at that," Ray said with a smile. "You see how chummy we are."

Pete raised an eyebrow at this use of the word chummy.

"Now, moving forward. Thugs for hire are hired to be thugs. Makes sense?"

I nodded my head in agreement.

"So," Ray continued. "If you hire a thug and that thug becomes difficult, you know what you do?"

"Put a bullet in him?" I said.

"Or her. Don't forget about the world we live in now. Everyone has an equal opportunity to fill any position to be a criminal."

"You're an equal opportunity employer," Janelle said.

"Yes, and we employ only the best. Marvin here sadly was hired because his cousin is one of our commanders down in Florida. Marvin's cousin is a strategic genius. Marvin was an idiot."

"Won't his cousin be upset that you shot him?" Janelle asked.

"Heavens, no. Marvin's cousin follows the boss. We all do. We don't question. And besides, he knows his cousin is a fuck-up. When he hears the news, it won't surprise him. That's why he begged the boss to get him the job as a henchman, 'cause he figured Marvin was going to end up dead on his own. Henchman was the only job where you can afford fucking up and making a mistake. I mean, we take your life, but that's the payment. He had already given himself up for dead, so he could easily afford the payment."

"This is all very fascinating about the philosophy of henchmen and thugs for hire. However, I really would like to know what's going on at this very hour," I said. "I mean, I'm dying to know, Man, what Dave is up to. What is this organization that you all have built?"

"That the boss has built," Ray said interrupting me.

"Right, my apologies for trying to give you credit also."

"I can't take credit where none is due."

"Wow, he's really got you believing his shit. I knew Dave was good, but not this good. I can't even fathom what the fuck is happening. But you all aren't connected to the coalition or to the First World Coalition. You all are an independent terrorist unit fighting for justice. I assume this justice is selected by your boss?"

"The justice we fight for is the justice inherently assured from birth because we're human."

"By who? Who is this justice assured by?"

"The sanctity of life."

"This isn't making much sense."

"That's because you have not taken the vow of 'The Flawed.'"

"Right, that's what you all call yourselves."

"That's what the boss calls us."

"But you call yourselves it, too."

"Because the boss told us to."

"So if your boss chose to change it and call you something else, then you would go by that name from that point on?"

"That is correct, Cecil."

"How can you give such blind loyalty?"

"Once again, you are not a member of 'The Flawed.'"

"Which could change its name to something else any day?" I interrupted.

"And therefore, there just is no way for you to understand."

"I understand just fine. I went through the United States military indoctrination."

"Yes, we know about that. That is why you are being offered this chance. But first you've got to be cleansed. You all who are not yet part of 'The Flawed' are tainted with the filth of the First World."

"Haven't you heard?" Janelle interjected. "The First World is no more."

"No, I'm sorry to burst your bubble with some current information. The First World has no power. That doesn't mean they are no more. There are plenty of First World leaders who have plenty of aces up their sleeves. Part of it is finding a way to activate the programming they've spent the last twenty years plugging us all up with."

"What do you mean?"

"The social media. You think all of that was freedom? Everything that was allowed to swim through on the information superhighway was embedded with a mind control code."

"Ok, this is all starting to sound like bullshit," Janelle said. "The Flawed and all of you are starting to sound like a whacked-out fanatical religious group that's been waiting for something like this to happen and are capitalizing on the confusion that's been created from the blackout."

"That's the accelerated programming you were put through when the government enlisted you. You all don't know this, but throughout America, the draft was reinstated following the blackout. The riots started and the destruction of the First World from the inside by its pissed-off citizens began. In the midst of the confusion, the military swarmed in and gave everyone a choice."

"Yeah, we remember that choice," I said, feeling the mental scars my training had left on me.

"You'd be surprised how many chose to sign up. All those who talked big turned tail instantly when they were faced with their own mortality, although there were those who refused to fight and chose to be executed. There were lots of executions following the draft. So many people died, the military started to throw the bodies out to sea. They thought of burying them in mass graves, but it just felt too eerily close to Nazi Germany with the Jews. That's why they closed the beaches."

"I didn't know they closed the beaches," Janelle said softly. "So they're not letting people leave the country?"

"Well, no. But even if they did, there's no chance they'd survive in a boat and just hop out to sea. There's no longer any way to chart the sea with the radar being gone. The entire First World was held up by Benjamin Franklin's great discovery."

"Actually, it was the 6th century BCE Greek philosopher Thales of Miletus who experimented with amber rods and sparked the first studies into the production of electrical energy," I said. "Benjamin Franklin just established the connection between lightening and electricity."

"Regardless of who discovered it, the coalition burned out all the components of every machine that ran on electricity. With non-nuclear electromagnetic pulses set off by e-bombs going off around the biosphere. The entire attack took less than two minutes. And then we were back to zero. The beaches are now the graveyards of America—and we assume other nations, too."

"What is a non-nuclear electromagnetic pulse?" I asked Ray.

"I'm going to let Pete explain all of that to you. Pete, do you mind going over basic NNEMP information for these two while I tend to our friend, Marvin?"

"No problem," Pete responded. Clearing his voice and taking a centering breath before beginning. "An NNEMP is a weapon that creates an electromagnetic pulse without a nuke. The concept of the weapon was thought up by Andrei Sakharov of the Soviet Union in 1951. An explosively-pumped flux compression generator for generating an electromagnetic pulse was achieved through the use of microwave generators. The NNEMP was deployed with the use of over a thousand drones that struck key targets of First World nations simultaneously around the globe. It's known that the United States and other nations were aware of this technology being developed. However, the aligning of the powers was missed and it wasn't thought that harnessing this technology could do such large damage. How wrong we were."

Ray had emptied Marvin's pockets and removed the tactical gear the three of the henchmen were wearing. He handed Marvin's vest to Janelle.

"You should put that on. Law and order doesn't exist in this land anymore. Like I said, there's only survival. That's all that matters. Thanks for explaining that, Pete."

"No problem, Ray.

"I was thinking about those beaches when I was fooling with Marvin's body," Ray said to Janelle and me. "It's a good thing you've never seen them. So many bodies were dumped there that now there are thousands washed up and decaying. Disease has spread so rampantly that they are saying 70% of the United States population is dead. Out of us 30% who survive, 20% are carrying some form of contagious disease. There really is no happy ending to this. But we of 'The Flawed' have the solution and our boss is positioning us to unleash his great plan."

"What's the great plan?" I asked.

"Now, Cecil, you know I can't tell you that."

"I can always hope."

"Didn't you hear me? There's no longer any hope. The First World's arrogance has gotten the best of us and the nations that we have consistently shit on over and over have finally snapped back; and snapped harder than any of us thought was possible. Now we're frantically trying to gather whatever power we have, and I don't mean electricity."

"But, I thought you all had the secret plan that would save us all."

"I never said that the plan will save humanity. I just said the boss has a great plan. And from what I know about the boss, you being alive means that you are a key piece in his great plan. I suspect your lady here is going to play a role in the end, too."

"So where is your boss, then?"

"Hey, my orders were to get to this location and then wait. I've achieved what I was ordered to do."

"That's all you do is obey orders?"

"Look around you, Cecil. I'm not the one to try and lead anything. But, having collected strong united people will help us move forward."

"And Dave's plan can guarantee that? Knowing Dave, I highly doubt that things are anything like they seem."

More Sweets

Memories of Smitheran Sweets.

The great hotel adventure began for me about the time that I was three. There was a sparkle of excitement I remember as I was carried by the policeman up the steps to Smitheran Sweets Adoption Agency. I knew the word "hotel" because my parents were dashing and elegant. I believe this to be true since I was in hotels from my memory of the first two years of my life and that brought about a feeling of acceptance in high society. Little did I know, but how I would learn, the falsity of my imagination.

I was accepted and doted over until the policeman went away. Then I sat in front of the inside front door for the next two days. Neglected, I cried to no avail. It wasn't until a little boy of three who took to calling me "C," dragged me away from the front door and into Smitheran Sweets. I would learn from the nurses that this boy's name was Zenek.

Zenek moved among the orphans with a respect that was given without knowing why. His way of speaking, once he finally learned to talk—which didn't take long at all, really—-by his fourth birthday, he was rattling off the radio stations he had heard the nurses listening to their soap operas stories on, his re-telling's were so accurate that the nurses used to gather around him just before bedtime and have him retell their favorites. He would do so with perfectly accurate detail.

His curiously inappropriate over-attention from the nurses enraged the head mistress, Miss Penerperkle. She saw to it that Zenek was locked away frequently in the closet of solitary confinement.

The solitary closet was among the scariest places in the entire enormity of the large hotel that was Smitheran Sweets Adoption Agency. Located on floor thirteen, it was the closet in the room of

Head Mistress Miss Penerperkle. Miss Penerperkle was also a dominatrix, who dominated over three men a week. She was part of a call in a dominatrix agency. Because of her unbreakable rigidity, she become something of a legend among the partakers.

Zenek and others like him would be locked in the closet of solitary confinement before every show; they would be chained up in the closet and forced to watch the spectacle. Miss Penerperkle was not faint of heart and would ravish the hell out of the men, and sometimes women, she would dominate. There wasn't a single moment in the entirety of time that the theatre of torture would cease before all but Zenek would pass out from disbelief. It was only Zenek, however, who would be present when the bitch would leave and Miss Penerperkle was finished.

"She would take her time when she came to open the closet of solitary confinement door," Zenek once told me at Smitheran Sweets. "I would hear her moaning in all these weird ways and wonder what she was doing. The sounds were something almost otherworldly, as if a king were gargling."

"What is otherworldly about a king gargling?" I asked him. "And what's he gargling?"

"Have you ever listened to a king gargling?"

"Of course not. And even if I had, why the hell would I want to?"

"Well, it's otherworldly."

"I'll take your word for it. Continue."

"Don't mind if I do. The click-clack of her heels on the wooden floor would crumple up my stomach into a knot. I'd succumb to a panic attack and my entire world would turn upside down; literally upside down. I would think that I was falling headfirst into I don't know what. The click-clack would last longer than I could ever imagine it would take for Miss Penerperkle to get from the door after dismissing her bitch across the room to the closet of solitary confinement. It was insane to think. There I was. The witness to a sexual act punched full of shock that no treatment could ever explain. Now, I'm not saying that my trauma was any worse than all the others. Even you, Cecil. 'cause I know once or twice you, too, were subjected to the tortures of the closet of solitary confinement. Where all of our stories change is when the head mistress opened the door. Only I was forced to endure the next phase of her dominatrix game."

"What did she do to you?"

"More than I can ever say; more than I ever will say. I have nightmares about it every time I sleep. There has been absolutely no point since the first time that I had my frightful experience with Miss Penerperkle that I have been able to move beyond it and not be overcome by anxiety."

"This seems like it would be worth reporting," I said naively.

"Report to who? Do you not know what this place is?" Zenek asked me. I was five at the time and he was six. "This is hell and Miss Penerperkle is the devil. There is no one else like her and everyone that is in her path is subject to her wrath."

The conversation with Zenek was heading into a depressing place, as they so often did; and I wasn't encouraged to any degree to participate. Zenek continued on his ramblings and I began thinking:

I remember from the first two years of my life dancing to be a wonderful thing, filling the empty hallways of my undiscovered brain with the James Brown similes of, "Baby. Please, please" eroding through the 45's my mother danced to when I was in her womb; a secret comparison to an angel and her baby escaped through the clear lens of what would be called a better or worse relationship added on by two and eventually extinguishing never to be seen past that year and the tragedy of everything is that I never was able to know just how elegant a queen my mother was and how royal a king my father proved himself to be. It's interesting that as an orphan I still found a family that treated me like a king and then I think of Zenek and wonder what will become of him. He sits there and talks these magnificent things that he has really gone through, but the hopeful discovery is that he just made it all up and I know inside deep, deep down that that is just my underbelly wishing for a happy ending; but this ending is neither happy nor sad; the story is not my friend Zenek's. As far as I know, he is at the bottom of the sea.

But in actuality, years later I would discover that he was not at the bottom of the sea, but had embarked on the greatest escape from Smitheran Sweets and then lived the life of an outlaw, biding his time for the opportune moment that came when the electro bomb went off, causing what has since become known as the Squared Dark Age. Why was it squared? Because it was supposed to be times meaning the second, or the Second Dark Age.

I didn't make the name up. That is just what it's called. Talk to Wikipedia if you have a real problem with it.

"Did you hear about what happened to Timothy?" Zenek said, breaking through my internal journey through my imagination's wonderings.
"What happened to Timothy?" I asked. How could I not be intrigued?
"He was attacked by a Freak."

You remember The Freaks. I've told you that Zenek always talked about them.

"What happened to him?" I asked with naiveté.
"What usually happens when you're attacked by one of the Three Freaks running around Smitheran Sweets Adoption Agency?"

There were no words to express the horror I felt as Zenek described the goings-on when attacked by a Freak from the tales of surviving victims, unlike Timothy, unfortunately. Timothy was raped and killed and then chopped into pieces by the most diabolical of the Freaks named Susan Sweets.

Susan Sweets was the last remaining relative of the Sweets family, starting with Smitheran, the oldest child in the family of four. From top to bottom: Smitheran, Alice, Zool and Susan. Three daughters and one boy were what Theodore and Rachael Sweets were blessed with. They doted over them for the years they were able to. The rest were taken from them for tax evasion; locked up, but able to secure the family fortune in a hotel called Sweets Hotels. All was left to the eldest Smitheran.

Smitheran oversaw the family fortune and sent his three youngest sisters off to school. He raised each of them as he was ten years the senior to the oldest of his sisters, Alice. They lived a life of comfort and Smitheran took care of all the family's deeds. There was nothing any of the sisters could ever ask for as Smitheran was always one step ahead of the game. It was an amazing treat, this Smitheran fellow.

Bred from the best of families, Theodore and Rachael Sweets each came from the historically epic Yarling family. Rachael was Theodore's second cousin. Traditions adhered to for hundreds of years cast the eldest to marry the second cousin of the Tweeny family. Family traditions were carried over by Smitheran to his three sisters who each were younger than they were able to comprehend that they were close family. I learned all of this, of course, from Zenek.

"That family was fucked up," he said to me in one of our last conversations before his eleventh birthday which he had miscalculated and thought was a year sooner than it was. "By the time that guy Smitheran was old and grey, he was crazier than a hare. His three sisters were so dependent on him that they could never survive without his presence. When he died, he invested his entire fortune in the hotel that at that point was known as the hottest and most frequented in the world: Sweet's Hotels. When Smitheran died, he secretly created an instruction in his will that demanded his entire fortune go toward the care and tutelage of abandoned children for the next century. His sisters did not like this one bit and they all vied to take control of the Sweets Empire. But Smitheran was no dummy and he locked away the family's money in a web of legality that would never be unraveled. The three sisters lived in the hotel for ten years in a life of solitude. One would believe they were content and happy, but it's so hard to know such things. Once the ten years passed and the message was delivered that the hotel was to be transformed into an adoption agency, the sisters' lividity rose to heights seldom seen by boogie bitches such as these."

"Lights out, you slithering toads that are the bane of my existence," Miss Penerperkle barked through the intercom she used to communicate with the population of Smitheran Sweets Adoption Agency. "If I so much as hear a whisper from any of you sniffling little brats, I assure you that you will spend an entire weekend in my closet of solitary confinement. There hasn't been anyone who has had the pleasure of attending my shows for quite some time. I wonder why? Could it be that you little twerps are actually beginning to learn that I run this place and now that you are here, none of you will ever leave? Oh, there will be one or two of you lucky sons of bitches that are able to escape my clutches and some rich, bored couple that can't have kids will latch upon you. Consider yourself lucky. But most of you—nine out of ten of you—are going to be here until you are old enough to work the mines. I'm sure all of you know the age when that happens. Now, for current events, we have one of your own who has earned the honor of reading the daily report put together by our lovely janitor every day. You may begin when ready," Miss Penerperkle said to the chosen orphan.

"There is a multitude of terror occurring outside of these walls. There is nothing that will be able to quench the thirst for destruction so many living beyond our sanctuary are embarking upon. Power is sought at a schizophrenic pace that can never be captured. Human beings on the outside are killing themselves and each other from pettiness that we of Smitheran Sweets Adoption Agency never have to deal with. We pity those who are chosen to rejoin this life outside. We are all lucky to have lost our connections with our parents and become able to disconnect from the machine that runs humanity. This machine is not connected to Smitheran Sweets. Those on the outside don't think we're strong enough. They don't think we are smart enough. They don't care about us. They don't believe we can be anything but what we are, and that is unwanted orphans. But we know as taught to us by the Head

Mistress: We are the orphans of change. And if we are able to survive the harsh tutelage of this most fortunate position we are in, then after a decade of living, we will be allowed to begin work in the mines that will create the foundation of the new world just waiting beyond the machine. Our job is to disconnect humanity from the machine; this humanity that has shunned us, the orphans. They will be saved by those they so arrogantly discard."

"Thank you, Betty," Miss Penerperkle, the head mistress, said, replacing her voice over the overhead speaker blasting through the entirety of the Smitheran Sweets Adoption Agency, all day and every fucking day. "You mumbled just a bit during your reading, so it seems you will be the lucky orphan to break the streak of vacancy in my closet of solitary confinement."

And she was. Betty was never the same after that. Everyone knew her. She was bright and positive. After her night in Miss Penerperkle's closet of solitary confinement, she was a tragic mess of nervousness.

...

"Cecil?"

Nothing

"Cecil?"

Still nothing

"Cecil. Wake up."

I stirred a bit, but quickly brushed away my stepmother's attempt at waking me.

"Cecil. Wake up!" Alice said with motherly forcefulness.

I popped up. There was never a moment of hesitation when my stepmother was ignored or treated without respect. She commanded a presence of obedience that seldom meant she had to yell or scream. It was nothing strange for a mother to command her family, but Alice was able to conduct each of us who lived under the same roof to be perfect little helpers. Alice ran her home like a gentle drill sergeant. There was never a dull moment.

"Always working toward progress. That's our motto, right?"
"Yes, Ma'am."
"Cecil, there should be more base in your voice."
"My apologies, Madam. Will that be all you need?"
"Yes. Did you finish your homework, Cecil?"
"No, Ma'am."
"Then you best get your ass up to your room and get to it."
"I finished my homework, Mommy," Laurel said. She was always a suck-up.
"Yes, Sweetie. I know you did. You are dependable. Therefore there is no reason for me to question you."

And she rarely did. Laurel was treated with a vague discomfort that kept Sherrie, her father and myself from ignoring the elephant in the room. There was a certain disrespect that was thrown at Laurel. After many years of thinking on why, I have come to believe that my stepmother was compensating for her son Johnny's death. There was no way for a mother to overcome such a tragedy as the murder of her baby.

Johnny was playing ball in the Hemingway Park across the way over by the lake. He was with two of his friends from school who never seemed to appear ahead of time, but always afterward. And it was afterward that they were lost in the wind of accomplices and it turned out that they had set up Johnny over the Jordan's he wore. Two boys had another boy killed for one pair of shoes. Did they share it?

Hemingway Park was dedicated by the alderman of the Fifth Ward, Leslie Hairston. She unveiled the park in the autumn. By summer, Johnny's blood along with dozens of others was spread across the pavement of the park. There were swings. There was a full basketball court. There was even a sit-and-spin and a sand pit for the little kids. Suffice it to say, after the bloodshed, the alderman's great effort was washed away by demolition trucks, replaced by an overpriced condo that served those from the top pile of money in the world.

When they shot Johnny, they left him bleeding on the court. It was four hours before his body was discovered. He was beyond saving and the officer who responded was forced to send the small boy away with positive words and prayers.

Johnny's death sparked an outrage throughout the city of Chicago. There wasn't a single story bigger than poor Johnny being shot for his Jordan's. Never mind that such crimes had been taking place for all the time that the Nike shoe existed.

The only thing that knocked it off the headlines was when the mayor's son was decapitated on a rollercoaster at Six Flags. That blocked out most of the news in the state of Illinois; not that we had a shortage of news, what with the police killing black men like prize games and the Police Accountability Authority put in place but not doing anything to stop bad cops from making all cops look evil.

The mayor's son having his head chopped off on a rollercoaster shut down Six Flags for a few days, which is all that could be expected. It was up and running by the time my junior class at Hales Franciscan was able to go to Six Flags for Physics Day.

"Cecil, did you ever get a chance to talk to Ms. Brown?" my friend Jepedo asked me.

I didn't have many friends in high school and Jepedo was probably the closet I had there. He was the only one who actually came to the house of the family that adopted me in Evanston. It wasn't that I was ashamed of my life. It was more that I just felt it was strange. There was too much to explain; always having to say that I was adopted and that all my blood relatives were dead and that this white family really was my family, the only family I knew, in fact.

"No, Ms. Brown had already left for the day by the time I got out of detention," I answered my friend.

"That's too bad, man. What was it she was going to help you with?"

"We were going to go over the writer Yukio Mishima from Japan."

"Who was Mishima?"

"He was a fiction writer and political activist of sorts during the modernization of Japan. His writing was hailed from the very beginning of his career at an early age as being otherworldly. It was said that he had a command of the Japanese language as if he had jumped into a time machine and found the greatest scholars and poured their knowledge into his brain. It would seem that that was the case, for he continued to write at an alarming rate until he killed himself the day he completed his Year of Fertility saga by committing ritual disembowelment, better known as seppuku."

"Seppuku?"

"Yeah, it was what samurai did when they lost their honor."

"How exactly does one lose his honor?"

"There are a number of ways honor can be lost. Primarily, a samurai would lose his honor after his lord was defeated or they themselves were fired from their position as a retainer. Once you were no longer a retainer, if you couldn't find another boss, you became a Ronin, a dishonorable thing to be. And committing seppuku was a way for a samurai to regain his honor in death."

"Sounds pretty stupid."

"It was tied up a lot in ritualistic Buddhism as well. There was something that I forgot to mention. When seppuku was done, the samurai would take a knife and insert it into their abdomen and then slice horizontally across, spilling out their intestines, and then their closest companion and also usually gay lover, would chop his head off and complete the ritual."

"That's crazy. I just don't understand the point of killing yourself because you made a mistake."

"It was the value they put on perfection. There wasn't a single thing done by accident and it was for this reason that when something was neglected, it was taken as the gravest of all offenses."

"Honestly," said Jepedo "it all sounds pretty stupid to me."

"It sounded stupid to a whole lot of people, but many people adhered to it."

"Including, Mishima?"

"Well, Mishima was trying to make a point. He felt that the Japanese military, as well as the country as a whole, was moving away from tradition and losing their respect for self. He was adamantly opposed to assimilating Western modernism into Japanese society. Even though he benefited greatly from the social status given him by his international fame through his novels, Mishima formed his own independent military command and trained them into a pretty impressive combat force. The day he finished his last novel in his Sea (or Year?) of Fertility Saga--I think it was called Runaway Horses--he staged a coup with a ranking general and addressed the guard."

"What did he say?"

"He basically told them that they needed to stop embracing everything Western and return to the traditional ways of the samurai and put the emperor back in power."

"Wait. The emperor wasn't in power?"

"You missed everything from history class, huh?"

"I wouldn't say that I missed it. I heard it and processed it. I just dumped it quickly after the period ended by smoking a joint."

"You're still smoking, Jepedo?"

"Yeah, Man. I personally don't see how you were able to stop so easily like you did."

"I never smoked as much as you."
"That's true."

"Doesn't it bother you?"

"What?"

"To lose all your memory like that."

"Not really. So what happened with the emperor?"

"Well, after World War II, he was dethroned and following the occupation that MacArthur was in charge of, he was allowed to be emperor, but had no power."

"How can you be an emperor with no power?"

"How indeed, Japedo. The answer is that you can't. So the people of Japan were not only decimated because of the nuclear bombs dropped on Hiroshima and Nagasaki, they were also left disillusioned because their emperor, who was supposed to be a direct descendent from the Sun Goddess was nothing but a man. And he was so weak that the Occupation Forces just let him be himself, a regular man that's no different from anyone else."

"But isn't that the case with all of us?"

"Yes, it is. But you want to believe that your leader is a descendant of god 'cause it makes you feel like you have protection."

As the two of us were talking in the cafeteria about all of this during our junior year at Hales Franciscan at 4930 S. Cottage Grove, there was a load explosion that tore away all traces of normalcy.

A pipe bomb that a student had put together from directions online blew out of his locker and severed the arms and legs of a dozen students. No one was killed. The blast turned the school into a war zone for the day. Locked down, the FBI and lots of really large bear-like men with guns swarmed the building, looking and searching. It didn't take them long to find the kid. He was a Muslim student named Akeem; which was unfortunate for blacks and Muslims across the nation.

We become something of celebrities, Hales Franciscan and the students themselves. But no one was more famous than Akeem. He was something like a genius. Nice, soft in speech, and he never wasted a moment in pettiness. His composure was that of a king who chooses to take the lowliest of jobs in order to do his share of the work in addition to maintaining his kingdom. So why did Akeem have a pipe bomb in his locker? And why did it explode? Well, the why it exploded is easier to answer. So let's get that out the way. It exploded because Akeem had failed to properly secure the bomb in his locker. He had lost his keys the morning he decided to bring the bomb to school. He wasn't going to set it off on that day, but he was prepping for the attack he had been planning for over a year.

The final touches for what Akeem often described as his power move on change were at the point of completion. As he put the pieces of his master plan into place, a stupid mistake ended what was intended to have been a great demonstration of violent protest.

The pipe bomb was sitting on the top shelf of Akeem's locker. Under normal circumstances, this would have been okay. But on this day—the first that Akeem chose to begin the staging of his movement of change—a fight broke out in the hallway. An argument had begun in the biology lab and worked its way up to blows being thrown. Flooding out of the classroom into the hallway, sides were taken and a full-on brawl ensued. Two beefy athletes entangled themselves and waltzed their way into Akeem's locker. The pipe bomb shifted as the locker was dented and then a punch was thrown that gave the pipe bomb just the right thump to set it tumbling down.

Boom!

The Akeem bombing, as it would later be called, came two years after two planes slammed into the World Trade Center causing both towers to collapse. This was the beginning of the outright war on terror. Such a war had been taking place against nations, but the First World powers were never given the opportunity to just say that it was bombs over Baghdad.

The two students who were locked in that violent embrace and slammed into the locker caught the full brunt of the homemade pipe bomb. They each lost their left arms. Onlookers who had gathered during the brawl that started in Mr. Sullivan's class and spread out into the hallway received shrapnel wounds to the face for their gawkish curiosity.

It was an absolute disaster. There were literally hundreds of lockers in the school and hundreds of days when this all could've taken place. At first it took some time for the confusion to work its way out of the brain. All around, students and teachers were in a daze. I was on the other side of the hallway when the explosion took place. I was considering if I should have a slice of pizza or a turkey sandwich. I just happened to look precisely at the moment the flash of light and shockwave of the explosion shattered any semblance of regularity.

It was as if someone had pushed a hard restart on reality. We blinked away and for a few seconds I found myself nowhere; a place where time didn't exist, space didn't exist, memory didn't exist and neither did I. There I was in nothingness.

I had just read about it in philosophy class a few days before the pipe bomb went off and had been thinking about it almost obsessively: the idea of emptying the mind entirely of anything and becoming everything that exists in the universe was fascinating. I knew from my stepfamily a little bit about Buddhism.

Sherries's daddy was a God-fearing, Bible-carrying traditionalist; a conservative white man if there ever was one. Sherrie's mother on the other hand was a Nichiren Buddhist. Alice started practicing Buddhism when she was in college. A girlfriend of hers had introduced her to the philosophy and taught her how to practice correctly.

"Janet, this is crazy," Alice said the first time her friend pulled her aside and encouraged her to chant with her. "I don't even know what it means."

"Nam means devotion," Janet began to explain. "Myoho means cause and effect or Mystic Law. Renge means lotus flower. And Kyo means sound. So, all together it is devotion to the Mystic Law through sound. Try to say it."

"Nam," Alice began, but abruptly halted as her nerve faltered. She laughed embarrassedly.

"It's okay. This is an entirely different language. You have to take your time and be patient. You'll get it. Practice makes perfect. Let's say it together. Nam-myoho-renge-kyo."

"Nam-myoho-renge-kyo."

"That's great! Perfectly said. Now, just keep repeating it over and over until you feel a waterfall of overflowing joy and energy."

Sherrie's mom, Alice, continued to practice Nichiren Buddhism chanting Nam-myoho-renge-kyo through the rest of her time at college and she continued until the last time I saw her before heading for Wuxi, China.

At 4:00am on the dot every morning, Diane woke up and chanted Nam-myoho-renge-kyo for two hours, then she would recite from the Lotus Sutra. She did this every single day. She was like a machine. I liked that I had joined a family that had a practicing Buddhist. For me it had been about the literature. After I went through all the books on the giant bookshelf, I moseyed over to the slender bookshelf next to the altar where Diane chanted to everyday.

At that point, I had never read anything about philosophy. My cup was empty and ready to be filled. The books I devoured opened up a new way of thinking. Life became no longer about gain and loss, but value. Tasks were no longer just to be accomplished, but to be explored and used as a tool to develop the self. My identity as a human being began to become important. It was a concept that altered the direction of my life significantly and made me take an interest in bouncing out of the country. It was a concept called the sanctity of life.

In a nutshell, the idea is that life has value just by virtue of being life. There is an inherent right to exist and to exist happily and joyfully. It's also a responsibility to protect the sanctity of life from those who would try to deny that sanctity.

"China! Why do you want to move to China?"
"Because that's where the globe stopped."
"What do you mean that's where the globe stopped?"
"I mean, I spun the globe to see where in the world I would travel."
"Why do you want to leave in the first place?" Sherrie's dad asked me.

It was a question that took me off guard. Why did I want to leave? I asked myself. I couldn't understand the question. I was faced with the same question when I returned from China just in time to walk across the stage and receive my high school diploma, the only diploma I have to my name. Why would I not want to leave? I would always answer with that response.

"John," I said to Sherrie's father. "There's just too much in the world to see to not have the thirst to go out and see it. This world's too big; there are too many people on the planet. I want to see everywhere and speak to everyone."
"Quite ambitious, aren't we, young Cecil? Kid, you don't know nothing about the war. They'll chew you up and spit you out, crying back home for us to take you in. Well, that's not going to happen. If

you want to go off on your own, you are more than welcome to do it, but once you leave, you have to make it on your own. Don't come back until you have made it."

"Why do you think I'm going to come back?"

"Because we're your family. You mean to tell me you're not going to come back and visit for the holidays?"

"You are not my family. You're just a nice group of people that took in an orphan black child. There is nothing that will change the fact that I have no family. I am all alone in this world and it's for this reason that I want to set out to discover this large globe. What's the point of reading all these books if I can't go to the locations that are described? I want to see Paris. I want to see Rome. I want to see Russia. I want to see beautiful women who know nothing of the horrors of poverty in America; women who truly believe in the American Dream and are wishing to be captured by a dashing young thing, whisked away back to the States and live happily ever after."

"You've got this very naïve and stupid view of the world," John said. "Things don't work like that, Cecil, in this country or any country. And out of everything you just said, you know what makes me the saddest? The fact that you've said repeatedly that we are not your family. I should've left your ungrateful black ass in the alley 'cause you were on an accelerated path to death."

"Maybe you should've, Old Man"

"How dare you? I get it. You're confused. You have no roots. And as hard as we have tried to provide you with a happy, stable and prosperous environment, you have no idea what evils lie beyond this country."

"Well, that's why I'm leaving so that I can experience these great evils for myself."

"This isn't a funny game you're playing here, Cecil. I will never let you back into this house if you step out. Do you understand what I am trying to tell you?"

"That if I go on my great China adventure, you'll disown me."

"OK, good. I'm glad we're clear on this. And I'm not giving you any money if you get stranded, robbed or sick. You're totally going to be on your own."

"I've always been on my own."

"Hah! See, that's the thing. You think you've done all this shit by yourself. You have no idea how much I maneuvered things to work in your favor. I have given you bodyguards, sent you to a good high school, fed you as much as you want. You have all the newest electronic equipment as soon as it comes out. You are smart and what's worse, I let you into my library and gave you access to the jewels of knowledge. I even talked to you and explained things to you; gave you helpful hints on which books not to waste your time on. I treated you like my son."

"I appreciate the help you have given me."

"No, you don't. If you did appreciate it, you wouldn't be doing this to us. Why are you being so selfish?"

This unproductive conversation developed into a heated argument that ended with John slapping me in the face, knocking me down onto a glass table with me needing several stitches. When I was finally leaving the hospital after the whole crazy episode was over, John didn't say a word to me. He drove me to the ER as my leg was gushing. The artery had severed and thanks to a last-minute emergency surgery, I didn't bleed to death.

"That was damn close, Son," the doctor said to me after it was done. "But you're patched up and good to go. If it weren't for your father's quick thinking there may not have been a chance for you to survive."

"He's not my father," I said to the doctor.

On the drive back, silence overtook the two of us. I had nothing to say to John. As far as I was concerned, he was a nonexistent entity, a person I had cut off and would never speak with again pending some civil order or other thing where we were contractually obligated or if my life and his life and the lives of thousands of others depended on our working together. Those rare and extreme circumstances are the only examples of when I would acknowledge the existence of the man who found me in the alley robbing a dead man when I was ten-and-a-half.

"Powerful stuff, ain't it?" Ray asked me.

We had been waiting for his boss, my friend Dave, for a long time now. The sun was still high and it was beating down on us every minute.

"I don't think you guys should be drinking that in this heat," Janelle said with genuine concern on her face.

"And be sober through this shit, instead? No, I'll pass."
"What do you need to be drunk for?"
"'cause I have a problem."
"It'll be okay" I said to Janelle, trying not to let any divides come between Ray and us. "Let me have another swig."

I took back the canteen and cringed inside as I drank down the gasoline.

"Stuff's basically useless now. Everything runs on fucking computers. If it uses gas, it has electrical shit in it."
"That's not true," Janelle said.
"It used to not be true. Now it's as true as that pretty little thing you got tucked between those luscious thighs."

I darted my eyes at Ray. He was already looking at my own. Silence engulfed us as the wind gusted, throwing sand everywhere.

"My apologies," Ray finally said, nodding.
"And to Janelle?"
"I am sorry."
"Thank you."
"Why don't you let me have that drink back, Cecil?"

"Quid pro quo," Ray said.
"What? I asked confused.

The sun had finally dropped out of the sky and the vicious desert cold breeze was beginning to pick up. A faint blue hue appeared on the horizon where we had been waiting for Ray's boss, my friend Dave, to arrive.

"It's all because of quid pro quo," Ray said continuing with his thread.

"You mean like, I'll scratch your back if you scratch mine?"

"Yeah, basically. After that last election, everything was in shambles. And then, the one we were going to have if the electro bomb hadn't gone off, was looking to bring down the entire Republican Party."

"Now, there just aren't any parties."

"I know. Ain't it ironic, fighting and squabbling over things instead of going for the main source? That's why you have to give it to the coalition. They were able to suppress their egos, group together, come up with a comprehensive plan, execute it, and then have a plan in place for the aftereffects of what they've done to the globe. It's actually quite impressive."

"So you're sympathizing with the enemy now?"

"Cecil, there is no longer an enemy. Now it's just about survival. And who is best to take back control of the world and govern once again? And we're on our way."

"Is that what your boss, the All-knowing, tells you?"

"That sounded dangerously close to a stab at the boss."

"I don't think I disguised it. But at the same time, he's my friend."

"Well, you're going to get the chance to ask all the questions you want to your friend. Here they come now."

Personal Bodyguard

I turned my gaze to the point on the horizon Ray was motioning toward. There was a cloud of dust that seemed to be moving toward us. At first I thought it was an optical illusion and then I started thinking about the genie from Aladdin and that whole story. Of course, all I saw was the Disney movie with Robin Williams doing the voice. I had read *The Arabian Nights* at some point during the seven years from ten to seventeen when I lived with Sherrie and her family. I watched Aladdin during those seven years, too. Most of my adolescent fun things happened with Sherrie's family. The time before that, those first ten years, were something I never wanted to relive again.

Thinking of Aladdin made me think how great it would be if I had a genie that could grant me three wishes. The first wish I'd make was that everything would go back to normal, back to this past Memorial Day in September 2016 – I didn't even know what date it was any more at that point. I figured it was close to New Year's 2017, but maybe I'd lost count somewhere between hitting my head in the bunker, being drafted into the military and brainwashed to obey, wandering the highways after finishing up basic training with Janelle who also was fucked up from the training and the Press Secretary on our first mission, getting ambushed by bandits and watching the Press Secretary die from a bullet to her stomach. I'm sure I lost track during the time following the Press Secretary's murder when I lost my mind and Janelle protected me in a motel suite. Then, after recovering, finally making it to Washington DC and delivering the letter from the Press Secretary, thus accomplishing my first mission. A coup d'état takes place in the White House conducted by a terrorist group led by my best friend, Dave, with no allegiance to anyone or anything. Then the kidnapping happened and the car crash and the second kidnapping and now this waiting. After having endured all of this, I was ready to have my questions answered. Or poof, go back to the beginning.

My second wish for the genie if I had three wishes would be that this never happened and never would happen. The reality of life after the electro bomb is that it all could have been avoided if nations respected one another's right to exist and leaders had protected the sanctity of their citizens' lives. If we had just protected human life, we would never have fallen to this point. Poor people were pushed down so far that it actually united them and made them see that power is the weakest force of all. It so depended upon a single source that is so large and all-encompassing that it's unable to be protected. All they had to do was turn off our lights and we couldn't survive. The coalition is used to fighting in the dark. We're the ones who outgrew our night vision 'cause we left the village for the big city and forgot to bring wealth back to the 'hood.

My final wish was that I could take Janelle back with me to the beginning, this past Memorial Day. As I sat there going through my make-believe wish list waiting for Dave to reach us, I realized that I was in love with Janelle. The shock of this was overwhelming, but I couldn't understand why. It made sense. We had been in the closest proximity for months. We had experienced death, had our lives threatened constantly and protected one another when the other was helpless. We did all this together. We'd shared the memories of our lives. I had apparently shared my subconscious thoughts in my dreams. And now we were here, about to find out what was to happen next. A small part of me, the exhausted part, was hoping that Dave would just put a bullet in both our brains.

But, unfortunately, we weren't so lucky.

The steam-powered Range Rover slid to a halt as the dust cloud it had caused began to settle. There was the feeling of hundreds of prickles hitting my bare eyeballs as the sand granules scratched the irises of those stupid enough to have kept their eyes open during the grandly overdue entrance.

Dave opened the driver-side door and hopped from behind the steering wheel. The passenger-side opened and out stepped Akeem, the pipe bomb maker from Hales Franciscan.

The two of them walked over to where we stood. Akeem looked exactly the same as he did back in high school. It was simply stunning. His body was adult, his voice was adult, but his face seemed to be perpetually young.

"I see you've got the magic elixir, Akeem," I said extending my hand and embracing him in long-time no-see fashion.
"Can say the same about you, Cecil."

I said, "Hey," to Dave and got right to it.

"So what the fuck is this all about!"
"Well," Akeem started to say.
"Wait," Dave interrupted him. His gaze had caught the boot of the third stooge Ray had killed. His body had been buried well by Pete, but during the time we had waited, the wind had shifted the sands until the boot was revealed. It also probably had a lot to do with the way Dave rolled up super swift in the steam-powered Range Rover. "What the hell happened to him?" Dave asked both Pete and Ray.

Neither said a thing. I inched my way back over to Janelle and put my arm around her waist and held her near me. She leaned into me and seemed to let go of a breath she had been holding for some time.

"Am I going to have to ask again?" Dave asked the two of them.

I must admit that it was nice to watch these two of the three goons that had kidnapped us from the car accident scene that was the aftermath of the first kidnapping, be treated like underlings.

'cause that's all they really were. I felt sort 'a bad for Ray. But once you pick your way, it is what it is.

"I guess so," Dave said answering his own question. "What happened to him?"

"Why?"

"Because he wasn't being cooperative and complying with your instructions to not hurt this man. I was only trying to serve you, Sir."

"So, you shot him?"

"Yes, Sir."

"Well now, that's quite unfortunate for you. This is my top general's cousin. I can't tell him that his little cousin is dead; not now; not with what we are about to launch. I appreciate your willingness to ensure that my orders were carried out, but your defense can't cause a disturbance in the unbreakable organization I have put in place. Does that make sense?"

"Yes, Sir. It does. I had no idea that it would affect the general, Sir."

"If someone put a bullet in your cousin's head, would it affect you?"

Ray seemed to really consider my friend Dave's question seriously. It was apparent how much respect Ray had for Dave. It was easy for me to understand. I had always respected Dave. Dave was my best friend since I was twelve years of age. We met at that horrible private school I had to attend before high school after Sherrie's dad found me in the alley robbing a man whose head had just been blown off.

"Would it affect you?" Dave repeated the question.

"Yes, Sir. It most certainly would."

"So you didn't think, 'cause I know you knew who his cousin is—everyone knows who his cousin is—and everyone knows that he was in our organization because of his cousin. His cousin knew he was a moron. Shit, he knew himself that he was an idiot. His cousin wanted him in our organization to keep him safe. In this after-the-electro bomb world everyone needs protection. Especially idiots like you just killed over there."

"I hate to be the person that's going to have to tell the general his cousin was killed," Akeem said, breaking his silence.

"Must we tell him?" Dave asked seeking his council.

"I'm afraid so. They were close. The general made his cousin report to him every evening, or report that he'd be unable to report for that evening when he was away on missions."

"So what you're saying is, by the end of this evening, the general is going to know something is up with his cousin."

"And then he's going to come directly to you to try and find him."

"So we let that happen. Then what happens?"

"Depends on what you say."

"What can I say?"

"Well, you can stall. Stalling's always nice 'cause it gives us till morning to create something."

"A scenario from an alternate reality."

"There you go."

"What's the activity been like in this area?"

"Same as normal. Not too much, but there have been a few incidents with bandits."

"I've heard rumors there's supposed to be a main base of operations around here somewhere. A safe place for bandits to sleep is how I've heard it described. Has such a place actually been confirmed?"

"Yes, as a matter of fact there is a bandit hideout not too far from here."

"Ok, let's employ their help."

"Bandits don't like us, sir," Ray interjected, for reasons I don't know why.

Dave slapped five fingers sternly across his face.

"We are having to take the time to create all this because of you. It's for your benefit that we're not going to tell the general that it was you who killed his cousin. If we did that, what do you think the general would do?"

"Kill me."

"Now that you're caught up, shut the fuck up unless I talk to you!"

"Sir."

"How were you thinking of employing them," Akeem asked, once Ray tucked his tail between his legs and he and Pete were told by Dave to wait in the steam-powered Range Rover.

"Burn one of our informant bandits we've been holding. Once we've squeezed everything we need out, make sure it's noticeable. Get them out of their hideout. Put the bodies of these three fucks in there. And then launch a retaliation that the general can lead."

"Splendid. When do you want us to receive the information that the three henchmen were ambushed by bandits? You can send the Morse code out as soon as we get back to base. One good thing about the electricity being gone is there's no way to communicate directly from the field. Morse Code can only be done in a set place."

"How do you want it phrased?"

"When we arrived, we found the three henchmen executed by bandits. We halted the execution of the prize package plus one-- that's the two of you--and then tracked the fleeing bandits to their hideout at this location. Give the latitude and longitude then send it over to the general, Priority One. Extend our condolences and that we place full command into his hands."

"Sounds good. Shall we?" Pete said removing a pistol from the holster at his side.

"Let's begin," Dave said, removing the one from his holster.

Janelle and I watched as the two walked to either side of the Range Rover, opened the right and left back doors and fired shots inside, executing the two.

After disposing of Ray and Pete's bodies. Dave and Akeem told Janelle and I to hop into the backseat where the dead men had been. The steam-powered Range Rover was started and off we went.

"How is it that this car's electrical components didn't short out in the electro bomb?"

"'cause this car is from a country where there was no electro bomb. You should see it, Cecil. These poor nations now are the sole suppliers of resources and the First World can't hold power over their heads and take what they want. Now, everyone's got to pay the same and everyone gets the same."

"Somehow I don't believe that's true," I said as Janelle and I bounced up and down, around and around, in the back seat of the Range Rover.

"You will have to see it to believe it, I guess. But you will see it, very soon."

"How so?" Janelle asked Dave.

"Well, now that brings me to something I wanted to ask both of you."

"What would you like to ask us, Dave?"

"I have a proposition for you ... of sorts."

"Of sorts? Is this the reason we've been kept alive until now?" I asked

"Yes, it is, indeed, depending on your answer it will determine whether you live or die."

"But of course, it will. It wouldn't be any other way, would it?"

"I'm afraid not, my old friend."

"So, what's your proposition?"

"Well. I would like the two of you to join the team."

"I figured it was something like that," I said. "But you know, we are at something of a disadvantage because we don't know a damn thing about you."

"Yes, I am fully aware of that. However, you understand, given the nature of our operations, the organization doesn't divulge, well, anything to anyone at any time."

"How do your people work if they don't have information?" Janelle asked.

"Well, the majority of them are following blindly. After 9/11 and the overall violence and fear that are plaguing humanity, people were grasping for stability, a community that people could gather strength from and use as a platform to bring out undeveloped ideas and help them express those ideas in a way that reaches a maximum population. Now, following the electro bomb, there has been an influx of rogue bandit groups springing up all over the First World nations. Murders and rapes are rampant. There is no longer a local police force. There is just the military and they are focusing all of their energies on providing the First World Coalition with protection."

"The Coalition is gearing up to attack?"

"Honestly, they don't know what the fuck the Coalition is doing."

"Dave, where is the President?"

"Ah, I see you're finally starting to connect it all together."

"Bit by bit. But fill me in on that, at least."

"The President is safe and sound. His family is safe, too."

"Why did you kidnap him?" Janelle asked.

"To protect him. He was unaware that this whole attack took place because the White House was infiltrated to the point of collapse. No one knows how or why because all trace of the scheme was erased when the electro bombs went off. We know it was a systematic, disciplined and tenacious attack, geared to do exactly what it has done. In the words of John Galt, Stop the motor of the world. Only in this instance, the motor could be stopped by flipping off the light switch."

"Who is John Galt?" Janelle asked.

"Ayn Rand. *Atlas Shrugged*," I responded.

"Oh, I see. That thick book," Janelle said.

"Yeah, stupid thick. I still have your copy, come to think of it," Dave said.

"You've got lots of my books."

"Well, if you join the team you can get them all back."

"I still need to know more, Dave. You know me. What the hell's going on?"

"Ok, I suppose a little bit of info can't hurt nobody."

I saw Akeem, who was driving, look over at Dave in the passenger seat, twisted around talking to us. His look said he greatly disagreed.

"It'll be ok, Akeem," Dave said, brushing off our friend's caution. "Ok, I can tell you just this." Dave seemed to consider how to begin. "Do you remember after Akeem's pipe bomb exploded in high school and he got taken away by the FBI?"

"How could I forget that? That commotion lasted until I left for China."

"It continued after you left as well," Akeem chipped in. "They had me bouncing around all over the United States in different holding facilities. They tortured me and tried hard to get information out of me. They were convinced that I was working for terrorists and that I had a trove of valuable information in my brain that they just had to get at."

"And then, what eventually happened?" I asked.

"They realized what I, my lawyers, my parents and everyone in the media was saying all along. That I was just a troubled kid who wanted to blow up his school because he was dissatisfied with life. By the time they let me out though, I was a fucking mess."

"Yeah," Dave jumped in. "I kept in contact with Akeem and Japedo the entire time you were in China and even when you came back and worked at the Fairmont Hotel making beds and cleaning up rich people's waste."

"Thanks," I said looking at Janelle and feeling a twinge of embarrassed self-deprecation come over me.

"No problem," Dave responded, feigning oblivion.

"Why didn't you tell me you were still hanging out with Akeem and Japedo? I'm the one who introduced you to them."

"You are, indeed, and I'm grateful for it. But, you weren't trying to hang out with anyone, Cecil. You kept to yourself and would only hang out if I showed up at your apartment with a bottle of bourbon and Nas's Illmatic CD."

"You still listen to CD's?" Janelle asked.

I couldn't see how, given the enormity of the tragedy happening and our survival depending on accepting a proposal to join Dave's organization—which I wasn't even sure was good or bad yet— that Janelle could care that I still used CD's. The entire scene was very perplexing.

"I figured you barely wanted to see me, so I didn't want to impose."

"Well, you could've at least let me know."

"We all agreed it best not to overly stress you. I gave them updates on your condition. We were all very worried about you."

"What happened to you?" Janelle asked. "It sounds like you were in the midst of depression or something."

"Oh, she doesn't know you were married?" Dave asked both me and Janelle.

"No, I know about that. But I didn't know you were an alcoholic mess. It's such a difference from the man you are right now."

"He's still an alcoholic," Dave put in for good measure.

"We're all alcoholics," Akeem added from the driver's seat.

"You two had been divorced for a while when you came back from China, right?" Dave asked, trying to continue on with why he failed to tell me he had kept in touch with two of my oldest friends. He was also conveniently not talking about the team he wanted Janelle and I to be a part of.

"Yes, I was a mess and, yes, I was an alcoholic. Not any more though. Haven't really had much to drink since the electro bomb as a matter of fact."

"Well that's not good," Dave said, taking out a flask that was identical to the one Ray and I had shared before he received a bullet for putting a bullet in the henchman, Marvin.

Dave handed me the flask and I happily took a sip. As the liquid warmed my belly, I felt my abs relax and my breathing begin to calm. It's always after the liquor hits that I realize I was in the midst of or still in the middle of an anxiety attack. I passed the flask to Janelle who took a few sips before passing it back to Dave. The flask was handed to the driver Akeem and he sipped while driving. Dave finished off the flask and then threw it out the window of the speeding steam-powered Range Rover.

"So much for that. The last piece of the henchman, Ray; never to be remembered and so easily forgotten," Dave said, smiling as if he had just said something clever.

"You know the man you killed, Ray, was actually a pretty good guy. When the other guy Marvin, lost his mind and started to stop following your orders, it was Ray who prevented him from causing us any harm."

"Yes, I know. Ray was a good guy. He'd been a henchman for a while. It was an unfortunate thing to have happened. But you know once the doors been pulled open, the light's coming in, no matter what you do. You can close it so no more gets in, but it doesn't matter, 'cause it's in."

"So that's why you killed him?" I asked.

"Had to be done."

"And if I, we, choose to not join, you're going to kill us the same way?"

Akeem stomped his foot on the Range Rover's brakes and the vehicle came to a skidding halt. I heard a gun cock and watched as Akeem pointed a pistol squarely in my face.

"Unfortunately, my dear friend, and his beautiful woman. Yes, I will kill you in exactly the same way."

It was a lot to think about. I was happy that Janelle didn't say otherwise when Dave called her my beautiful woman. She was beautiful and I did hope she was mine, but then this got me thinking about living. If I were to be killed now, after all of this, it made everything that's happened since the electro bomb seem like one big waste. What was this all leading to? What was the point? And the Press Secretary's made me promise with her last breath to save the world. She said only I could do it and she trained me to do it, but I just couldn't blindly agree.

"How long before we arrive at our destination?" I asked thinking of whatever I could to not answer right away.

"Hah! You're gonna try and stall this? For what purpose?"

"I just need time to think. It's not like I even know whose side you're on."

"I already told you. I'm on neither side."

"Yes, I know that. But what side of morality are you on?"

"Ah, morality."

"Still not believing in morality? Even after all these people you've killed?"

"Cecil, morality is just a word, principles concerning the distinction between right and wrong or good and bad behavior. You're a Buddhist. You know such things don't exist. You know there just is."

"Is what?" Janelle asked David.

"Is happening at the moment its being observed."

"What is the 'it'?" Janelle asked Dave.

"Cecil would call the 'it' Nam-myoho-renge-kyo. Wouldn't you, Cecil?"

"I would," I responded. It was true. "But your whole argument is all twisted up."

"How is it twisted?"

"Well, for one, you don't chant, so it's all just theory for you. How can you be objective if you've never even done the damn thing?"

"Now, you know, I've done the thing."

"Not necessarily true, but I won't contradict you. Anyhow, what side are you on, Dave?"

"The side of justice, of course."

"Ok, that's all I needed to know. Did you know the Press Secretary?"

"Look at this guy, using his brain," Dave said to Janelle. He had a smile on his face that took me back to the days long ago when David, Japedo, Akeem and I would play Goldeneye on the Nintendo 64 while eating pizza and drinking coke.

As the Range Rover raced across the desert to who knows where, the four of us lapsed into silence. Akeem drove, Dave sat in the passenger seat and drifted off to sleep, and Janelle had her head in my lap and was trying to sleep as I rubbed her hair. Looking out the window as the ground zoomed past, I thought of many things...too many things:

What have I agreed just now to do and why is it that if I chose not to join we would be killed? How in the hell did Dave even put all this together and this whole question of whether or not morality is important or should be considered part of an archaic and forgotten time that needs to stop being applied to today's society in hopes that it will give children a chance to grow up big and strong and maybe one day be able to oppose those things that are being put in place trying their best to shut them down? That's what the Coalition has shown with what they did versus any other revolution with the exception of when the initial electro bomb went off and there were a few planes that crashed and then it is tragic that there were a number of households that caught fire and people were electrocuted and other such things, but for the most part the Coalition carried out a rational and highly detailed movement to shut down the power of the First World. And they did it. All other revolutions have been many times more bloody and they weren't even successful and if there was ever a moment in a time such as this that needs to be recorded, this will be forever remembered as the moment in history where the shift took place and those standing up to take the reins will decide the next two decade's direction and that is both amazing and great, but that is also scary. If you ask me, there's no reason to look back and this is how and why we need to try our best to create a unified mind that will enable us to collectively overtake the evils seemingly engulfing our entire beings. That would be such an amazing feat; to be able to look people in the eye and not fear for your life, but right now, we are the farthest from that reality that we've ever been.

Janelle stirred in my lap. I guess she had been sleeping. She nuzzled her face deeper into my crotch and woke her new friend and my longtime companion. I wasn't as embarrassed as I had been at other times and continued to watch the desert pass by. When I couldn't grow any more, the strain of my pants and Janelle's head in my lap began to cause a slight ache. I heard her breathing return to a sleeping pace and enjoyed the feeling of having a woman that I had fallen in love with in my lap.

Dave woke with a yawn and pulled out three Newport cigarettes from a pack on the dash. He lit all three and took a drag. Keeping one in his mouth. Dave grabbed the other two in both hands. Extending his left hand in Akeem's direction, he offered the square to him. Akeem happily obliged. Taking his time, Dave turned in the passenger seat toward me and offered me the other burning Newport.

"How's she doing?" Dave, softly said.
"Think she's ok. Been through quite a lot," I responded through drags. Man, it felt good to smoke a cigarette. Now, I just needed more of that liquor that was in Ray's flask, may he rest in peace, I thought to myself.
"We've all been through a lot."
"Yeah, and you caused a lot of what we're going through right now."
"Now, that's not fair, Cecil."
"Why isn't it fair, Dave? You kidnapped us. Twice. Three times if you count this one."
"No we're not going to call this one a kidnapping. You joined the team. This is an escort to Headquarters."
"Dave, seriously, what did I just join up for?" I asked, flicking the spent Newport out of the back window of the speeding Range Rover.
"I can't go into any more details than I already have, my friend."
"You've barely gone into any details. You just said you're fighting for justice. Lots of people say they are fighting for justice.

Hell, lots of people even believe they are fighting for justice when, in fact, they are only feeding their own inner selfish tendencies."

"And that's what you think I'm doing?"

"I don't know what the fuck you're doing! You won't tell me."

"You should keep your voice down, Cecil. You'll wake your woman."

"Her names, Janelle," I said starting to get irritated.

"Do you want another cigarette? You seem to be getting irritated?"

"Don't patronize me. You owe me, Man. Tell me what's going on."

"How do you figure I owe you?"

"Who bailed you out of jail when you got arrested for drunk driving?"

"You did."

"And who convinced his stepdad to use his contacts to have the case expunged from your record?"

"You did."

"And who took you in and let you stay in my small-ass studio apartment when you lost everything in a damn poker game?"

"Well, you did that partially because you were depressed and lonely after you got the divorce. But, yes, you did. Do you still speak to her at all, by the way?"

"Who? Chelsea? Hell, no!"

"Just asking. No need to get defensive."

"I wasn't getting defensive. Just answering aggressively."

"You let her really do a number on you, huh?"

"Yeah, Man," I reluctantly said to Dave. "I let her all the way in. I guess I was just too young to be able to handle the torment that was happening inside."

"Well, she didn't help any; always getting angry; always interpreting what you said in the most negative of ways. I couldn't believe when we were out eating that one day and she threw her glass of wine in your face. All because you said she was becoming rather demanding. I know you meant it as a joke and I know you would never disrespect your wife on purpose."

"Could we not talk about this?"

"Yeah, sorry. Just that dinner was shocking to me. I couldn't believe she was so irritable all the time."

"She was going through a lot. It wasn't all her fault, I was going through a lot, too. So we just weren't in a position to support each other. We could barely support ourselves. I was just too weak to be able to see that and then admit it. She was a great woman; just horrible circumstances and I was too messed up. I tell you, I wish I had met her at the airport and begged her not to leave me."

"Don't say that. Look at how your life blossomed after you divorced."

"My life didn't blossom. It spiraled down into a horrible abyss of suffering and pain. I fled to China again. Got more depressed. Returned to Chicago and sat in a stupor until that job in Japan jumped off. That job probably saved my life. And then I even tried again to fall in love."

"That's the one that fell apart on you, right?"

"They all fall apart. Over and over I replayed that last night in the club when my entire heart disintegrated and I felt like jumping in front of a train."

"Well I'm glad you didn't. What I meant was that you survived it and then started working for the Press Secretary. You can't tell me that working for that woman wasn't an awesome time."

Janelle woke in my lap and sat upright in the back seat.

"Morning," she said.

"Morning," Dave said back. "How'd you sleep?"

"About as comfy as can be speeding through the Nevada desert to get to some location no one is telling Cecil or me anything about," Janelle replied.

"Glad you got some rest," Dave responded, nodding his head. "I'll leave you two to some privacy. We still have quite a ways to drive."

"How is this car still running? Should we have had to take a stop and refill it with, what, water?" I asked.

"It's not necessary. Do you remember all the rain from the other night? That was enough to ensure that this car will be able to last us for as long as we need to drive. We'll probably have half a tank when we arrive."

"How is that even possible?" I asked Dave.

"Cecil, enjoy the ride and talk to your woman. I'm done talking to you. I'm tired, Man. Leading a revolution is exhausting. Especially when you're fighting against both sides."

"Thought you said you were on the side of justice."

"I am. Neither side is with me though."

"So whoever's with you is with justice?"

"No. I am with justice. If you're with me you're not fighting for me. You're fighting for justice."

"But who determines this justice?"

"Humanity," Dave answered.

"How do you know what humanity wants?"

"You know, this conversation is becoming a little annoying," Janelle chipped in, breaking the monotony of the philosophical banter Dave and I were engaged in.

"I concur." With that said, Dave turned around and went back to sleep.

Silence did its thing for a time as Janelle and I listened to the Range Rover bounce its way toward what Dave said was Headquarters.

"How long was I out?" Janelle asked.

"I'm not sure, couple of hours. Did you sleep ok?"

"Yea, it was alright. Felt you getting hard."

"Sorry about that," I said, embarrassed.

"It's ok. It was nice."

"Did you have any nice dreams?" I asked, trying to change the subject away from my penis poking Janelle in the head. The thought did little to relax me.

"Actually, yeah, I had a crazy dream."

"What was it about?"

"Well, I don't remember much of it. There was a school and I was a student. The rest of the students were elementary age, so I assume I was, too. You were there, but you were a little boy. I barely recognized you, but it was this glint in your eye that shined every time you smiled. It's the same thing that I see when you smile at me. The bell to start class rang and we were running late."

"Me and you?" I asked.

"Yes. I think we were flirting by the lockers."

"We were flirting?"

"Yeah, of course, if I was going to be dreaming about you, I would see you as my romantic interest. When we made it into the classroom at the bell we took our seats. Mine was in the back and yours was in the front. I think that's because you talked a lot in class."

"Why do you say that?" I asked laughing.

"Because after a point you started talking and the teacher scolded you and you were sent out."

"I'm not liking where this dream is going."

"It gets better."

"I can't wait."

"After you left, the class continued."

"What class was it?"

"I really don't remember. I didn't pay attention to all of that because of what was in my desk."

"What was in your desk?"

"A dead cat."

"What the fuck?"

"Yes, a dead cat. It seemed like it was run over by a car, but it was fresh."

"What do you mean fresh?"

"It was still gooey. When I put my hands in my desk to pull out my notebook after you were dismissed from the classroom, I felt the cold wetness of the cat's blood and the minced flesh of its squished body. I let out a horrible scream.

Water poured forth from the giant faucet leading into the cave. We stood at the giant iron fence circling around the hole that seemed to be endless in depth.

"Took us months to dig this."

"I don't understand," I said shaking my head. Looking away from the cave I turned to Dave. "What are you doing?"

"Creating water reserves for the future."

"Why?"

"Because water has become the new currency my friend, Cecil. It hasn't quite hit the sweet spot of the economy yet, but soon, it will. Right now, the two coalitions are trying to come to terms for an agreement. After that, the damage will be assessed and a standard of living will be reached. Eventually, it'll all balance out."

"How do you balance this out?"

"Well, you don't balance it out. What I mean is, unbalance will be balanced. It's not a solution. It's more of a let's reach homeostasis so that we can continue living from day to day. Once that happens, then everyone's going to realize that water is the most valuable treasure we possess. The main problem is purifying it," Dave began to explain as he led Janelle and me into the headquarters of The Flawed.

"Why is purification a problem?"

"Because we ain't got no power and the amount of water we'll need to purify on top of the sheer need to have healthy drinking water is going to create a panic that no one's going to see coming."

"Except you," I said.

"Has to be someone. We've developed a purification technique that uses the sun to clean water of the harsh chemicals in it. What's crazy is that the technology has been around forever. Well, forever by millennial standards. They were just sitting on this and hundreds of other technologies that use solar energy and have no electrical components. They planned for every contingency and let popular opinion determine what was developed aggressively and that was shelved as a great idea, but not necessary. Given our current Dark Age, I bet there's a lot of United States officials kicking themselves for that now."

"The grass is always greener, I guess," I said.

"There ain't going to be no green grass or grass at all in not too much longer, Cecil. This is what our organization is about. This is how we fight for justice: by defending the future. You see, we've been tracking the United States infrastructure and technological development for a long time. We're the ones that made the drones capable of dropping electromagnetic bombs on specific targets."

"The United States created that?" Janelle asked as we climbed into an elevator leading to the top floor.

"Yes, of course, we created that. We create everything that's great at destruction."

"Well then, how did the Coalition get their hands on it?" "Stole it?" I asked.

"No. It was easier than that. We sold it to them."

Both Janelle and I stood stunned and silent as the elevator made its way up.

"Of course we sold it to them," Dave continued. "The United States knew about the damn coalition before it even got started. I've heard actual tapes from top officials talking about how the nations were beginning to gather together."

"Wait, how do you know all of this stuff?" Janelle asked

"I already told you I'm not gonna talk about any of that."

"But then, how do you expect us to trust you?" Janelle asked.

"By virtue of you being in this elevator means you trust me," Dave responded. "You all joined up. There's no going back now. It's the same option as before: either you are in or you are dead. It's your choice and you made it. So now live with the decision."

"I never said I wasn't going to live with the decision," Janelle said. "But I do want to know how in the hell you know so much."

"Janelle does have a point, Dave. You're asking for a lot and we've gone alone with it. We are going to go along with it. But you haven't given us shit in terms of information. Just give us a little so we can feel good about something; make us feel like we are part of the team. I don't even understand what the team is, what it does, who is on the team and what the hell Janelle and I will be doing as new members of this team."

The elevator dinged as the doors slid open. We walked off the elevator.

"You guys are perfect for each other," Dave said after he showed us to his office on the top floor of the building that was The Flawed organization's headquarters.

"Can I get either of you something to drink?"

"I thought water was the new currency," snapped Janelle.

"Oh, very soon it will be. But even then, we'll have control of the majority of the supply. The goal is to own all the water in the world."

"But people can continue to produce clean water. It will just take more time."

"That's very true, Cecil. That is why we are going to poison the remaining supplies."

"That's crazy. You're going to kill thousands, probably millions of people. How can you call yourself a fighter for justice? You're just a thug. No different than those three henchmen you killed earlier today."

"For the record, I only killed two. It was Ray who killed Marvin and made us have to waste a lot of time designing the story that we could tell his cousin. But, I understand what you mean. Yes, I am a killer. But I am not a cold-hearted killer. I am a very calculating, patient and smart killer. I'd go so far as to say brilliant."

"Aren't we patting ourselves on the back quite nicely? Too nice," Janelle said. She let out a sigh and closed her eyes. I took that as meaning she was turning her attention away from this conversation.

"What happened to Akeem?" I asked, exasperated.

"He went to take care of the story we put together."

"I see. That makes sense. What does he do in the organization?"

"We don't discuss one another's functions in the organization."

"Of course not, Dave. How the hell am I supposed to do anything? Am I going to get any kind of briefing or anything like that?"

Dave slid a brown folder over to me that he pulled out of a drawer in the desk where he sat.

"There you go, Sherlock. Your first mission. Take your woman and this file and I'll show you to your barracks."

"Our barracks?"

"Yes, where did you think you were going to live?"

"Honestly, I hadn't thought that far ahead. I was still waiting on information from my friend, Dave."

"Well then, its good your friend Dave went on ahead and prepared everything for you."

"How'd you know we'd make it to this point? How'd you know I'd agree to join your little organization? That's looking to be more and more like a terrorist group bent on stroking your overbearing ego."

"Because I know you, Cecil. Plus, this was the Press Secretary's instruction to me."

"You never told me how you knew the Press Secretary."

"I haven't told you a whole lot of nothing. So, I know I never told you anything about the Press Secretary. But, since we're friends and you have been through a whole lot, I will let you know about my relationship with the Press Secretary."

Dave leaned back in his swivel chair and pulled out a new pack of Newport's. After removing the cellophane and tossing me a square, he pulled out the Zippo I bought for him and Pandy and lit mine first, then his. We sat in his office on the top floor taking drags and filling the room with smoke. Janelle didn't stir so I assumed she was still asleep.

As the silence wafted around the room, intermingling with the smoke, I started to think about how it was amazing that two people who didn't know each other, given the correct circumstances, could fall into a pattern and in love and now Janelle was my woman. I wasn't even sure if I wanted a woman. But here you go; I got one. The little ticks and pulls of my heart over the years had left me drained before the electro bombs went off. In a lot of ways, there was a saving grace to the power outage and spending all that time in the bunker. It was like being a caterpillar and then turning into a butterfly. However, I didn't quite feel like anything as elegant as a butterfly. And if I did, I felt like one that had been pimped.

"This is bullshit, I just have to say," I said abruptly to Dave.

"Whatever do you mean?" he asked snubbing out his cigarette in the glass ashtray on the desk.

Dave slid it over to me and the sound of the glass scrapping against the oak desk woke Janelle.

"There's so much smoke in this room. Can you open the window?" she asked Dave.

"Sure thing. Quite demanding, aren't we?"

Dave rose from the swivel chair and walked over to the window behind where he sat. He opened the window and the cold evening air swept in. I watched as the clouds of smoke that had gathered at the ceiling crept out the open window.

"Is there anything else I can do for you, Madam?"

"Something to drink if you don't mind," Janelle answered.

"Ah yes, the water. I was just about to get you all some when Cecil distracted me with quite an intriguing question. Tom!" Dave yelled out.

"Sir," a bellowing voice responded from the other side of the closed door to Dave's office.

The door opened and a large man dressed in all black tactical gear and a black ski mask appeared.

"Do you mind getting these two some water."

"Clean or dirty, Sir."

"Clean. These are our distinguished guests. My good friend, Cecil. And his wife, Janelle."

"Pleased to meet you. I'll just be a moment," the solider said before exiting and closing the door behind him.

I didn't feel like correcting Dave about me and Janelle not being married. Janelle didn't say anything either, so I figured she was cool with it.

"Now, back to your question. The Press Secretary is an old family friend."

"I never knew that."

"Why would you? You know how large my family is."

"That is true. Every time I would come over to your parents' to hang out with you, there'd be another new cousin or uncle to meet. How many were there in all? I remember meeting like ten."

"I have twenty-two uncles."

"How do you have twenty-two uncles?" Janelle asked.

"And one niece," Dave continued. "Both my of parent's parents were married three times each. Each marriage had at least two kids. I think you met two of the uncles. I am pretty sure I had just met them for the first time that day, too. The Press Secretary was dating one of these uncles, very briefly. But she was liked by everyone, just like she always was. So, after they broke up, my mother continued to invite her to family festivities."

"Ah, I miss you all's block parties. That was the first time I ever got drunk."

"How old were you?" Janelle asked.

"Ten or something, I think."

"Yeah, I think that's about right. You were something else. I think that's the only time my mother was angry with you."

"Yeah, I still feel bad about that to this day."

"She always told the story with a laugh."

"That's even worse. Who did she tell the story too?"

"Everyone, Cecil. The Press Secretary, too. My mother and the Press Secretary were very close. There was something of a spiritual connection with them. They helped calm each other.

"Come, take a walk with me, Cecil," Dave said after more conversation about his mother's parties and the shenanigans we engaged in as children. A few bits of information were thrown out about the Press Secretary, but nothing worth mentioning to enhance this story. The three bottles of water the solider brought to us at Janelle's request were crushed and sitting in a waste bin by the time Dave abruptly made this statement.

"Janelle," Dave said addressing her. You're welcome to head to your and Cecil's barracks now to rest. There is a full bath and shower and I assure you that you will be doing the chef an honor if you would put him through the ringer as far as the menu is concerned."

"I thought this was supposed to be the Dark Ages," Janelle responded, but I could tell that the thought of a bath peaked her interest significantly.

"It is the Dark Ages, my best friend's Woman. However, that doesn't mean some of us aren't able to maintain a certain level of elegance and comfort," Dave said.

"That sounds exceptionally unfair," Janelle responded.

"It is unfair. I wholeheartedly agree. However, it was also unfair for the First World nations to rape the countries for as long as they did. So, I guess it is, as they say, Move your meat, lose your seat."

"So now you're the one sitting in the seat of power?" Janelle asked Dave.

"No, not yet. But yes, very soon."

"With your poisoning the world's clean water supply and ensuring that you are the world's only major supplier of the most precious resource?" Janelle said, laying out her position.

"You're an incredibly smart woman, Janelle," Dave said. "That is exactly what I am doing. It's amazing how you figured it out so succinctly, even when it seemed like you were just sleeping the entire time Cecil and I were talking."

"Nothing is ever what it seems," Janelle said.

"Yes," Dave said with more excitement than either of us expected. "Then that means, one of you is waiting for the opportune moment to strike me dead."

266

This last sentence shook all rationality from my brain. However, Janelle seemed to pale. Her breathing became noticeably quick and she kept clenching her fist over and over again. Suddenly, in a rush of bursting violence, Janelle sprung upon Dave. Jumping over the large desk, Janelle clasped her hands around Dave's neck and squeezed with all her strength. The two of them tumbled back and hit the ground. Janelle's grip didn't relax. Dave's face began to turn bright pink and slowly fade to purple, which was alarming to watch as I had never seen a white face turn purple and for a moment the whole concept of race and the categories of colors seemed obsolete to me; if a white man can turn purple, then what really was a human being?

This thought was shattered quicker than it was allowed to begin, however. The solider who had politely fetched us three bottles of water at Janelle's request, burst through the office door with an automatic pistol, locked cocked and ready to blow a hole into both me and Janelle, who was strangling Dave with all her strength. I watched him take aim at Janelle. Before I knew it, I had hit him with the chair she had been sitting in before swan diving over the desk and locking her fingers around Dave's windpipe.

The automatic pistol went off as the chair I swung at the solider made contact. It shot up into the ceiling and the recoil provided me enough time to slam my foot into his groin. All that was left was a ridge hand to the throat and the solider dropped to the ground. His eyes bulged as he realized he was dead as he fell.

I knocked the automatic weapon from the dead soldier's hands and checked his pulse. He was dead. When I turned back toward Janelle and Dave, Janelle was doing a similar thing. Dave's face showed that he was dead, too; purple and twisted. I didn't know what to think.

I looked at Janelle. Waiting for her to explain.

"We have to get out of here," she said.

"I'm not going anywhere until you explain what's going on."

"Cecil, we really don't have time for this. Your friend Dave had a tracking device that was to be activated when his heart stops. I'm sure the signal's already been sent and it won't be but a matter of minutes before this place is surrounded and they will shoot us dead."

"You've still got to tell me what's going on."

"Cecil, Baby, I love you. I really do. And the reason I haven't disagreed with you being my man is because you are. But I'm going to need you to trust me and listen to what I'm saying. We have got to get back to that steam-powered Range Rover and get the hell out of here."

"This is just a little bit too much to process."

"Stop being a pussy. You were trained by the Press Secretary. I know what you can do."

"How do you know what I can do?"

"Because I was trained by the Press Secretary," Janelle said knocking away all sense about this parade.

"Everybody was trained by the Press Secretary, it seems," I said, feeling dejected and not as special as I thought I once was.

"No, everybody was not trained by the Press Secretary. Just you, me and Dave over there were the only students she ever had. But truthfully, you were her star student. She told both me and Dave."

"Why did you kill Dave?"

"Baby, not now. We gotta go."

As if providing incentive to further sell her deal, bullets began to fly through the window Dave had opened to let out the cigarette smoke not too many moons ago. We both hit the deck, we felt and heard the whiz of bullets flying overhead. We crawled toward each other. In the span of a few seconds after the barrage of shooting took place, not a sound could be heard. Glass poured from the sky and landed on top of us as we tried hard to protect one another and make it to the office door. We crawled our way outside, with no way of knowing what lay on the other side. The gunfire continued, but we were safely out of the office. We hit the emergency stairs and ran as fast as we could down the never-ending number of flights.

After about five minutes of frantically hopping down steps, a door opened from somewhere below and the footsteps of what sounded like a battalion of soldiers made its way up toward us. With nothing to do but continue gaining distance between us and the enemy, Janelle and I entered the floor that we happened to be on. It was the 57th.

The 57th floor of the organization known as The Flawed was set up to look exactly like a retail department store. All the products, however, looked to be geared toward whatever operations and overall work the organization had been participating in. The array of goodies was astounding. It seemed almost as if Dave had been busy building his own commune and was on his way to forcing the United States to enlist into his vision and live life the way he said it should be lived.

He was dead now, I remember thinking, as we ran our way through the retail store and tried desperately to find a place to hide. Janelle was sure they had heard us open the door and she figured they had the building locked down tight. So all things considered, we were trapped like rats and there wasn't a whole lot we could do about it.

Once we found a good hiding place, we tucked ourselves under a mattress and bedframe that was on display for newly birthed couples. It was a tight fit but we didn't mind squishing our bodies into one another.

We heard the footsteps of the soldiers as they searched for us. After about twenty minutes, it all finally died down and we figured they were busy searching the rest of the building.

"So, this seems like as good a time as any to tell me exactly what the hell is going on," I said to Janelle after about an hour of dead silence had passed.

"Would you keep your voice down? You're going to get us killed. We're barely alive."

"Ain't nobody on this floor? They are looking for us, but they ain't on this floor. They figured this floor is empty. You saw how long they was searching."

"I just don't trust it. They could have left one guy whose job it is to wait just in case we try to escape."

"Isn't that a bit over the top?" I asked feeling like Janelle was just stalling from telling me about what exactly was going on.

"You and I have an entirely different perspective on these things. Our trade crafts are different, just as Dave's was. You're the best rounded of all of us, but we were trained to be good at just one thing."

"And what was that?"

"Mine was tactical and Dave's was strategic. You were the missing link. You were the operator. You're the guy who can do both in the moment. It was the Press Secretary's vision to create a complete team capable of fighting against terrorism, domestic and foreign. It was her hope that the three of us could put a stop to the Coalition's efforts before they got underway. Dave ensured that didn't happen, though."

"What happened to Dave?" I asked. It was all starting to click.

Bit by bit, the Press Secretary had been dropping hints to me about the other two students she had trained. For whatever reason, I was trained last. Dave was trained first. Janelle went on to tell me about how she first linked up with the Press Secretary.

"It was my first day at the American Embassy in London. I hadn't stepped foot off the plane more than a minute when this woman approached me at baggage claim."

I recalled to myself how my own first meeting with the Press Secretary had taken place at a baggage claim. I wondered if Dave's was the first time, but then, I remembered that he had known the Press Secretary for quite some time. He claimed I met her once but I just couldn't recall it. And the Press Secretary never brought it up to me.

"I had mistaken her bag for mine and we shared a joke about it. Afterward, when I was outside waiting for a taxi she strolled up to me. We made small talk and she told me that she was the Press Secretary for the President of the United States.

"What brings you to the capital?" she asked me.

"I'm starting school at UNI," I replied with no reason to lie to as nice and elegant a woman as she seemed to be.

"Oh, how nice. I remember my first entrance into undergraduate school. The butterflies from just being away from my parents were remarkable. Is this your first time to DC?"

"Yes, first time," I responded.

I listened intently as Janelle spoke. The air was growing stale under the mattress where we were trapped, I guess, until Janelle felt it was safe to step out. She continued to tell her story.

"If this is your first time," the Press Secretary said to me. "Then let me take you out to dinner. My treat."

Legacy

Janelle and I cruised in the same Range Rover we had confiscated after Janelle strangled Dave to death. Where we were headed was anyone's guess. I sat silent in the passenger seat for most of the ride. It was a long ride. When we finally arrived at our destination, the sun was high in the sky of the next day. The majority of the night ride I pretended to sleep. I didn't know what to say to Janelle. She had just killed my best friend. It wasn't that I was upset that she had killed him. Dave needed to die. You heard what he was talking about. Craziness.

But Dave was my best friend. How could I excuse the taking of his life? Sitting there while Janelle drove through the dark in the desert, I allowed my mind to process all that had occurred. There was nothing I could do to comprehend the terror that was attacking me at that moment. It was a great test of restraint that I did not open the passenger door and dive out onto the pavement we were driving on at such a fast speed. It wasn't even the question Janelle asked that made me feel the way I did.

"Are you ok?" she asked.

Instead of answering, I sat there and thought about how stupid that question was. I always wondered, when people didn't know what to say they said things that they obviously knew the answer to. Wasn't the point of asking a question to find out something that you didn't know in the first place? If you knew the answer, then why the hell would you be asking questions? But this is coming from a guy who doesn't like to talk much. So, take my words with a grain of salt.

"No, not really," I responded to Janelle, revealing that I had been pretending to be asleep. At that point I couldn't care less whether or not she was upset with whatever the fuck I did. She killed my best friend.

"Do you want to talk about it?"

"Not particularly. Would you want to talk about it if your woman killed your best friend with her bare hands?"

"I suppose, no. I wouldn't care to speak with her.

I had to give her respect for being honest. Interestingly, it helped a lot.

"Well, then, I don't really feel much in the mood to talk at this moment. I know you did what you had to do. You did what I would have probably had to do in the end. But none of that takes away from the fact that you did kill my best friend. So for that reason, you can understand why it is hard for me to just sit here and be cool with everything."

"If you were able to sit here and be cool with everything. I'd be concerned about your mental health," Janelle honestly responded.

"Well, that's good to know. I would hope in spite of me not being able to sit here all collected and copasetic, that you would still be concerned about me."

"Trust me, Cecil. I am very concerned about you. But at the same time, there is a specific mission that we must achieve."

"You know, that seems to be something the Press Secretary left out in her tutelage with me. It seems she only gave you and Dave specific missions."

"Don't you see? That was her way of providing you with freedom."

"What do you mean?"

"By not assigning you a specific mission, the Press Secretary was giving you the option to live your own life, to choose your own path. Do you think I wanted to do this for my life; that I wanted to dedicate my entire existence to a cause that I will never understand? She knew all of this was going to happen a decade ago. When she and I first linked up, she already had the plan in place and I was just a piece in the Grand Master chess game she was playing with good and evil."

"What do you mean, playing a chess game with good and evil?"

"What I mean," Janelle explained, "is that she was on her way to creating the greatest master plan that anyone had ever done."

"What are you talking about, Janelle?"

"This whole electro bomb shit was the Press Secretary's plan. She made all of this happen."

"Why would the one woman who wanted above everything to keep the country together and unite human beings devise a master plan to bring down the very source of power that could provide that care she was so desperately trying to get all nations to adhere to?"

"So that the United Nations would grow a backbone and take control."

"That can't be what this was all about."

"Why not?"

"It just seems way too farfetched. There was nothing that the Press Secretary cared more about than peace. Why would she allow thousands upon thousands of people to die in order to construct a plan that seems absolutely ludicrous to me? I can't imagine that the Press Secretary would even entertain such a thought."

"Shows how little you actually knew about your boss," Janelle said as she navigated the steam powered Range Rover across the Nevada dessert to where I still didn't know.

"What the hell is that supposed to mean?"

"Just what I said. You didn't really know the woman as well as you thought. Between the three of us—you, me and Dave, may he rest in peace—we probably all know something that the other doesn't."

"Well, Dave is no longer in a position to let us know if your little theory is correct. In case you hadn't noticed, he was strangled to death."

"Now, why you gotta go and say mean things like that? After we were off to such a great start. I wonder, do you really want to save the world or not?" Janelle asked point blank and straight up.

"Where are we going?" I asked, ignoring her question.

"It just so happens, we are on our way to the President."

"The President? I thought Dave had him hostage. Or killed him. Honestly I figured him for dead already."

"Well, you would lose a lot of money on that bet. The President is alive and well. And we are on our way to report our mission's success."

"What mission?"

"Take down Dave."

"Why was Dave so important to take down? Besides the obvious, obviously."

"Because Dave was the one who manufactured the drones that committed this evil act of terror that knocked our nation and the globe back into the Dark Ages."

"I take it you're not a fan of the blackout," I said stupidly.

"You're sitting here making jokes at a time like this? Do you know how long I have dedicated myself and how much I have sacrificed to carry out this mission? My orders were given to me directly by the President of the United States before this one. Do you understand what's going on here?"

"Nope, I still don't' get it."

"The Press Secretary was in charge of everything. I don't know how. I don't know why. But the Press Secretary was the one who orchestrated the entire show that was the United States."

"Now you've lost me completely," I said beginning to think that my girlfriend had gone crazy. Then she started to make sense.

"About twenty-five years ago, Antoinette Stalk, the Press Secretary, was privy to some pretty risky footage of the President at the time with a number of his interns engaged in a flamboyant orgy that ranked up there with the Greeks. This footage was priceless. The Press Secretary knew it. The President knew it and the First Lady, who was a participant in the lewd and crude act, knew it too. So the President did what any good man would do. He bargained for his life and he handed over the executive seat to the Press Secretary. It wasn't legal by any means, so they devised a simple machine where the President was the puppet and the Press Secretary was the Queen."

"So the Press Secretary ran the country like Dick Cheney?"

"To a certain extent, yes, you could say that," Janelle replied with a slight shrug of her shoulders.

"How is it that successive presidents afterward adhered to the agreement?"

"The footage was enough to totally destroy the very fabric of our government. Diplomacy as we know it would become a joke if this video was ever released to the public."

"Jesus, how bad is the video?"

"The other reason that everyone allowed the Press Secretary to rule this long was because the majority of the interns went on to become valuable members of parliament."

"Quid pro quo?"

"Exactly."

"Why didn't she tell me any of this?"

"I told you," Janelle replied. "You were the one that wasn't given any mission. Only the Press Secretary knows the answer, but cherish the gift. You were the only one of us three who got to have a life."

"You have a life now. We can have a life, together," I said. I tried to make it sound cool, but it came out all sappy. She huffed at me and chuckled once.

"Let's see if we survive this last part and then start thinking about our futures. Right now, my main priority is reporting our mission's success to the President."

"Why is that so important?"

"Because he is waiting on us, Stupid."

"Why is the President waiting on us?"

"Because this is all part of the Press Secretary's plan."

"I still don't see why the Press Secretary went through all of this in order to just give the country back."

"It's because this President is good. This President will be able to solidify peace."

"But if the Press Secretary didn't set off the electro bombs, we wouldn't be in such a dire need for peace."

"Are you kidding me? There hasn't been a single moment when we haven't been wanting peace. Think back on your life. What was the one wish everyone in the world wanted? What's the one wish everyone has now?"

I thought seriously about the question Janelle.

"To be happy, safe and healthy for self, family and friends."

"That's right. And do you know how that kind of peace is obtained?"

"No, but I'm guessing you're going to tell me."

"By taking it off the choice factor. Submit the human race to such pain that you force unity."

"You're all crazy."

"That's why the Press Secretary didn't give you any specific mission, Cecil. You're meant to make the choice of the path you will take, not have one given to you. You will soon see what was in that letter the Press Secretary had you deliver to the President before he was kidnapped by The Flawed terrorist organization."

The conversation died away. Neither one of us picked it back up again. Eventually we came to a wire fence that stretched across the entire horizon. There was an armed guard and a tank positioned to greet us. Janelle knew all the codes and provided all the credentials.

"The Press Secretary gave them to me as a care package while we were hibernating in the bunker," she told me after we were through the checkpoint and driving to meet with the President of the United States.

We were escorted into a large basketball court once Janelle stopped the Range Rover in front what only could be described as the biggest factory I had ever seen. It stretched for at least three blocks, just sitting there in the middle of the Nevada desert. US military were posted everywhere the eye could see...probably some placed where the orb couldn't see.

"Cecil, it's good to see you made it. Good work keeping him alive, Janelle," the President said embracing us both and inviting us into his makeshift Oval Office.

Once we got seated and were comfortable with glasses of Scotch, I had to come out and say it.

"Mr. President. What the fuck it going on?"

The President looked at me with cold eyes. The silence was thick enough to cut. I thought about, how could one cut silence? I guess it's meant to emphasize the thickness of the absence of noise. Whatever I felt, it was a good phrase to describe what I felt in the makeshift Oval Office in the large gymnasium somewhere in Nevada.

"Well," the President said, finally beginning to speak. "There's no easy way to tell you this and all I know is to be direct. So I'm just gonna' come out and say it."

Those icy eyes of his continued to cut through me.

"Cecil," the President of the United States, who was beginning to seem not too united anymore, continued "It was Miss Antoinette Stalk's final request that you inherit her status as Press Secretary."

The air in my lungs completely escaped.

"This must be a mistake," I said. "There's no way you can expect me to become the Press Secretary to you, Mr. President."

"Why not, Cecil? You were trained directly by Miss Stalk to do this very job. There can be no one else but you that steps in and takes over. I'm going to need you, Cecil, especially now as we try to rebuild not only our nation, but the world as a whole."

"But there's still no electricity. How is there going to be a press? I haven't heard a news report in months."

"We are actually now in the final stages of massive negotiations with the Coalition to determine an agreement to share the planet's harnessed resources."

"Why are we making deals with the Coalition?" I asked.

"Because we have no other choice," the President responded. "We are in a new age, Cecil. Through the efforts of Antoinette Stalk, the world's been forced to confront the problems that have been disrupting humanity's unity since the inception of civilized society. The class system was eliminated thanks to the blackout. Every citizen from every nation has now fallen in status. Ironically, the nations that are thriving are primarily those who know how to survive with minimal resources. We made sure they got very good at it."

"When are you expecting this agreement to be reached?" I asked the President.

"Within the next twenty-four hours, Cecil. That is why I need your answer immediately."

"Can I at least have an hour or two to think all this over? I'd also like to talk to my girlfriend, Janelle, if that's alright with you, Sir."

"That seems reasonable. Yes, we can give you two a room where you can talk.

Cecil?"

"Yes, Sir, Mr. President."

"Time is of the essence. The world is urgently waiting on you. Don't take too long to make you're decision."

"Yes, Sir," I replied.

Those icy eyes continued to cut into me, freezing my heart and slowly killing me softly. We were escorted out of the makeshift Oval Office into a barracks that was no bigger than a closet. When the door was closed and Janelle and I were alone, we embraced in a much-needed hug of comfort.

"This can't really be happening," I said, as she pulled her arms from around my neck and started to unbuckle my pants. "What are you doing?"

"What's it look like I'm doing? You only asked for an hour or two. So this is our only chance. I want you inside me."

And I wanted to be inside Janelle, but I also really did need to wrap my mind around what was happening. Before I could get a chance, however, Janelle wrapped her lips around my hard penis that she had grabbed and removed from my pants. Suffice it to say that my mind was cleared of all anxiety...except the thought of whether or not someone was going to walk in before Janelle could finish. It mattered not. With her skill and my excitement at the unexpected happening, it didn't take long for me. Janelle nursed my tool as it recovered and then tucked it back into my pants and re-buckled them.

"Feel better?" she asked, wiping her chin.

"Tons. Thank you."

"You don't have to thank me. It's my pleasure to please you."

"So, I guess it's fair to say that you're happily my girlfriend?"

"I hope to be more, Mr. Press Secretary."

Janelle snapped me back to reality after she had sucked me out of it for a brief moment.

"How can you be so sure?" I asked Janelle.

"Cecil, look at all we have been through together. I've never shared the emotional rollercoaster we've had to endure with anyone. We were together at the beginning. When the blackout started and the era changed into what is being built now, there is no one else I want to embark on this new world with other than you."

Janelle's words melted my heart into my stomach. Words escaped me and I looked into her eyes and could only see sincerity there.

"But first we've got to get through this," she said moving to kiss me on the lips.

We kissed and let it linger for longer than I can remember. All the fear and anxiety that had been swimming through me evaporated. My lips were wet from Janelle's tongue. I liked them and faintly tasted her. A warm happiness overcame me and a spark of determination ignited.

"Does this mean that I am to continue running things the way the Press Secretary did?"

"No. Lucky for you, this is a restart. We are at the beginning. The leverage Antoinette had is no longer a factor. Character assassination is the least concern for all the powers. Power is what everyone is scrambling to grab at this point."

"I thought the President was saying that a unification of humanity was what was trying to be grasped," I said.

"That's what he and some others like him are striving for," Janelle explained. "The majority of people are clawing at whatever source of power they can get a footing on and command. In one swoop, everything was set back to zero and power has been scattered around the globe. Whoever is able to gather the most will be the head nigga' in charge."

"How do you know all of this when you've been with me the whole time?"

"I told you, Cecil? The Press Secretary had been working on this for decades. I was trained to be here for you...to protect you."

It made me feel happy to hear Janelle say this. The reel of memory activated with a click in my brain as my past relationships were replayed for me. They weren't all bad, but seldom do we recall happy memories. Flashes of the worst scenes with my ex-wife; the woman whose heart I broke and who broke mine in Tokyo; the happy but depressingly brief rendezvous I had with the woman in China. The list was long enough and the pain was overbearingly harsh. Horrible self-deprecation filled my brain as regret tried its best to pull the steam out of my engine of hope.

"Cecil," Janelle said, interrupting my sad reprise. "Let all that go, Baby. It's not part of reality anymore."

I looked at Janelle. She placed her hands on the sides of my face and pulled me closer to her. She kissed me lightly and then shook my head from side to side like a compassionate mother comforting her child.

"You don't have to be tormented by all of those demons," Janelle continued. "Free yourself from them. Love yourself. You've earned it. It is your right."

"It's not that easy," I said, removing Janelle's hands from my face.

"I know it's not that easy, but it's just not worth holding on to. You're about to be the Press Secretary to the United States President. You have a front row, active seat in the rebuilding of the nation and the world. We can do it right this time. We can have peace."

"I didn't realize you were such an optimist, Janelle."

"I believe in you, Cecil. You've given me hope. I wouldn't have been able to make it through all of this if not for being beside you. You don't realize it, but you've taught me so much; lessons that Antoinette never taught me. You are the missing link to this incredible equation that's going to bring about a great force of unity and positive change in society."

"Why am I the missing link? I'm just an orphan."

"Who was trained personally by the Press Secretary specifically for this day? Let go of all that self-hate, Cecil. You don't deserve it. Through your talks in your sleep, I believe you have spilled to me everything from your past," Janelle said. "At least the most important traumas that have been thrown at you and those of your own doing. You're not as bad as you think you are, Cecil. Think about all the horrible people we've met on this journey from London when the power went out all the way to this military base where the President of the United States is hiding out. You are nowhere like any of them."

"How do you know that?" I asked, unconvinced.

"Because your heart is warm, Cecil. You are a good man and you care. You've just got demons. And given the life you've had, it's not surprising. I'm actually shocked you were able to maintain for this long with all of that madness going on in your brain. I'm sure I would've taken it into my own hands to silence the movies you seem to be forced to watch inside your brain."

"Yeah, it's my own little personal movie theatre. No happy movies though. And it's always exactly what I need to see in order to break down my confidence and confirm my worthlessness."

"Well, you're about to be the Press Secretary now. If that doesn't confirm your worth then maybe this will."

And with that Janelle and I made love. I pushed all of the excess energy swimming around in my brain in her and emptied out all of my sadness. Drained and exhausted, I felt the calming feeling of Janelle's heartbeat atop my own. We were lying naked on a cot that barely fit in the tiny barracks after the President offered me my mentor's job. A knock on the door resounded through the barracks. The sound startled us both as we were beginning to doze.

"Sir?" came a voice from the other side of the iron door. "The President has requested your presence in his office immediately."

"Thank you. Give me moment, I will be right there."

"Very good, Sir. I'll notify the President."

"Well, this is it," Janelle said as we dressed. I admired her body and felt a rush of pride at the thought that she was mine. I realized that I had given myself to her from the beginning.

Janelle stayed behind and I walked with the armed guard toward the makeshift Oval Office. When I was allowed in, the President was sitting behind his desk. A chalice of whiskey was set in front of him and two glasses were laid out, one in front of him and one in front of the empty seat meant for me. I took a seat and the President poured me a healthy four fingers of whiskey.

"So what's your decision?" he asked bluntly.

"I accept your offer to fill the position of Press Secretary for you, Mr. President."

"Outstanding," he said raising his glass. We clinked and each polished the four fingers in a single gulp. The President refilled my glass and his own and then lifted it again. "You've made a good decision, Cecil. We are going to rebuild this nation, you and I, for the better."

"I hope so," I responded.

The President got roaring drunk. I was more than tipsy. The two of us were a merry sight indeed. To ourselves, we seemed the most gorgeous pair of idiots ready to lead the not-so-united, not-so-free and no longer first, but definitely Third World.

"You have been a great gift sent from the heavens, Cecil," the President said to me after we sang merrily. Yes, we sang karaoke for a dozen or so minutes.

He had a song he wanted to sing. And then I had a song. Which spawned another song in the President's mind leading to an encore of bad singing.

"I haven't had this much fun since I was in college," the President continued. "Pushing and fighting has been my life. I've dedicated everything to the service of the people and now the world has become a disunited and nasty place. In college, things seemed so free and new as I realized I was attaining mastery of myself. Embarking on studies that unlocked communication through different languages and learning the languages of science and math. College was the highlight of my life."

"What about being president. That has to count for something."

"It does. Being President of the United States is great. But, I've never felt the joy and exhilaration of my college years since; even when I was inaugurated and even when I won a second term. Now it seems I'll get a third until we can complete this peace treaty negotiation between the First World and the Coalition. Thank you for bringing me back to that time. I needed it. It seems we are all starting over, individually and collectively as a nation. There's no reason not to take such an opportunity to reflect on the brilliance and passion contained within the innocence of graduating high school and seeing the entire world before you. What school did you go to, Cecil?"

"You mean what high school, Sir?" I asked, startled. I had been spacing out during the President's soliloquy.

"High school and college," he responded.

"I went to Hales Franciscan High School, Sir."

"Ah, you were a Spartan?"

"How did you know that, Sir?"

"I lived in Chicago for a couple of decades. My wife also happens to be part of that fun group of people who like to eat thick pizza and root for teams that seldom win."

"Except for hockey."

"Go Blackhawks! And you're a Cubs fan?"

"No, I'm a fan of the Chicago team that swept the World Series."

"I see where your allegiance lies."

"My allegiance is to the flag."

"Very funny. And what college did you go to?"

"The college you probably never heard of. It was in Aliso Viejo, California. Small Liberal Arts College, very steeped in eastern philosophy."

"That sounds very unique."

"It was. It is."

"What did you study there?"

"Literature and history. But I also took a lot of political science classes."

"What'd you end up getting your degree in, literature?"

"Mr. President, I don't have a degree."

"You're joking. Really?"

"Yes, Sir. I never completed my undergrad. It seems like such a thing doesn't really matter much anymore."

"Why do you say that?"

"Because of the state of the planet. Its people who tried to be god and control the planet, instead of flowing with it. But that doesn't mean things aren't going to return to some kind of normalcy. By next year, the Dark Age will be the new normal and people will be living in an entirely different system on every level except one."

"What is the one?"

"Religion."

"Religion? What do you mean?"

"Religion is the one thing that can't be replaced. As much as people run from it, as much as they deny it, religion is going to be around for as long as humanity survives."

"Religion helps society," I said feeling the liquor energize my confidence.

"Religion helps everything," the President said, standing up from the chair and wobbling unsteadily to the chalice of almost empty whiskey sitting on his desk.

He refilled the glass he was holding with two fingers and then held up his glass toward me, offering me the same. I rose from my seat and walked over to him. The President poured the rest of the whiskey from the chalice into the glass I had been sipping from. After that glass, I was pretty tight.

Luckily the President's security detail escorted me back to my barracks where Janelle was in the shower waiting for me. I stripped down and stepped into the shower with her. She felt my rise in attention brush between her butt cheeks and turned, surprised to see me.

"I missed you," she said, putting her arms over my head and pulling me to her by the back of my neck.

"I missed you, too," I said after she finally allowed me to breathe.

"How was your meeting with the President? Wow that sounds cool to say!"

"It was good. We shared some stories and drinks."

"I can tell. You can't even see straight. Well, I'm glad this is still working," she said giving me a yank.

"It always works for you."

"It better, 'cause it does good work. Mama need good work done to her."

"I'm at your service, Ma'am."

"In that case, allow me to service you."

And she did. When Janelle stood up from her knees, we showered each other and then dressed in the nightclothes provided by the President's people and hopped into bed.

"What were some of the things you and the President talked about while you were drinking?" Janelle asked just as I was entering a dream.

"What?" I asked, trying to figure out what reality I was in.

"What'd you and the President talk about?"

"College mostly. There was some talk of religion but never extensive. He's a Christian."

"Yeah, that's common knowledge."

"There's a lot of things that are common knowledge that people don't know."

"Point taken. I knew."

"I knew you did. He was talking a lot about how he missed his college years."

"That's pretty normal. I miss mine."

"Really?"

"Yeah. College for me was an experience of opening up myself. I had never dealt with so many major things in my life as when I was in college. The sheer amount of work was staggering in itself. But that is expected. I feel like you come into college knowing it's going to be a lot of hard work and so you get mentally prepared to be put through the ringer. At least I did."

"What school did you go to?"

"Morehouse."

"Good school."

"It's a great school. A bit isolated in the sense of exposure."

"What do you mean?"

"I mean it was a whole lot of black people and not a lot of anything else."

"It's a historically black school."

"Yeah, I know that. I'm just saying it made things difficult when it was time to assimilate into society."

"You mean up here," I said tapping Janelle's temple with two fingers.

I rested my hand on the side of her face and she put all her weight on it, resting her head. I lowered her head, scooped her body up in my arms and pulled Janelle to me. She pressed her butt against me and let my essence slip into her.

"Let's sleep," she said wiggling her way into a comfy position between my arms.

Her wiggles enlarged my desire, but sleep overcame me. Before I realized it, I was awake. The sun was coming in from the one window in the tiny barracks. I freed my arm from under Janelle's athletic body and tip-toed to my clothes. Once dressed, I set out toward the door to explore just where the hell we were.

A large solider carrying an MP-5 stood a couple of steps directly in front of me. The sight of him was startling.

"Good morning," I said, unable to think of anything better.

He nodded in return. Is there no speaking to the guards, I remember thinking as I stared into his cold dark eyes.

"Thank you for protecting me and my wife," I said, trying to sound as sincerely as I felt about him being there. "Were you here all night?" I asked, trying to get him to speak.

He nodded again. Affirmative and correct, the gesture conveyed more than words, but with the succinct punch of assuredness.

"Have you eaten?" I asked desperately, trying my hardest to stretch the conversation until I could get this guy to talk.

He nodded yes, of course.

"Great. Am I free to wander around?"

This time he actually hesitated and I saw the corner of his lip stretch just slightly. It was the very beginning of a grin he suppressed. Then he shook his head. I was in awe of the soldier's control. Encouraged by the smile that almost was, I continued to ask questions.

"Is this basically the new White House?"

He nodded, yes.

"Do you know how long before the President will be finished with his peace treaty negotiations with the Third and First World Coalition?"

The soldier shrugged. His eyes never wavered a degree, however.

"But once that gets worked out, the President will return to the White House, correct?"

Again the soldier shrugged. His eyes revealed nothing. So if he didn't speak, it was impossible to read him.

"Good talking to you," I said giving up on my information gathering game. "So now that I'm awake and ready. Where am I supposed to go?"

The soldier tilted his head to the left motioning for me to follow him. We took off down the corridor. At first it was difficult to keep up with him. His stride was enormous. Just a brisk morning jog, I thought to myself as I caught up to him. The soldier returned me to the entrance of the gymnasium that led into the President's office.

"Thank you," I said.
"Don't mention it," the solider responded, finally speaking.
"Why'd you wait so long to say anything?" I asked, legitimately curious.
"I usually don't speak. I could just see that you were trying hard to engage me. You also are a nice guy. So I decided to break my rule for you."
"Well, I appreciate it."
"You should," the soldier said lightheartedly. He knocked on the door.

"Yes," the President responded.

"Cecil, Sir."

"Send him in."

The soldier gestured for me to go in and pulled the door open for me. He nodded again but this time his lips were stretched wide in a grin. His eyes were also warmer.

"Thanks. Have a great day," I said walking into the office.

"You, too," the soldier said with a nod. He pushed the door closed behind me, shutting me in with the President of these not so United anymore States.

"Good morning, Cecil, the President said rising from his desk and walking toward me. He extended his hand and I shook it.

"Good morning, Mr. President."

"How did you sleep?"

"Surprisingly well."

"Good. Are you hungry? You must be. You couldn't have eaten in, what days?"

"Something like that, sir."

"Would you like something? I have one of the best chefs in the world."

"Even now, while we're in the midst of the Dark Ages?"

"I'm still the President, Cecil. The only reason I'm here is because I needed to be off the grid. When the power outage first happened, we had no way of determining where the attack was coming from or if there would be more. We didn't even know who did it."

"But you do now?"

"Of course. It was all in the letter you delivered to me."

"The one from the Press Secretary?"

"Yes. She explained everything very succinctly. Would you like to read it perhaps over breakfast?"

"I just may have to take you up on that, Sir."

"Very good. I'll have a menu sent over to Janelle as well and she can have breakfast in bed."

"Sounds lovely."

"What are you saying?"

"I'm saying I have a letter for you. A letter I know you want to read," the President of the United States responded to me.

"How do you know that?"

"Cecil, come now. I thought it was understood that we're friends. Relax. Sit down. Have a drink with me."

"It's still pretty early, Sir."

"Does that mean you're not drinking? No problem with me."

"I'd love a drink, Sir."

"That's what I thought."

The President brought out the favored chalice that seemed to never be drained of whiskey. We drank a healthy two fingers each and I was more relaxed. Good thing, for the President reached into his jacket pocket and pulled out the letter that I had carried after Antoinette's murder and delivered personally to this man before me. Carrying the letter through such circumstances created an attachment to the words sealed within it. The bloody envelope was torn open and I gathered the President had read the letter. He never spoke of it until now. Dave and his organization of terrorists called The Flawed prevented any chance for that to happen.

"Thank you for delivering this to me?" the President said, handing the letter to me. "This is sort of Antoinette Stalk's last will and testament. And the last half of the letter is addressed to you. I removed those pages that were written for me and pertain to matters of United States security. The rest is all for you, my friend. I did not read them for they clearly are directed to you. In fact, it was two separate letters written on entirely different stationaries in different colored inks. She made a point of making sure I knew this portion was for your eyes only."

"I don't understand," I said turning the envelope with the letter over and over in my fingertips."

"I believe that's why she wrote the letter to you. There was a lot I didn't understand, until you delivered her letter, that is. Then everything was clarified for me and I knew what my mission was to be and the course of action I needed to take in order to accomplish it. I have a strong feeling that your letter will be the same."

"What makes you say that?" I asked skeptically.

"It's how the Press Secretary graduates her students from her tutelage."

"You were also a student of the Press Secretary?"

"I was her first student. But you, Cecil, you were her favorite. I think it's because you didn't have any family?"

"You know about me?"

"Of course. I know all about you. I am the President of the United States. But also, Antoinette always talked about you. In fact, she raved about you. I remember when she first told me about you. She had returned from a business trip and said she met the most energetic young man at the baggage claim area. I can't remember where she had been coming from."

"Chicago," I answered for the President.

"Right, cause that's where you're from. Of course, how could I forget that? It practically is the reason you are you."

"Because I'm from Chicago?"

"Yes. You can't say the city has not had a profound effect on your development."

"Well, when you put it like that, I would have to agree with you. Chicago was responsible for molding my external armor."

"But internally, I would say it's done a number of things to you, especially when it comes to your heightened concern for safety. I took the liberty of going through your military record."

"It's a pretty short record."

"These are very special times, Cecil. You scored the highest marks recorded in a number of fields. Tactical planning, operating and final analysis come naturally to you. It's like you have an instinctual way of seeing the patterns and knowing how to present them in a way everyone gets. You're not rigid, yet not soft and you stay poised and ready. Your psychological evaluations also show a heightened awareness of yourself. Your ability to control your emotions and how you've been able to organically mold that so as not to cause damage to your life condition is astonishing. I've never met nor heard of anyone who can do the things you do. It seems the

Press Secretary made the best choice in picking you to be her final student."

"How many students did the Press Secretary have?"

"That's difficult to say. Between you and me, I've met ten. There was a period of five years where I didn't hear from Antoinette. She said she was on sabbatical, but you never knew what to think with that woman. Whatever she was telling you was almost certainly a lie and she could hide the truth in plain sight under obvious lies. You know this, it's how she trained us to be."

"Yes, the perfect liars."

"Perfect sociopaths, you mean?" the President said refilling our glasses with whiskey. "You know, I rarely ever think back on my formative years with Antoinette."

"How old were you when you became her student?"

"I was seventeen. I had just graduated from high school and was all set to travel the world. My mother suggested I meet Antoinette Stalk. She was just a consultant at the time. Consultant to the powerful is the way she was presented by my mother. My mother was Catholic and didn't approve of Antoinette's tactics."

"She did have a 'whatever it takes' way about her when she conducted business."

"It wasn't just business she was like that with. Her personal life was just as much 'whatever it takes.' But instead, serving at the pleasure of the client was a fight for constant happiness. She believed there was no point in being alive if not to be happy."

"If she believed and felt that, why would she put into action the short-circuiting of the entire First World?"

"So that you and I could be sitting right here, planning how we are going to rebuild this country and the world. Lots of people talk about revolution, taking control of the government, etcetera etcetera. But nobody actually does it. Antoinette did. And then she didn't take the power she had ripped away from the First World and allowed the nations that she had unified, mobilized and weaponized to take advantage over those that had for so long taken advantage of them. Don't you see, Cecil? She wiped the slate clean. Everyone went back to equal footing by falling to the lowest point in history, the Dark Ages, and now we can rebuild. And do it right this time."

"But so many people died. And so many more will as we try to make order from this chaos."

"Yes, many people have died. Many more will die. But imagine if we get it right this time—and you know we can. We were both trained by Antoinette Stalk.

I didn't respond and the President stopped talking. I finished the glass of whiskey I had been holding and politely waved off his attempts to refill it. I needed to think, not get drunk. The letter was sitting on the coffee table before me. It had burned a hole in my pocket while I carried it. Now it had burned a hole into my very existence. The President saw me staring at it.

"Why don't you take my office and spend some time with the letter," he suggested. "I have a good deal of work that I need to attend to."

"I can just read it here on your coach while you work. There's no reason to leave."

"Oh, no, that wouldn't be right of me at all. Whatever the Press Secretary wrote, she wrote especially to you. It is a sacred connection shared only between the two of you. This is the strongest thread you have connecting you to Antoinette. I'm certain you will appreciate reading and taking in the letter in your own private space."

"So you're giving your office to me?" I asked with skepticism.

"Yes."

"Why, Sir?"

"'Cause that's what friends are for. Help yourself to more whiskey and whatever else you find. Just knock on the door when you're done."

And with that, the President walked out of the room and shut the door, closing me in, alone. I took the letter off the table and went back to flipping it around and around with my fingertips. I paced the room while the envelope performed a series of acrobatics with my fingers as the puppeteer.

I felt like a puppet. The Press Secretary had used us all to fulfill her own ends. She wanted to set the world in motion by shutting its power off. And then what, a massive power on? It just didn't make sense. Everything the Press Secretary taught me revolved around the principle of flowing water; to not resist, to use no force, to flow and wait for the opportunity to arise where change could be made without interfering with the flow of the environment. We were to be assistants, not operators; interceptors not obstructers.

I decided that enough was enough and it was time to know all and get to the bottom of everything–or, everything that was in the letter from the Press Secretary, which hopefully was everything.

I poured myself another glass of whiskey and walked over to the President's desk. Feeling right at home, I sat in his chair and placed the envelope on the desk. I traced the lines and splashes of blood with my eyes, trying, but failing to not recall the horrible moment when she was killed by the nomads.

We had been traveling for at least six weeks after reuniting following basic training. We had been assigned our first mission and the Press Secretary took the lead. She was excited about working with two of her students. I didn't know Janelle was a student at that time. She knew about me. Apparently, a lot of the Press Secretary's students knew about me. But I didn't know any of that at the time. I was still half crazy from basic training.

As we traveled toward DC, our destination, so that the Press Secretary could deliver personally to the President what I imagine was what I ended up passing on to him myself. We passed each checkpoint and reported successfully. Then, one night as we neared a checkpoint, the Press Secretary veered from our set method and chose to help a woman who was walking on the street. She had a small baby in her arms and neither she nor the child had shoes on their feet and minimal clothes on their backs.

Why the Press Secretary veered from a set protocol I will never know. It proved to be a fatal mistake for her, however. Something she had instilled in me would be the result of slipping up. I guess this was her way of welding that point with this lesson.

The woman had stashed a tiny hand pistol in the blankets the infant was wrapped in. As she cradled the baby to her breast and hysterically praised God in whispers for our arrival. She took out the pistol. I had been driving the steam powered vehicle we were able to obtain from the military base before we embarked on our mission. I saw the metal glint in the rear view mirror and turned my gaze to the back seat in time to watch the Press Secretary grab the woman's hand and pull the pistol toward herself.

The two wrestled in the backseat but not before the woman threw the infant out the window to free her hand. I kicked myself for not taking notice that she had lowered the window for seemingly no reason just before pulling the gun. I slammed on the brakes and the two lunged forward. Janelle, who was in the passenger seat, ripped off her seat belt and hopped out of the car. She opened the back door on the side the woman we picked up was on. And then a shot was fired. Just one. Directly into the Press Secretary's belly.

Janelle wrapped her arm around the woman's neck and pulled her out of the car in a chokehold. She didn't let go until the last breath had left the woman's lungs. As Janelle choked the life out of the woman, I jumped in the back and tried to tend to the Press Secretary. There was an ungodly amount of blood pouring from the hole in her stomach. Blood was spewing from her mouth. She kept choking. She tried hard to speak, but only gurgles came through. I applied pressure to the bullet hole in her stomach and she screamed. I didn't know what to do.

Janelle got behind me and whispered into my ear that there was nothing we could do. She wrapped her arms around me and rested her forehead on the back of my head. The Press Secretary smiled and closed her eyes. It was the next morning that she said those final words I told you about earlier and then died.

I shook my head clear of the tragedy and refocused on the letter that was before me. I picked it up and pulled out the papers. There were four pages in all. This is what they said:

Dear Cecil,

Eisenhower's Press Secretary 'Iron man' James C. Hagerty was the reason I wanted to become a Press Secretary. They called him Jim at the White House. He meticulously informed reporters with competence and candor.

There's this famous story that, a little bit following the start of Eisenhower's campaign in 1952, the soon-to-be president lost his temper about something that had happened in Mr. Hagerty's department. After snapping at some length, Eisenhower stopped and looked at Hagerty, who was struggling to keep his Irish temper cool.

"You don't scare easily, do you?" Eisenhower said.
"No, Sir, I don't," Hagerty replied.

Hagerty, having been a reporter himself, understood the emphasis on deadlines, transmission facilities, prompt texts of speeches and statements and the frequent necessity to ask seemingly irrelevant and inconsequential questions. During the first meeting with Hagerty and White House reporters, he laid down the rules that for the most part have been the model for the president's press conference ever since. He said:

"I would like to say to you fellows that I am not going to play any favorites, and I'm not going to give out any exclusive stories about the President or the White House.
"When I say to you, 'I don't know,' I mean that I don't know. When I say, 'No comment,' it means I'm not talking, but not necessarily any more than that.

"Aside from that, I'm here to help you get the news. I am also here to work for one man, who happens to be the President. And I will do that to the best of my ability."

Mr. Hagerty pioneered the practice of regularly scheduled presidential news conferences. And for the first time, everything the President said at a press conference could be printed verbatim. In 1955, he was responsible for bringing television cameras into presidential news conferences. He was also the only Press Secretary who served under the president for all of his two terms.

I'm sure you are wondering why I'm writing to you at such length about James Hagerty. The reason is because you're like him, Cecil. You shall be a pioneer in the position of Press Secretary to the President of the United States. I will pass everything that I have accumulated--business and personal--over to you. I have taught you all that I know. You have been my best student. You have a monumental task before you. To bring order to chaos and justice to the unjust is what will be expected of you. I know you can do it. Always remember that life force determines victory. Fight joyfully. Win gloriously. I will see you again in eternity.

> *You are my family. For that reason you are never alone.*
> *You are unique and for that reason made for this task.*
> *It is yours and yours alone, to accomplish it.*
> *I have no doubt that you will.*
> *I love you dearly.*
> *Thank you for enduring my cruel tutelage with a smile.*
> *Your smile puts a smile on my face.*
> *Never give up on yourself, your country or the law.*

Love,

Antoinette V. Stalk
Press Secretary to the United States of America.

The End   09/06/2016 - 10/26/2016

About the Author

Stanley Ish is from the low end of the South Side - Chicago, Illinois. The great grandson of American Actress and contralto vocalist, Etta Moten Barnett. And, great grandson of Claude Barnett, founder of the first international news agency for black newspapers. Stanley was born and raised Buddhist and has lived in both China and Japan studying the languages of each country. An alum of Soka University of America. Stanley currently lives in Los Angeles with his girlfriend.